Drive Me Crazy

ASH HOSKING

Table of Contents

Chapter 1

ALEX

"I'LL NEVER LEAVE you, Alexei. I love you."

I wake up, shivering in a pool of sweat and frantically kick the suffocating covers to the floor.

I swing my legs over the side of the bed to sit up, bracing my elbows on my knees as I take slow, deep breaths to calm down.

Whoever said, '*It's better to have loved and lost, than to have never loved at all*' can kiss my arse.

I would give anything to remove the void that's been eating away at me for almost seven years now. It never lets up or fades, and it refuses me just one full night of sleep.

If I could, I would go back in time to warn my thirteen-year-old self to never kiss his best friend. Or even further back, to my six-year-old self and convince him that Hope is *not* the exception and *all* girls have cooties. So no—don't invite your best friend's sister to play with you, and definitely, don't fall in love with her.

Things would be so much easier.

Of course, right after these thoughts that I have every time I'm desperate for a reprieve, I'm slammed with guilt for thinking it because my mind flashes the slideshow of all the good times I shouldn't want to lose. But I'm exhausted, and even the happy memories cut like a blade.

I just want some *peace*.

I check my phone for the time and groan because it's only midday. Four hours since I crashed onto my bed after getting home from my bartending shift at Ruby's and following after hours activities.

I head to the shower to wash off the layers of sweat, cologne, and cheap perfume I feel coated in. Worse since I didn't bother to shower when I got home after dropping the new dancer off, whose name I think was… *Sapphire*?

I didn't even get her real name before seeing the inside of her bedroom and getting inside of her. Yeah, I'm a douchebag. But to be fair, she wasn't real interested in talking.

I have the water as hot as I can handle pummelling my neck and shoulders until it runs cool and then shut it off. I towel off briskly on my way to the kitchen to see what I can scrounge up for breakfast.

Mouldy bread, expired milk, and a container of something that looks biohazardous that I don't even recall what it originally was. I throw it all out and trudge back to my room to get dressed since I can no longer put off food shopping.

I hate food shopping. I hate the numerous over-stocked isles and having to search them all because everything is so spread out. I think there should be a row of shelves at the very front, filled with everyday necessities, so those of us who don't need the extras don't have to waste our time. It would be a great idea, but managers never take my suggestion seriously.

The looks I receive never fail to amuse me, though. From the old people who see my ink and move out of my way immediately as if I'm a serial killer to the young mum's in their workout gear, fiddling with their wedding rings, biting their lip as they eye me wantonly. The harried mothers, juggling a little one or a tribe of them, who take a moment to appreciate my appearance before moving on. Or even the cougars, who don't try to hide their perving before finding a way to slip me their number.

It almost makes grocery shopping worth it.

Today, it's the young checkout chick who blushes up a storm as soon as she sees me approaching her register. She's cute with her strawberry blonde locks, pale skin, emerald eyes, and awkwardness. Barely looks over the legal drinking age though, so I reign in my natural urge to appreciate her body and keep my eyes above her neck. Yeah, even I have limits, and jailbait's one of them.

"How's your day going, beautiful?" I ask when she squeaks out a hello. I start loading my trolley of goods onto the conveyor belt, watching with a grin as her blush deepens. I may not be interested in anything with her, but I flirt harmlessly. My mother always says, 'Flattery will get you everywhere, ' and there's nothing wrong with giving her ego a boost.

"G-good. Yours?" she stammers, looking away to scan my items. I smile as I push my now empty trolley ahead to park beside the bagging area.

"Much better since your smile has brightened it," I reply then watch her squirm self-consciously with a small smile as she reads off my total. I pay with my card then give her a wink as I wish her a good day while taking my bags.

After all that shopping, I end up detouring through a drive-thru to get breakfast because I'm just too hungry to wait any longer. The food is long gone by the time I complete the five-minute drive home.

Within minutes of putting away the groceries, I'm sick of my own company. I decide to drop by Ink fix, my best friend's tattoo parlour since it's the place anyone I want to see will be.

I haven't heard much from Dec since he's busy with his new business and on a health kick, no longer interested in hitting up our usual spots for girls and drinks every other night. Now he's got himself a gym membership and barely touches alcohol.

I miss my wingman, and it's not just because no one can get the girls to flock like he can with just a flash of his dimples and intense eyes that feel like they strip you bare and see to the heart of you when focused. I don't do so badly without him, but there's no denying, the guy has a whole other level of game when it comes to the ladies without even trying. I swear, if I didn't love him like a brother, I'd hate him for it. But I do—love him that is, and miss him.

I pick up some beer on the way since it's now late enough in the afternoon to be acceptable, and it is my day off.

When I get to Ink fix, Dec is seeing a client out the door and grins when he sees me approaching with the case of Coronas.

"You do know we don't close until ten, right? You encouraging my staff to drink on the job?" he mock-complains while turning in the doorway to let me pass, and I give him a shrug of my shoulders.

"I'm only supplying the goods. It's up to them to handle their own responsibilities," I reply before setting the pre-chilled box on the counter and opening it to get two out, offering him one.

"But you're the boss so you can do what you want. And by that, I mean, drink up, or be labelled a bitch."

I grin smugly as Dec swipes the bottle from me with an eye roll, walking around the counter to take the stool Kit usually occupies, which draws my attention to her absence.

"Where's the kitten?" I ask as I pop the top off my drink.

"With a client." Dec points over his shoulder to the hallway as he replies, then looks at the clock on the wall while opening his bottle. It's the second time I've seen him check the clock in the two seconds I've been here, and it makes me curious.

"You waiting on a client?" I prod, but he shakes his head, taking a sip of beer.

"No, I'm free for an hour." He starts to pick at the label on

4

his bottle. I'm about to ask what's up with him, but we're interrupted when a door opens down the hall. I hear Skunk instructing a client on tattoo aftercare before he exits the hallway. He gives me a nod in greeting before turning back to the hot little piece following him with a bandage covering the length of skin from her left ribcage to hipbone. It's clearly noticeable because she's only wearing a navy blue bikini top that barely contains her plastic-fantastic tits and tiny denim shorts that barely cover her arse. I take a moment to appreciate the view, but I came here to hang with my boys and don't have the urge for any tail, so I let her go without introducing myself. Girls like her are easy to come by on the Gold Coast.

"So, what's up, man?" Dec asks when he sees I'm done with my perusal. I turn back to him with a shrug as I sip my drink.

"I have the night off. Thought I'd come chill, see if I could talk you all into going out tonight."

Dec turns me down without even thinking about it.

"Sorry, bro. I have a late client tonight."

Skunk joins us, helping himself to a beer as he slaps my back.

"I'm in. Even though I'm still recovering from last night," he adds then we're distracted again as Kit exits the hallway with another hot chick who is walking gingerly behind her. I watch curiously as Kit hands her care instructions and a small phial of cleaner. She rattles off what to do and what not to do. I notice the other guys' heads follow the chick out also before Kit turns back to see us, shaking her head in admonishment.

"You guys never stop being pigs for a second, do you?" she complains before walking over to grab a beer.

"What did she have done?" I ask when curiosity gets the better of me. Kit expertly pops the top off her bottle using the top of the counter.

"Clit and navel piercing," she answers offhandedly, and

Skunk almost chokes on his beer as I lean back to see if I can catch a glimpse of the chick again, but she's gone.

Too bad. It could have been fun to see her again once she's healed if I could have committed her face to my memory bank, which was already a long shot.

I spend the next couple hours annoying Kit while Skunk drops in and out with clients and Dec makes himself comfortable on the couch to finish drawing up a wicked tribal elephant piece. A huge Samoan guy turns up a little later, and Dec takes him back to do his thing.

The guy is an amazing artist. I have the proof in the ink covering the top half of my body. From my fingers to my lower back are all his. My body is a showcase of Dec's career from the first piece he was allowed to do on a person—the shadowed skull on my right arm—to my epic chest piece from last year of a mean phoenix, its claws embedded in the skin over my heart protectively. Its colourful body covers my left shoulder and trails down my arm where it catches fire, which is set off by a Japanese style, green and gold dragon on my right side that's snarling and seems to be glaring out of my skin with warning. The detail in the feathers, scales, and eyes is insane and took many sessions, and the characters seem to pop out of the curling grey smoke shadows. They're the most personal of all my tattoos, and it means everything to me that my best friend created them.

Before I know it, Dec is walking his client out, handing Kit the camera to upload the photos of his work from the day to their Facebook page, before heading back to clean and prep for his next client.

I lean over Kit's shoulder to check out the impressive pieces, which annoys her. She shoves me hard enough that I have to tuck my feet around the legs of my stool to keep from falling off.

"Personal boundaries. Learn them and keep out of mine," Kit growls, making me grin. I wrap my arms around her to pull her back into my chest playfully. Messing with her never gets old.

"I'm aware of the personal boundaries. I just like getting into them," I murmur against her ear. Then I gasp in pain when she elbows me in the ribs making my arms go slack, instantly releasing her.

"Keep out of mine or next time, it'll be a junk shot," Kit warns smugly as she returns to the Mac. Skunk comes back in the room with a cute little Asian chick who has her wrist bandaged and wearing a brilliant smile, clearly proud of her new ink. He gives her the care spiel then says goodbye before coming to fall into the stool beside me that Kit vacated.

"Thank fuck that's over. This day has been too long," Skunk complains as he leans back against the wall and scrubs his hands over his shaven head. Kit silently hands him a Corona which he gratefully takes.

"I'm going to need something harder than this soon," he complains after guzzling half the bottle.

"You continue like that, and you will be passed out before we even head out," I warn just before Kit spins around to glare at him.

"You are not seriously going out again after not sleeping last night. You have to work tomorrow also, remember?" She accosts Skunk, who scrunches his face at her yelling.

"Easy, woman. Hell yeah, I'm going out, I may not be twenty-one anymore, but I can still do it *and* show up for work," he assures her which just makes her scowl more.

"Why don't you come too, Kitty? Then you can make sure he goes home at a reasonable hour like a good boy."

I smack Skunk's cheek playfully until he shoves me away.

"I have better things to do with my time off than watch you two drool over skanks at a bar." Kit snubs my invite, but I hold my hand up to stop her from turning away,

"Dec's coming," I add which, for some reason, has her

7

snorting in laughter.

"He is not," she argues looking smug like she knows something I'm missing.

"You know what, if you get him to go, I will too." She chuckles to herself, sounding much too amused. I rub my hands together with a grin.

"Challenge accepted. I hope you have your dancing shoes ready," I reply, before grabbing another beer.

Dec comes out with another happy client who pays up with Kit before leaving. I hand Dec the beer I had just opened and grab myself another. Dec looks at the beer in his hands as though he doesn't really want it but takes a reluctant sip anyhow when he sees me watching expectantly.

I'm about to comment on it when Skunk jumps in to brag. "Honestly, dude, you have to come out tonight. Last night was off the hook. I went home with two hot as hell girls on holiday from Japan, who took me back to their hotel and had their wicked way with me. I'm talking Harajuku, crazy-sexy chicks who did things I've never done before. I was in love. I almost didn't want to slip out on them this morning to come here." Then he pulls his phone from his pocket, scrolls through a few photos, and then shows Dec something on the screen that has his eyes bugging and throat pausing on its swallow of beer. He looks away with a shake of his head.

"I need to bleach my eyes. Warn a guy before you shove a picture of your naked arse in his face next time," Dec complains as Skunk turns his phone my way.

I hold my hand up to block the screen while turning my head the other way.

"Some things, once seen, can never be unseen. I love you, bro, but I never want to see your pale arse." This has Kit giggling until she clearly gets an eyeful because it cuts off suddenly with a protest which has me chuckling.

"You're disgusting, Skunk." Kit starts ranting, dragging me into it also, as she says I'm just as bad and our mothers would be so disappointed to know what we do.

"I resent that. I'll have you know I wine them, dine them and only *then* do I sixty-nine them," I protest when she's done, earning a high-five from Skunk and a chuckle from Dec before he goes back to his room to prep for his next client.

"Bro, you work too hard. I really think you need to come out tonight," I yell after him over Kit who is expressing her outrage over my statement—though she should know by now, it doesn't affect me except to make me want to poke at her more.

Skunk and I continue trying to persuade Dec to come out when he returns until I notice his attention is elsewhere. His eyes keep flicking to the clock, and he's still holding the same beer from hours ago that is still three-quarters full.

"Dude, have you come down with something that sucks the fun out of you as it turns you into an old man or what?" Then we all start arguing. I ask with concern if he has an STI from the last woman he was with, as I try to understand why he is so adamantly against coming out.

My mind fills with all these horrible possibilities before Dec looks at me as if I've lost my mind and assures me his Lady Pleaser, is perfectly fine. The banter continues until Kit drops the bomb that his next client is 'his girl.'

The guy used to share everything with me—seriously, we even shared chicks once. Now he's suddenly different and not telling me when he makes such a huge change?

I watch as he glares at Kit like he didn't want me to know, rubbing salt in my emotional wounds.

"What the hell, bro? You went and got yourself hooked on a girl and didn't tell your best friend?" I complain, seconds away from jumping on him and demanding to know what's going on. I cross my arms over my chest to contain the urge for now.

"She's just a friend, and I've told you about her. It's Aela from the gym." He tries to defend himself. He and Kit get into a debate about stuff that makes no sense at all to me. Then I'm distracted by two gorgeous chicks approaching the glass door of the shop.

One is a tiny little thing with long brown hair, in a cute little dress. Her dress would look sweet and virginal if it weren't for how it clings to her curves, displays the right amount of cleavage to *just* be modest, and the expanse of leg shown. She's stunning without being in your face. She's exactly the type of chick we stay away from because this type would never have a one night stand.

They're *real* women who deserve the whole package. Basically, she's relationship material—the planning a future kind and one who scares the fuck out of us. Well, it used to. If she's who I think she is, it's just me who is terrified of the R-word now.

I turn to her friend who is a little taller and leaner but just as gorgeous. Short blonde hair is tucked behind one ear, showing her brilliant smile as she laughs at her friend. My eyes get stuck there for a moment before moving on down to the dark blue floral, strapless top reminiscent of a corset. A heart shaped top showing a lot more delicious cleavage than her friend and is paired with dark skinny jeans and black kitten heels. It's a hot as hell outfit that showcases her delicious curves without being trashy like I'm used to seeing.

I'm instantly imagining peeling those skin tight jeans off and exploring all her soft skin with my hands. I'm torn between hoping she isn't this Aela chick so I can do all the things I'm imagining, and praying she is so I have a reason to stay away from her because she looks like the type of girl who will have me bending my rules or dropping them completely to have her.

I look away just as she turns back to face the shop and pull out my phone for something else to focus on as Kit and Dec continue talking.

The door slides open, and I hear a sweet, melodic sounding voice reply to Kit's greeting. I look carefully to see it's from the cute little one which has me breathing a small sigh of relief before I focus on Dec and the little chick as he gravitates towards her immediately.

If I didn't know better, I'd say my guy has a crush, but he's never crushed on a girl in his life. Not even in high school, when the majority of the population fell in and out of love every other week with a different person. Well, except me, since by then, I only had eyes for one girl. Of course, back then, he was too busy making sure the male population stayed away from his twin sister, unaware his best friend and comrade in guard duty had already stolen her heart. I still wonder what would have happened if I'd not let her convince me not to tell Declan about us, but Grace thought it would ruin our friendship, so I kept it from him. Even now, I have days where it's on the tip of my tongue ready to be blurted out.

"Oh, damn. You've gone and got yourself a real girl. Are you crazy?" I blurt out when I come back to the here and now, barely registering what comes out of my mouth before all eyes are on me—and Aela's adorable face pouts before she challenges me,

"As opposed to what? A blow-up doll? Sorry to disappoint you." That angelic voice should *never* be talking about blow up dolls and such depraved things. I become so distracted by the wrongness of it that, before I know it, Dec is gesturing for her to go to the back room without even introducing her to his best friend, which is wrong if she really means anything to him.

I intervene and take her hand, politely introducing myself while Kit says something typically snarky in the background. I ignore Kit while I'm caught in Aela's mesmerising eyes. They

11

clearly display all her emotions and are beautifully coloured in patches of blue and green. Dec kicks me as though I'm taking too long, and I continue my lean down to kiss her hand. I mean, it is the gentlemanly thing to do. Not that I'm a gentleman, though.

"I guess you're the mysterious Aela, who has turned my bro into a teen girl." I must be right since she doesn't return my greeting. She looks speechless, actually.

That's okay, babe. I get that a lot, but you're safe from my magic because my boy has dibs on you and you're too sweet to be my type.

I grin good-naturedly at her before Dec smacks me in the back of the head and snatches her soft, tiny hand from mine and sends a territorial death glare my way.

Idiot, I'm not interested in losing my balls.

I smile back at him, so he knows it's all good, watching as he looks down to Aela. His expression instantly lightens into a small smile when he sees her little grin.

Yeah. The poor sucker is *so* whipped.

"Like I said—ignore him. I don't know the guy. Whatever you do, don't feed him, or he'll follow you around like a stray too."

Oh, no, he didn't.

Seriously, he wants to play me like that?

I've been the ungrateful arsehole's best friend since kindy.

"Whatever, fucktard."

We trade barbs until Aela giggles when I drag her into it. This seems to be Dec's drawing point because he gives me a hard look as he tugs her hand that he hasn't released since he took it from me and they head down the hallway.

I watch them go with amusement until Dec turns to look back over Aela's head and calls out to her friend Kara. My eyes happily steal the chance to go to the blonde.

She's leaning down on her elbows over the counter with her

hands clasped in front of her, pushing her tits out beautifully. I can't take my eyes of the creamy flesh on display. My mind happily fills itself with images of touching, licking and nibbling all the exposed skin. I have to tear my eyes away to look casually around the room before my dick makes itself known.

"I'll be in soon. I want to catch up with Kit for a bit."

I hear her speak and have to close my eyes to savour her voice. The woman could make a killing at phone sex.

Her voice is sultry, low, and smooth as a fine whisky. It's pure bedroom, and I could listen to it forever. *Forever?*

I don't know where that came from, but I don't think so—for twenty-four hours straight, maybe.

My eyes open and my gaze is drawn back to her, lingering for only a moment on her tits before lifting to her face.

Kara is already looking my way when I meet her grey eyes, and I'm fascinated as I watch her gaze harden. She stands back from the counter and gives me an expectant look as though preparing for battle.

I don't understand it. Especially when I caught a split second of the heat in her gaze as she appreciated me before practically slamming down steel shutters behind her eyes. Colour me intrigued.

"And who is this beauty? Hey, I'm Alex, but you can call me Mr Licks. It's what the ladies call me round here."

I don't know what possesses me to use that line. I've only ever introduced myself like that once while rotten drunk. It's so sleazy, and I'm usually much smoother, but the anticipation in her eyes made me nervous. I want to put her in the same box as all the other chicks I fool around with.

Of course, Kit calls me out on it. The chick can never pass up an opportunity to dis me unless she's blind drunk and telling me she loves me like the annoying brother she never wanted. Yeah, she knows how to dish out the love.

13

I let it go because I know it's only fun for her to get a reaction from me. Right now, I'm solely focused on Kara.

"I'll be more than happy to show you how I got the name," I push further as she stares at me. I can clearly see her warring with herself about how she wants to respond which keeps me grinning in amusement.

"I'm Kara. You can call me Kara and keep that tongue of yours to yourself. Lord knows where it's been, but it couldn't be anywhere good to cop a lame nickname like that. It's probably short for arse licker, right?" Oh, she can bite back. This gives me a little thrill because there's nothing I find hotter than a good looking chick with a smart mouth, quick wit, and dirty sense of humour.

I step up closer to Kara, feeling like I'm stepping up to bat. My grin deepens as her arse licking comment repeats in my head.

"If a rimming is what gets you off, I can get down with that, no problem, babe," I reply then watch her shiver in response while her mouth opens and closes like she doesn't know what to say.

My ability to leave her speechless with just a comment makes me smile in anticipation of her reaction when I kiss her. *When* not *if*, because I will. And soon.

I watch Kara scrunch her nose as if she copped a whiff of something bad. Then she haughtily replies, "No, not babe—*Kara*. Are you deaf or dim, or do I just need to say it slower? Again, I. Don't. Want. Anything. To. Do. With. Your. Tongue."

It makes me laugh which causes me to miss my chance to reply before Kit forces her way between us with a snort. Kit takes Kara back behind the counter with her as if that will deter me from pursuing her.

Not likely.

"She's feisty. I like feisty—especially between the sheets." *Where I can work it out of her.* At least half of that thought was

14

out loud because Kit groans a complaint while Kara fights a smile. Before I know it, she is retreating towards Dec's workroom to see if they want coffee.

"Kit, if you get her to come out tonight, I will owe you one, including sexual favours. Not by me, but I'll help you get laid since we all know you could do with a release. You're far too crabby," I murmur quietly to Kit. She whacks me in the arm with a cry of outrage.

"I do not need your help, or anyone else's for that matter, jerk. Why should I subject Kara to your shit?" Kit demands, so I take on a more pleading look,

"I will do anything you want. Pay for all your drinks, be extra nice to you all night, and I'll be a perfect gentleman to Kara. No worries," I promise. Then I try to wait patiently as she stares hard at me while thinking it over. I fail in my attempt to not squirm under her gaze and lean back to make sure Kara isn't coming back.

"Okay. You agree to shout the two of us drinks all night and refrain from being your usual slimeball self, and I'll ask her to go out. *But*, the second you resort to being a douche, I'm bailing and taking her with me," Kit concedes. I could lean over the counter to kiss her. I control the urge though because that would be a fatal move on a sober, sex-deprived Kitty.

"Deal," I reply instantly, and she smiles winningly. She then collects her bag as the sound of Kara's heels announce her return just before she rounds the corner.

Kit makes her way over to link their arms and asks if Kara wants to get some drinks when she gets off work. After a thoughtful moment, Kara shrugs with a nod, and Kit turns to me with a grin.

"You're on, arse-licker."

Kara looks between the two of us curiously as Skunk chuckles, and I nod my acceptance.

15

"What are you two up to?" Kara asks suspiciously, but no one replies as Kit tugs her to the door. I refuse to watch them leave, so I make my way down the hall to interrupt Dec. I'm sure now he can be talked into coming out. But when I get to his door, I can't help turning back to watch as Kara shuts the glass door behind her and walks away—swaying hips drawing my eyes to her perfect arse and legs that go for miles.

I face the room again once she's out of sight and see Dec flick me a quick glance over Aela's shoulder. I watch the two of them while trying to figure out the best way to get what I want. I decide Aela is the best course.

"Aela, have you got any plans after this, honey?" I ask as sweetly as possible. Dec looks up to glower at me, knowing exactly where I'm going with this.

It takes a lot of convincing, and a little pleading, for Dec to finally give in when he realises I'm not going to let it go. I fist pump the air victoriously. A moment later, Aela agrees to come also, which makes me laugh happily because this is going to be a great night.

Dec orders me to get out of the room so he can get some work done, which makes me chuckle. He's never had a problem focusing before, and I can't help but point it out,

"You've never made me leave before. But then, you've never had an Aela distracting you. I'll go, for the sake of the art, a great night, and for Aela to put in a good word for me with her friend with the legs."

I waggle my brows at Aela, who giggles. Then I duck out of the way with a chuckle when I realise Dec intends to throw his water bottle at me. He's going to be so much fun to mess with tonight.

Chapter 2

KARA

I KNEW ALEX would be trouble for me the moment I laid eyes on him—before he even opened his mouth.

It wasn't the ink covering his arms and his bad boy demeanour, nor the fact that he was the embodiment of everything I hated in the male species. It was because he stirred something in me I've never felt before. Not even with Nate, the guy I had given everything I had until he tore my heart out.

I feel my blood heat as it rushes through my body, and my heart gives a weird lurch as my pelvic muscles clench. I casually lean against the counter so I can cross my legs to try to alleviate the tension between them.

And that's all before he turns his attention to me. Those jade green eyes lock onto mine, and I watch as they slowly lower to peruse my body before making their way back to meet my gaze. He smiles a grin I've seen too many times on too many handsome, cocky faces to count. It's a grin that says he's making plans to get to know my body a whole lot better, minus clothing, and that he's assured I'll love every second of it.

Too bad he doesn't know that smirk and gleam in his eyes is an instant libido killer for me. I've been there, done that, got the shirt to prove it, and once is enough for me.

Unlike some girls, I learn from my mistakes.

I straighten both my stance and spine and harden up as I put a lockdown on all my girly bits that are trying to roll out the welcome mat.

He introduces himself, and his deep, rough voice does *not* cause a quiver in my lower belly. Nope. It doesn't because I won't allow it. That shit is on lockdown.

I hear a snort and turn to Kit, my new friend and kindred spirit, who works here and is as colourful as my bedroom with her tattoos, pink makeup, and matching streaks in her white-blonde hair. I laugh along with her and Skunk, one of the good looking tattooists here, before she turns to face Alex snidely.

"The only reason they call you 'Mr Licks' is because it's the only name you give them. By no means has it got anything to do with your sexual prowess," Kit states, but it doesn't seem to affect him at all as his grin remains. Then he continues as though she never spoke.

"I'll be more than happy to show you how I got the name." I cringe and use the moment to establish my disinterest of ever being with him. The others laugh as he steps towards me with a playful gleam in his eyes. His voice dips deliciously lower with his reply, but I'm still on lockdown, so it just flows right over me.

Well, that's what I try to convince myself and blame my shiver on the air conditioner I'm standing beneath.

I scrunch my nose but struggle with a comeback because I've lost my ability to speak. My brain has drained all words, containing only whimpering sounds I refuse to release.

Because of the cold.

From the air-con.

Alex's grin turns into a knowing smile, and my brain seems to recall how to curse at the sight of it. The guy gives a good smile. Equal parts boyish and charming, with just enough sexual intent to have most women throwing their panties at him. Too bad I'm *not* most women. I deliberately pronounce each word of my rebuttal slowly, pausing between each word, so they have a second to soak into his self-absorbed head. Alex doesn't get a chance to reply. Kit shoves him with a disgusted noise. She moves to take me by the arm, leading me to sit on a stool behind the counter with her and Skunk, who gives me a guy nod in greeting as I sit beside him.

"She's feisty. I like feisty, especially between the sheets," Alex comments a moment later, not the least bit perturbed, which causes Kit to let out a frustrated groan. I fight to not show so much as a twitch of the smile that tries to break out on my lips.

"I need more caffeine if I have to put up with much more of this. Come for a coffee run?" Kit turns to me for a reply, so I nod and slide back off my stool. I could really use the fresh air right now.

"I'll go see if the other two want anything," I offer and then walk down the brightly lit, white-walled hallway to the last room on the left.

As I approach the door, I hear Aela downplaying how good she is at school. She always does this, and I don't understand it. My girl is at the top of her class and gets high distinctions for practically all her grading. She has earned those bragging rights. I step up to lean against the doorframe. Then I take a second to admire the walls covered in art before I focus on my best friend-slash-housemate-slash-practically my sister and her crush. Dec is finishing the tattoo on Aela's back tonight. Every time I see the two of them together my hands itch for my camera. They complement and balance each other so perfectly. Not just in the looks of Dec's golden tan to Aela's fair complexion, his blond hair to her dark. It's also in their auras. Aela is so light, caring, and sweet, while Dec has a dark, wary barrier like he doesn't want anyone to get too close to him.

Don't get me wrong. He's perfectly charming to everyone

and a genuinely great guy, but there's something that weighs him down and has him keeping people at arm's length.

Except for Aela. They've only been around each other less than a handful of times, but each time, they just fit together seamlessly like he couldn't keep her out if he wanted to. I love that. I love the way he looks at her and constantly reaches out for her like he needs to, and all the while trying to be casual about it.

I also love watching Aela because it's the first time I've seen her become tongue-tied at just the thought of a guy. It's good to know even the smartest of women can become fools for the male form, and although it's early days for them, they give me hope that maybe there could be a guy out there for me—one who isn't a piece of scum and won't let me down like the men in my life have so far.

Dec's looking uncomfortable with the way I'm watching them, so I smile as I comment,

"Don't let her uncertainty fool you. My girl is a science genius. She's going to cure cancer and shit," I tell him adamantly. I watch as his eyes slide to Aela, and he grins when she rolls her eyes, which is her usual reaction when I talk about how great she is. I get their orders—one mocha frappe and a short black. Then I leave them in their little bubble to rejoin the others in the front reception area.

Kit has her sugar skull tote over her shoulder, waiting with a big smile when I come out, and links her arm with mine. She then invites me out for drinks when she's clocked off work. I shrug then nod my acceptance since I don't have to be at work until eleven in the morning.

"You're on, arse-licker." Kit grins at Alex. I watch curiously as he nods his assent with his own mischievous grin. I look between the two of them suspiciously and then ask what's going on, but Kit tugs on my arm as she heads for the door.

"Arse man is paying for our drinks tonight and agreed to not be a douche to either of us for the entire night," Kit informs me happily. I halt her forward momentum when I come to a standstill just outside the door.

"Wait. Alex is coming too?" I ask stupidly. Kit replies with a nod as she tugs on my arm for me to continue moving. She looks back impatiently when I don't move.

"Well, yeah. It was his idea to go out in the first place. Why? Do you have a problem with that?" she asks curiously with a tilt of her head. She eyes me, and I shake my head while doing my best to look unaffected by the news.

"Nothing. I just didn't realise." I try to cover up my moment of hesitation. Kit watches me for a silent moment before shrugging turning to continue on our coffee mission.

I release a slow breath and send out a silent prayer for strength because I have the feeling it's going to be a *long* night.

IT FEELS LIKE twelve hours—not four—by the time Aela and Dec finally finish and come out to join us.

We all cheer, and I excitedly pull myself up off the couch to check out Aela's finished piece. I gasp when she turns her back to reveal it. I had seen it with just the outlines and some shadowing and thought it was beautiful then, but this… Dec is truly a talented artist.

The roses and lilies pop out of her skin, the butterflies look insanely lifelike, and the script is beautiful. It brings a tear to my eye that I quickly blink away. Instead, I squeal and pat Dec on the back for a job well done. After we've all had a good look, Dec takes Aela behind the counter where he covers the ink with cling wrap and tape, and Aela gingerly pulls on a light cardigan.

"Can I book the taxi or do you need to pretty yourself up before we can leave?" I assume Alex is talking to Aela and turn, ready to snap at him for the mocking tone he used because it's rude and uncalled for. However, I see his focus is on Dec, who shakes his head good-naturedly.

"Piss off. I don't take half the time to get ready as you do. I just need to grab my wallet so go ahead and call it."

Dec heads back down the hall as Alex uses the booking app on his phone.

I don't even realise I've spaced out and am still watching Alex until he finishes and looks up, catching my stare.

His lips tilt into a half grin as he holds my gaze while lowering his phone. The gleam in his eyes has me biting my bottom lip. I can feel my body temperature rising for no good reason as my stomach flutters like I have butterflies.

Oh, hell no.

I do not do butterflies. Definitely not over a guy.

My back stiffens as I mentally shred wings and make sure those bastard butterflies die a horrible death. I struggle to tear away from our eye connection though. That is, until Aela shoulders me, sending me stumbling to the left before I catch myself and turn to see her with an expectant look.

"You totally spaced out and didn't hear a word I said, did you?" She assumes correctly as I fight the urge to look back to Alex.

"Sorry. What's up?" I ask, trying hard to shake Alex off and focus on my best friend.

Aela searches my eyes back and forth for a moment before shaking her head with a small smile. "Nothing. It's fine."

Dec re-enters the space and immediately makes his way to Aela's side. I get a whiff of his fresh cologne as he passes me which is damn mouth-watering. I watch as he places his hand at Aela's lower back while saying something too low for me to catch. This gets her blushing, and I can't help smiling at the two of them.

"So, what do you do, Kara?"

It's an innocent enough question. But the way Alex murmurs it, and the way his breath skates over my shoulder, sends a tingling sensation across the bare skin it reaches.

I spin to face him and immediately take a couple steps back to put some distance between us. My turn put us almost chest to chest because he's standing so close.

"You mean for work?" I ask, and he shrugs lazily.

"It's an open question you can answer however you like really. Like, what you do for fun, your occupation, how you get yourself off..." His sentence trails off, his eyes never leaving mine. I raise my eyebrows at his comment before controlling my reaction.

"I'm a junior photographer and a graphic arts student. Yourself?" I refuse to give his masturbating comment any response.

"I'm a bartender and piece of meat. I have sex for fun, and I haven't had to get myself off since I was fifteen." Alex answers all of his own suggestions. I roll my eyes at his refusal to let it go.

"What do you mean by 'piece of meat'?" I ask curiously as Kit calls out the taxi has arrived. Everyone starts to move towards the door.

"I do some modelling but mostly—I get paid to walk around shirtless for ladies' nights at a few of the clubs in Surfers," Alex replies casually. He waits for me while I collect my bag from beside the leather couch, and I turn to look at him sceptically.

"Seriously?"

He shrugs with a proud grin as he gestures for me to go through the door before him.

"I get paid to pose for photos, pour some drinks, get felt up, grab chick's arses, and rile them up with a bit of bump and grind every other night. It's a dream job really."

Alex shuts the door and checks that it's locked for Declan. Then he falls into step beside me as the others climb into the van.

"So, you're a stripper," I conclude.

He shakes his head with a chuckle. "Not quite." He waves for me to climb in while holding the sliding door open.

I'm sure there's an art to getting into these things gracefully without revealing more than you want that I haven't mastered yet. But I do my best as I bend down on the second step and press a hand in between my boobs to keep them contained. I'm unable to do anything about the expanse of lower back I expose, though. I take the first seat available next to Kit and hike my jeans back up into place.

Alex slams the door shut and slides into the bench seat facing backwards in front of me with a wicked smirk.

"Love the purple lace."

Alex lets me know he caught the view of my G-string as he rests his head back into the headrest.

I glare at him. "Shut up, Chippendale," I snap back.

He chuckles before pulling himself up and leaning over me, his hands braced on the top of my seat.

"I don't strip off my clothes to music for money, but I'll give you a show for a good time if you want, baby. No need to be grumpy," Alex murmurs. Then he places one knee between Kit and me and the other braced on the floor beside my seat. He lowers so he is sitting in my lap and gives me a little grind before my brain catches up. I push him back into his seat with a snort. I laugh with the others as Aela catcalls encouragement for him to continue while he smiles mischievously.

"We haven't even reached the bar, and you've already broken our deal, Alex. I knew you couldn't last!" Kit complains. His attention leaves me to give her a grin before he winks. "I can last all night, Kitten. And that so didn't break any of your stipulations because Kara enjoyed it. Look, she can't wipe the smile off her face," Alex exclaims as he waves his hand at me.

I instantly lose my smile and grit my teeth.

Damn it. He's hardly even trying, and I'm falling for his crap.

"Okay, maybe she can. Wow."

He tilts his head with a curious look, but I ignore him and resolutely turn away to talk to the others for the remainder of the ride.

When we pull up, Alex is the first one out since he's right beside the door. He turns back, offering a hand to help us out like a gentleman. I ignore him as I duck out and avoid so much as looking at him as I pass. Kit takes his help since she's wearing dangerously high heels and gives him an approving nod when she's safely on the ground. Skunk jumps out behind her and instantly lights a cigarette.

Alex turns back to offer Aela help, but Dec smoothly passes her with a hand on her hip. He jumps down in front of Alex and puts his hands on her waist before lifting her out. It's as if it's a higher jump than it really is which makes me laugh along with Alex and Aela.

We head up to *The Beer Garden,* and the bouncer obviously knows the guys. They greet him with that handshake back slap thing guys do, and then he lets us in without asking for our I.D.

It's packed inside, but most of the crowd is in front of the stage for the band that's playing. Alex finds us a free spot in the corner with an available pool table which is a lucky score. I dump my bag on the table and shove it against the wall along with Kit and Aela's bags. Skunk racks up a game, and Alex goes to get our first round of drinks without bothering to ask what we want.

Dec and Skunk negotiate game terms. It's decided we'll play in teams of two. Dec instantly asks Aela to be his partner, and Kit demands Skunk be with her, and they high five. *Great.* That leaves me with Alex, who is returning to our little corner with a tray of drinks and a huge grin. He hands Kit and Aela raspberry vodkas, and the guys get beers. Then he offers me a glass of something mixed with coke.

"Tell me I got it right. I figured Aela would like one of those sweet girly drinks Kit loves. But you, I think you like the harder stuff, so I picked Jack. If I got it wrong, though, I'll get you something else."

I feel there's a challenge or test in his offering and his gaze. I'm not sure if I'm imagining it, though. I don't really understand, but I take the drink without comment because he's mostly right. I can enjoy the sweeter, softer drinks as good as any other girl when the mood takes me, but nothing hits the spot like a good whisky.

I tilt my glass in salute to him and then take a drink, enjoying the mixed sensations of cold, warmth, and bubbles as it goes down. Alex continues to watch me with heat and approval in his gaze which makes me feel the need to squirm. I look away from him and hike myself up to perch on the stool behind me. This way I can watch the first game being played, trying to look interested while Alex's gaze burns into my skin.

I fight to ignore it until I can't take anymore.

"Will you turn your eyes to something else? You're creeping me out," I complain. Then I take a sip of my drink, keeping my eyes glued to the game.

"I'm trying to figure you out. I don't think it's creeping you out. It is affecting you, sure. And maybe making you uncomfortable, but not in that way," Alex states confidently. This causes me to snort indignantly as I drop from my stool and finally meet his gaze.

"You've only known me for a handful of hours. Don't go thinking you have me figured out because you don't know shit. If I say I'm creeped out, it's because I am," I insist. I turn and walk away to stand on the other side of the pool table between Dec and Kit.

"Is he being a douche?" Kit asks, turning to look at me. I shrug it off as I take a long sip of my drink.

"I can handle him," I assure her and then throw back the remainder of my drink.

I watch Aela step up for her shot, contemplating her options silently. I can't help my knowing smirk because she's going to kill it. Aela may look meek and girly with her size and innocent style with those sundresses, but the girl is a pool shark. She begged my dad to teach her to play after he got his billiard table when we were six. She took to it like a pro. She even won a few competitions Dad took us to where the grown men didn't mind getting beat by a kid.

Aela doesn't disappoint. Sinking all her balls in the one turn, she looks up like it's no big deal. I turn to see the others all looking at her slack-jawed in stunned silence and laugh as I step up to offer her a high five even though we're on opposing teams tonight.

Skunk pats Aela on the shoulder. "Holy fuck. I was not expecting that insane shit. You more than earned this round, little lady." This makes her grin. He then heads to the bar.

"Guess my money's safe for the night," Dec gloats with a huge grin. He draws Aela in so she is leaning back in his arms and then kisses her head.

"Hey, you haven't seen Kara's skills yet, so don't be so sure," Kit points out while racking up for the next game, which makes me laugh self-deprecatingly.

"If it comes down to me, trust me, your money is safe. We may have learnt together, and I can hold my own, but in no way do I have Aela's skills. Poker is my game," I state as Aela passes me her cue. Dec nods admiringly while I try not to get hung up on his dimples from his grin.

"Challenge accepted. We'll see what you've got our next poker night," Dec offers. I smirk my assent before Alex joins our side of the table and sidles up beside me. I still when his arm brushes mine.

"I'd like to test that. How about you, me, and a game of strip poker on my bed to make it interesting. What do you think?" he asks quietly, leaning towards my ear to be heard over the music. The back of my neck tingles at the caress of his breath which causes me to shiver. I steel myself before facing him with the best impartial expression I can give.

"I think I'd rather have a root canal by a student dentist than get you naked."

I put my hand up to stop him when he looks about to comment. "Don't bother turning that into something dirty. I'm not interested, Alex. I'm sorry, but you're not my type."

I turn back to watch Dec break but not sink anything. H then steps back to reclaim his beer as Alex snorts beside me.

"You keep telling yourself I'm not your type, baby. But I don't believe your words. You say one thing, but your body and eyes scream another. I don't know why you're fighting it, but I do know you want me," Alex states self-assuredly with his arms crossed over his chest. Now it's my turn to snort as I turn back to him.

"I'm not playing with you. When I say no, I mean it. So whatever you think you see is all in your head." I step up to take my shot, looking over the table for the easiest lineup.

The little burgundy seven is practically in the pocket across from me already, so I lean over to make sure. Then I recheck my line up before gliding my cue through the fingers of my right hand that's braced on the table to get the feel of the cue. I take my hit with just a little push. The seven goes in perfectly, and the white ball stops in line to sink the four in the left corner pocket— as long as I'm careful.

I walk around the table, and my eyes roam of their own volition to Alex as I'm leaning over. I find him leant back against the railing dividing us from the small lounge area above. He's chatting to a couple of tarts in barely-there black dresses, who are giggling and hanging on his every word as he eats up their attention with a cocky grin.

I roll my eyes in disgust and then focus back on the table, but I'm distracted, and the white ball goes wide. I step back, disappointed in myself for letting Alex's stupid skanks distract me. Aela comes over to pat me on the shoulder and take the cue back for her turn just as Skunk finally returns with our drinks.

I'm so thankful for the much-needed drink that I could kiss him.

I spy Alex out of my peripheral, climbing the railing to be on the airheads' level as they clap enthusiastically. They squeal with delight as though he had just done something much more heroic than pulling himself up a two-foot wall using a handrail.

Please.

I resolutely turn my back on them. I suppose I should think nicer of the bimbos. They did, after all, remind me why I should keep Alex at an arms distance. The guy is a horndog who will hump anything within reach. While it may be fun to try him out for a night, I like to be the one in control of the hookup and the first to walk away with my head held high. However, with Alex, I get the feeling he will rob me of it all, so what's the point?

I contemplate all this as I watch Aela methodically sink her balls one after another. Without seeing her, Kit bumps me, and I turn to see what's up—just in time to see Alex be pulled head first over the rail into one of the girls as she mauls his mouth with hers.

"What's up, chick?" Kit asks while bouncing to the heavy drum beat of the band up on the main floor. I shrug as though I don't know what she's talking about. She looks to where Alex is detangling himself from the girls to jump back down.

"Arse-licker, we need some more shots over here, stat," she calls out. Alex gives her a nod of acknowledgement over his shoulder before making his way through the crowd.

"I need to dance. You're coming with me," Kit drags me upstairs to the main floor before I can object—not that I really want to.

The band is playing a heavy cover of Gnarls Barkley's *Crazy*, which is actually pretty good. I get lost in the rhythm, shouting the lyrics along with everyone else squished into the dance area whileKit forces them to make room for us.

I only last two songs before the heat of all those bodies pressed together is too much for me. I motion to Kara that I'm heading back. There's a guy wrapped around her from behind, and she seems comfy where she is. She gives me a thumbs up but doesn't move to follow me. Alex is leaning against the railing on the three stairs back to our claimed spot with a smirk as he watches my approach. He offers me a shot which I take gratefully to relieve my dry mouth.

"You were beautiful out there," he tells me as he leans in close. I roll my eyes as I move past him, but he takes hold of my wrist and tugs me back hard enough that I stumble into his chest.

"Do you have something against compliments? I'm serious. The way you let go and lost yourself to the music… if you do that in bed, goddamn."

I push away from him with disgust, shaking my head.

"It's not a compliment when all you're thinking about is getting in my pants, Alex. Enough already." I storm off, feeling him follow close behind, but he stops me again just before I break through the crowd.

"Okay, okay. I'm sorry. I'll stop with the sex talk no matter how amazing I know it will be. Let's kick some arse in pool, partner."

I give a hard laugh at the sincere look he gives me.

"From what I've learnt about you in the last few hours since meeting you, I don't think you're capable of it," I argue. He smirks as he places a hand over his heart.

"I'm not saying it will be easy. But for the rest of the night, I'll keep it to myself," Alex promises, so I match his smirk.

"We'll see," I reply doubtfully and then turn to step by the last few people between us and our friends.

Aela offers me another drink from the table she's leaning against when I approach. I smile when I notice her eyes are already glassy.

"Shut up. I need to pee," Aela yells a little too loudly. Then she takes my free hand while slipping off her stool. I take a few mouthfuls of my drink and return it to the table as Aela tells Dec we'll be back. Dec moves over to take her seat while Alex takes his turn in the game.

I guide Aela through to the toilets when she starts heading in the wrong direction. She laughs and sighs audibly when we get to the entrance.

"Shut your hole. I'm a lightweight. I know, and I don't care." Then she runs to the cubicle that just became free. I don't want to break the seal yet, so I just wait by the exit until Kit walks in, heading to the sinks with an annoyed look as she grabs a pile of paper towels.

"Some arsehole spilt his drink down my top." She meets my questioning gaze in the mirror. Kit mops up her cleavage before patting at her shirt. Lucky for her it's black and not noticeable. Aela stumbles out and joins Kit at the sink to wash her hands. She flinches when she bends down and presses a hand to her inked shoulder, the movement obviously having aggravated it.

"Do I have a hairy back?" Aela asks my reflection.

I laugh as I sputter, "*What?*"

She straightens and grabs some towels before facing me.

31

"Each time Dec started my tattoo, he had to shave my shoulder first. Am I really that hairy? Like one of those gross old guys?" she asks. This makes Kit and I burst out laughing. Aela turns, peeling the unmarked shoulder out of her cardigan to show me.

"Babe, any bit of skin has to be shaved before a tattoo. Your back is fine," Kit assures Aela through giggles.

Aela looks between us warily.

"You would tell me if I did so I could get it waxed, right?" We both nod and swear we would. Kit links her arm with Aela's to lead her out.

We rejoin the guy's game, and Alex keeps his promise of being a better behaved and encouraging teammate.

Until he decides to make a toast.

"To great friends, great sex, and the awesome possibilities of combining them both!"

I laugh and then swallow the shot before giving him a look that has him shrugging playfully before leaning into me. "Sorry. Last one, I promise."

I don't believe him for a second. I shake my head as I laugh. The buzz of all the alcohol he's kept coming makes me not care so much while I set up the table for the next game.

"You're an excellent ball handler," Alex murmurs beside me, and I laugh out loud.

"You have no self-control at all!" I exclaim as I turn to face him. Alex slides even closer with a sexually playful look in his eyes that just screams trouble for me—because I like it.

"I have superb self-control. I'll prove it to you whenever you're up for it," Alex challenges. I just laugh again, turning back to placing the balls in the correct order in the triangle. I'm a little disappointed when he backs off to annoy Aela and Dec, who look rather cosy at the table.

Chapter 3

ALEX

I'M HAVING A good time. I keep the drinks in a steady supply as promised while enjoying a sort of tug-of-war game with Kara and then riling up Dec by messing with Aela as much as I can. I've never seen Dec like this.

The more drinks Aela consumes the more talkative and fun she gets. I'm enjoying getting to know her until Kit suggests moving on to a bar in Coolie where her friends have a gig.

I don't like their *music*—if you can even call it that. However, I'm not ready to call it a night and Kara's going, so I agree, but Dec and Aela bailout. Damn Pikers.

But then, going by the hot as hell make-out session I witnessed, I'm sure they have much better things to do than endure a possible ear bleed.

So the rest of us make the half hour cab trip down the coast. Three of us fall out of the car in relief when it pulls up to the venue so we can escape being gassed to death by Skunk. He just shrugs as he pays the driver before climbing out, totally immune to his own funk.

The place is packed. There's a long waiting line outside, but Kit's name was left at the door, so we get in without a problem. Krush is the band of one of Kit's friends. They are opening for a much bigger band that's touring the country, which explains the crowd. We get to the bar just as Krush starts their set. I grin when Kara scrunches her nose at the growled first chorus. At least she has taste in music. Kit yells that she's going to go by the stage, and she rolls her eyes when the three of us don't move to follow her.

"Are they normally good but the singer has a cold?" Kara leans against me to ask while watching what she can see of the musical massacre on stage.

"What? You don't like this?" I tease. She turns to give me an incredulous look before realising I'm messing with her. Kara smirks while pinching my side hard enough to make me jump. "If you can ignore the lead singer, who sounds like a dying cat, the band is decent." She snorts at my response.

"Yeah, because his noise is so easily ignored," Kara mocks as our drinks are placed before us on the bar.

We stay there, cringing through the singer's worst with amusement until Krush is finished. We leave Skunk getting busy feeling up a chick at the bar and go find Kit for the headliner's performance. I spy her leaning over the barrier to the left of the stage and force our way through the crowd, ignoring the disgruntled complaints from others. Kara grabs hold of my hand, so we don't get separated. The feel of her hand in mine feels so unexpectedly natural and comfortable that I pause for a split second before shaking it off and continue politely shoving our way through.

"Hey!" Kit squeals and launches herself at us when we get to her. She bounces and squeals about how great Krush supposedly was. I don't know what she listened to, but it sure as hell wasn't what I heard.

The equipment on stage is quickly switched out, and the lights go back down as the lead singer strolls out to his position at the front. The crowd surrounding us loses their damned minds and begins pushing forward with excited screaming and shouting before he can even say a word which has him grinning in appreciation.

Without a second thought, I slip behind Kara and brace my arms on the barrier in front of her protectively when she stumbles. She shoots me a confused look over her shoulder for my efforts as I push back to give her some room.

"What are you doing?" Kara asks after turning in her space in my arms to face me. I hold off on replying to reach out and drag Kit back beside us when she's pushed to the side by a couple of ignorant guys making their way to the front. I'm not too concerned for her, though; I know she can handle herself. She's had more than enough experience in some crazy gigs.

"Making sure you're not swallowed up by the masses. You fall in this, and it could kill you." I foolishly expect some sort of gratitude for being her hero. Instead, I get a glare as she pokes my chest indignantly.

"I can handle myself. This isn't my first mosh pit," Kara complains, which amuses me because this crowd isn't anywhere near a 'mosh pit.' I give the crowd behind us back an inch or two, until I'm pressed to Kara's chest.

"Just like you warned Dec to look out for Aela, I expect she'd be pissed at me if anything happened to you. So keep your mean, pointy little fingers to yourself, turn around, and enjoy the damn show." I fight a smile when her eyes flare at my demanding tone.

The girl gets hot being ordered around. I can work with that. Kara hesitates for several seconds before I raise my brow with mock impatience. With a long blink, she starts to turn, so I push back to give her some room again.

The band starts up with their latest chart-topper, which has everyone bouncing around to the beat, and I enjoy the show immensely. Not just because the band is tight or because of the soft body pressed up and personal against me—that caught my

35

appreciative attention for a moment when the strange woman cheekily cops a feel—but because I get a show of Kara letting go.

She bounces and sways those curves of hers to the beat like a snake charmer, shouting the lyrics to her favourite songs and squeals excitedly when she recognises their intro.

It's not only my attention she garners, either. I notice the lead singer has paused his stage-strutting above us for longer than usual. I look up to see his eyes flicking between Kit and Kara repeatedly as they swing their clasped hands between them in the air to the beat. They don't even notice his attention because they're too busy laughing, serenading each other with the lyrics in amusement.

The guy drops to his leather clad knees on the stage before them as he belts out a line, gaining their attention as the crowd behind us swarms in an attempt to get to him.

He points his index and middle fingers in a V at the two of them and his thumb to himself before moving it over his shoulder in clear invitation—and singing a line about having "one crazy night to change your life." Then he uses a break between vocals to lean out, grab Kit's wrist, and draw it towards him to kiss their entwined hands.

Oh, hell no.

I give him a glare as I step up against Kara's back, releasing my grip of the barrier to place my hand over her stomach in what *looks* like a territorial move. He gets the idea, bouncing back up off his knees to continue revving up the rest of the crowd. I artfully make it feel like the surge of the crowd caused me to lose my stance and grab hold of Kara protectively so she can't be mad I sabotaged her possible night with a rock star. Not that it would've happened. He's *so* not her type.

Yeah, I can be a clever cookie. So clever, in fact, Kara doesn't even fight my hand on her. A couple songs later, when the band breaks into a slow ballad, she even leans back into my chest. I'm fucking brilliant. I mentally pat myself on the back for my pure genius.

When they announce their last song for the night, Kit shouts over the noise to ask if we want to go backstage with her for the after party. Kara declines as she sways against me to the beat, and I shake my head also with a shrug. Kit turns with a wave to make her way to the stairs on the side of the room where I recognise the guy from Krush waiting at the top for her.

After the encore, the lights go back up, and everyone starts clearing the room. I'm a little reluctant to release Kara, and she doesn't step away from me as she tilts her head back to give me a small smile.

"That was so awesome," she says exuberantly while I turn us to face the bar. I move my arm wrapped around her to rest it over her shoulder.

"You want a drink?" I ask as we slowly make our way through the crowd, but she shakes her head as a yawn escapes her. "You want to get out of here?" My voice dips lower as I lean more into her, and she nods her acceptance. I release her from under my arm but take her hand to lead our way out through the crowd and then up the street to the taxi rank. The line is long despite the constant pickups. After the first twenty minutes of standing, Kara ends up leaning against me as she sits on the metal railing. We're both dead on our feet and breathe a sigh of relief when we slide into the backseat of a cab half an hour later. Kara instantly reclaims her spot against me after I shut the door, and she snuggles in with a yawn that has me watching with amusement.

"Don't go over thinking this, Alex. You're not getting laid tonight. I'm just tired, and you're warm and comfy," Kara warns as though she can feel my gaze. I chuckle as the driver impatiently clears his throat for our destination.

Kara leans forward to give her address and then resumes her

snuggling. I wrap my arm around her shoulders, rubbing the slight chill out of her arm with my palm, I can't help continuing the caress of her smooth skin long after it warms, content with enjoying getting to touch her any way I can.

I'm not usually this touchy feely or patient. Any other time, I'd be putting on the moves, and the driver would be getting more than he bargained for in his rear-view mirror, but this chick has gotten under my skin and has me acting like a pansy. Maybe if I just man up and get the deed done, she'll just be like all the others to me. I need my sanity back.

I lean down to take the tip of her earlobe into my mouth.

I drag my lips down it, nibbling, and sucking around the stud there.

Kara emits a small whimper before suddenly shoving herself across the seat to lean against the other door with a glare and finger pointed my way.

"Not happening, damn it." She then buckles herself in. The click of the latch sounds final, but I slide towards her persistently.

"Come on, Kara. Why are you fighting this? I can see you want it just as much as I do," I insist knowingly. I wouldn't be so persistent if I thought for a second she genuinely wasn't interested.

Kara shakes her head before turning to look out her window. I slide closer until our knees meet, and she yanks her knees up to curl up against the door.

"I guarantee you will enjoy every second if you give in," I add, then wait with my hands clenched to keep them to myself. I'm not going to fucking beg and plead for her—yet.

Four heartbeats later, she turns with a small smirk. I can feel the adrenaline of the win coursing through me as I match it.

"You guarantee it, huh?" she purrs then slowly lowers her feet to the floor space. I momentarily forget her question at the sudden change in her attitude. I am distantly aware of the cab slowing as she releases her seatbelt to turn the rest of her body into mine.

"I promise you all the orgasms you can take until you beg me to stop," I murmur as she draws closer, her tits pressing against my chest. My eyes dip down to watch them push up over her top as she makes a throaty rumble of approval.

"I only have two problems with that," Kara whispers as she runs a hand down my chest, which threatens to short circuit my brain as her hand nears my belt.

"Problems?" I tilt my head so my mouth is just below her ear as I speak and get a shiver from her for the effort. I feel her intake of breath ruffle my hair. She pushes more against my chest as her hand cups my hard-on that twitches in a silent demand for bare contact with her palm.

"Yes. You see… for one, I don't beg for anything. Especially not mercy from orgasms—and then there's *your* part of this scenario—because that's not going to happen. You're exactly the type of guy I need to stay away from. So, thanks for the company, but no thanks."

In the handful of seconds it takes me to wrap my muddled brain around her unexpected rejection, Kara hands the driver a fifty dollar note, telling him to take me wherever I need to go—anywhere but here—and then slips out of the car.

The slam of her door breaks me from my stupor. I finally make a move after her but stop and put the window down instead, as I watch her walk away without a second glance. Her hips sway invitingly, and her blonde hair glows in the streetlight as she goes.

"Say what you want, sunshine, but I'll have you begging for mercy soon," I call out, amusement clear in my voice. The only reply I get is a dismissive wave over her shoulder which has me chuckling.

I sit back in the seat and watch Kara safely get to her building's elevator and then turn to face the smug looking driver as I consider my options of where to go now.

I could make it into Surfers just before lockout for the clubs and find someone willing to take care of the tension Kara deliberately left me with. Or I can just head home to take care of it myself and have an earlier than usual night.

I catch my reflection in the rear-view mirror, notice my happy grin, and give the cabby my address because despite the need she's left me with, I haven't had this much fun and interest in a chick for a long time. I'm not ready to forget her yet.

I want to relish in this light feeling for as long as it sticks around, though I'd much rather it be with some sexual satisfaction. Oh, well. I can be patient when I need to, and something tells me I'm going to be testing that virtue to its limits as far as Kara's concerned.

But I'm game.

I see my cabby off with an added tip then head straight to my shower as soon as I get inside my flat, stripping off my clothes as I go. I don't bother with the lights since there's enough filtering in through the blinds from outside for me to make out where I'm going. I flick the light switch when I hit the bathroom.

The harsh fluorescent bulbs burst to life three times, making me wince before they stay on. I get the water running then grab a towel as I wait for it to heat up. Then I adjust the temperature and step under the spray.

I let the water pressure work on the knots in my shoulders and neck muscles while my mind wanders to what Kara might be doing right now. I palm my ridged cock as I picture her bending over to slip off those tight jeans, revealing that hot pink scrap of lace I'd gotten a peek of that frames her perfect arse.

I groan as the image switches to her kneeling before me, those deliciously plump lips of hers replacing my hand around my dick as I run my hands through her sunlight-coloured hair. I pump my fist harder as I tighten my grip with that image firm in my mind, complete with Kara's grey gaze looking up at me with the same playful look in her eyes she had before she pulled that stunt in the cab.

It doesn't take much before I'm releasing hard into my hand. The relief flowing through my tensed muscles as I throw my head back under the downpour is euphoric.

I wash up quickly and dry off on the way to my room where I climb into bed with my hair still wet. I'm out like a light without even needing to bother with the usually controlled breathing ritual I normally have to do in order to fall asleep.

For the first time since Grace passed away, I sleep right through to morning, waking up in the exact same position I started out in.

No nightmares, sweats or needing to vomit. I lay there and just luxuriate in the peace of the moment. I'm unsure of the *whys* of it, but thankful nonetheless.

I stretch until shoulder and back joints pop and crack then check my phone to find out its midday. *Ten* hours of sleep. I laugh and feel like I can take on anything today.

Third world hunger.

The war in Syria.

Hope jacked up on sugar.

Getting Kara naked.

I could conquer it all.

My stomach grumbles, so I pull myself up out of bed and put my mental to-do list aside until I get some breakfast in me.

41

Chapter 4

KARA

IT'S BEEN ALMOST two weeks since I met Alex, and that night has been replayed fondly in my mind only *every* day, despite my best efforts to brush it off.

Seriously, it's become annoying.

Regardless of being busy with work, classes, and studying, I keep finding memories triggered by the littlest of things, as though any excuse will do, for it to recall moments with Alex.

Mostly the ride home and his parting comment, along with the time I spent cocooned in his arms. Which, at the time, I fought to convince myself I was just enjoying the music and not the feel of being wrapped in him, but I've chosen to stop lying to myself.

I can admit—to myself at least—that it was the first time I'd ever felt protected, regarded, and comfortable with a guy, especially one I'd just met.

If I close my eyes and picture it, I can still conjure up that feeling, which is scary and addictive at the same time—and of course, is what I'm doing this morning as I lay in bed, not yet ready to get up and greet the day.

I'm class free and don't have to be at work until three, so I'm just enjoying the lazy moment while I can after all the early mornings I've had.

I hate early mornings.

I force myself to stop thinking of Alex but stay curled up in bed reading until my stomach churns, demanding food. I trudge out to the kitchen in just my singlet and underwear to make myself some vegemite toast and coffee.

The brewing coffee sounds extremely loud in the silent apartment. I'm the only one here since Aela's in class, so I turn on the television for some background noise even if it is just the midday news.

I take my breakfast into the lounge room and curl up against the arm of the two seater sofa. I relish the aroma of my mocha before my first sip, but I hear my phone ringing from my bedroom, and pause with the mug to my lips. Damn.

I place my plate and mug on the coffee table forlornly then scramble to catch the call before it ends, cursing whoever is interrupting my sacred first coffee of the day.

The screen displays a number I don't recognise, so I'm hesitant as I slide my thumb across the green icon to answer it— considering the weird texts and calls I've been receiving lately.

"Hello?"

"Hey, sunshine. Are you doing anything today?"

I recognise the deep rumble down the line that really shouldn't be so familiar to me.

"*Alex*? How did you get this number?" I hear him chuckle at my incredulousness, the delicious sound of which has me biting my lip before I give myself a mental slap.

"It's good to hear from you too, sunshine. I got your number through Dec because I need you urgently if you're free right now."

My jaw drops and his words leave me speechless for a moment that stretches so long, he starts to think the connection has dropped. I hear a rustling on his end then. "Hello... Kara? You there? Can you hear me?"

I attempt to clear my throat of the lump that seems to have formed there then force my words out. "What the hell, Alex? I told you the night we met I wasn't going to sleep with you even with all the alcohol in my system. What makes you think I will just drop what I'm doing in the middle of the day, stone cold sober, to come screw you?" My voice is high with shock then I hear him laugh out loud. This really pisses me off.

"Is it always about sex with you, sunshine? I love your dirty mind. We should definitely set up a playdate for it with mine. But right now, I need you in a professional manner. You said you were a photographer, right?"

I close my eyes and smack my head against my bedroom door in embarrassment at my presumption. But come on, what else was I supposed to expect coming from him?

"Yeah, but I don't see how you could need a photographer urgently? What, you can't get the right distance for your perfect selfie, and your hair looks really good right this minute?" I reply sarcastically, and he chuckles again.

"No, smartarse. We're doing a promo shoot for work, and the photographer has walked off set with food poisoning after doing an impressive rendition of the girl from *The Exorcist*. We have no replacement, so my boss is freaking because she's paying us to just sit around right now. I may have suggested I knew a chick and was begged to call you. So please? If you can, come make me look good to my boss?" Alex pleads. I shake my head even though he can't see it.

"I'm a *junior* photographer for Sharpe Images, not a freelancer. I can't just take any job I want. Not to mention I have to be at work soon, so I'm sorry, I can't."

There's a heavy pause before he replies, "Got it. I'll speak to you later." Alex abruptly ends the call, and I pull my phone away to stare at the screen for a moment before going back to my coffee.

I'm halfway through my cup when my phone rings again, causing me to groan. It's going to be one of those days, I guess. It's work calling, so I clear my throat before answering though it doesn't matter. I barely get out half a greeting before Isobel is talking over me.

"Hey, Kara. Are you able to start early today? Josh just requested you get to a job down on the coast ASAP before you head up here to the studio."

I spring to my feet and run to my room to get dressed as I reply, "Sure. Can you text me the address he's at?" I ask as I strip out of the clothes I had slept in one handed.

"I just sent you the address, but Josh isn't there. You're going to be solo on this one. He says you can handle it. Congratulations."

I pause with my shirt half over my head as I take in her words. "I… but. Are you sure he said me?"

Isobel huffs indignantly, and I wince, knowing she's taken it as me doubting her ability to do her job correctly. Isobel is the receptionist slash assistant slash Josh-handling extraordinaire at Sharpe Images and is used to being called incompetent and blamed for all of Josh's mess ups by the man himself.

"Yes. My hearing is perfect, and Josh said it clearly, several times. Don't forget your camera and equipment," she bites out and ends the call before I can apologise or explain.

I sigh as I lower my phone and read the address she sent me before rushing to get ready. The job's only about a ten-minute drive away at one of the bars in Surfers Paradise, which must be why Josh gave it to me since the studio is up in Brisbane.

I slip into a plain black tee and dark wash jeans, quickly brush my teeth and hair, putting it up into a messy bun, and swipe on some deodorant. One of the perks of being a photographer—I don't have to primp much to work behind the camera. So long as you are decent enough to be in public and have your camera, you can get away with little effort, because no one's judging your appearance. It's much better than being in front of the camera getting judged and primped to death. Plus, I get to eat whatever I want at the refreshments table while the stick-thin fashion models at most of Josh's jobs, glare in envy as they hog the veggie sticks.

I grab everything I'll need and then put the address into my GPS. I slide into my car and try to ignore the nerves from being given this job to do solo. I turn the music up loud until the vibrations from the bass massage my back through the seat. I sing along with every song that plays until I'm pulling into the parking garage Isobel instructed to. I collect my main camera bag but leave all the rest of the equipment until I see what I need rather than lugging it all out unnecessarily. Then I walk over to *Sinners.* It's daytime, so there's no bouncer at the door like every other time I've been here. I pull open the heavy door myself and walk through the eerily quiet and pitch black entrance, struggling to make out the way without the blue overhead lights. I turn a corner and hit the brightly lit main floor where the bar area is occupied by at least twenty people, kicked back chatting or on their phones.

The club has a totally different vibe in the middle of the day with the lights on, and the music turned down to just background noise.

"You the photographer?" A striking blonde in a black high-waisted pencil skirt and white blouse asks as she approaches from my right. I try to keep my eyes away from the overly large breasts trying to bust out the buttons of her top. It's like a car accident on the side of the road, though, and my eyes go there against my will before I pull my gaze back up to her face with a nod. I watch her exhale in relief through her red-slicked lips. She takes me by the arm to lead me across the room with a firm grip as though she's worried I'm going to turn and bail on her.

"All right, you lazy arseholes, time to get up and earn the money I'm giving you," she calls out before turning to me. "I'm Ruby. What I want are shots of the guys around the bar for promotional work, and I need it done as fast as possible since I've had everyone sitting around on my dime for far too long already. So I want you focused on your camera view only. There's plenty of crew and lighting equipment, so if you need anything, yell out, and I will make sure someone gets it done," Ruby insists as she hands me a memory card.

I nod my understanding of Ruby's request, watching in amusement as everyone immediately moves at her orders.

"Alexei and Max, where are my boys?" she yells again, and someone from the crowd replies they're on a smoke break. Ruby curses under her breath and yells for someone to get them inside immediately. She looks around and gestures to a buff, blond guy propped against the bar, flirting with the woman behind it.

"Tyson, we'll start with you. Over here."

The guy pushes away from the bar with a wink, peeling off his loose tee as he approaches.

I gulp as my eyes soak in his naked, perfectly bronzed torso. Tyson is ripped with abs of steel that beg to be licked. My eyes trail slowly up his body, and now that he's closer, I can admire the handsome face. He has a strong jawline and cheekbones, plump lips, broad nose, and playful blue eyes that are currently looking back at me knowingly. I return his smile as Ruby pats my shoulder, saying she'll leave me to it as she walks away.

"Where do you want to start?" Tyson asks, his rough rumble making my stomach flutter before I shake it off to reinstate my professional façade. I observe the angles of the three-sided bar and point to a vacant spot with dim lighting.

Tyson is easy and fun to capture as we play with shots on both sides of the bar. Ruby comes over to look at the shots and is happy with what we've got.

"Ty, you take a break until the group shots. Alexei!" Ruby calls as she looks around. I grab the opportunity to take a drink from my water bottle.

"My turn?" I hear the familiar voice and choke mid-swallow. I fight to not let the mouthful of water spill from my mouth or nose.

"You all right, sunshine?" he asks in amusement. I turn to glare at him, mentally questioning why I didn't see this coming. Ruby watches us with a confused look as I glare at him. Just then, her phone rings and she excuses herself.

"You did this." It's a statement, not a question because I know it—though I don't know how. Alex slips off his open shirt before moving to lean back against the bar. He hauls himself up to sit on the top of it and shrugs, nodding to the camera in my hands that I momentarily forgot I had—because holy, hot torso. He's all perfectly defined—chiselled abs and impressive ink that seems to come alive as he moves. I'm especially drawn to the phoenix covering the left side of his body. I almost want to reach out and pet it to see if it will bite. To top it off, there's a silver barbell glinting through the left nipple, begging to be played with.

"You said you couldn't do the job outside of the company you work for, so I called and booked you through your boss. No problem."

I lift my camera and take a few photos, so I'm not standing here just staring at him while on the clock. However, I pause to glare at him over it before continuing.

"I say no, so you go around me to get what you want and don't think I'll have a problem with that?" I ask quietly. Alex is silent for a moment, just staring thoughtfully, so I pause again and wait for him.

"You said you were sorry you couldn't do it. I made it so you could. I don't see the problem."

I shake my head because the guy is impossible.

"Jump behind the bar. Can I get another light from the left?" I yell, and immediately, another light is on before Alex can finish sliding over the bar. The make-up girl moves in to attempt to move the hair that has fallen into his face, but I call out for her to leave it where it is.

"Turn your head down but keep your eyes here. I need the light higher but angled down also." I take a few more shots until Ruby returns and calls out for some of the bar girls that have been sitting around to join Alex behind the bar. Three of them wrap themselves around him all too eagerly, pressing their singlet covered, overly fake boobs against him, which he watches with a grin before looking up at me. He lets out a chuckle at whatever my expression must be.

I ignore him, dutifully taking more photos. Another girl joins in, lowering herself before him behind the bar. Then she reaches up to run her hands over his phoenix and dragon affectionately.

I pause, gritting my teeth before continuing, and of course, Alex catches my hesitation.

"You feeling all right there, sunshine?" I capture the teasing gleam in his eyes as his hands move to caress what I guess is the skank's hair.

"Peachy. I don't think I need to ask how you are. It's written all over your smug face," I reply which has him chuckling.

"I'm feeling pretty good right now. I'd be better though if you joined in over here, and we could get down to some real business."

The girl lowered in front of him must lose her footing or something, because there's a sudden thud followed by a lot of smashing glass. A bunch of the crew run over as Alex hauls her up by her hands and effortlessly lifts her out of harm's way by sitting her on the bar top with his hands at her waist.

"May as well take five while they get that disaster cleaned

49

up," Ruby growls beside me and then stalks away.

I hit the display icon on my camera to flick through the images until I feel someone approaching. I look up, expecting Alex but am surprised to see Tyson grinning as he leans in to peek over my shoulder.

"You're pretty talented with that camera," he compliments as his eyes flick to mine. I have to bite off an appreciative smile.

"You guys are just easy subjects," I reply dismissively, turning back to the pictures.

He continues, "No. You know exactly what you want and how to get it without making us feel like awkward posers." There's a pause after he says this, which I ignore because I don't know what he expects me to say to that... *Thanks?*

"So you and Alex..." he trails off meaningfully, and I turn to look at him sternly.

"Are barely even friends," I finish for him and don't ask why he's enquiring because I think I know where this is heading. I'm not interested, so I won't make it easy on him.

"Don't tell me you're the only woman here immune to the pretty boy? I'll have to buy you a drink or maybe kiss you for existing."

I laugh at that, which makes Tyson grin triumphantly. I feel a little sorry I'm about to burst his bubble by turning him down, but we're interrupted. A warm arm settles over my shoulders while a solid body settles against my side.

"Sunshine, Ruby wants me oiled up, so can you put this on for me?" Alex is holding out a bottle of baby oil with his free hand, and I snort before pushing him off me.

"I am not rubbing you down with oil. Ask one of the other girls that either get paid to do it or will enjoy it," I refuse adamantly. Alex shakes his head and steps closer to me.

"I need you. The others will think too much of it and get carried away. Please?" he insists, but I shake my head in reply which makes him huff impatiently as he thrusts the bottle at me.

"Stop being a chicken. It's only my shoulders and chest. It's not like I'm asking you to give me a fucking hand job or anything."

I glare at him as I put my camera down on the bar then snatch the bottle. Alex turns to the side, holding his left arm out to me, so I pour more oil than necessary over his shoulder then angrily rub his soft, warm skin.

I catch his smug look at Tyson who emits a quiet, humourless laugh before walking away.

"What the hell was that?" I demand quietly. Alex turns his head with a questioning look as though he has no idea what I'm talking about. I just roll my eyes.

"Do you know Tyson still lives with his mum and is a total momma's boy? He lets her run off the chicks he brings home like a champion cock block," Alex tells me. I stop to raise my brow as I move to stand in front of him.

"So, if I want to screw him, I should get a room in the hotel next door or take him back to my place? Good to know." I then continue to spread the oil over his chest roughly.

"I hear he also has a kinked dick."

I choke out a laugh, my hands stopping on his chest as I meet his gaze. "Okay, what are you playing at?"

"I noticed the flirting going on here and just thought you should know. Wouldn't want you to end up disappointed." Alex shrugs, and I fight to control a grin. If I didn't know better, I'd say Alex was jealous.

"Well, thanks. But I happen to like a little kink in my sex," I joke, then realise my hands are resting against his bare chest, so I make them move. I experimentally run my hand over his pierced nipple and he shudders, his eyes closing.

"Good idea, Kara," Ruby commends. I turn to see her watching as I finish. I wipe my hands on the towel Alex offers me and turn to give him an accusing look as he smirks back.

"I thought this was Ruby's idea?" I cross my arms over my chest with an accusing look.

"Did I say that? My bad. But I've gotta say, I haven't ever enjoyed a rubdown as much as I did just then."

Alex shamelessly grins before leaning in to kiss my cheek in a super quick move before I can even begin untangling my arms to ward him off.

I glare at him in warning as he backs away with an unrepentant smirk while the other guys make their way over to the bar now that the clean-up is complete and we can get back to work.

Two hours later, a very happy Ruby announces we're done, and I can't help but watch the guys putting their shirts back on even though I've just spent the last few hours staring at their half-naked bodies.

Yeah, it's a hard job for sure, I feel so sorry for myself.

I snort at my own sarcastic musings, catching Alex's attention. He steps closer while buttoning up his shirt, covering those washboard abs I'm grudgingly sorry to say goodbye to.

"We should get a drink," Alex states, making me look at him dubiously.

"I have to go to work," I point out. He frowns in disapproval.

"You just finished a job. Call it a day and have a drink with me."

I laugh at that as Alex bends down to take the strap of my camera bag and hauls it over his shoulder.

"Of course, a stripper like you would think four hours counts as a day of work, but it doesn't for me. I have to get to the studio and back to my day job," I counter as I lead the way to the back door where everyone is leaving.

"You've finally decided to dance, Alex?" Ruby exclaims excitedly at overhearing me. Alex holds his hands out to halt her enthusiasm with a chuckle.

"No. Definitely not, boss. Will you tell the woman I don't strip because she won't listen to me?" Ruby purses her lips in disappointment while reaching to pinch his cheek as she turns to look at me.

"Sadly, this boy doesn't go beyond losing his shirt for me when he's on the clock. It's a shame because he's already a popular favourite." She ends with a chuckle when Alex pulls out of her grasp and rubs his reddened cheek as though her grip hurt.

I don't miss the hint behind her "on the clock" statement and take in the two of them as a couple. I can see the cougar being a fireball in the sack, but my stomach threatens to revolt at the mental image of the two of them bumping uglies. I turn away to focus on anything but them.

Only, Alex makes it difficult, pulling me in against him under his arm as he leans forward to see my face.

"See. Now stop calling me a stripper unless you're going to take me up on my offer of a private dance in a bedroom or anywhere I can lay you out when I'm done." Alex waggles his eyebrows suggestively. This gets me giggling—which is most unlike me—before I can control it. I jab my elbow into his ribs to get him off me.

"I would say *in your dreams,* but I don't even want an imagined form of myself subjected to that, so just stop, Alex," I state firmly, holding a palm out to his face, but he just grins without flinching.

Damn infuriating, edible man. Wait, I retract that edible part. I have no idea. Oh, hell. I can't lie to myself. He is totally edible. If we were alone right now, I would gladly lick him up. Damned be the consequences and despite how annoying he is.

"You keep telling yourself that, sunshine." Alex breaks me from my mental dialogue, and I catch the knowing look in his eyes before I shake myself and turn away.

"I haven't got time to fight about your delusions. I have to get to work. Ruby, thank you. It was a pleasure working for you. Isobel will send you the payment details once I give her the hours."

She takes the memory card when I offer it. I hold my hand out for a professional handshake, but the woman steps in to hug me, slipping a small envelope into my hand and whispers, "A bonus for saving me and doing such an excellent job." Then she rushes off when someone calls for her. I peek into the unsealed envelope, and my eyebrows rise at the wad of cash inside. It has to be at least five hundred dollars. Who the hell carries around envelopes like that and just gives them away?

"Don't go thinking she's generous with however much is in there. You saved her a fortune. And don't try to give it back— you deserved it. Not to mention she'll be insulted, and you'll just waste time arguing when you have to get to work. That is unless you've decided to blow them off to come have a drink with me?" Alex suggests. I shake my head.

"I've got to go."

He follows me silently to my car and seems reluctant to put my gear away when I open the back door.

"Last chance, sunshine?"

I resolutely point for him to put my bag in the car as a reply, so he complies—with a deep overdramatic sigh that causes me to bite the inside of my cheek to keep from so much as grinning.

"We should have that drink soon, though. You know, to show our support of the happy new coupling of our best friends?" he says after shutting the door and leans against it.

"How would having a drink without them—you know what? Call me, and we'll see since you have my number now. I have to go." I give up on understanding his convoluted reasoning because he's just stalling me.

I move to go around him towards my door, but Alex reaches

54

out to pull me to him, pressing a kiss to my temple then pauses, looking as though he's unsure where the urge came from.

"You can bet your sweet arse I'll call you. Later, sunshine," Alex murmurs, stepping back to open my door. Chivalry might not be dead after all.

Chapter 5

ALEX

I HAVEN'T BEEN able to get Kara out of my head since the day we met. She's like an annoying fly constantly buzzing around my mind that makes it difficult to focus on anything but the buzzing.

My sleeping pattern—or lack thereof—went back to normal after that one glorious night, and in my sleep deprived mind, I've convinced myself that she was the difference that let me sleep. As if she has some kind of magic power over me.

I've been trying to find a way to see her. Hanging out at the shop as much as I can or seeing what Dec is up to when I'm free, waiting for him to be with the girls, with no success.

Well, until the drama with the photographer and Ruby asked if anyone knew someone who could stand in.

I recalled Kara mentioning her job. It was just the reason I needed to ask Dec for her number without drawing his attention and seeming like a stalker. I called her the second Dec gave up her digits. I don't remember so much as saying goodbye to him before ending the call. Then I heard her voice, and it was like an automatic balm to my frayed nerves, even though she sounded less than pleased to hear from me.

I needed to see her and did all I could to ensure I got my way.

I notice Kara the moment she walks through the entrance and can't take my eyes off her. She's not dressed to impress, but she does nonetheless—in her skin tight jeans and oversized tee that hangs off one shoulder and flirts with the curve of her breasts. From my spot in the dimly lit corner where I'm hiding from Ruby, I watch as all heads turn her way. The male eyes linger too long for my liking, giving me the irrational urge to mark her as mine, but I grit my teeth and bare it. I remain in my spot to watch her interact with Ruby, unseen because I have the feeling she wouldn't look so happy once she finds out my part in her being here. I don't so much as twitch when Ruby calls for me, her voice barely registering as background noise before some idiot tells her I'm outside. I'm happy for them to think that so I can watch Kara work for as long as I can. I'm feeling like a creeper but not enough to care or to stop.

It's not until I have to watch that dickhead Tyson flirt with her as she's trying to work that I step down from my seat.

I don't approach her just yet, but I'm sure to get Tyson's attention to send him a wordless warning to back off.

I can't hide my amusement when witnessing her react to my voice before even seeing me, followed by her adorable glare that I'm sure would make weaker men crumble.

Me? It makes me want to push further, to see how riled up I can get her and then sex her up to see how sweet she can get.

I bet she would be *really* sweet too.

We get down to business, and I decide since she gets to ogle me, it's only fair I spend the time admiring her right back while she bosses me around.

Kara hesitates when Ruby orders the promo girls to get in on the shoot. She lowers the camera just enough to reveal the territorial jealousy in her gaze before hiding back behind the camera.

I chuckle because it makes me happy to see, and I take the

57

opportunity to push her more. Before I can enjoy her reaction though, the chick crouched down before me takes me too seriously and starts unzipping my pants.

Seriously? I'm all for having a good time and known for not minding an audience, but we're working right now for Christ's sake—and not putting on a porno.

I push her away from me, meaning to be gentle about it, but she lands on her butt and bumps her back into the bottles on the shelf below, causing a domino effect as they come crashing down around her.

I immediately take her hands from me to tug her up out of danger, lifting her onto the bar for good measure as she squeals, meaning to be playful, but it grates on my nerves.

Ruby suggests a short break while the mess is cleaned up, and I can't get out from behind the bar fast enough.

"We can use those five minutes in the backroom?" the chick on the bar leans in to suggest as I step away. I don't reply or even care about watching for broken glass in my escape from her. I become even more annoyed when I round the bar to find Tyson has already swooped in on Kara.

I almost laugh out loud when I take in the clear disinterested body language she's throwing down that the stupid arse isn't picking up on. Or he's trying to work around it, maybe?

My amusement instantly dissipates, and I search for something to butt in with before I just jump in and lay claim to her. Something tells me Kara really won't appreciate that. I spy a bottle of baby oil in the makeup artist's case that sits wide open on a table before me, so I grab it and storm over. I force my way between the two of them to ask Kara to put it on me. Genius really—although I hate the feel of the stuff suffocating my skin with its sliminess, but desperate times...

Of course, Kara tries to be mad at me afterwards when she finds out it wasn't necessary. The woman should never quit her job to be an actress though because she stinks at it. I could clearly tell she more than liked rubbing me down.

When we wrap up the shoot, I try to talk Kara into going somewhere else with me, but she insists she has to go to work. I help carry her things to delay our parting for as long as I can. Of course, she can't help ribbing me about being a "stripper." Then Ruby butts in excitedly when she overhears, and I work to nip that in the bud before she can get carried away. Ruby has been trying to get me to dance for ladies' night since I started, and often reminisces about her time as a dancer before she decided she was too old and went into the business side of things. As Ruby talks to Kara, she also slips in a hint of a history between us, and I try not to physically cringe while Kara does.

I did. Once. At my first and only Australia Day celebration at Ruby's house where I got so drunk, I also had alcohol poisoning and, thankfully, can't remember doing the deed. Not that she hasn't held up well for her age because she has—but there have been way too many plastic surgeries done to that body for me to find it attractive.

I attempt to distract Kara from Ruby's words with a strong come-on, which works perfectly. Before I know it, the two of us are at her little Kia, and I have to give up her bag. I don't want to, but I can't see kidnapping her turning out well, which is my only other option.

I make one last ditch attempt to stall and have a little freak-out when she moves to her door. I reach out to grab her before I can think it through or acknowledge it, and I pull her into me, breathing in her intoxicating coconut and peaches scent and kiss her silky hair. I bite back a groan because she smells and feels so goddamn good.

I let her go before I can't do it and then open her door. I wave as she pulls out of her parking space and then head to my Jeep, trying to get my head on straight. I don't know what's going on here, but I don't like it.

A WEEK LATER, Kara is still avoiding my calls. I haven't seen her apart from the night the group got together at the pub after Dec's shop was vandalised, though I didn't know it was her at the time.

That witch made me eat my thoughts on her bad acting skills when she walked in looking like a punk princess, dressed in black with long black and blue hair and then acted like her own twin.

It wasn't until the next day when I texted to invite the twins out for the night that she revealed it was her all along. I was pissed by her duplicitousness for a good while before seeing the humour in it. She had been flirting up a storm, leading me to fantasise about a threesome with the hottest twins alive.

At first, I didn't believe her. I called Dec and asked Aela if it was true. I then went through the stages of loss—grief then anger and acceptance. Then I realised if she was that good at acting like someone else, she'd be wicked good at role-play sex.

I've decided I need to step it up and make sure she can't ignore me. I have her work details thanks to good ole google, so I sent her flowers. Then I sent her chocolates, candy, coffee, but it wasn't until I sent her edible underwear this morning that I get a reaction even better than I had expected—she shows up while I'm at work.

"Hello, sunshine. Are you here to see me?" I lean over the bar and have to yell to be heard over the music.

"Your phone is off so I stole your move and asked Dec where you would be so I can yell at you. Alex, what the hell do you think you're playing at? It's my workplace you're sending all that stuff to!"

Someone's grumpy. She either didn't eat any of the sweets or ate so much that she made her stomach hurt.

"Well, you've been avoiding my calls and texts. I had to get creative to get you to talk to me. Don't be mad. It's your fault really. Now, can I get you a drink?"

Do I sound smug? I'm feeling rather smug.

"I'm not staying. I have classes in the morning. I just came to tell you to stop sending me shit." Kara stands there with her arms crossed, creating a shelf to prop up her beautiful tits that threaten to spill out of her black singlet.

"I'll tell you what—I'm off tomorrow night. You agree to get that drink with me, and I'll stop the deliveries. Otherwise, there'll be more surprises to come," I offer, grinning as Kara's eyes widen.

"I already have plans. I'm going to a party with Aela," she grumbles.

"I like parties," I point out, but she shakes her head immediately.

"You are *not* coming to this one." She's so adamant that it intrigues me.

"Pre-drinks?" I counter, and she emits a hard laugh.

"No way."

"What's the party for?" I try to fish for details, but Kara shrugs and looks away, which really gets me curious.

"Just a student party," she adds vaguely, unwilling to give me anything that explains her reaction.

"Lunch Saturday. I know a place that makes a hangover-curing, all day breakfast," I offer.

After a long hesitation where I ignore the customers calling out for service, unwilling to take my eyes from her, Kara grudgingly nods her acceptance.

"If it's the only way I can stop your deliveries, fine."

Win! I smile while she glares back before the crowd of

disgruntled patrons catch her attention. "I'll let you get back to work. I have to get home anyway. Text me the address for Saturday." She smacks the bar and begins to step back, but I lean over, gesturing for her to come back. There's no way I've gone to that much effort to see her that I'm now going to just let her walk away. Kara looks wary but complies, stepping forward and leans in a little. I reach out quickly to wrap my left arm around her waist and pull her closer until our breathing collides.

"Bye, sunshine. Save those edible panties if you still have them. I'm looking forward to eating them off you soon." I lean further in to nip at her ear, taking advantage of her shocked stillness that my words have just caused, chuckling when she catches up and pushes away from me with a scowl. Kara just shakes her head. She then hightails it out of the club as if the bar's on fire. I'm laughing as I turn to serve the crowd with a huge smile.

It's only when I'm finishing that I remember Kara's curious behaviour over the party. I Decide to drop by Ink Fix in the morning to see what Dec knows about this party his woman is going to.

I WALK INTO the shop to find Aela curled up on the sofa, quietly reading a large textbook. Kit is wiping down the glass display case. The two of them pause to look up at my arrival.

"Hey, pretty ladies." I greet them with a smile which Aela returns as Kit pretends to gag herself with her fingers.

"Please, don't. I don't want my breakfast to reappear."

Wow, someone's in a top mood today. I would poke the kitten, but I don't want to be side-tracked from my mission right now.

"What's our guy working on back there?" I ask Kit when I

spy Dec's door is closed, which usually means he doesn't want to be interrupted or he's working on skin that requires privacy.

"A chick's chest piece," Kit replies while moving to cut open a large box on the floor behind the counter. Right. Not going in. No one can say I don't learn from my mistakes.

"You two lovebirds have plans for when he's done?" I ask Aela as I take a seat beside her.

"No. I came to hang out between classes. Kara's forcing me to go to a party with her that he can't come to and Dec's sulking a little over it," Aela explains, grinning as though a sulking Declan is the cutest thing ever. Which it isn't. *Chicks are weird.*

"What's the special party?" I attempt to keep my question casual though I'm fighting off a grin because I may be about to get my answer.

"It's a Sexual Fantasy costume party."

Aela winces and blushes as she explains, and I laugh in surprise.

"Dec is seriously letting you go without him? Are we talking about the same caveman who growls whenever I get too close to you for his liking?" I ask incredulously as Aela glares in offence.

"Letting me? I'm a grown woman, perfectly capable of making my own decisions. Although I'm only going because Kara guilt-tripped me into being her wing-woman," Aela explains defensively before a butch looking punk chick walks out of the hallway. She's chatting to Dec who gives Aela a brilliant smile when he spots her.

"Okay, Kit will get you paid up, and if you need anything, you have my card. Have a good one," Dec bids farewell to his client comes to lean over Aela, kissing her with his arms braced on the back of the lounge.

"Just let me clean up and get prepped for my next booking then I'm all yours, sweetheart," Dec murmurs when he finally comes up for air, and Aela acquiescently nods. "What's up, bro?"

He finally acknowledges my presence then gestures for me to follow him to the back room. We shoot the shit with small talk until we get in the room.

"Do you really know about this costumed orgy your girlfriend is going to tonight?" I ask as soon as the door is shut and he groans.

"I'm aware." Dec holds his hand up for me to pause as he messes with his phone before putting it to his ear.

"Hey, man, are we good or not?"

I frown impatiently as he listens to the gruff voice on the line.

"Two hours of a sitting for free. Done, man. Thanks a lot." He ends the call with a winning smile as he looks back to me.

"Like hell, my girl is going to something like that without me to keep the leeches away. You cool to go back out there? I want to see this, make sure it's done right."

I nod curiously, and Dec leads the way back to the main room as I hear Aela answer her phone. Dec falls into a comfy lean against the counter with a grin as she begins complaining and arguing with whoever is on the line before giving in and hanging up with a cute little growl.

Aela looks to Dec, who schools his face into a look of concern.

"Malcolm needs me to work tonight. Kara's going to be pissed." She looks down at her phone and begins taking her frustration out on the screen with her thumbs as she types.

"That's too bad. I was looking forward to seeing you in your costume. Tell Kara I will bring drinks and keep her company until you get home?" Dec offers, trying to sound sympathetic, but he can't mask how pleased he is with this outcome. I finally catch on, giving him a shake of my head and a grin as he smiles back smugly.

Aela's phone starts ringing seconds after her text is sent and she cringes as she swipes to answer.

"Hey... I know, sorry... No. I can't... you can't go alone, don't even think it. What about..." Aela looks up, her eyes catching mine, and I can practically see her scheming before she puts her hand over the phone.

"Are you doing anything tonight, Alex?"

I could kiss the little genius.

"I'm not. I can take Kara and look out for her, no problem," I offer, receiving a brilliant smile of appreciation in return. Aela gives Kara the *good news* as Dec chuckles quietly and nudges me with his elbow.

"Generous of you, bro. Giving up your spare time to go to a sex party with a chick you're hot for," he muses, and I fight off a smile.

"Right? I should be sainted for it—or at least knighted," I joke. Then we're distracted by Aela raising her voice to an obviously less-than-happy Kara.

"If you're going—he is too, so I don't have to worry. Deal with it, or I will find a way to trap you in your room and don't think I'm not inventive enough to come up with a way because you know I am. *Please*, for me?" There's a long pause before Aela smiles again. "I love you too. Bye."

She ends the call then chuckles, looking at me with amusement.

"Do you need a costume? Because I have an unopened Naughty Nurse one."

I laugh as Dec tells her she is keeping it to wear for him later, and I assure her I've got something.

Aela gets up to make her way over and snuggles into Dec, and they start making out. I take that as my cue to leave while my text alert sounds.

I step out of the shop as I retrieve my phone from my pocket and chuckle at Kara's text;

"I know you had something to do with this. Lunch is off if I have to deal with you tonight, and you're still not getting laid."

I wait until I'm in my car before replying;

"Saturday was a done deal that has nothing to do with tonight. It still stands unless you want more deliveries at work. Just a hint, the next will be sex toys or lingerie… I'm thinking something red to match your temper. See you at 8. Xx"

She doesn't reply, which doesn't surprise me. I can imagine her stewing indignantly, which has me chuckling as I slide on my aviators and then climb into my car.

Chapter 6

KARA

I'M FUMING. I can't believe Aela just pulled this on me, and I *know* it was all somehow Alex's doing, just like the photography shoot.

This was meant to be a girl's night where we can dress up, have a bit of fun, and let off some steam. I don't even really want to go to the stupid party now without her. But my stubborn streak has kicked in, and I refuse to let him ruin my night.

So I'll get dressed up and lose Alex at the event, even if I have to throw girls at the man-whore to distract him. Then I will have fun if it kills me.

I try calling Kris—my friend from media class—in one last attempt to talk him into taking Aela's ticket, but it goes straight to voicemail. I leave a quick message and try not to growl aloud as I shove my phone into the pocket of my denim skirt and rush to my next class.

I climb the stairs of the auditorium, ignoring the looks from the other students, and slip into the first available seat. My mood has soured so badly from the phone call that I don't even bother acknowledging my lecturer, who complains that I'm late.

Ten minutes later, though, it's clear I shouldn't have bothered coming in. I can't focus and haven't taken any notes. Good thing I recognise the familiar strawberry blonde head of my friend Mel a few rows over, furiously taking notes. I'll beg to borrow them when we get out of here. Maybe I can bribe her with the ticket for tonight and will be able to tell Alex to suck it while I'm at it.

I like this idea.

I'm grinning with anticipation for the remainder of class and scramble to Mel's side the second we're let out. She has no problem letting me copy her notes. But Mel adamantly refuses to come to the party, saying it's not her scene and she has other plans, which she won't reveal or let me talk her out of no matter how much I plead or barter.

I have half a mind to drop by and give Aela's boss, Mal, a piece of my mind and maybe work some magic on him, but I accept defeat and head home.

I slam the front door behind me in a show of my continued sulking and hear Aela's bedroom door shutting as I drop my bags on the couch.

"Cheer up, buttercup," Aela teases as she rounds the corner to find me glaring at her.

"I'm not talking to you," I inform the traitor. This makes her laugh as though I'm joking, so I tighten my glare to prove I mean business.

"And yet you just spoke to me. Stop trying to be mad at me. You know you can't do it. I had Alex promise to look out for you and be on his best behaviour, so you're going to have a super good-looking chaperone and designated driver. What a tough life you live." Aela's sensible sarcasm is damn annoying.

"What if I wanted to get lucky tonight? That idiot hanging around is going to be a major vag block."

Aela wrinkles her nose at my word choice and then shrugs off my complaint while stuffing her work apron into her bag before sending me a smirk.

"Give it up to Alex, then. I'm sure he would appreciate the

gratitude for being your designated dick. Pun intended." She laughs at her own lame joke while I look on unamused.

"Laugh it up, bitch. You'll get yours. Just remember, I've witnessed *all* the embarrassing moments in your life you'd like to have forgotten... Oh, the stories I can entertain Declan with," I threaten with a mockingly sweet voice. Then I grin when her smile disappears as she pauses to glare at me in silent warning.

"The same can be said for you, so don't go there, bitch. I've gotta bounce. Have fun, love you." Aela leans in to air kiss my cheek on her way past me. She heaves the strap of her bag over her shoulder and is out the door before I can reply with more than a wave.

I remain in place for a moment, just taking in the silence of our apartment. I take a deep breath and let it out slowly.

You can do this. You will stop complaining. You will have fun, and you will not *fall for Alex's moves.* I finish my mental pep talk and straighten my spine as I head to my room to get ready.

I start with a thirty-second scrub down in the shower since I don't have to wash my hair. I brush my teeth even though I still have to eat dinner. I put my hair up in the smallest bun at the top of my head since I'll be wearing a wig, and then I apply my make-up, going with a dark smoky eye and blood-red lips with some bronzing over my cheekbones.

I unwrap my towel from around me and let it fall to the floor as I step out into my room and then into my closet just beside the bathroom. I collect my "Russian Army General" costume I bought from e-bay and the long, curly, black wig and take them to lay out on my bed. I can't help the laugh as I take it all in.

I put on a pair of lacy black underwear with the matching bra, and slide on the gaudy fishnet stockings you can only get away with wearing on occasions such as this. I fight to attach the suspenders and then slip into the dark grey button front dress piece. It barely covers my butt and has lace-up sides from my hips. I pull on the Epaulette shrug with the red detailing and do up the buckles that sit over my collarbone. Adding the black belt around my waist, then the knee high boots, I then fight to get the wig secured into place. Top it all off with the hat, I walk over to the mirror and really laugh as my eyes bug out.

If women really dressed like this in the army, young guys would be fighting to join.

The feminist in me hates the sexist costume, but I tamp her down as I go back to my closet to retrieve the props.

I decide to leave out the gloves because I already feel too hot, but I grab the riding crop with an image in my mind of using it on Alex when he pisses me off, which is likely to happen. I enjoy the mental picture way too much and shake it off as I leave the room to the buzz of the intercom, which has my stomach clenching nervously. I immediately start second guessing my costume choice. It seemed fun at the time I bought it, and I loved the idea of messing around with the whip all night. But now Alex is involved.

He's been persistently trying to get me to have sex with him, and now I'm going to parade around in front of him like this? It will be like throwing petrol on a flame.

The intercom buzzes again and continues as if it's jammed, so I run over to answer it, pushing away my second thoughts. *Too late now.*

"What the fuck?" I complain irritably into the mouthpiece, and then I'm greeted by Alex's deliciously deep chuckle.

"About time you answered, sunshine. If you're done putting on your face, your ride awaits. I thought we could get a feed before we hit this orgy."

My irritation skyrockets. I'm tempted to make him wait out there in hopes to return the favour. Instead, I grit my teeth and grumble out, "I'll be right down." I go to return the receiver, but he continues.

"Take your time. I think the neighbours are enjoying my costume."

My curiosity is peaked by his playful tone, so I hang up, make sure I have everything I need in my small black leather bag, and grab the riding crop as I rush out the door.

When the lift opens up on the ground floor, I have to bite off a laugh at what's revealed. Alex is hunched over his phone, casually propped against the back of one of the couches with his legs kicked out before him, crossed at the ankles. He's totally at ease while no less than seven women around the lobby have come to a standstill as they stare at him. Their reactions range from slack-jawed disbelief to keen interest. He's a *fireman*. Although, I use the term loosely since his costume consists of only a pair of khaki pants with black patches over the knees, black boots, red suspenders, and a fireman helmet. No shirt.

I guess I really have no room to judge since he probably resembles one more than I do a Russian General.

I shake my head at the women as I make my way over to Alex. He looks up with a playful smirk when he feels my approach.

The smirk instantly dies when he find me, his mouth dropping open and eyes widening comically as they slowly wander down my costume and then back up.

"If you really wanted me to stop calling you a stripper, you should have chosen a different costume. Or at least more of one," I comment with a smirk after a long silent moment.

Alex swallows hard while reaching up to adjust his helmet, his eyes glued to my boobs.

"Fuck. Me. You have to go up and change. Seriously, as much as I want to stare at you for forever in that hot-as-fucking-hell get-up, if you go to this party like that, I will end up in jail or dead. Oh, fuck. You even have a whip?" Alex ends with an incredulous lilt to his words and then scrunches his eyes shut like he can't bear to see me anymore.

I huff while crossing my arms in annoyance.

"I'm going like this. If you have a problem with it, you don't need to come. I'll get a cab."

His eyes flash open instantly, and he levels me with a straight-faced stare that means business.

"You're not going without me. Especially not like that. For fuck's sake, you look like a fucking wet dream. Arseholes are going to cause a riot climbing over each other to get to you, and I'm going to have to put them on their arses. I'm begging you, Kara. Please, change."

Alex gives me these huge, ridiculous puppy eyes, and I shake my head resolutely.

"You're being over dramatic. The only one who will be swarmed is you when the ladies mistake you for a hired stripper. Now let's go." I start walking towards the glass doors and hear him hiss in a breath behind me.

I look back to see his eyes on my legs with a pained expression.

I thought women were meant to be the drama queens?

I shake my head once again, turning back to watch where I'm going. I'm unable to stop myself from putting a little extra sway of my hips into my walk and then grin when I hear Alex curse.

I take back all my complaints about his presence tonight. Playing with Alex is going to be so much fun.

ALEX CHANGES HIS mind about going somewhere for dinner because of my costume. He opts to get drive-thru KFC, parking his Jeep across the road where we have a view of the moon shining over the rippling Broadwater while we eat.

I still can't stop chuckling at his actions since we left my place. From him deliberately standing behind me while helping me up into his Jeep to block the view in case I flashed anyone to his inability to keep his eyes on the road, and then to snapping at the poor kid at the drive-thru, whose eyes bugged when he leant out to hand Alex our order and noticed my getup.

I don't think Alex appreciates my laughter one bit if the silent glare he's throwing me is anything to go by. He leans back against his door and demolishes two burgers before I'm even half through my wrap. His glare doesn't bother me in the least, though. If anything, it amuses me more. Plus, I can see he's fighting a smile of his own as another giggle erupts from my chest that I can't stop.

"You know, I would feel a whole lot better about this if you were laughing *with* me and not *at* me, sunshine," Alex complains between mouthfuls while I breathe deeply in an attempt to control my giggles.

"Well, if you stopped being so stupid, I wouldn't laugh at you," I counter, I watch him raise a brow before leaning forward to steal a handful of my chips from the packet on my lap, despite having his own. I make a protesting grunt since my mouth is full and try to turn in my seat so my chips are out of his reach as he chuckles.

"Don't make me use my whip. You have your own chips," I warn once I finish my mouthful, but Alex just gives me a challenging look.

"Yours taste better, and I finished mine anyway. But if you pull out your whip, I'm going to pull out my hose." His brows wag after that statement, and I frown while looking around the car for a hose prop before catching his drift. I slap his shoulder with the back of my hand in disgust as he chuckles. I take a couple of chips then offer Alex the packet, but he shakes his head as he collects his wrappers into the paper bag.

"You need more to line your stomach than just a wrap if you plan on drinking tonight. I'll grab something later." I eye him in disbelief then let my eyes wander down his chiselled torso on display. "You had two burgers, six wings and a large bag of chips. Where the hell does it go?" I ask in amazement as he restarts the engine with a boyish grin.

"I have a high metabolism, so I'm always hungry. Where am I driving to for this orgy?" Alex changes the subject while slowly reversing from the parking spot, and I shake my head at him.

"Dress-up party—not orgy. It's at the tavern across from campus," I inform him, and he turns in the direction we need.

I play with my phone for the duration of the short drive in an attempt to cover my amusement when Alex makes up his own lyrics to the songs playing on the radio. He is singing them at the top of his lungs and nudging me to join in, but I refuse. His playfulness is affecting me more than I'm willing to admit, and I'm liking it way more than I should.

I hop out of the car before he can even remove his keys, and Alex is frowning at me as he rounds the front of the car.

"You could have waited for me to help you out," he complains while placing his helmet back on his head. I smirk while tugging the hem of my dress down.

"Thanks, but this isn't a date, and it's the twenty-first century, dude. We womenfolk are more than capable of getting out of cars unassisted. I didn't even flash anything."

Alex shakes his head at my statement.

"I applaud said womenfolk, but you're wearing heels high enough to break your neck in a fall and very little else. My mama worked hard to instil some gentlemanly qualities in me and would smack me upside the head if I didn't at least open doors for you. So you'll have to get used to it when you're with me, sunshine."

He turns to face the tavern and places his hand at the small of my back where he uses a little pressure to get me moving beside him. I quicken my steps though, so I'm no longer under his touch.

"You're poor mum must be so disappointed then. Because you are the furthest thing from a gentleman that you can get. They could put your picture in the thesaurus as the antonym of the word."

I'm pulled to a standstill just as I step up onto the footpath as Alex takes hold of my right wrist, pulling me back to face him.

He's standing in the gutter so our eyes are level, and the look in his gaze stalls all thought process in my head as he pulls me closer until we're barely a breath apart.

"I can be a gentleman. I just haven't been with a *lady* worth the effort for years. But you, you deserve it. So, shut up and let me charm the shit out of you."

He grins playfully as I laugh and step out from his arm that he'd slipped around my waist while I was caught up in his gaze.

"So charming." I roll my eyes then turn back towards the bouncer at the doors.

The place is already packed, and many heads turn at our entrance. Three guys sitting at the table beside us dressed in medical scrubs take a keen interest in my costume. I feel Alex place a proprietary hand on my lower back again, but I'm too taken with admiring the sea of costumes to bother protesting.

We make our way to the bar through the throng of people, and Alex calls out in happy surprise when we get there. I watch as the guy behind the bar looks up from the draughts he's pouring, smiling at Alex in recognition.

I take the moment he turns back to the drinks to admire the bartender over the bar. Tall, with a swimmer's lean and toned build, showcased in a pair of well-worn, skin tight black jeans tucked into biker boots, and a sleeveless, vintage Led Zeppelin tee that reveals tattoo-covered arms. His black messily spiked hair that has a large part artfully falling over his left eye and fair skin with a smirk that promises sin with a ring through the middle of his plump bottom lip that's just begging to be bitten.

He makes his way over to us, and I squint to judge if he's wearing make-up because his lashes are ridiculously dark.

"How the hell did you get in here? I know you're not a student. You hated studying in high school and still hate paperwork in general," he asks Alex suspiciously with a thick British accent that makes something twinge in my belly. Hot damn, there is nothing sexier than a man with an accent… except maybe a man in uniform with an accent.

"I'm this one's date to the orgy." Alex gestures to me with his thumb, and the bartender gives me a once over.

"For the last time, Alex, this is not a date *or* an orgy." I roll my eyes with a shake of my head as Alex shrugs while surveying the room.

"Take a look around, sunshine. This scene is one more PDA away from becoming an orgy. And this *is* a date. I picked you up, we ate, and now we're having drinks. Sounds like a date to me."

I growl under my breath while his buddy laughs out loud before leaning over with an outreached hand and an amused smile.

"I'm Lawson. Nice to meet you. Let me know if you get sick of this non-date date, and I'll have his arse thrown out of here to keep you company myself. But in the meantime, what's your poison?" I shake his hand with a grin at his words and flick a considering look at Alex, who is glaring at Lawson before I reply.

"I'm Kara. It's great to meet you. I'll have a Jack and coke, and I'll keep your offer in mind." I wink as I watch his dark eyes gleam with humour before he nods and turns to get us drinks.

"Don't get him worked up, sunshine. The guy wears his

jeans so tight he'll probably split them if he gets a semi," Alex warns, making me laugh at his cheekiness.

I watch Lawson bend down to grab a beer from the fridge, getting a great view of his arse in those jeans. It certainly has me biting my bottom lip.

"Eyes off his arse, sunshine. Before you hurt my feelings and I'm forced to rough him up on principle. Friend or not," Alex growls. I turn a grin on him as Lawson returns.

"Don't worry, *babe*. You're still prettier."

I pat Alex's cheek patronizingly, which makes him glare.

"These are on me. Al, we'll have to catch up soon, bro," Lawson announces as he places our drinks before us and then slaps the bar before moving to serve other customers. I take a sip of my drink and wince when the burn down my throat is stronger than expected. I give a big exhale and then smile when I notice Alex's lifted brow as he waits with his bottle tilted towards me. I happily clink my glass against it in a wordless toast.

I take a moment to survey the people surrounding us and their costumes. I roll my eyes at the unoriginal group of playboy bunnies in the corner, but I laugh with amusement at the guy in a banana suit, busting out his best running man before them. He may be failing to impress them, but he's having fun with it nonetheless, which has me silently cheering him on and tempted to join in.

"I'm going to dance. Have fun," I tell Alex before throwing back the rest of my drink and placing the empty glass back on the bar.

Alex grabs my wrist when I turn away. I look back with a dark look over my shoulder as he slips off the stool.

"Let's do this." He sips his beer and tugs me out to the dance floor.

"Uh, Alex. I said *I* was dancing. Not *we* were."

He ignores my complaint as he turns to face me and pulls me

against him.

"You're out of your mind if you think I'm going to sit there and watch these little punk arseholes try to make a move on you. Fuck that. You want to dance, then you dance with me." Alex lifts the wrist he's still holding to place my hand on his shoulder, finally releasing his grip to place his now free hand on my waist. He then leads me to sway against him with the music.

"You're being irrational," I point out, pulling his hand back up when it starts sliding towards my arse.

Alex grins at my warning glare.

"I'm being completely sensible. You see… if any of these idiots get their hands on you—which will happen if you dance alone—it will piss me off. This way no one gets hurt. I get these delightful curves all to myself, and you get to dance all you want. Everybody wins."

His overly pleased grin makes me want to stomp on his foot. Instead, I lift my free hand and slide it around his ribs as though I'm giving in. I then pinch him in his side, enjoying his flinch and very unmanly squeal of protest.

"Fine. I'll dance with you, but if one of these 'punk arseholes' gets up the nerve to approach—despite you hanging around—prepare to be ditched, because I'm on the lookout."

"The lookout for what?" Alex asks, his forehead scrunching up in displeasure as his hands tighten on my lower back.

"For my next guy," I reply simply. Then I get the breath squeezed out of me when he pulls me against him so tightly that my boobs are forced up and threaten to bust out the top of my costume. He clearly notices, because his eyes stop searching my face to dip down and become glued to my heaving cleavage. Alex gets a small pleased grin before I pinch him again.

"You can quit your looking. I'm right here and up for anything you have in mind. Literally," he murmurs then grinds against me, so I feel just how *up* he is.

78

"I'm not having sex with you, and do not grind that thing against me again, or I'm ditching you now." I meant for it to come out sternly, but the feel of his rigidness against my hip stole my voice and made it breathy, which has his grin deepening until a dimple is revealed in his cheek.

His eyes veritably smoulder while his hips grind even as I glare at him to stop. I do the only thing I can think of to break the heated moment. I flick my wrist still holding the riding crop so it whips a soft part of his exposed lower back, startling him enough to break his hold on me so I can step back, biting off a grin.

"I mean it, Alex." I move to turn and walk away, but he's suddenly pressed against my back. His hands trail down my arms towards my hands, locking me against him.

"If you think that was a deterrent, you are sadly mistaken. You should know I don't mind a bit of kink, and I'll happily be your whipping boy as long as you return the favour, sunshine," Alex growls against my ear. His words and breath on my overheated skin give me tingles of anticipation. I gulp and stiffen as his erection is pressed against my behind.

Not because I'm intimidated, but because the feel of his solid length has my eyes rolling to the back of my head, and I have to fight not to melt against him with a purr.

I need to put some distance between us and regroup before I give in and demand he take me right here on the dance floor.

"I… I need a drink," I stutter, struggling out of Alex's hold. I weave my way through the crowd until I reach the bar. My heart is pounding, and I'm breathless as though I had just run a marathon instead of being pressed against a body that screamed its promise to give me the best sex of my life.

By the time Lawson gets to me, I've got myself back under control and am able to clearly yell, "Double Jack and coke." He lifts a questioning brow but fills my order.

I hand him a twenty dollar note when he places it before me, then slam back the drink before placing the empty glass on the sticky bar top. I tap the glass for a refill before he can even finish collecting my change, making Lawson chuckle and put it all back into the register before collecting my glass.

"You all right?" Lawson asks as he hands me my refill. I nod as I take the icy cold glass.

"Better now," I reply then take a small sip, deciding to nurse this drink since I can feel the effects of the first one calming me down already. Lawson moves away with a wink, and I straighten myself with a bracing breath before turning around to find Alex.

I grin when I see he's been waylaid by a couple of slutty nurses, grinding up on either side of him as he tries to politely dislodge them. He looks up in agitation, eyes locking on mine, and I'd say he isn't happy with my amusement at his predicament if his scowl is anything to go by.

I salute him with the drink in my hand, which makes his scowl deepen, and I chuckle as I look away.

"Hot damn, babe. You look hot enough to have every guy in this place melting at your feet. Both the straight and gay ones."

I turn expectantly at the familiar voice and squeal when I see Kris's cheeky grin and gleaming hazel eyes as he holds his arms out for a hug. I am so excited to see him that I might throw myself into his arms with a little too much enthusiasm after putting down my glass. Kris stumbles back a couple steps as I wrap my arms and legs around him. He has to prop me up with his hands under my behind to keep us upright as he turns to lean against the bar.

I squeeze him in my arms and lean back to smack a big, wet kiss on his cheek, giggling when he scrunches his nose.

"I'm so happy you're here. Why didn't you tell me you were coming?" I ask. He gestures with a tilt of his head to his left, playful grin back in place. I turn and finally notice his boyfriend, Corey, standing beside us patiently with an amused smirk on his much too handsome face—totally unconcerned that I'm practically mauling his man.

"I didn't know I was until this guy dropped in with costumes. I tried to call you, but you didn't answer."

I drop my legs from around Kris, and once my feet are on the floor, he releases his hold so I can move over to hug Corey, using a little restraint this time.

Corey chuckles as he wraps his arms around me, and I groan when I'm enclosed in his David Beckham cologne. These two are just too much. Both look like Abercrombie and Fitch models— tall, chiselled, bronzed with perfectly styled blond hair, and always smell amazing.

It's a real loss to womankind that they aren't even a little bit bisexual, which I've accepted after numerous drunken attempts to talk them into a threesome. Don't judge.

Any sane woman would kill to be sandwiched between that perfection. And did I mention they are both dressed in army camo tonight? So not fair.

"Babe, do you know Mister Tall-Dark-and-Yummy who is making his way over, promising me a beat down with his eyes?" Kris asks, sounding amused and not the least bit threatened. I grin, not bothering to turn and see who he's talking about because it's a pretty safe bet I know who it is.

"I might." I shrug. I lean in so I can playfully hook my finger through the chain of his fake dog tags with a wink. Thankfully, Kris doesn't need prodding to play along since he's a pot stirrer like me and has been my douche repellent many times. He pulls me into his side by one muscly arm and chuckles under his breath into my hair.

"I think you're playing with fire with this one, babe. He looks too determined to give up easily," Kris murmurs conspiratorially.

He's the only person who knows the skeletons in my closet

from my past by name, so he knows exactly what he's talking about. I sigh as I lean into Kris more in an attempt to soak up some of his strength. I feel my barriers weakening against Alex, and I can't let that happen, as great as one night with him is starting to sound.

I know guys like him, and I know me, so I have to stick to my guns, especially since I will be seeing more of him thanks to our best friends being together.

"I know. He also has me struggling to remember I don't want to get burned."

"Friends of yours, sunshine?" Alex's gravelly voice is both questioning and accusatory. I turn to see him glaring at Kris's arm that's still around me before his eyes move up to meet mine.

"Alex, this is Kris and Corey. Guys, Alex." I gesture between them all with a wave of my free hand, and they exchange head nods. Corey and Alex shake hands while Kris pulls me to him in a move that is meant to be reassuring, but I'm sure it looks like he's staking his claim on me to Alex since his eyes and jaw harden while he watches.

"I thought we were dancing?"

I shrug then collect my drink.

"I'm fine here. Go, have fun. Find those two hot nurses or someone else willing to dance with you," I urge dismissively.

Alex takes a determined step closer, levelling me with a dark look before he turns his attention to the guys, mainly Kris.

"Sorry to ruin any plans being made here, but I'm going to be a cock-block all night as far as this one's concerned. She's mine tonight, so don't get your hopes up for anything happening with her." Corey grins while Kris chuckles at Alex's words.

I swallow the rest of my drink indignantly before levelling him with a hard stare.

"I'm *not* yours. Tonight or any other night. Kris, we're dancing. Right now. Before I convince myself it's okay to put the heel of one of my boots through his eye."

I grab Kris by the elbow and drag him away, shouldering Alex as I pass him.

Chapter 7

ALEX

"FUCKING HELL." I scrub my hands over my face in agitation and the other guy chuckles while slapping my back. Corbin, Corey… Casey? I can't remember his name. I was too busy watching his friend all over Kara.

"Let me buy you a drink?" He waves down Law, and I turn to watch Kara wrapping her arms around Kris' neck as he places his hands on her hips, making her laugh at something he says as they move closer.

"Not if you're just distracting me so your pal can make a move," I reply as I turn back to the bar with gritted teeth and he laughs.

"Nope. You're safe as long as she's with Kris. Kara's not his type, and neither is he hers. They really are just friends."

I snort in disbelief, which gets him turning from the bar to look at me again.

"Don't try to bullshit me. Look at her. Seriously, what kind of guy could look at her and not think she is the hottest fucking thing around and make a play?" I ask sceptically as I gesture to where she is now swinging her hips, dropping down low while holding the douchebag's hands, and he grins down at her.

"A gay one?" Corey suggests, and I swing back around to get a read on his expressionless face.

"But he's not gay," I argue, turning back to watch the two dancing as he pulls her back up and leans in, resting his forehead against hers. He doesn't look the slightest bit gay to me, just an average bloke. Broad shouldered, taller and more muscular than I am so he clearly looks after himself. A little product in his hair and a diamond stud glinting in his left ear… I stop my scrutiny when I realise I'm being a stereotyping arsehole, looking for a "sign" in his appearance that he's gay when I know better than to be so stupid.

Seeing him and Kara so affectionate towards each other has really thrown me for a loop.

"Is he?" I ask Corey for confirmation while he's ordering two beers, then he turns to face me.

"I sure hope so considering we've been together for almost a year," he replies with a daring look as though he's expecting me to react badly.

"No shit?" I'm more than a little surprised because it's the complete opposite of what I thought when I first saw them. But again, Kara had been clouding my head.

"Do you know a straight guy who would say he's gay to help a mate in some convoluted scheme to get laid?" He laughs out loud. Law drops off the two beers and change, then makes to move away, but I wave my hand to make him pause.

"Something tells me Kara's set on testing my patience, so I'm going to need something stronger to get through tonight. I'll have a double-shot of tequila for me and my new friend here."

Law chuckles as he pulls out the shot glasses. I turn to see Corey grinning gamely while I pull my wallet from my pants.

"Kara's going to do her best to push you away with their little game. But don't fall for it or rat me out. I was supposed to be the designated driver, but what the hell. We can taxi it home." He says, and I slap his back proudly.

"Don't worry. It'll be our secret. I drove tonight too, but I like your taxi idea. Cheers." I take a glass Law places before us, and we toast and then throw them back, wincing in sync as the tequila burns its way down our throats.

We're four drinks down, watching the other two dancing in between Kara stretching out to playfully whip people she knows. Corey shares some funny stories about Kara that I'm happily soaking up. We're laughing when he suddenly stops to stare me down, which gets me raising a brow, silently waiting for him to voice whatever it is.

"I like you, Alex. I also think you two could be good together, but I need to tell you that if you hurt her, we will make you pay. Don't lie to her and don't promise or say things you don't mean. The girl has been let down by too many deadbeats in her past, and it's made her jaded. So if she does give you a chance, I will make you hurt if you blow it," Corey vows sternly.

Both my brows go up at that, and then I take a sip of my beer.

"I don't intend to hurt Kara. I just want to get to know her," I reply, his words making my stomach twist.

Not in fear but at the thought of Kara being hurt.

"What are you two gossiping about. You look like a couple of old ladies?" Kara pops her head between us, alleviating the tension of the moment. I smile as I turn in my stool to face her, my hand reaching out to push strands of her wig over her shoulder before I can even acknowledge the urge to do it.

"Corey was just telling me about how you vomited on him the first time you met."

I smile at her groan as Kris hands her a drink from his stool on the other side of Corey. Kara sips what I'm guessing is a Jack and coke by the smell of it.

"You owe me a dance, and I'd like to claim it now if you're up for it?" I lean down to ask, my breath reaching the overheated, glistening skin of her neck going by her shiver. Kara bites her lip as she considers me.

"Let them have some time together. I promise to be good," I urge when her eyes flit to the guys for help, so she gives me a sceptical look.

Kara finishes her drink then snags Corey's untouched glass from the bar before nodding her acceptance. I lead her away before she can change her mind.

I take her in my arms and notice how the sweat-dampened fabric of her costume is clinging to her as she writhes against me to the music. My mind conjures up images of similar sweaty writhing, only in my bed.

I need that to happen *so* badly.

I grip her hips, feeling the way she sways before grinding against me, and I groan, dropping my head to rest against her forehead when she looks up at the sound.

I search her glassy eyes and see the want there that faintly mirrors my own before she bites her bottom lip. She's wasted, and I can't take another second of this teasing.

I need to get out of here.

"We're leaving. You're coming back to my place," I all but growl to her. She gives a small nod before I drag her over to say a quick goodbye to the guys.

Kris eyes me warily, but Corey happily shakes my hand as Kara says a few words. Then, with a wave to Law, we're headed out the door while I pull up the taxi app.

Luckily, there are a few parked out front, so we slip into the backseat of the first one in line. I tell him my address as Kara winds down the window on the opposite side and leans back against me where I'm slouched against the door.

"You're still not getting laid," she mumbles. She struggles to remove her wig, sighing happily when she tugs off the stocking looking thing underneath it and loosens her hair.

"It wouldn't be happening even if you wanted to—you're

too drunk for me." I kiss her sweaty hair that still smells good. Tropical. Something coconut and fruity that makes me want to inhale her, but she pulls away to face me with a look of outrage, her tits pressed against my chest.

"I am not. Are you seriously turning me down?"

I have to bite off and swallow a laugh. She's a cute drunk.

"No. You didn't offer anything." She blinks several times before huffing and lowering her chin to my chest while hooking her right leg between mine.

I grin down at her because this is beginning to feel damn good, despite the rough rubbing of her thigh against my hard-on.

It looks like Kara doesn't even realise what she's doing as she gets comfy, making little content noises that remind me of a kitten before she falls asleep on me.

Unfortunately, my place wasn't that far. I'm not ready to move her when we pull into my driveway. I lift my hips to retrieve my wallet and struggle to hand the amused looking driver a twenty. I wave my hand in a silent gesture for him to keep the change, then open the door and gently manoeuvre us around since Kara's out cold.

I hold her against my chest with one arm, her legs draped over the other, then slide out of the cab and close the door with my side. Walking to my door, I curse myself for not getting my keys out of my pocket first. I have to put her feet down to fish them out, and she wakes up enough to stand, which makes it easier for me to get the doors unlocked.

I stumble inside with her under my arm, flipping the first light switch we reach. The illumination wakes her a little more because she stands on her own to appraise my apartment.

I look around to see what she would be seeing for the first time. The forty-two inch LCD on the wall in front of the leather sofas, the large dark wooden coffee table on a black and a red rug my mum bought in an attempt to add some colour. Then there is a square four-seater wooden dining table, tidy kitchen, and several black and white pieces of art by Dec that hang around the place. I admit it's not much and doesn't look homey, but as far as bachelor pads go, I think it's pretty decent.

"Nice. Still not having sex," Kara murmurs as she stumbles in place. I laugh before scooping her up.

"We agreed on that," I remind her, heading to my room. I place her on the bed and kneel down to free her of those ridiculous-but-sexy boots, unable to stop myself from running my hands down her smooth, warm calves in her stockings as I do. Kara sits there watching me, eyes barely open. She sighs in relief and wiggles her toes once they're free, causing me to chuckle. I lean up to press a kiss to her nose which she wrinkles but doesn't comment.

I stand back up and move to the closet to fetch her a shirt to change into and laugh when I see Kara's laid down, struggling to free her stockings from the back suspenders.

"Don't laugh. I'm stuck," she complains pathetically. I walk over to take a look. It's a pretty simple clip I'm familiar with, and I try not to get distracted by the bare skin of her thighs between the stockings and garter belt since she's inadvertently flashing me with her leg bent up in the air.

"I'll help you with them and then leave the rest up to you, okay? There's a shirt here you can change into."

I place the shirt beside her head as she nods her acceptance. I focus on quickly unlatching the clips of the garters from the stockings, not letting my hands or eyes linger anywhere.

"Done," I tell her as I take a step back.

Kara struggles to sit up, her hands going behind her at awkward angles like she's doing some weird stretching routine before she sighs and drops them into her lap, giving me a sheepish look.

"Do you mind getting the zipper, just until I can reach it, at least?" I take a slow deep breath then step toward her again with a nod as she turns to face the window. My hand trembles with anticipation and need, but I ignore it as I move her hair out of the way then tug the little zipper down. The sound is loud in the room, as is our breathing. The straps of a lace bra are revealed with the bare skin of her back. I have to step away before I fall to the temptation to touch it or lean in to kiss her.

"There. Call out when you're in the shirt, and I'll bring you some water and then let you sleep."

I make a hasty retreat but overhear her snicker as I get to the door. "I won't be able to sleep in the shirt. I sleep naked," she mutters, and my grip on the door handle has never been harder as I curse under my breath and close my eyes at the image of her naked in my bed, green sheets tousled around her, golden hair spread across my pillow. *Goddamn.*

"I… water. Call out when you're in bed."

I shut the door and escape down the hallway. I duck into the kitchen to grab a water bottle from the fridge. I take a moment to lean against the open door and breathe in the cold air that rushes out to meet me, cooling my heated skin. I crack open the bottle and guzzle it down before grabbing another and then let the door shut.

I hunt down some Panadol to give her in anticipation of a coming headache and slowly make my way back to the bedroom. I can't hear anything behind the door, and I hesitate to knock, reluctant to go in there.

A chick has me scared of my own room.

I smile at the absurdity of it all as I shake out the tension in my shoulders and run a hand through my hair. I lean my ear against the door to see if I can hear anything… Silence, except for the weird noises the fridge always makes, so I knock.

"Sunshine, you covered?" I hear an indecipherable mumble, so after a pause, I crack the door open and slowly enter. Kara's curled up in the centre of my bed, covers tucked up under her chin, looking child-like as she watches me.

I place the bottle and pills on the bedside table as I point out what they are. I grab a pair of boxers from the drawer that I haven't worn in ages since I sleep naked also.

"You need anything else? Want me to leave the bathroom light on?" I ask as I make my way toward the door, and she shakes her head.

"Okay, goodnight. Holler if you need anything."

I make my way out of the room and take a deep breath when I reach the door.

"Where are you going?" Kara asks quietly, so I turn around with my hand on the doorknob.

"I'm taking the couch. No, don't fight me on this," I add when it looks like she's about to protest. "You're taking the damn bed because I won't be able to sleep with you out there thanks to my mum's lectures, and no way can I sleep in here with you either. So rest that gorgeous head on the pillow, close your eyes and go to sleep," I order sternly. After a moment, she does so with a sweet smile as her hands slide under her cheek.

Huh. She *really* likes being bossed around.

"Goodnight, Alex," Kara murmurs softly as I switch off the light. I head back down the hall, stopping to take a spare blanket and sheet from the linen cabinet.

Of course, once I'm settled in my makeshift bed, I'm wide awake. My mind is back with the beautiful and infuriating naked woman in my bed. I imagine slipping in there with her, feeling the silkiness of her warm skin beneath my hands... and my mouth.

It's a long night of tossing and turning with a mind full of dirty images and little sleep for me. I even try to rub one out in an attempt to ease some of the tension to no avail. I'm still staring off into space at the window when it starts to gradually lighten with the coming sunrise. I internally groan as I flip around to face the back of the couch and silently beg for sleep.

I'm so getting her back for this hell.

I smile as I plot ways to make her uncomfortable, and I guess I must have dozed off because I wake up suddenly when I fall to the floor and see it's now nine a.m.

I groan as I struggle to lift myself back up onto the couch while kicking to free my legs of the blanket tangled around me. I slouch until my head meets the top of the sofa and stare at the ceiling for a beat before getting to my feet to get something for breakfast.

My head is pounding and all my muscles hurt. I can't tell if it's from sleep deprivation, sleeping on the couch or the drinks last night. I try stretching out the kinks in my back, feeling several pops and cracks that do little to make me feel better.

I'm craving fried crispiness, so I pull out bacon, eggs, tomato, and mushrooms and then get the large pan heating before I start chopping it all up. I hunt down the TV remote to put on a music channel as I hear my bedroom door open. I turn back to the kitchen and what I see is enough to make me pause as my brain short circuits.

Kara still looks half asleep as she walks my way, eyes focused on the carpet before her while gathering her hair at the top of her head in a messy pile. She's wearing the shirt I offered her last night that is flashing a scrap of her lace underwear with her arms stretched up like that.

She must feel my presence because she looks up while she finishes securing her hair in its elastic band. I watch as her sleepy eyes take in every bare inch of my torso before meeting my gaze sheepishly. Kara swallows hard then gives me a small smile.

"Morning, sunshine. Sleep well?" My voice is still rough with sleep, so I clear my throat as I head into the kitchen with her following.

"Good morning. I did, but please tell me you have coffee?" Her just-woke-up voice is even huskier and hotter than normal, which I didn't think could be possible. I want to drag her back to my bed to hear her moan, curse, plead, and whisper dirty things with that throaty voice.

Instead, I turn the bacon while flicking the kettle on. "Coffee coming right up."

Kara pulls herself up to perch on the bench behind me, watching me cook.

"I hope you don't mind if I borrow the shirt? I couldn't slip back into my costume when I got up. It feels and smells gross," she explains, and I shake my head.

"I offered it to you last night. It's yours as long as you need it."

"Thanks. Aela said she'll bring some clothes and pick me up when she finishes work. Only if you have nothing to do and don't mind the company for a few hours, though. I can call a taxi to go home now if you want." Kara's rambling nervously and it's adorable, but I don't like her being uncomfortable around me. I miss her confident snark, so I put my hand up to stop her.

"My only plans for today are having breakfast with you and vegging out with some Assassin's Creed, so you're more than welcome to stick around."

Kara winces with a sheepish smile and a blush that is just too freaking sweet as she ducks her head.

"Sorry. I shouldn't be listened to until I've had my first coffee of the day."

The kettle turns off just as she says this, so I gesture for her to help herself.

"Go for it. And there's nothing wrong with your rambling. It's just really sweet, and I'm not used to that side of you. Weirded me out a little." I chuckle at my own joke. She slaps my arse for it before sliding from the bench.

I watch in awe as Kara correctly guesses her way around my kitchen as though she's been here before, collecting what she needs before pausing while stretched up to the mugs in the cupboard to look back at me.

"You want one?" The curve of her arse is peeking out from the shirt with the way she's stretched, and Kara catches me admiring the perfection, giving me raised brows when I meet her gaze, so I give her a winning smile.

"I really do."

She knows I'm not talking about just coffee, but she rolls her eyes while pulling down two mugs.

"How do you want it?" Her voice is suggestively sweet, which makes me laugh as she pours her own cup.

"Strong, creamy, and sweet." I lean over to murmur against her ear playfully and watch her shiver before I back away to put the toast on.

"Can I help with anything?" Kara asks moments later. She places a mug in front of me and then wraps both her hands around her own cup while checking out what's in the pan.

"I've got it. Go make yourself at home. I'll bring it out in a sec," I reply, focused on adding the eggs.

I don't see, but I hear the grin in her voice when she says, "I could get used to this." Then she heads for the lounge.

"Hope you like your eggs sunny side up," I call out as I turn to see Kara curling up on the couch. I grin when I receive a thumbs-up because she's too busy sipping her coffee.

"You want any sauce?" I finish plating everything up then head to the fridge to get tomato sauce for myself.

"I'll have maple syrup if you've got it?" I pause with the fridge door open to look over the kitchen bench that separates us to see if she's serious.

"With bacon and eggs?" My face matches the distaste I feel at the thought of the combination, and she smiles.

94

"Hell, yes. You don't know what you're missing," Kara enthuses, so I grab the syrup from the cupboard, tucking it in my elbow with the tomato sauce and grab the plates to take to the coffee table.

I sit beside Kara and watch with a look of horror as she drizzles the syrup all over her bacon and eggs with a happy grin, only noticing my attention when she puts the bottle down.

"You want to try?" Kara cuts some of her bacon and egg then offers me the forkful. I adamantly shake my head, turning to my own plate.

"And ruin my meal? I don't think so. The only breakfasts maple syrup belongs on is pancakes, waffles and the like. You're a crime against food, so no thanks. I'll stick with my tomato sauce."

This turns into a debate that ends with Kara moaning comically loud with every bite she takes, making me struggle to not laugh while eating my own meal as I watch her enjoy her abomination.

"Mm... thanks for that. It was delicious. Do you mind if I have a shower?" Kara asks as she finishes her last bite and rests back against the lounge with a hand on her stomach.

I grin as I stand, collecting our empty plates to put in the dishwasher but pause before I exit the room to answer. "You can, so long as you're willing to pay the fee."

I walk through to the kitchen and see her turn to look at me in her seat.

"Fee?" Kara asks curiously. I nod while focusing on rinsing the plates, trying to keep a straight face.

"You want to get naked and soapy in my shower, then you've got to let me join or leave the door open."

I can't look at her as I say this or I'll laugh, so I bend down to place the dishes in the washer as I hear her huff of indignation.

"What happened to being a gentleman?" Kara challenges,

and I have to work at keeping my voice even when I reply.

"I spent the night being tormented by the fact I had you naked in my bed, but you were too drunk to have any fun with. Any intentions I had about being a gentleman in the light of day were beaten to death by how badly I want you."

I stand back up, shutting the door of the machine with my foot as I grip the bench top with both hands.

I lean over and risk a quick peek her way. Kara's gaze rests on my abs for a moment with a glazed look before trailing up my chest. Her distrustful frown makes me grin again as she shakes her head.

"Too bad. You're not watching me shower or joining, you perv. I'll just wait until I get home."

My chuckle finally escapes me, and I shake my head. "You can use the shower and anything else here. Really, you don't have to even ask. I'll leave you to it if you want, but you can't blame a guy for trying."

Kara glares as though she doesn't see the humour in my joke, but I see her lips twitch, so I wink and step away to fetch a clean towel from the linen closet.

I throw the soft, fluffy towel to her and fall down on the sofa with my right leg kicked over the arm of it.

"Dickwad," Kara complains as she passes, hitting me in the face with her towel.

"I'm a guy, what do you expect?" I call out as she retreats down the hall, her only response the bathroom door firmly shutting and the resounding click of the lock latching into place.

This makes me chuckle as I lean over to grab the Xbox controller.

"OH, MY GOD. Stop killing me, you cheater!" Kara complains

from beside me. Then she begins beating me with her controller as I lean back and try blocking her attack with my arms up and crossed in front of me.

"How am I cheating? That's the whole point of the game, sunshine," I protest and manage to pin her hands to her lap while trying not to laugh at the sore loser.

"Stop repeatedly picking the ninja dude with all the swords and stabbing me to death before I can even get a hit in for one. And go put a shirt on. Or pants," Kara retorts indignantly, and her huffy little pout has me laughing.

"Sorry. Is my irresistible nakedness distracting? You can't handle all of this?" This makes Kara growl and try to break free of my grip on her hands, but I hold tighter so she squirms her way to sitting on the edge of the sofa—as far away from me she can get.

"Aww... show me your owie, and I'll kiss it better, you sore loser," I taunt. She silently flips me the bird through my grip on her hand before yanking on my hold harder this time. The force of it has me colliding into her, which causes Kara to lose her balance, and we both fall to the floor. I let go just in time to stop most of my upper body from slamming into her, my hands landing on either side of Kara's head. I instinctively go to pull back, but then my brain catches up. I slowly lower myself to take advantage of this opportunity while her eyes are still shut in anticipation of the crash landing.

"Hmm... this is nice," I murmur when I'm cushioned by Kara's lean but soft body from chest to groin, her legs between mine and her tits squished under my weight perfectly so I can feel her hard nipples poking at me.

Kara's eyes burst open, and she pushes her head back into the carpet as though she didn't expect to come literally face to face with me. That or she's trying to escape me again.

"Get off me," Kara instantly orders, and then starts pushing at my sides with her little hands, but I shake my head so our noses brush.

"Not until you stop being grumpy and give me a smile." I lean back a little to see her full face, but she only glares at me, so I shift my weight off one hand and grab her wrist again, leaning back on my knees and grabbing the other wrist. I lean back over her and trap them in the one hand against the floor above her head.

"Fine. You want to do this the hard way… Let's see if you're ticklish." I trail my free hand down her arm softly and feel her twitching a little as she protests loudly and tries futilely to buck me off when I get to her armpit. I grin but continue my trail down, over the shirt and around her breast that I fight to ignore. I reach her ribs, and that's when she really starts squirming and bucking as she screams.

"Come on, give it up to me, sunshine," I prod and continue tickling her ribs as her legs kick like crazy beneath me.

I hear a loud, feminine throat clearing behind me and pause, turning my head to see Aela in all black, leaning against the doorway looking amused.

"Have I come at a bad time? Are these no longer needed?" She holds up a cloth bag, clearly holding Kara's clothes. I shake my head as Kara begins yelling for Aela's help.

"Na. We're good, right, babe?" I grin back down at Kara and watch her glare turn glacial before she swiftly brings her leg up between us to knee me in the tender spot just above my hipbone. This causes me to instantly lose all strength in my limbs, and she shoves me to the side as I collapse.

"Do *not* call me babe. It's not sweet and cute. It's derogatory, and it pisses me off how you arseholes use it to try to get your way."

Kara jumps to her feet as I curl into the foetal position, clutching my side while I try to breathe through the pain. *Fuck*. It

98

feels like my kidney is going to burst.

I hear the girls talking but can't focus to make out the words before Kara heads down the hallway where I hear a door slam.

"Sorry. Kara hates guys using *any* generic pet names, just so you know. Sweetheart, baby, babe, darling, the lot of them." Aela gives me a sympathetic cringe.

"Noted," I choke out then try to haul myself up into a sitting position against the sofa with controlled deep breathing but can't help panting once I come to rest.

"Can I get you anything or help you up?" Aela asks when I calm down. I shake my head as I hear a door opening down the hall seconds before Kara appears, still looking mightily pissed off.

"Let's go," she suggests to Aela, walking straight out the front door without so much as a pause or a look my way.

"You're not even going to... say goodbye?" Aela mumbles the last bit of her question when she's cut off by the screen door slamming. "Right. See you later, Alex. Hope she didn't get you too bad."

She gives me a small awkward wave of her hand as I assure her I'll be fine.

The apartment feels too quiet after I hear them drive away. Too empty. As though having Kara here had filled something that's now noticeably empty, and I don't like it one bit.

I sit there until the pain fades enough to be ignored, then get up and make my way to my room. The bed is made with the shirt she wore sitting on the end, but nothing else is out of place, almost as though she was never here. Except for the riding crop I spy peeking out from the gap between the wall and bedside table, which makes me grin. I collect it then take it back to the lounge with me, grabbing my phone to text her;

"I wasn't trying to be insulting, but I'm still sorry for hurting you. Also, you left something here I think you may want back so let me know when you're free next."

I'm expecting an instant snarky reply but wait for five minutes before I realise what I'm doing. I throw my phone to the couch as I get up to pace the length of the room.

I'm hanging for any attention this woman gives me like a complete *chick*. This is not me, and I don't like or understand it. She's consuming my thoughts, both awake and asleep, every other minute of the day. How can my mind so callously and easily shove Grace aside for someone new? Guilt burns like acid in my chest at the thought. How could I do that, just forget about the girl I loved for more than half my life for a chick I barely know?

The apartment suddenly goes from feeling too big and empty to feeling like the walls are closing in on me and airless. I need to get out. I rush into a pair of shorts, grab my smokes, phone and keys, then slip on a pair of flip flops at the door, only to come to a standstill once I'm outside. *Shit.* I forgot my car is still at the tavern.

I light a cigarette with shaky hands and call Declan to see if he's free to drop me to my car. Even though I work at keeping my voice even and the conversation short, Dec clearly senses something's wrong because he pulls up much sooner than expected. He is leaning over the centre console with a concerned frown peeking over his mirrored aviators before I can even get the passenger door open.

"What's up, bro?" he asks, turning the stereo down as I slide into the leather seat. I shrug, wishing I had my own shades to hide behind.

"I'm just tired. Didn't get much sleep last night."

It's true. Just not what has me rattled, but I'm keeping my mental shit to myself. Dec has enough on his plate with the bikies wanting to bring trouble into his shop, so he doesn't need my issues. Especially when that means I'd have to come clean on my past with his sister, something I plan to take to my grave after all this time and avoid him giving me a beating. Not that I can't take him, but I would deserve it and not lift a hand to defend myself.

"I heard Aela had to pick Kara up from your place. Dude, you are one smooth fucker to get into her pants. I thought for sure she hated your arse—enjoyed teasing you but would never give it up. I'm buying you a beer for that."

Dec punches me in the shoulder, and I shake my head before taking the last drag of my cigarette, crushing the butt in the ashtray.

"I didn't, bro. I gave her my bed and slept on the couch. Well, barely. Do you know the chick sleeps naked? I suffered through the night with the worst case of blue balls I've ever had, knowing she was naked in my bed but too drunk to take advantage of the moment."

God. Just the thought of it still has me shifting in my seat.

Dec throws me a commiserating grimace between watching the road. "Been there, man. I reckon you've earned something harder than beer. We'll hang for a bit," Dec suggests as he pulls into the tavern's parking lot.

"This is all your fault, you know?" I complain as I take a seat at the opposite side of the bar from where I'd been last night. My eyes wander over there as my mind replays images of Kara in her hot-as-hell getup, dancing, laughing, and having fun. *Damn it*. I resolutely turn my back on that area of the bar and focus my accusatory glare on Declan, who looks amused as he awaits my explanation, face tilted my way expectantly. I almost want to shove him from his stool for enjoying my misery.

"You went and let yourself get domesticated by your sweet little thing, which brought her evil best friend into our family of misfits. If it wasn't for you, I wouldn't even know Kara existed with her irritatingly bitchy, impenetrable wall of defence," I point out. I then wave over the guy walking in through a door behind the bar.

"*Domesticated*? I'm not a fucking pet. Arsehole." Dec laughs, shoving me in the arm before ordering two Gentleman Jacks.

"Might as well be, the way you follow Aela around like a puppy. It's sick, man," I tease once the bartender walks away.

"You mean sick—like how you begged and bribed for Kara's number in order to work with her, or how you so eagerly went to that party last night?" His brow quirks smugly because he knows he has me there.

"Touché," I concede, taking the chilled glass bottle from the bartender before he can place it in front of me. I toast Dec with a tilt of it before taking a long pull of the refreshing drink.

"I'm over it. I'm not interested in a relationship, so no one night of sex is worth jumping through all her hoops. No matter how great that sex might be." I voice my resolution as I place the bottle on the bar but avoid Dec's eyes because while I'm determined to stick to it, ejecting Kara from my mind feels as though it will be easier said than done.

"Whatever you say, bro." His tone sounds just as unconvinced as I feel, but I choose to ignore it and finish my drink.

We shoot the shit for a while but only have the one drink before Dec has to leave for an appointment. I have to work tonight anyway, but I still feel too restless. I stop at home to grab my board and wetsuit and then head to the beach for a surf, hoping it will clear my head. There's an inner peace I can only find when I'm out in the water, where I can leave all my worries on the shore and focus only on the waves and the necessary motions to ride them. It makes me appreciate any time I get to surf, so I stay out until the last rays of sun sink behind the mountains, then leave, feeling loose-limbed, refreshed and recharged, despite my lack of sleep.

I notice my phone is lit up as I peel off my soaked wetsuit, so once I'm in a dry pair of shorts, I pick it up from the centre condole of my Jeep. My stomach tightens when I see a text from Kara and open it hesitantly.

"Sorry I bitched out and hurt you. Brunch tomorrow, my shout?"

I'm not replying. I'm determined to stick to my resolution. Let Kara hate me. I'll give her whip to Dec to pass on.

Chapter 8

KARA

I'M A BITCH. I feel horrible for my literally knee-jerk reaction to Alex calling me babe. It pissed me off at the time, but my anger wasn't directed at him. Not really. In the back of my mind, I knew Alex meant it innocently, but in my head, it was spoken by a different voice from my past that brought with it the memories of betrayal and hurt that's best left behind. Damn lying, cheating, arsehole, brother-of-my-best-friend, Nate.

Aela didn't try to hide the disapproval on her face but remained silent the entire drive home until pulling into her parking spot. My anger had died by then, and I just felt tired and stupid. She questioned me quietly, and I tried to shrug it off as PMS and a hangover before escaping to the elevator.

But that wasn't it. Not only did I have the flashback, but Alex had also been slipping through my walls during our time together with how thoughtful and playful he'd been. I hadn't noticed how much until Aela's arrival. I'd been seconds away from just giving in and letting Alex have whatever he wanted.

Aela had to rush to keep up with me to the lift and gave me her disapproving look again but didn't bother commenting.

I shut myself in my room, threw myself onto the bed, and groaned into the quilt. I lay for a while before deciding to drown my problems in a bubble bath. I pulled myself up, gathered the essentials to head into the main bathroom, which has the only bath in the apartment. It's a wonderful little spa.

I realise I left my stuff in Aela's car while looking for my phone to play music, but I let it go. I can't deal with her again just yet. I need some time to get my head on straight—a soak in water hot enough to melt off my skin and bubbles. Lots of bubbles.

I wake up to pounding on the bathroom door and Aela asking if I'm alive. Clearly, I've been in the tub a good while, because my fingers and toes are seriously waterlogged and the water is lukewarm. I murmur affirmatively as I haul myself out.

Aela must have brought in my things from her car, as I find my bag dumped on my bed. I retrieve my phone to find a text from Alex, amongst a couple of my daily hate texts that I now automatically delete without reading.

It's timed hours ago, around the time we left his place and I feel even guiltier. Without over thinking it, I send him a text.

An hour later, I'm sitting on the edge of my bed, biting my nails as my phone sits silently beside me. I try not to look at it or will Alex to reply, but I can't help it.

I hate myself for acting this way and try to stop the nail biting by keeping my hands busy braiding my hair. Aela's already in bed, so I don't have her company to distract me. I turn on my television then scoot up to my pillows, making sure to drag my phone with me. I channel surf but find nothing of interest. Then I try to read for a while, but my brain doesn't retain a single word of three pages, so I do the only thing left—I retrieve a small tub of Chunky Monkey ice cream from our emergency stash and hack away at it while randomly searching the computer for videos to watch.

Before I know it, it's four thirty a.m. I shut my laptop with it still on the latest makeup tutorial so I can watch it when I wake up, and then get comfy in bed. I don't even think about uselessly checking my phone or even about Alex as I wait for sleep to take me.

Nope. Not at all.

Until the vibration of my phone drags me back from that in-between state. My hand snaps out for it before my eyes even open. Thankfully, it's Alex and not the unknown number of hate.

"No worries, sunshine. Shit. I can still call you that without being attacked, right? Because you're sunshine to me—until you spill hateful words from that mean, lickable mouth of yours ;-) Next time I piss you off, try not to go for vital organs though, please? I like brunch. When and where?"

The stupid grin I feel growing on my face has nothing to do with his words. Nu uh. Yeah, okay, my denial isn't even fooling myself.

I bite my bottom lip to control my stupid facial muscles. I noticed the first time he started calling me sunshine, but it never irked me like generic pet names usually do. I think because the look in his eyes whenever he's said it has never been scheming, only genuinely affectionate and playful. Same with the tone he says it in, which is free of the condescending mollycoddling I'm used to hearing.

"Your 'vitals' are safe with sunshine, but I can't promise their safety if you piss me off. And, if you try to lick my mouth, you'll find my teeth are just as bad. How about the café across from me on the corner at 11?"

Not as witty as I'd like to be, but the best my brain can do this late with the buzzing of sleep deprivation in my ears. I snuggle deeper into my pillow and barely read his instant confirmation of the date before I succumb to sleep.

I'VE JUST SNAGGED us a booth against the bank of windows

the sun is shining through when Alex arrives looking a little rough but still edible.

He has his Ray Bans on protecting his eyes from the harsh morning light. His hair is a sexy mess, there's a hint of dark stubble shadowing his jawline, and his loose singlet leaves very little to the imagination. Even his cargo shorts show a delicious set of calves and hug his arse perfectly—if the looks of the girls he passes on his way to me are anything to go by.

I notice the knowing tilt of his lips as he slides in the bench opposite me, so I yank the chain on my thoughts clear away from the gutter.

"Morning. Fun night?" I ask cheerily as he removes his shades to reveal those jade green eyes that still manage to be striking as bloodshot as they are.

"Could have been better. Sorry if I woke you this morning with my text, I'd just got off work and didn't even think about the time," he explains, rubbing his eyes as though still trying to wake up before he lifts the menu to check it out.

"It was fine. I was just going to bed."

Alex's eyes snap up from the menu to look at me with speculation.

"Fun night?" his voice is growly as he repeats my question, making it sound as though he doesn't really want to know.

"If you call stuffing your face with too much Ben and Jerry's while surfing YouTube a fun Saturday night, then sure. It was great fun," I joke and watch his brows rise in disbelief.

"Ben *and* Jerry?" It takes me a moment to understand his shock. I laugh out loud, drawing glances from the other people in the café.

"Ice cream, you perv!" I explain through my laughter.

Relief washes over his face before he looks back to the menu with a small smile.

"Thrilling night. My grandma would approve," Alex mocks

from behind his laminated menu, and I flick the back of it.

"Not all of us can work at a strip club or get paid to walk around half naked."

His eyes peek over the menu with a glint of mischief in them. "I'd pay you to walk around half naked."

I roll my eyes but refuse to comment.

"Do you know what you want to eat?" I grab my wallet, preparing to get up to order since it's my shout while I watch him expectantly.

Alex's menu lowers as he looks at me salaciously, leaning towards me with his elbows on the table. "I do. I *so* do."

Oh, boy. The invitation in his growly tone.

"Okay, stop. I'm talking about food, Alex."

He chuckles at my exasperation, leaning back and putting the menu away.

"I'll have the all-day breakfast and a coke, for now."

I ignore his leering and head for the counter to order, making sure I get the biggest serve of coffee they have while trying to contain my vitriol for the overly bouncy and cheery blonde who serves me. It's just not natural to be that perky so early. The one cup I had before leaving home wasn't enough to deal with Alex's innuendos and drool-inducing yumminess—and then this server's perkiness combined, it makes me want to stab some eyeballs.

"Can I ask something without you getting mad?" Alex asks as I take my seat again. This makes me smirk as I meet his inquisitive look.

"You just did," I point out smartly, receiving a lifted brow as his only reply, so I wave my hand in approval.

"You can tell me where to go if it's too personal, but considering how intimate your knee got with my kidney, I think I deserve to know. What's up with your total hate of pet names, and is there an arse I have to kick for it?"

The bubbly server interrupts, placing our drinks on the table and leans in suggestively to get Alex's attention, but his eyes never leave mine as I mumble my thanks to her.

"I don't think you could handle the list of names. Let's just say I grew up surrounded by arseholes who use meaningless sweet talk to get what they want. I picked up on how belittling it is." I fiddle with my napkin for something to focus on and avoid eye contact as I feel the weight of Alex's stare.

"How? Give me something so I can understand."

I don't like his pushing. I hate to think about this, let alone talk about it. The emotional wounds tied to the memories still cut deep. I work hard to lock them away, to move on while making sure it never happens to me again. Lesson learned.

Alex reaches over to cover my hands that I'm so focused on as I destroy the napkin, forcing me to stop and look up at him. The patient concern in his eyes only works to piss me off. Because while I hate the memories, I hate looking weak or vulnerable in front of a guy even more. I steel my spine and use the anger to shut off any other emotion as I keep my eyes locked onto his.

"Why, so you can figure out a way around it and get me to trust you enough to give you what you want? It won't work, but I'll tell you the headliners just so you know how aware I really am. Let's see... There's the story of my best friend's older brother I crushed on for as long as I can remember growing up, which everyone knew and teased me about, including him—until four years ago, when I grew curves, and he started looking at me differently. That douchebag was my first everything, and I stupidly believed every word he fed me. I was over the moon even though he said we had to keep our relationship a secret for a few months until my eighteenth birthday so no one would get mad at us. I was his *beautiful girl* until I went looking for him at his family's New Year's Eve party and found him in his en suite bathroom, banging his ex-girlfriend and murmuring the same *sweet* words to her."

I take a breath as my brain registers my words, but I continue. "Nate saw me in the mirror before I ran out, and he found me an hour later, but didn't try apologising or explaining himself. Oh, no. He just wanted to make sure I still wouldn't tell anyone about us. Or there's the next day when I found my dad screwing his receptionist in his office. He tried using every pet name in the book to placate me after I went ape shit on his cheating arse. A few weeks later, I was watching idiots desperately try to hook up at a school dance when I figured out those words were used against the female population and weren't special at all. So, whatever game you're trying to play you can forget because no amount of pretty words will work on me."

I finally stop and realise I don't want to be here anymore. I didn't intend to go that far, but I couldn't stop the words from spilling from my stupid mouth. I move to slide out of the booth, but our food arrives, and Alex props his leg on my seat, blocking my escape.

"Sit back. Stay and eat. Jeez, give a guy a moment to process the shit you just unloaded."

I settle back to give him a moment, my eyes glued to the pancakes placed before me that look mouth-watering though my appetite has vanished.

After several silent moments, I take my cutlery and pick at what's on my plate for something to do because I feel awkward as hell.

"Kara."

I look up when Alex says my name but focus on his nose instead of meeting his gaze.

"I'm sorry the guys in your life have let you down like that. It's really shitty, but you shouldn't hold a grudge against all males and use it as a reason to not let anyone in."

I raise my brows and snort indignantly.

"Are you going to try to tell me you've never used *babe* or the like when you didn't care to know a chicks name before?" I counter snidely.

Alex is the one to look away with a grimace this time, but his eyes quickly return to mine.

"I'll admit, sometimes names aren't even exchanged in my hook-ups for me to forget, but when I use a pet name, I mean it affectionately, even if it is only in the heat of the moment. I never make promises I don't plan to keep or say things I don't mean, which is the difference I'm trying to point out. I'm sorry, but I think you're only denying yourself this small form of intimacy and that's just sad."

"No. It's about respect. Making sure the guy I'm with knows exactly who they're having sex with and not just any available hole," I argue a little too loudly, drawing attention from a few people around us. I shove a forkful of ice cream coated pancake into my mouth to shut myself up.

Alex laughs in disbelief at my use of words then shakes his head as he cuts into his food.

"I see your point, but we'll have to agree to disagree on some points. Now eat your breakfast and let's talk about something nicer. What are you wearing under that sexy little skirt?"

I choke on my swallow of food at his question, and Alex grins unrepentantly as I look at him in shock.

"You're a bastard," I complain, smacking my chest with the heel of my left hand in an attempt to clear my throat as I cough and struggle to regain my breath.

"Nope, my parents were happily married long before I came along. I'm just a bit of a dick," Alex remarks and I roll my eyes, pausing with my coffee halfway to my lips.

"A huge dick," I correct, instantly regretting my words when I realise how he'll take them.

Sure enough, Alex winks with a proud grin,

"You know it, sunshine."

I laugh in amusement as I shake my head reproachfully while Alex's grin transforms into a tender smile.

I realise how quickly and effectively his playfulness lifted the mood in our booth. For maybe the first time since we met, I can appreciate his brand of boyish charm.

"But you haven't seen it yet. We should go somewhere I can show you so you can be certain, and in turn, I can find out the answer to my question myself since you're avoiding answering."

And then he goes overboard.

"You really need a filter for that mouth of yours," I object, not bothering to comment on his actual suggestion.

Alex places his cutlery on his plate then leans over towards me without a hint of a smirk on those tempting lips. "Believe me. I've got one. You would've fled ages ago if I shared all the inappropriate thoughts I've had since entering this shop to find you sitting here, looking like an angel of sin, bathed in the sun coming through the window."

Why did I think having breakfast together was a good idea? I'm blaming sleep deprivation because that's the only logical reason.

"You wanted to have breakfast to apologise for nearly rupturing my kidney and because, really, you want to be around me."

I don't realise I'd spoken out loud until Alex replies to my musings.

"Just FYI, food is good, but a better apology would have been to kiss it better. Preferably while naked and in my bed. Though, I'm not picky about the location so long as there's no clothing. Just saying for future reference if you ever need it." Alex continues eating after his crass statement, but I drop my cutlery to my plate and wipe my hands with finality of both the food and the conversation.

I don't know what I'd been hoping our conversation during breakfast would consist of, but the sexual innuendos are getting piled on too thick for me to find amusing. I have no intention of sitting through it for another minute.

"Right, I've had enough. I was hoping we could maybe be friendly since we're bound to see a lot of each other while our friends are together, but I guess not. Enjoy your breakfast. Maybe the waitress will enjoy your conversational skills more than I do."

I grab my belongings and slide out of the both, dumping his foot to the floor before he can protest with more than the sound he makes through his stuffed mouth.

I force a smile and thank the waitress as I pass her on my rush out the door. I'm halfway to my building and am just thinking I may get away without being stopped when a hand grips my left arm just above the elbow, and I'm jerked to a halt.

"What the hell, Kara?" I've turned around and facing Alex, his expression a mix of confusion and a little annoyance as his eyes flick between mine.

"You were laughing at the crap I was spouting a few minutes ago. I was just trying to keep it going because your laugh is warm and sweet as fuck. I don't know why it suddenly offended you, but I'm sorry. You could have just told me to shut the hell up instead of storming off without finishing your food."

I break from his grip and back away several steps until he follows. I put a hand up to stop him.

"I don't know why I'm surprised it's all about sex with you—you're just like every other guy. Forget about it, okay? It's fine."

I turn to walk away, but he stops me again.

"No, it's not okay. Jesus, you make my head spin with your mood swings. I—"

"*Mood swings*? Like I'm some unstable, crazy woman? I'll show you mood swing—" My rant is cut off in an embarrassing squeal when Alex suddenly pulls me against him, slamming his mouth to mine.

His lips are hard and unyielding for a moment, but then soften as he pulls back slightly and then loosens his hold on me. His plush, perfectly soft lips tenderly place little pecks on mine before sucking my bottom lip between them. He playfully nips at it with his teeth then releases my lip with a small popping sound, emitting a low growl from the back of his throat that sends a tingle of anticipation down my spine.

Alex slips his tongue out to glide over the seam of my lips seeking admittance. I give in with a deep inhale of breath before he blocks the passage of air as his mouth seals to mine, his tongue teasingly prodding my own into action. He's good at this. Too good. My hands are clutching at his biceps as my body practically melts into him.

Alex's kiss is slow, tender, and thorough, as though he has all the time and not a care in the world.

Really, neither do I, as everything but this kiss ceases to exist. I don't remember why I was mad or why it was important to keep him at arm's length. All that matters is his hands gently holding my face as though I'm something precious and fragile, his mouth on mine and… the unexpected barbell through his talented tongue.

Our kiss seems to last forever yet not long enough when he slowly pulls back. I open my eyes to see him blinking at me as though he's coming back to earth. I know the feeling because I feel off balance. Like the earth has tilted on its axis, but as I take in the people gawking as they pass us, it's clear to only have affected the two of us.

"Golden syrup and coffee have never tasted as good as it does on you," Alex murmurs, his voice husky as he slips a hand from my cheek into my hair at the nape of my neck, the other hand lowering to rest at my waist. I lick my wet lips, watching his eyes zero in on the movement hungrily. I give him a smile as my stomach flutters at how affected he is by me.

"You seriously just kissed me into submission. I should be mad or at least annoyed about it, but I'm struggling to give a damn. You're talented with that pierced tongue of yours. Didn't know you had that," I muse.

Alex grins smugly. "Wait until you see what my tongue is most talented at, sunshine. It'll rock your world."

I laugh light-heartedly, reaching up to move some of the hair that has fallen into his eyes.

"Your ego is impossibly huge. How do you fit through doorways with that massive head of yours?"

"Easy. I mostly keep it in my pants." He winks, and I slap his chest as I really laugh at that one.

"While you're in a slap happy, S&M mood, I have your whip in my car if you want to come get it."

"That's what I forgot that you thought I'd need?" I laugh as I step back out of his embrace. Alex shrugs, stuffing his hands into the front pockets of his shorts.

"Hey, I don't know what you do when I'm not around. You could work as a dominatrix at night for all I know—which, by the way, is a totally hot image. You in all that leather…" his eyes slowly travel down my body, clearly projecting this fantasy in his head onto me.

"Okay. Let's go get it before I remember how to be mad at you." I wave for him to lead the way. Alex chuckles and takes my hand to wrap it around the crook of his elbow as though he's escorting me like a gentleman.

"If you recall it on the way, feel free to use the whip on me once we get there."

I elbow him lightly in the ribs in reply, struggling to contain a goofy smile.

Alex leads me to his beat up old Jeep and extracts my whip from the passenger seat with a flourish.

"My lady." He presents it to me with a dramatic bow, and I laugh as I take it. "Now that you have it back, what do you say we go upstairs, and you test it out on me?" Alex wags his brows eagerly, so I playfully tap the handle of the riding crop against my chin as though I'm actually considering it.

"Tempting. But I can't. I have a lot to do on an assignment due tomorrow."

Alex doesn't look the least bit defeated.

"I could come help. I've been told I'm a great study buddy?" he offers with that mischievous smirk that promises distraction.

I shake my head adamantly as I push him towards his car door. "I'm sure you have, but no thank you."

Alex braces his legs to stop me from pushing him just before he reaches the gutter.

"All right then. How about you give me a thank you kiss since I went out of my way to return it?" I raise my brows at his suggestion.

"You already got one—don't push it."

Alex shakes his head this time.

"No. I stole one, and I don't recall you complaining at the time. In fact, I know you *loved* it. So shut up and give me those delicious lips," Alex leans in expectantly.

I want to. *So* badly. But I can't encourage him to continue pursuing whatever it is he wants from me, and I can't start liking the guy. No good can come from it. I panic and do the only thing I can think of—I turn without so much as another word to him and run for the lobby of my building. I take the stairs without pausing until I'm three floors up, and then step out to take the elevator. I collapse on the floor, heaving for breath once I'm safely locked in my apartment.

Chapter 9

ALEX

WATCHING KARA'S EYES, I knew the second she decided to run, and I mentally cursed myself for pushing my luck while watching her disappear into the apartment building.

I could have chased after her—I wanted to—but I couldn't see the outcome being any better, so I let her run away and have her space for now.

At least, I have some insight into why she's so hot and cold. *Fuck,* just remembering her story has me gritting my teeth against the need to punch something—preferably the face of the dickwad who took advantage of her. Kara deserved better than that for her first time.

I take a slow, deep breath meant to calm me down but don't feel any different as I climb into my Jeep. I try to force it to the back of my mind, thinking up another plan of attack because I can't let her go. This infatuation with her is now critical after my failed attempt at moving on yesterday.

It was pitiful, and it pissed me off that a woman could get me so wound up without even trying. I was mad to the point that when I first came to breakfast, I was set on getting under her dress in a misguided act of revenge to steal back the masculinity she'd robbed me of.

The second my eyes found her sitting in that booth, though,

it all faded away. Kara looked like a damn angel basking in the sun. I received a huge, genuine smile the moment she saw me, as if she was happy to see me, and she damn near had me kneeling at her feet. Then that kiss. Jesus. I know I stole it, but that didn't make the way she reciprocated any less giving. The surrender of her soft, warm body melting into me and the sweet taste of her mouth as her tongue eagerly introduced itself to mine was intoxicating. I swear I can still faintly taste the mix of golden syrup and coffee.

I need more.

I MANAGE TO hold off contacting Kara for three days, taking another hit to the ego when I don't hear from her in that time, but I let it go.

Just because the woman is stubborn, doesn't mean she isn't missing me. I send her a picture message of my ugly mug Wednesday night while on my break, asking if she's missed it, anticipating a sarcastic reply. She doesn't disappoint. A few minutes later, I get a picture of her fresh-faced and messy-haired while pulling a face with her eyes crossed that I'm sure she's aiming to look unattractive with, but it just makes her cute. The accompanying text states: "You missed this more."

I have to agree—though I notice her reply wasn't a denial.

I take it as a win. We wind up texting away my break, and I return to work with a grin on my face and a plan in mind.

The next morning, after my typical nightmare awakening, I make my way to Ink Fix to talk Dec into my double date plan. I instantly forget all about it, though, when I slide open the door to find the front of the shop looking like a war zone and overhear arguing coming from down the hall. The debris of broken glass and fragments of the television and the shelving unit crunch loudly under the soles of my chucks as I make my way across the room towards what sounds like Kit and Aela giving a very disgruntled Dec a tongue lashing of the not so fun kind.

He places himself in the doorframe, barring Kit and Aela behind him just as I get to the hallway, then gives me a relieved look when he recognises it's me. I shoot him back a questioning one of my own.

"What the fuck happened in here?" I exclaim when he doesn't answer my silent question.

Kit forces him out of her way, looking mightily pissed off and determined like she's ready to kick some arse with the broom she's wielding, though I catch the wobbling of her bottom lip before she bites it, facing me with a daring look. I'm smart enough to keep my mouth shut. I don't want my rectum to be the new home for her broomstick.

I turn back to Dec but catch sight of Aela trying to get by him also and feel my eyes go wide.

She's wearing a tight, white singlet that leaves nothing to the imagination and her nipples are high beaming. I don't know if I'm more shocked that the sweet little thing has such a spectacular rack, or because Dec lets her be around other people like that. Either way, my eyes are glued to her tits as my brain short circuits in shock.

Dec curses and blocks my view while ordering her to go upstairs. I turn when I feel a presence at my back to find Skunk there, giving the couple a questioning look as they have a standoff. I silently hold my hands out in front of my chest in the universal gesture of boobs. He follows me as I try to get another peek over Dec's shoulder—only to find out what's going on... she is my boy's girl, after all—but Declan feels us there and shrugs us off while placing his body even more in the way to block our view.

Aela laughs then skips up the stairs when Dec growls like an animal in warning and begins shoving us backwards.

"Dude, I need to get in there to grab some ink containers," Skunk complains as he tries to fight Dec's pushing while his feet slide along the tiles uselessly.

"Oh, hey, Aela. Didn't see you there. Come give me a hug, girl," he adds when Aela rounds the landing to the second lot of stairs, which makes her laugh as Dec elbows Skunk in the stomach.

"Bro, you've got to work on your social skills. We're just trying to say hi to your girl," I tease before Dec turns with a glare.

"Fuck off, arseholes."

I chuckle at how unhappy he looks but then glass crunches under my shoe as I step back, reminding me of the destruction of the shop, and I lose my amusement.

"You going to tell me what happened to the shop now?" Dec runs his hands through his hair then down his face, dragging the skin of his cheeks with how hard he rubs it, like it's all just too much for him.

"A couple of guys came in and started busting up the place while Kit was in the back. She called me when she saw them on the surveillance feed through the TV and decided to go after them with a baseball bat instead of waiting for me to get here." He sounds bemused, as though he can't believe Kit would do that, but I can totally picture it. The girl has balls of steel and loves this shop as if it's a living child of hers, as well as everyone in it. I so want to get a look at the footage of that momma bear chasing the punks off—that shit will be priceless.

We head back to where the hallway opens to the front of the shop, and the three of us stop to take in the destruction, trying to pick where to start cleaning as Kit sweeps a corner free of glass.

"Wow. Someone really had a grudge against the TV," Skunk remarks after several moments of silence, and we all look to where a lot of effort was put in to pull the television from the brackets bolting it to the wall. I don't know how they managed it, but a couple of the bolts have been pulled, so the whole thing hangs on an angle, pieces of the plastic shell smashed off and the screen shattered.

"Kit, let me do that. Can you make a call to the cabinet guy you know for a replacement?" Dec rushes to take the broom from her as she curses when a piece of glass she'd been sweeping flicks up and cuts her just above her right ankle.

Kit looks up with a glare as she blows away some of her pink fringe that fell into her eyes, but she softens when she meets his gaze.

"Knock yourself out." She passes him the broom then carefully makes her way over the mess to grab the cordless phone. She then takes it outside as Skunk tackles removing the television. I watch Kit curse and pace outside for a second and then move to take the broom from Dec, who shoots me a questioning glance.

"Talk to Kit. She doesn't look as okay as she is acting, and we know she'll take your concern much better than mine." I tilt my head in a gesture towards her which Dec follows. We watch for a moment before he nods with a sigh, releasing the broom to me. I turn my back to give them some semblance of privacy and pick up where Kit left off in the sweeping.

I notice in my peripheral when they both return, but I continue working until I'm halfway across the waiting area and Dec approaches.

"I need you to walk Aela home to make sure she gets there safely," he murmurs with his head close to mine, so I pause my sweeping to meet his anxious gaze.

"You think something's going to happen to her?" I ask, schooling my facial features and avoid looking over to the woman in question. I feel her eyes on us and don't want to alarm her.

"I don't know what to think right now. I just need her safe and can't go with her myself. Just keep an eye out for me?"

I give in to his pleading with a nod and slap his back as I release the broom to him. I make my way over to where Aela is talking to Kit who is in the clean corner, righting the magazine table. I feel how tense Aela is when I put my arm around her, so I do my best to lighten the mood while ignoring Kit's unnecessary bitching.

"Just so you know… I'm taking my duty so seriously that I'm willing to make you the Whitney Houston to my Kevin Costner. I'll carry you home while simultaneously kicking arse *The Bodyguard* style. Feel free to bust out in song about how much you will always love me. I'm down with that."

It gets a laugh out of Aela, and she loosens up, which I can't help grinning proudly about. That is until Dec snaps at me to get going. I wait for her to say goodbye and then lead the way out the door. I doubt anything is going to happen in public and in broad daylight, but I still keep a vigilant eye out for anything nonetheless. I keep Aela entertained with my musings while I'm at it.

"Look out. The hipster with the handlebar moustache looks shifty to me. Quick, jump into my arms." I hold my hands out and bend my knees as though bracing myself, but Aela shoves me with a giggle as she looks at the guy sitting amongst a group of smokers in business suits that have congregated around the water feature out front of her building.

"Well, thanks for walking me. It was fun despite the circumstances." Aela makes to turn away from me dismissively, but I grab her arm as I recognise an opportunity. "Is Kara home?"

Acla shrugs with a thoughtful glance. "She should be."

I keep hold of her arm and start walking to the glass doors.

"I'm going to have to come up with you, make sure the

premises are safe for you both."

Aela barks out a laugh, shooting me a knowing look, but still goes along with it.

Aela enters their apartment in a rush, heading straight through to the hallway as I shut the door behind me.

I spy a sleep-rumpled Kara, clinging to a coffee mug with both hands where she leans against the kitchen counter. She's wearing an oversized white shirt and a concerned frown, as her gaze tracks her friends hurried movements. I take a free moment to admire her state, since she hasn't noticed me, before stepping forward and gaining her attention and an instant scowl—which makes me grin in return.

"Morning, sunshine," I greet her cheerfully as I take a seat on one of the black leather and chrome stools at the bench beside her.

"What's going on?" Kara demands, looking back the way Aela went, though she's no longer in view.

"A couple of punks smashed up the reception area of the shop and ran off when Kit went after them with a bat. Dec was concerned for Aela, so I walked her home." She bites her lip while turning back to face me.

"Is there a reason to worry about her?"

I shrug because I honestly doubt it, but it's better to be safe than sorry and wouldn't hurt for them to be cautious, especially when Snake has been sniffing around.

I tell Kara as much, and she nods gravely.

"Hey, nothing's going to happen to you two. Come here." I pull her into my arms, and she comes willingly, gripping the side of my shirt in one hand as I kiss her temple. "I promise."

Kara shoves away from me at my words with a scowl. "You can't say that. You don't know what these guys are going to do next anymore than I do, and even if you did, you couldn't stop them," she says with a hiss as she puts down her mug harder than necessary.

"You're overreacting. Nothing happened to Aela, and nothing's going to happen to you. I would glue myself to your side if I thought it would. Or just lock you in your room and distract you with amazing sex until we get the all clear." I wink, trying to calm Kara down or distract her, but she shoves passed me with a look of disgust to storm down the hall, her arms wrapped around her waist.

Well done, Alex.

I hear her talking quietly with Aela, so I decide to give them some time, hoping Aela will calm her down better than I did.

I stand there not knowing what to do with myself for several seconds before I get bored and restless. I begin to wander around and check out their pad. I inspect the photos on display around the living space and stuck to the fridge, then check out the contents of the fridge, noticing the stash of Mexican beer that Dec always drinks on the bottom shelf, which makes me grin. I shut the door and head to their movie collection in the case beside the TV unit. I cringe when the majority of it is romance or comedy romance, with a handful of horror flicks.

Not a single porn, which is disappointing.

As I'm about to stand back out of my crouch, something bright red in the drawer that's slightly ajar on the TV unit catches my eye, so I curiously tug the drawer open more and have to fight to keep from shouting out in victory.

Jackpot.

I retrieve the DVD cases stashed in there to inspect and am impressed with what I find. Those dirty, *dirty* girls.

I spread them out on the floor to take a photo on my phone to keep for evidence before returning them.

I head down the hall to confront the girls, following the sound of their voices. I peek my head into the room but keep as much of my body hidden, because I'm pretty sure I know who the porn belongs to, and I'm anticipating an attempt of bodily harm from her.

"You girls really shouldn't leave a guy alone in your apartment to amuse himself for so long. I found some interesting things in the TV unit drawers."

Sure enough, Kara goes from looking calm to embarrassed and outraged in a split second and swings her hand around to smack me in the shoulder while Aela looks on, confused and curious.

I grin playfully and step into the room, deciding capitalising on this moment to tease her is worth the risk but keep a wary eye on all her limbs. Kara immediately starts shoving me back, yelling for me to get out, which makes me chuckle and stumble backwards, but I don't relent.

"I should have known they were yours. Great selection. Can I borrow *Wild and Raw* or maybe we can watch it together? Watching porn while snuggling is the best way to watch it." Then I put up my hands protectively as she begins squealing indignantly and shoving me away while Aela laughs behind her.

"Never, will I *ever,* watch porn with you," Kara replies scathingly, but I catch the glint of interest in her eyes. I drop all semblance of playing with her. I just can't take her pushing me away good-naturedly anymore. That shit is getting tiresome.

I grab hold of her elbows and pull her in against me so she can feel how deadly serious I am when I say, "Never say never, babe. One day, I might get fed up with this little 'hard to get' game you have going on and give you what you really want." I pointedly press my groin against her lower stomach and then force her feet together between mine, expecting a knee to the balls—or at least a verbal bashing for the pet name—as I stare her down.

But it never comes.

Her only reaction is in her eyes and *wow* is it a reaction.

There's a mighty storm of emotion in those steely grey eyes as they stare up at me with fear, doubt, anger, lust, and a little spark of hope. The fear is winning though, her eyes welling up with tears as I stare back helplessly. The only thing I can do is hope she sees the promise and determination in my eyes in return and knows I'm not messing around with her.

I give Kara a moment, but her tears threaten to spill, and she starts looking frantic for an escape, so I give her one since we have an audience. I don't want to push her until she breaks and cries, especially not in front of her best friend. I'd be branded an arsehole for life even though her tears aren't because of me. I look to Aela with as much of a smile as I can force.

"I'll get you to drop me off at the shop on your way if you're ready to go." I release Kara to walk back to the living room, but not before I catch her swiping at a tear that escapes.

I hear a muttered, "Arrogant hot-as-hell arsehole."

Which makes me chuckle as Kara makes her escape, slamming a door shut behind her. I fight the urge to follow and wrap her in my arms. I lean against the wall beside the front door, instead, with my hands in my pockets to wait for Aela. She is flitting around the apartment gathering stuff in a hurry between shooting me puzzling glances.

I give her a questioning look in reply then follow as she heads out the door.

"You're a bit of an enigma," Aela finally replies on the way to the elevator. I'm not sure where she's going with this so I play it off as a compliment and try to act like her continuing to stare at me during the ride on the lift doesn't affect me. I fight the urge to fidget nervously. I last until we get to the parking lot, where I cave and shoot her another questioning glance.

"Just don't hurt her. I know Kara acts like she has a thick skin, but it's only because she's been burned in the past. And don't tell her I told you that, or she'll kill me."

126

The fact Aela felt the need to warn me pisses me off since Kara's issues stem from *Aela's* brother. I have to bite the tip of my tongue to keep from saying something because I know Kara never told her, and I don't want to cause trouble. I work on reigning in my temper as Aela leads the way to a tiny, black Suzuki Swift, and I'm forced to cram myself inside.

"I may be a man-whore, but I don't lie or make promises I won't keep. The chicks I hook up with know the score beforehand. It's not my fault some are batshit crazy and delude themselves into thinking it can be more. I don't deliberately hurt anyone."

Unlike your arsehole brother, I add silently and then stare sightlessly out the passenger window to avoid continuing this conversation so I can calm down.

The short drive feels twice as long as the silence weighs heavily inside the small car. I practically fall out of the car in my eager escape the second Aela pulls up in front of the shop. I hurry inside with a plan to get stuck into the cleaning in order to clear my head. Unfortunately, everything's been handled and cleared up. Kit's even talking to a guy about cutting a niche into the wall to make the next television flush and protect it with a plastic faceplate. When she sees me, Kit pauses her conversation to point down the hall, letting me know it's safe to go find Dec, who is in his 'office' prepping some ink containers.

"What happened?" he asks as soon as he looks up at me, shooting up off his stool. I shake my head to calm him down before he goes storming off to the rescue when no one needs it.

"Nothing at all. Aela's safely on her way to school."

The rigidness of Dec's stance slackens in relief as he takes a step back, but his frown remains.

"Then why do you look like someone kicked your puppy?" I shrug as I walk over to his drawing desk to check out the sketch sitting there.

"Kara and her fucked up issues. The woman makes my head spin." I sigh as I admire his wicked sea monster design. I can feel Dec's eyes on me but avoid looking over until he speaks.

"This isn't just the thrill of the chase for you anymore, is it? I've never seen you hung up on a chick for so long without getting a little action."

I glare at the teasing glint in his eyes as he smiles with amusement.

"I don't know what this is anymore. I want Kara so bad. It's gone beyond want and more of an all-consuming *need,* but not just for sex. I'm desperate for any time I can get with her. I want to be there for her and can't stop thinking up things to do to make her smile, despite her continuing to reject me at every turn. I also love pissing her off because she's hot as hell when she's all fired up. That witch has my stomach in knots and my balls in her purse. I can't even get it up for another chick but am constantly fighting a semi when she's near. I don't get it, and I don't like it. This isn't me." I take a deep breath in the silence after the verbal spill of my frustrations before Dec starts laughing out loud with glee.

"I'm glad my misery entertains you so much, arsehole," I complain and shove him in the shoulder.

"It does, it really does." He continues to chuckle, so I shake my head.

"Right, I'm out. Smell you later, dick face," I grumble and then turn to walk out of the room.

I replay my outburst as I head to my car, thinking of all the stupid shit I've been doing to gain Kara's attention. I have a revelation that brings me to a standstill while climbing into my Jeep. All the stuff I sent to her and constant bugging draws forth memories of doing the exact same thing for Grace. Like how I used to make it my mission to covertly slip her favourite sweetheart lollies into her bag every school day. Or the time I paid to have roses 'anonymously' sent to every class she had one Valentine's Day until she had so many she needed a bucket to carry them and wore a brilliant smile whenever I spotted her. My mind is assaulted by a barrage of happy memories I fought to keep locked away because of how painful they are. It causes me to fall heavily into my driver's seat and I lean my head back against the headrest, eyes squeezed shut, as I fight to breathe through what feels like an elephant sitting on my chest constricting my lungs.

By the time I get the onslaught of memories locked back up in my mental vault, my freak out steps up to the plate. *Batter* up.

I did all those things because I loved Grace and swore that part of me died right along with her in that hospital bed. But Kara seems to be slowly resurrecting it. I can't have that happen. If I fall in love with her, I won't survive losing that a second time, which is inevitable. Death eventually comes for everyone.

I don't know how long I sit until it passes, but I feel exhausted as though I've run a marathon, and my hands are shaky when I finally pull out of the carpark. I can't stomach the thought of going back to my place that screams with solitude, so I head to the comfort of my parent's home, which I'm supposed to be checking up on while they're on holiday anyway.

On the way, I make a call that has my stomach twisting, but I'm determined to exorcise Kara from under my skin and out of my head.

I INSTANTLY FEEL more at ease when I pull up under the awning off the garage of my family home and practically jog up the stairs to the front door.

The familiar scents of home surround me as soon as I step inside. A mix of my mum's perfume, lemon scented cleaning supplies, and my dad's aftershave all work like a comforting blanket as I breathe it in. It calms the ragged edges of my nerves, and even though the huge house is empty, I no longer feel alone.

I check everything is as it should be, then swipe a bottle from Dad's beer fridge just as there's a knocking at the front door. My breathing halts. My stomach twists and my heart hammers in disapproval of what I'm about to do, but I grit my teeth, force out a long, slow breath and then go to answer it.

I open the door to find Trixie with a bright red smirk I'm sure she means to be sexy but just looks smug to me. Her bottle-blonde locks sit over one shoulder and dip into the cleavage that's revealed by her plunging black dress that leaves very little to the imagination and is paired with silver strappy heels.

"That was fast, Trix." I open the door wider for her to enter.

"You haven't called me in a long time. I wasn't giving you time to change your mind. I've missed you." Her hand trails over my crotch as she passes. I could apologise for not contacting her, but it was deliberate, and I'm not sorry in the least, so I don't.

"Would you like a drink?"

"Where do you want me?" Our questions are simultaneous as she turns to face me, and I smile in appreciation of her not trying to waste any time.

"We'll go to my room," I reply first. With a short nod, Trixie turns to head straight to my old room.

"Water would be nice, thanks," Trixie calls over her shoulder, so I head for the kitchen. She knows where to go because we've been friends since our senior year, and she's been here plenty of times. The chick has a bad rep thanks to her open sex life when we were teens, then becoming a stripper the second she was old enough, and then getting involved with recreational drugs.

To me though, she'd been a godsend back then. She was the first girl I slept with a year after losing Grace, and she didn't judge me when I was an emotional mess throughout the experience.

She was always there when I needed someone, and she even got me my bartending job, until she got booted from the club for dealing drugs while on the clock. I don't know her full story because she never talks much about herself, but I've gathered enough to know she had a tough home life growing up.

I enter my room to find she's made herself at home, laid out in the centre of my bed with only a micro pair of black lace panties covering her.

"So… a mind block, huh?" she asks as she props herself up on her elbows. I nod while placing the water bottle down on the bedside stand. "You want an upper?" Trixie reaches to the floor on this side of the bed where she's left her clothes, but I put my hand on her shoulder to stop her.

"No. I don't touch any of that anymore. I just need to move on."

"Okay, handsome," she concedes, taking the hand from her shoulder to tug me onto the bed into a sitting position so she can swing herself over to sit in my lap. Trixie moves both my hands to her hips, just above the scrap of fabric covering her. She starts grinding against me enticingly, her fingers running through my hair and her lips kiss, nibble, and suck a trail up and down my neck. She knows what she's doing and feels amazing, but I'm struggling to keep my head in the game and not compare her to the feel of having Kara against me, which isn't fair.

After several minutes of this, and receiving only the barest of twitches from my dick in return, Trixie leans back with a determined glint in her eyes as she slides off me.

"Lean back against the pillows and relax."

I do as I'm told as she pauses to sip her drink. She then returns to straddle me, using my hands to cup her awesome, full tits that are enough to make any man weep at the beauty of—but again, my mind compares them to Kara's perfect handfuls that I've been dying to get my hands on.

I groan in frustration against Trixie's lips without meaning to that are also disappointingly not Kara's, and she pulls back with a thoughtful little, "Hmm."

I close my eyes as she retreats and I hear the rustling of her clothes being moved.

"I'm sorry." I sound pathetic and think she's giving up on me already until I feel the bed dip with her return.

"Don't be. We'll get there if it takes me all night."

She tries going down on me with her talented little mouth for a solid ten minutes but only gets a semi for her efforts and huffs, "Right. This is starting to get to me. Have one of these for now. I'm starting to wonder if it's more than just mental." Trixie is getting demanding, producing a little blue pill from her pile of clothes, and I shake my head firmly.

"Chill out. It's nothing bad, just Viagra."

I snort at her statement and shake my head again, but she holds it out determinedly.

"If anything happens to me that shouldn't, I'll find a way to return the favour and also get Kit to beat you up."

She snorts at my threat, shoving the pill towards me, so I take it, swallowing it with a gulp of her water she offers as I glare at her.

"That was too easy. Since when is Mr Licks compliant?" Trixie teases, and I jack up off the bed to grab her around the waist, hauling her on her back onto the bed.

"You're right. Maybe that's my problem. Your turn to just lay back and relax. You've more than earned it." I press a kiss to her collarbone then move down between her thighs until my nose meets the scrap of lace between her legs. I lean back to remove them then prop her left leg over my shoulder as I return, grinning when I look up her body to see her head thrown back. A little moan escapes her in anticipation of what I'm about to do. I lick and gently bite her tender folds that are slick and warm until she's squirming underneath me in need. I add two fingers to the mix, thrusting them inside of her and rubbing against her g-spot until she shatters around me twice and breathlessly pleads for me to stop.

I press a light kiss to her over-sensitive clit, which makes her whimper then grin as I lean up over her until our eyes meet. She pulls me down to lick my lips, moaning when she tastes herself there. I dip my hips, and Trixie emits a gasp as she smiles triumphantly when I prod her slick, warm folds with a more than satisfactory erection.

I'm eagerly pushed back so she can swipe a condom from the drawer I keep them in. She expertly applies it, then takes hold of my member to guide it inside of her in a rush as if I may go limp if she's not fast enough. I watch her face as I begin to thrust into her. I use one hand to brace myself on the bed while I slide the other hand between her head and the pillow to grab a handful of her hair. Picking up the pace of my thrusts, I'm disappointed to find her hair is coarse, not soft and silky like the other blonde I'm trying not to think about, but whose face flashes behind my eyelids whenever I close my eyes as I struggle to keep them locked on Trixie.

Her nails dig into my back, her moans and gasps get louder and near-constant as my pace becomes punishingly hard and fast, causing her to call out and curse. She suddenly tightens around me and pulses in ecstasy, gushing around my dick and dragging me over the edge with her into a hard, forceful, strength-stealing climax.

I collapse onto Trixie who squeezes her arms tightly around me for a moment. We gasp for breath before she pushes on my shoulder to roll me off to her side then curls up facing me with her hands tucked under her cheek.

The euphoria of my release doesn't even last until I catch my breath when the centre of my chest hurts. I'm wracked with guilt even though I didn't do anything wrong. "Smoke break?" I need to get out of the room and get my head right as much as I need the nicotine hit.

Trixie nods, so I grab my cigarettes and jeans from the floor to put on before stepping out onto the balcony. I take a seat at the little two seater table and light up before Trixie joins me in only my shirt, holding out my cell that's vibrating with an incoming call.

"Thanks."

I exchange the cell for a smoke and see Dec's name flashing. I answer the call with a wordless murmur as I take a draw.

"Alex, I need you to watch Aela for me tonight. Some place none of the club knows about. Snake attacked her on campus, and I'm not letting him get away with it." Dec's voice is laced with fury, and I choke on the smoke in my lungs with shock, almost coughing up a lung before I can reply.

"Bring her to my parent's place."

Not only do none of the bikers know of this place, but my dad invested in some top-notch security with camera surveillance and alarms, which Dec knows, so he should be less anxious about leaving her here.

"You okay, man?" I know he's anything but, however, I'm hoping he's not going off half-cocked and crazy because that can only end badly.

"I'm in check. Not about to storm the clubhouse if that's what you think. Buzz got us an appointment to see Joe all official like, but if Snake should happen to cross my path… well, I'm more than open to that."

I mutter a curse and drop my cigarette into the ashtray to scrub my hand over my forehead where I can feel a headache coming on.

"Just don't do anything that will get your dumb-arse killed."
I sigh when he snorts derisively.

His voice is gentler when he replies, "I'll do my best."
There's a hesitation before he adds, "I've gotta go, man. See you
soon." He ends the call abruptly.

I notice a bunch of missed calls from the shop and Kit before
I toss my phone onto the small table and take back my cigarette,
looking up to see Trixie eyeing me speculatively.

"You want to talk about it?" I shake my head before leaning
back until I can only see the dusk sky and focus on making
smoke rings. I try to force myself not to get worked up and
anxious about what's going to happen—at least not until I see
Declan.

"You hungry?" I ask, rolling my head on my shoulders until
I can see Trixie off to my side. She grins salaciously as her eyes
dip to my crotch.

"Are you going to feed me?"

I give a little chuckle as I lift my head to shake it at her.
"That can be for dessert. I meant actual food that I'm going to
cook," I clarify then stand as I wait for her answer. Trixie arches
her brows with a small smile.

"You've never offered to cook me a meal before. A girl
could get used to this." She takes the hand I offer to help her
from her seat as she says this. I drop her hand almost
immediately as guilt hits me.

I'm such an arse.

Trixie sits at the breakfast bar and watches me with a
childlike giddiness even though all I'm doing is reheating one of
the containers my mum left me. As an Italian mother, she
couldn't have me coming to her house and not get a home cooked
meal just because she's away.

Eating at the dining table feels too intimate, more than what
we've ever done together, which is stupid. But I'm jittery and

awkward nonetheless and rush eating my meal to step outside for another nicotine hit.

"I'm ready for dessert now," Trixie purrs behind me, her chest pressing against my back while her hands snake around to open my jeans and slide inside.

I turn around intending to stop her, but Trixie drops to her knees, taking my jeans along for the ride. She then pushes until my back is against the railing, taking me in her mouth with a moan. The vibrations hit me just right to stop me doing anything but leaning my head back with a groan.

My hands are in her hair, and I'm lost to her ministrations when I hear a loud banging from inside and then Dec calling out. *Shit.*

"Babe... Trix, I'm sorry to say it, but we've got to wrap this up. I have to do something for Dec." I push on her shoulders as she continues sucking until my dick falls out of her mouth with a *pop* that makes me whimper.

"All right. But you owe me now," Trixie says with a wicked grin as she bounces to her feet. She then goes inside at my gesture. I take a deep breath then collect my jeans from around my ankles, thankful I only have a semi as I zip up and adjust before going after her.

Trixie comes out from my room before I reach it, dress back on and shoes in hand, as she launches herself at me to seal her lips to mine. I automatically wince but stick with my resolution, returning the kiss with just as much fervour. I walk us backwards to the door that is still being pounded on. Trixie wraps herself around me as I open the door, so I give one last ditch attempt to make this work and hold her close as I tangle my tongue with hers. It's a good kiss. The chick knows how to work it like a pro but doesn't get my heart racing and blood heating like Kara does.

I give a small sigh of defeat as I extract myself from Trixie and gently prod her out the door.

"Call me, Licks," she orders over her shoulder then pauses facing Dec long enough that Aela becomes annoyed and glares accusingly my way. I get Trixie moving with a smack to her arse. I grin at Aela smugly, which is when I get a proper look at her in the dim lighting. She has cuts and scrapes down the left side of her face and a nice shiner blooming over her eye that is swollen almost completely shut. It makes my heart drop to my stomach. I can't believe anyone could want to do this to *any* woman, but *this* little woman? She's a damn sweetheart.

The sight of her injuries and the brave front she's putting on, which is betrayed by the skittishness of her good eye, just pisses me off and makes me want to hunt down the arsehole who did it.

I can't imagine how Dec must be feeling, but going by the storm of emotions in his eyes when I look at him, it's pretty safe to say he's out for blood.

I wrap myself around Aela for comfort—mine more than hers—and so I can assure myself she's still in one piece. I grin when she complains I smell like sex, cheap perfume, and smoke as she wriggles to escape me.

"Mm... you smell great too, like vanilla and coffee. Makes me want to lick you up," I tease as I breathe in her hair, but really, there's something about her scent that calms me more than anything. It was probably not the best thing to joke about—Dec looks murderous and distraught enough without me poking the bear. Aela retaliates by jabbing her bony little fingers into my ribcage, causing me to jump and release her with an undignified yelp.

I'd intended to question Dec about his plan for this meeting to make sure he's being smart, but Aela seems determined to play off the tense aura of trepidation surrounding the whole situation. The little lady has been through enough. So I let it go and follow along with her joking while Dec tries his best also until he has to go.

I'm suddenly an awkward third wheel, not knowing what to do with myself as they share an intimate moment.

I'm about to make myself scarce when Dec pulls back from their kiss, but Aela clings on in fear for him, and it damn near makes me tear up.

Dec turns to me, his eyes showing desperation and determination.

"Look after my girl. But keep your hands and all other questionable body parts to yourself. Keep your phone by you, ears open and no alcohol until I'm back," He orders and I do my best to put on a calm, confident face as I force out a laugh and punch him in the arm.

"I've got her, bro. Crack some skulls for me while we have a sober slumber party." I try to reassure him, receiving an eye roll for my trouble before he gives Aela a final kiss. He releases her and turns to leave in a rush as though he's afraid he'll change his mind.

Aela looks as though she's seconds away from running after him, so I put an arm around her as I steer us inside. I attempt to distract her by asking if she needs something for the black eye.

After dumping their stuff into the first guest room, we set up camp in the central family room. I raid Mum's sweet stash in the vegetable crisper, swiping a bag of skittles—making a mental note to replace them, so she doesn't find out I know about her hiding spot. I look for something we can both watch on the idiot tube, landing on the *Fast and Furious* marathon because those movies are awesome. If anything on television has a chance of distracting us, it will be these movies. Seriously. Action, hot chicks, mean cars, and bad arse dudes… there's something for everyone.

It fails to work, though, and the sugar I stuff my face with only amps up my edginess, making me jittery. I can't stand being inactive and quiet. Unlike Aela, who seems content to watch the flick without running commentary.

I try to think up a way to casually bring up Kara because no one's mentioned her, and I don't know if she's safe. What if Dec's been so focused on Aela that Kara's safety has been overlooked? I'm so worried about so many things that can go wrong tonight. All the people I care about who might be in danger if something does makes me feel like I'm about to burst out of my skin which feels too tight.

Aela gets fed up with my mindless rambling about what I see on the screen and exits the room with a frustrated sigh. Without thinking about the reasons I shouldn't, I pick up my phone and call Kara, breathing a sigh of relief when she answers, sounding tired and distracted.

"Hey, sunshine. Please tell me you're okay and not home alone?" I demand quietly and then hear a male voice in the background that has me sitting straighter. I press my ear harder to the phone as though it will help me hear better.

"Hey, uh… no. I'm fine. Crashing at a friend's place. No stop—" She squeals in protest and I hear a manly chuckle.

"Is that Kris?" I ask in vain hope as a pang of jealousy hits me that some guy is clearly touching her when I can't.

"N-no. Sorry. Is there something you needed? Is Aela okay?" The laughter in her voice dies when she asks about her best friend, so I guess she's been kept in the loop.

I bite my tongue to keep from replying with a barrage of questions. I have no right to ask about who the unnamed arsehole is or telling her I need *her* in my bed—like, yesterday.

I take too long fighting myself because I hear her calling my name over the phone as though she's not sure I'm still here. So I clear my throat that feels clogged with the words I'm trying to swallow.

"She's fine. I just wanted to check on you, but I gotta go," *before I say something stupid.* "Catch you later, gator."

I hang up and throw my phone on the coffee table with an exasperated sigh just before Aela returns.

She sets up her laptop, a pile of books, and her papers on the far end of the coffee table where she settles herself cross-legged on the floor. I watch curiously, stuffing more skittles into my mouth thoughtlessly before I return my gaze back to the television that holds no interest for me at all.

All I can see is Kara with a faceless guy all over her, which makes me feel worse than I did before my call. So I do the only thing I can to take my mind off her. I put all my focus on Aela, which is unfortunate for her as I talk incessantly about anything and everything, not even keeping track of what I'm spewing as though there is no filter between my thoughts and mouth. The chick puts up with it far longer than anyone ever has, I'm talking for well over an hour before she calmly tells me to shut up—which is a poor move on her part because now it's a challenge to test how far I can go until she snaps.

I obnoxiously chew on skittles, exaggerating my jaw movements in a way that would have my mamma slapping and cursing me out as I pretend to watch the movie.

It's not until I bug her about what she's working on and end up on a tangent about becoming drug dealers that she finally snaps at me. This makes me grin. I find myself liking the chick even more and so happy that Dec found her. Aela works as a distraction so well that I don't even question it when I receive a call from an unknown number. I don't even think to be concerned as I answer until I hear Dec's voice over the line sounding pained and tired.

"Hey, man. I haven't got my wallet on me to call a cab. Can you come get me from Southport police station and drop me at my car—if it's still where I left it?"

I had so many bad outcomes my mind had conjured up for tonight, but Declan getting locked up hadn't been one of them. It can't be good, but the relief that he wasn't killed overshadows my concern.

I almost burst out in laughter until he adds, "I won't ask you to speed, but the sooner, the better, man. I started a brawl just before the police raided, and I got tasered into submission. The cops don't look real happy about releasing me on just the MC's grudgingly given word that I'm not affiliated with them. They are trying to dig something up to keep me here in a cell with a bunch of bikies who are pissed at me."

My relieved laugh dies as I slide to the edge of my seat. "Got it. On our way," I assure him, ending the call as I get up and gather my shirt, keys, and wallet before facing Aela, who is already looking up at me curiously.

"We have to go get Dec from the cop shop." I have never seen someone move as fast as she does when she slams her laptop shut while fluidly getting to her feet and to my side.

SOMETHING'S OFF WITH Declan. I don't know what's going on in that head of his because he retreats to their borrowed room as soon as we return to my parents home, but there's something more than what's already troubling him. I can feel it. I stay up several hours after Aela turns in, hoping that he'll come out and spill it. Dec doesn't venture out though and I'm losing the fight against my drooping eyes. So I give up and head to bed, but of course, my mind is wide awake as soon as my head hits the pillow and decides to recount this messed up day. I went from wanting to do the double date bullshit as an excuse to be around Kara to realising my feelings for her are a whole lot more than I bargained for, freaking out and fucking Trixie, then getting pissed at Kara being with another guy.

I'm a nutcase. My stomach is knotted with dread, which has

me tossing and turning restlessly for the remainder of the night.

"You're going to find love again, Lex, I promise. She'll be amazing and beautiful and the luckiest girl in the world for having you," Grace says with a wistful smile as she squeezes my hand.

I fight to swallow a lump in my throat, shaking my head as I move to sit beside her on the hospital bed. I wipe a tear that spills from her watery eyes.

"No. I will only ever love you. You're going to get better and be stuck with me, I'm afraid, until we're old and wrinkly, and I'm sneaking into your room at the old folk's home for a little afternoon delight," I argue with a waggle of my brows that gets her laughing and her cheeks flush a beautiful rosy red that's vibrant against her too pale complexion.

"You have a big, wonderful heart in here, Alex. Promise me you won't ever close it off," Grace pleads as she places her hand against my chest where said heart is beating so hard in protest of her words that she has to feel it.

"It's yours. Always. Speaking of afternoon delight, you know something else I have that's big?" I add on the joke to change the subject because she looks ready to argue. I don't like where this conversation is going. It works. She laughs again, using her hand on my chest to push me away.

"Your ego, it's enormous. Luckily for you, I love it."

I wake with a gasp, and my face is wet with sweat when I run my hands over it.

Fuck. I'd forgotten all about that conversation. I kick my legs to free them from the tangled sheet and then get out of bed to go grab a drink for my dry throat.

I hope it's not from screaming in my sleep and if it is, hope the other two didn't hear it. When I pass their room, though, the door is wide open, and it looks as though they were never here.

"Dec, Aela?" I call out though I can feel in the stillness of the house that I'm the only one here. Sure enough, I get no reply.

My mind is such a mess of contradictory thoughts of Grace and Kara. With worry about Declan's problems too, I struggle to focus on one thing at a time. I curse when I pour juice in a bowl of cereal instead of milk and then spread vegemite on my toast before buttering it—which is just so wrong.

I scrub my face with my hands roughly, wishing I could do it to my brain. I right my mistakes and take my food outside to eat by the pool, taking a detour to collect my phone so I can call Dec when I've finished so I can find out what's going on.

The calming sound of the water lapping at the pool edges and the sun's warmth against my skin helps calm my mind some. I'm feeling more in control by the time I make my call.

"Hey, man, I was just about to call you." Dec's greeting sounds tired and troubled, which instantly has me straightening with awareness.

"What's up?"

Dec sighs heavily over the line. "Can you find a way to check the girl's apartment with Kara, but without her knowing it's for me? I should've before I ended it with Aela, but I wasn't really thinking straight, so now I'm scrambling to make sure she'll be safe without me. I'd do it myself, but I'm booked out. Plus, I have Hope here sick, and I doubt Kara will be happy to oblige me after she hears from Aela. There's probably nothing to worry about since their building is pretty secure but—"

"Whoa, dude, back up. You broke up with Aela?" I interrupt him, hoping I misheard.

"Yeah. Keep up, would you? Have you not had your morning coffee yet?" He's mocking me, but it falls flat.

"Care to tell me why? Did you hit your head harder than we thought?" My voice goes high in disbelief, and I can practically hear Dec gritting his teeth when he replies,

"No, knob-jockey. I fucked up last night and had to fix it,

you know? To make her safe. I can't have her get hurt because of me."

"You don't think dumping her hurt?" I ask cynically because I think this is the stupidest thing he's ever done—which says a lot because we've done some really stupid shit together.

"But she'll live, which is the whole point. Now, will you do it or not?" Dec barks, clearly fed up with my opinion on the matter.

"I'll see what I can do," I promise solemnly, though I'm not sure how I will be able to pull it off. Kara's moods are hardly predictable when it comes to me.

"Thanks, man. Let me know how it goes." I hear Hope calling for him in the background, so we say goodbye and disconnect.

I light up a cigarette then pinch the bridge of my nose while trying to think up a plan of action. I still have nothing by the time I stub it out, so I decide to try my luck and wing it. I call Kara who answers on the second ring.

"If you're not going to say something this time, I'm turning off my phone, so stop calling," she growls. I scowl and wonder who she thinks she's talking to.

"Sunshine, I have a lot to say about that alone. Is someone pranking you?"

"Alex? Hey, sorry. Someone's called me four times in a row but not said a word. Once, I could have written off as an accident. Twice could have been amusing, but now it's just pissed me off so if it was you, you're in trouble."

I snort indignantly before I reply. "That's not my style, and you know it. If I want to bug you, I talk and tease you, not sit there all silent-stalker-beating-off-to-your-voice like. Give me some credit, jeez."

Kara laughs then concedes, "You're right, sorry. So what's up?"

I take the fact I just made her laugh when she was mad as a good sign and forge ahead. "I was wondering if you've been home yet, and if not, could I meet you there to make sure the place hasn't been infiltrated by the enemy?"

"*Infiltrated* by the *enemy*? This isn't one of your lame x-box games," she mocks, which has me glaring off into the distance in outrage since I can't glare through the phone at her.

"They are not *lame*, woman. They're character building. They teach you how to be brave and loyal and about teamwork and sacrifice. Not that I didn't already know all of that," I argue, and Kara laughs out loud. It's a beautiful sound, don't get me wrong, but I want to pinch her for it right now. It's totally uncalled for.

"They do not. They turn grown men into boys, who don't leave the house and just sit in front of a screen, talking to like-minded losers while stewing in their own filth."

I gasp in outrage, gearing up to continue the argument but then realise we've gone off topic. She's happily amused, even if it is at my expense.

"You're so wrong, but we'll continue this at your place. When do you want me there?" I insist and then listen intently to the following silence, willing her to give in.

"Give me half an hour. Did you see Aela this morning? Is she okay? Did she go to her classes?"

Well, this is awkward.

"Uh… I didn't see her. They were gone when I got up. I've got to go jump in the shower, see you in half." I hang up without saying goodbye since I'll be seeing her soon anyway. Then I head for the shower like I'd claimed —although when I had said it, it was just the first excuse that came to mind. I want to avoid telling her about what my idiot of a best friend has done until I can make sure their home is safe.

Chapter 10

KARA

NOTHING'S MAKING SENSE to me today.

My emotions are all over the place, and I feel off centred, like at some point yesterday I tripped and fell into an alternate universe that looks the same, only it's not.

The things that happened yesterday just don't happen in broad daylight. Ink fix getting busted up, Aela getting attacked the way she did, and the surprise of finding a dozen wilted red roses, with a black and white photo of me asleep and naked in bed, somehow left for me on the passenger seat of my *locked* car.

The world has gone crazy, and I don't know what to think or do about any of it.

I probably should have called the police about my car somehow being broken into without being broken, but I'd just heard about what had happened to Aela, so my concern was more for her. Plus, Kris was with me at the time, so there was no immediate threat to myself. I just shoved the photo into my bag before Kris could see it, throwing the flowers in the backseat as he gave me a curious look I deftly ignored.

Kris tagged along while I dropped an overnight bag off for Aela and made sure she was okay. I was really shaken by her attack and Kris demanded that I stay at his place, picking up on my uneasiness and getting protective.

I didn't want to be alone, and we were already going to hang at his place for a group assignment, so it was easy to agree.

I also couldn't get Alex out of my head after our morning clash. It made my head spin because I'd wanted to jump him, scream at him, and run from him all at once. The look in his eyes as they met and held mine with determination is burned into the back of my eyelids and won't leave me alone. I felt stripped bare, like he could see everything I was feeling and I hated it.

Not long after the assignment was done, and the celebratory drinks come out, a bright idea hit me and mission 'Get-laid-and-forget-Alex' was put into motion. My target set on Max, a classmate I hadn't spoken much to before this assignment. He's a quiet guy and reasonably cute, broad shoulders, year-round tan, brown hair and eyes.

Unfortunately for me, just as I'd got him comfortable with my advances and was enjoying a pretty pleasant make-out session, Alex called. Dousing the fire that had been warming inside me for my new friend, and I wound up crashing in the guest bedroom solo and very drunk only to be awoken a couple hours later to someone prank calling me.

I was wound up, hung over, and pissed off when Alex called immediately after. But somehow, with his odd charm, he got me laughing and my spirit lifted. Then I found myself agreeing to meet up with him at my place.

"About time, woman. If I had known your half an hour was more like an hour, I wouldn't have rushed to get here." Alex's stroppy complaint greets me as he opens my door for me.

I can't help the smile that spreads across my face.

"I'm not even fifteen minutes late, Mr Grumpy." I take the hand he offers to help me out of the car like a gentleman.

I parked out on the street in front of the building instead of in the underground parking so it would be easier to find Alex. I stop to feed a few coins into the metre then check twice to make sure the car is locked before heading inside. Alex walking beside me grumbling under his breath about women lacking time management skills.

I use my fob to get us through the glass doors and into the foyer as Alex drops his sulking to wrap an arm around me. He starts pretending to act like a bodyguard, pulling me into his side so hard that I stumble and squeak in surprise.

I laugh when I turn to see his faux serious expression that's ruined by the appearance of his left dimple as he fights a smirk.

"Stay close to me, ma'am. I can't protect you if I can't reach you." He attempts to order me sternly when we pause to wait at the elevators, the old lady in front of us turning to watch us with amusement. When the lift arrives, Alex sticks his neck out pretending to scope it out, announcing, "All clear," before dragging me inside.

I slap him away as I laugh and try to ignore the people smiling as they watch us.

"Cut it out. Can't you be normal for just five minutes?" He slides back up beside me to wrap an arm around my shoulders.

"Normal is overrated, sunshine." Alex slaps a kiss to my cheek quickly. I turn to give him a warning glare but end up giggling at the mask of innocence he gives me.

We're the only two left on the elevator by the time it arrives at my floor, which is anticlimactically normal. I tense in awareness, though, when Alex does the same as we near my apartment door. It's as if he's anticipating something happening. I unlock the door, and no one jumps out at us as I push it open, but Alex still makes sure he goes in first then is off to check the rooms, though I can tell the place hasn't been disturbed as I enter. I make my way over to the kitchen to collect a water bottle from the fridge to pack in my bag for later, snagging a red apple from the fruit bowl. Then I slide up onto a stool to wait for my *big, bad protector*.

I snort in amusement at the thought as I chew on a mouthful of the crisp apple, listening to doors opening and closing down the hall.

When I'm halfway through, and Alex still hasn't reappeared, I curiously go after him to find Alex sitting on the edge of my bed, taking in the room thoughtfully.

I clear my throat to gain his attention.

"You comfy there? No big baddies hiding under the bed?" I tease, which gets me that smirk of his.

"Smartarse," he retorts. I snort with humour.

"Says the guy who was making a public scene about all this only minutes ago," I argue haughtily. Alex nods in ascension.

I move into the room, leaning against my chest of drawers in front of him, and then I tilt my head curiously as I finally ask, "What are you doing?"

Alex takes in my room before meeting my gaze. "This isn't what I expected your room to look like."

It's my turn to smirk this time. "Expecting whips, chains, and torture devices? Sorry. I told you I'm not a dominatrix."

Alex shakes his head. "It doesn't match the vibe you give off at all. No offence, but you're kinda moody and bitchy whereas this room looks like a Care Bear exploded, all bright and cheery with every colour of the rainbow."

"This is my sanctuary. My happy place where I can lock out the world. Stop judging," I complain defensively.I cross my arms over my chest as I take in the room, trying to see it from his eyes.

"I'm not judging, just trying to figure you out. You're like a puzzle with unexpected edges that I'm not sure what to do with. Just as I think I have you figured out, I stumble on another piece." Alex leans forward to pull me to him by my elbows until I'm standing between his legs. I don't fight him because, from the moment I saw him sitting on my bed, I've been fighting the urge to climb on top of him as my mind played devil's advocate, playing out scenarios of just that, distracting me.

"What's your favourite colour?" He eyes me curiously. and I don't even pause with my response.

"White."

Alex gives me a disbelieving look, and I raise my eyebrows expectantly.

"Seriously? White's not even a colour."

"White is more than just a colour. It's actually made up of *all* the colours," I argue.

Alex shakes his head with a quiet chuckle as he runs his hands down the back of my arms until his fingers tangle with mine. He then gives a small, experimental tug.

"So that's why you like it, cos you can't pick just one?"

I'm the one shaking my head this time at his guess and, absent-mindedly, start to swing our entwined hands.

"It's the possibilities of white that I love. The blankness of an untouched canvas, photo paper waiting to be developed, even a bride's wedding dress. It's a symbol of hope, of new possibilities… I don't know. I can't explain it. It sounds stupid out loud."

I expect Alex to laugh at me, so I look away self-consciously, but he doesn't. Instead, Alex tugs my hand to get my attention. When I finally give in, I find him smiling tenderly as he releases my left hand to reach up my arm.

"You're kind of amazing, sunshine. Don't be mad, but I have to kiss you right now." Alex tugs me down quickly until our lips meet before I can even *think* of objecting. His lips press sweetly and softly—almost reverently—against mine, and then he sucks my bottom lip between them. He grazes it with his teeth, sending a crackling of heat-like electricity down my spine to settle in my core. Alex's tongue snakes out to flick my top lip teasingly then invades my mouth. His hold on me tightens, surely anticipating I'll pull away, but I don't even want to.

This kiss is softer than our first, but no less earth-shattering and flammable. It lulls me into a fixated state.

Alex pulls away before I'm ready, leaving me floundering for a moment. I try to clear my throat as reality returns and I step back from his grasp.

"You've got to stop kissing me like that. I don't even like you." I try to be objective, but it comes out breathless and saturated with desire, which has Alex grinning knowingly like the Cheshire cat.

"You're a terrible liar. I don't know why you insist on dragging this out and torturing the both of us. It will be so much more fun just giving in to this inevitable thing between us already." Alex leans forward, wrapping his hands around the backs of my knees while I struggle to find words to string together in response to his remark in my lust-clouded mind.

He pulls me to him so suddenly that I emit a shocked squeal. I find myself straddling his lap with my knees on either side of him on the bed, hands gripping his shoulders. I'm chest to chest and nose to nose with him as he smirks like the proverbial cat that caught the canary. Seriously, I can picture feathers falling from his mouth as his eyes shine gleefully. He extracts his hands from where they're captured in the bend of my knees, sliding them out and then up the sides of my thighs to rest on my backside.

"You—" My protest is cut off by Alex sealing my lips with his, which is becoming an annoying habit I'm not too inclined to complain about just yet.

His hands grope the cheeks of my arse, moving me tighter against him before one hand trails up under my singlet to press warmly in the dip of my spine. He growls when I press deeper into our kiss with need, the sound sending a shiver of anticipation through me, which he no doubt feels.

Alex pulls back and uses his hand on my back to drag my

top over my head. I raise my arms to help remove the barrier between us before attacking his lips with mine as soon as I'm free. I can feel his body shake with a silent laugh of amusement until I bite into his bottom lip hard enough to make him hiss in pain, but his fingers dig into my flesh, letting me know he likes it. I begin to grind my pelvis against his lap like a cat in heat, which is exactly what I feel like. I'm burning up with need.

My skin feels as if it's only seconds from setting alight, and the little clothing that still remains on me feels suffocating.

I give in.

Because he's right, fighting this thing between us is exhausting. Maybe, if we just get it out of our systems just this once, we'll be able to put it behind us.

I yank his white shirt up, forcing his arms to oblige me when I impatiently tug it up beneath them. I wave it over my head in both surrender and victory, before throwing it to the floor.

Alex smiles triumphantly before I take those ridiculously sexy lips again as my hands explore the warm, smooth expanse of his back, delving into his soft, slightly damp hair.

In return, Alex's hands are everywhere. Travelling down my spine. Grasping my left breast. Releasing the clasp of my bra with a flick of his wrist. Trailing down my stomach then around my waist. Both hands settle on the straps of my bra and slide them down my arms. When the straps are resting in the crook of my elbows, Alex pulls away from my mouth, taking hold of my hips. I squeal again when he suddenly lifts up, then throws me down on my back onto the bed. He removes my bra that's rudely in his way before settling his body on top of mine.

The luxurious heat of our skin pressed together from chest to navel makes me moan in bliss, and I need more. I reach down to tug on the waistband of his jeans because I can't get to the fly, but Alex doesn't oblige me.

He lifts my left leg up by the knee until it's above his hip. He settles himself more snugly between my legs while trailing kisses down my neck to my collarbone where he nips gently with his teeth, causing my core to clench with need.

"Fuck. Alex." I'm panting shamelessly as I attempt to plead for more while he moves down to rain kisses, nips, licks and sucks on my breasts. His hands move up to get into the action also, cupping, fondling, and pinching unhurriedly.

"In good time, sunshine. I need to taste you first." Alex's throaty voice growls over my right nipple. I want to cry out in frustration and ecstasy simultaneously.

What he's doing feels amazing, but I *need* more. More than I need my next breath. I've never felt this much before with anyone else. It's simultaneously too much yet not enough. Tears well up in my eyes as one of his hands trail down my stomach and tug on the button of my shorts. My hips buck against him, and his hand moves to force them back into the mattress.

"Easy, precious. Calm down."

I give a hysterical sounding laugh at that, my mind picturing Gollum from *Lord of the Rings*, of all things, but it quickly turns into a breathless gasp when his hand travels down to cup me underneath my shorts, his fingers pressing into the wettest part of my underwear, right where I need him most.

Alex hisses as he pulls up off me. I immediately miss his warmth. I'm about to protest until I feel him tugging on my shorts and hear the zipper being undone, which sounds like music to my ears. His fingers slide into the sides of my panties at my hips then he removes the last of my clothes in one long pull as I lift up my bent legs to help. They're thrown over his shoulder to the floor as his eyes trail down my body. I would feel self-conscious if it weren't for the heat I see blazing in his eyes as he takes in every bare inch of me. His gaze meets mine, and he dips down to press a kiss to my left knee that is still bent up beside him.

"You're absolutely fucking perfect, sunshine. Fucking hell."

I lean up to make a grab for his jeans to remove them, but he stops me, taking my hands in his, and forcing them to rest at my sides.

"You do that, and this will be over faster than either of us want. I want the taste of your release on my tongue before I feel you come around my cock, but if you free him from his denim cage, I won't be able to stop from taking you."

I laugh at him talking about his penis in the third person, but then I fight to escape Alex's grip when he starts to lean down, so his face is nestled in my crotch.

"Wait, Alex, no. I don't... don't like *that*. Please come up here." I squirm until I manage to close my legs over Alex's right shoulder, cutting off his access.

"You don't *like* it? I don't believe you." He stares at me as though I just told him I have a pet unicorn that poops fairy floss stashed in my wardrobe. I look away self-consciously until Alex moves up to hover over me. I hesitantly meet his determined gaze.

"The only reasons not to like it are if the idiots who have tried before me didn't know what the fuck they were doing, or you've never had it. Either way, today's your lucky day because they don't call me Mr Licks for nothing. I'm about to rock your world."

The cocky arsehole bends his elbows in a push-up form so he can press his lips to mine in a promising kiss as I'm about to protest again.

"Just relax for me, sunshine," he whispers once I'm a compliant lump of goo. He then journeys back down my body, dropping kisses as he goes.

I squeeze my eyes shut, fighting the urge to push him away. Nate was the last and only guy I allowed this with, and that experience isn't something I ever want to repeat. It was embarrassing, uncomfortable, painful and awkward, long after I begged him to stop.

After our disaster of a time together, I quickly learned that if I wanted an orgasm, I had to take it from the guy I was with at the time. We went at my pace. I remained on top and in charge. The power play was such a heady thing and what I found I needed to climax.

So it's a big deal when I decide to give Alex three minutes of compliance before I put a stop to this since he wants it so much. I can handle three minutes.

Alex moves my legs apart again and settles between them, sliding his hands underneath me to palm my arse. I clench the bedspread in my hands as he presses kisses from the inside of my knee up to the inside crease where my thigh joins to my pelvis.

"Breathe and relax for me, Kara," Alex murmurs against the dip there, his warm breath against my skin causing me to break out in goose bumps.

One of his hands slides out from beneath me to glide over my leg in a soft caress, and I release the breath I'd been holding, working to relax every tense muscle in my body.

"Open your eyes, sunshine." His low murmuring makes my pelvic muscles clench every time, which doesn't help me relax at all.

I open my eyes to see him smiling up at me as his fingertips glide down over my clit, two of them pausing to run around my entrance, teasing me.

"Keep your eyes on me. I want you to watch and feel what I do to you."

My breathing is laboured as his head dips. I both see and feel his tongue introduce itself to my clit in a quick upwards flick before it swipes over my soaked opening, and then his mouth seals over my clit. I feel the cool metal of the bar through his tongue glide over my clit and moan shamelessly, my head sinking back into the pillow as first one, then two fingers get in on the action, sliding inside of me.

Alex sucks gently on my swollen nub, and his fingers start to thrust then withdraw. I take back all reservations I had about this when his talented tongue sweeps around my clit and those fingers of his curl, turning upwards and rubbing against a spot that feels *fan-freaking-tastic*.

My muscles lock up in anticipation again, but this time not in fear, but the familiar build up that's taking over my body. My hands fly up to clench the pillow beneath my head, my eyes go wide, back arched, and legs shake. Then Alex moans deep in his throat, and the vibrations shatter me as my vision blacks out.

I'm reduced to a mewling, rutting, gasping heap of flesh by the time Alex finally lets up after coaxing every last spasm of bliss from my orgasm that he can.

My heart feels like it's trying to hammer its way out of my chest as I fight to catch my breath. I open my eyes to see Alex grinning wickedly as he crawls up my body, his eyes lit with glee.

"Jesus. I've been missing out." I didn't mean to say it out loud but can't find it in me to be embarrassed or annoyed that I probably just inflated his already enormous ego. Though, in this case, it is well deserved.

Alex chuckles, leaning in to kiss me, his lips still saturated in my tangy juices, which I don't mind in the least.

"Not Jesus. Alex. I can see how you'd get us mixed up though, so I forgive you, sunshine," he murmurs against my lips. I freaking giggle like a *girl* while affectionately moving back the hair that has fallen into his eyes.

I don't even recognise myself right now.

I'm about to retort when there's a loud banging, which sounds like it's coming from the front door. We both pause with what I'm sure are mirrored *"What the fuck?"* expressions.

"Stay here. I'll check it out." Alex hauls himself up and off the bed, and then walks out of my room without bothering to stop to grab his shirt.

I can't help pausing to enjoy the show of his back muscles bunching as he moves. It's so totally drool-worthy. I *may* emit a happy sigh.

Once Alex is out of sight, my brain reboots as a ball of dread lands in the pit of my stomach. *Shit.*

What the hell was I thinking?

I'm already feeling more than just physical attraction to the guy, and we haven't even sealed the deal. *I can't do this.*

I slip out of bed, rushing to put on clothes to hurry after him because who the hell would be knocking at our door right now?

Pussy-blocker, whoever it is, even though they just saved me from making a big mistake.

I hear a disgruntled male voice I don't immediately recognise as I slip into the hallway, which gives me pause, but there's no arguing or sounds of a struggle, so I decide it's safe to show my face.

"How do you know Aela, and how did you get into the building without anyone here letting you in?"

"Why do I have to explain myself to you? What is going on? I'm Aela's godfather. I saw her down at the station last night and want to make sure she's okay. A couple ladies were coming in at the same time as me and let me in. Now, who are you and why are you answering the girls' door?"

"Since I'm the one on the inside of this door, I'm the one asking the questions, old man, and I don't believe your story. It sounds a little too convenient for my liking, so you're not coming in. But I'll tell you that Aela isn't here anyway. So… see ya."

Before I can reach them, Alex swings the door shut, spinning to face me with a determined look as though we can pick up right where we left off now that he got rid of the interruption.

157

"You dick. That was Kevin. He's practically family to Aela." I slap him out of the way, rushing to open the door and apologise, but when I stick my head out into the hall, Kevin's already gone.

"Well, she's not here, and we were in the middle of something," Alex states from behind me. Not the least bit apologetic, as he snakes an arm around my waist, pressing his front to my back. I can feel his erection grinding against me as though trying to force its length between my butt cheeks.

"You're an arse," I complain half-heartedly, trying to hide the effect he's having on me as my reservations crumble yet again.

"You like my arse," Alex murmurs against the skin behind my ear, and I feel myself melt into him. Good thing he has a strong grip on me, or I'd be a puddle at his feet right now because my legs seem to have turned into soggy noodles.

"It's a real problem of mine," I admit, feeling his chest shake against me as he chuckles moving me back inside.

The door shuts with a nudge of his foot, and I'm pressed against the hard wood. My hands are taken and held firmly on either side of my head as I turn so my cheek is pressed to the door. I can see Alex in my peripheral view.

"Now, where were we?" His hands slide in a light caress down my arms, leaving a tingling sensation on my skin in their wake, before he turns me to face him with a grip on my elbow. I gasp when his chest presses to mine while his hands get busy, one pressing me into him firmly by my lower back as the other trails down my side, hiking my left leg up over his hip before it dips under the dress I'd hastily put on. He palms my bare behind with a happy groan.

"So hot," Alex murmurs, and before I know it, I'm hoisted up over his shoulder, and he's heading back to my bedroom.

I happen to catch sight of the time on the microwave as I'm

about to protest his manhandling and thankfully remember myself.

"Stop. Put me down, Alex. I can't do this. I've got a class I have to leave for like, right now." I kick my legs for him to put me down and Alex hesitates at my door.

"Are you fucking with me?" he asks, wrapping an arm around my calves to protect himself. "Because I gotta tell you, this isn't funny, sunshine." He sounds uncertain, and I feel guilty for leaving him hanging after what he did for me, but I can't let this happen.

"I'm serious. Sorry," It's barely a whisper, but Alex hears it and slowly lowers me to my feet, grabbing my shoulders to hold me in place before him where he can search my eyes.

Alex lets out a huge breath, trying to expel some pent up tension, as his hands slide up to cup my face. Then he leans his forehead against mine.

"What's going on in that stubborn, beautiful head of yours?" Alex murmurs, his breath ghosting over my lips. The way his voice drops makes my mind blank.

"It can't be insecurities because for a chick like you to have them is insane. And you shouldn't have any doubts about my ability to complete the job after what we just did, so help me out here, sunshine. Let me in?" he pleads.

I stare into his beguiling jade eyes because they're all I can see from being held so close to him. I could drown in the depth of the honest, imploring look he's giving me.

It's a dangerous look.

"Nothing. Really, I just didn't realise the time, and I have class. I'm sorry." I pull out of his grasp and avoid looking him in the eye, but I see his mouth tilt up into an enticing little grin.

"You can't skip just one class?" He reaches out to play with a part of my hair that brushes my collarbone,

"I'll make it worth your while." Oh, God. Alex is an expert

in temptation, and I struggle to keep the mental grip on my resolve.

"No. Exams are coming up, and I can't miss anything, or I'll have no hope of passing." I turn away and head back to the lounge room and use my bag as an excuse to avoid looking at him, rifling through it as though I'm checking I have everything I need.

"Rain check then. Why don't you come over to my place when you're done? I'll make us dinner."

I shake my head and hear a disgruntled groan before Alex steps up to take my arm and turn me to face him.

"Why the hell not?" He demands, clearly fed up with my evasiveness.

I irrationally panic, feeling like I'm being backed into a wall, though I'm not.

I *am,* however, tired of this whole thing. How many times do I have to turn the guy down before he moves on and leaves me alone?

"Because you're *you,* I'm *me,* and I can't do this," I exclaim louder than intended. Then I feel guilty at the shock and hurt that flashes over Alex's face before he controls it, and his expression turns blank.

"You know what? I don't need this shit. I'm not going to be dragged through the mud for what some other pricks have done to you in the past. If you don't want to let it go, and move on instead of using it as an excuse to remain a bitter bitch and giving them that power over your future, then that's on you. You know how to find me if you pull your head out of your arse."

Alex turns away and storms into my room, emerging moments later with his boots in one hand as he tugs his shirt into place with the other.

"You might want to check in with your best friend sometime today, by the way. Dec broke up with Aela after last night ended badly, and he's worried he made her a definite target for the bikies to go after for revenge, which is why I had to come check the place out. So good luck with all that." Alex avoids looking at me as he says this on his way out, slamming the front door behind him.

The noise echoes in the resounding silence as I stare at the door, unmoving and unsure of how I feel about finally pushing him to his limit.

My eyes begin to blur from tears welling up, and I swipe at them in annoyance at myself before moving on and gathering my stuff to get to class. I make a mental note to stock up on ice cream on the way back. I won't be able to speak to Aela until she's home, and this day definitely calls for a tub.

Alex's words replay in my head as I walk out—in particular, the part about giving the men I hate power over my future, which causes me to pause mid-step.

Is that really what I'm doing?

This whole time I've been fighting to do the opposite to make sure I never fell for a guy like that again—to remain in control of any relationship I decide to have.

I can feel a headache forming and rub at the tension in my forehead as I continue towards the elevator.

The day isn't even half over yet, and it feels like one of the longest in history.

Chapter 11

ALEX

I'M DONE. I'M *so* fucking done. I impatiently jab at the button for the elevator with a shaky hand, then notice I'm shaking all over. I start to pace, willing the elevator to hurry the hell up before I go back to throw more hateful words at the damn cock-teasing witch. Dammit. I thought we were finally getting somewhere, that she was finally letting me in. But no, she ran the first chance she got. Again.

The doors finally open to the lift, and I take a deep breath in and attempt to calm down as I step inside the small space, pressing the lobby button on my way to lean against the back wall and throw my head back hard against it. I go to run my hands through my hair and catch the mouth-watering scent that's still clinging to the fingers I had inside her, and everything from that moment when she lost herself in her bedroom replays in my mind, which only amplifies my frustration.

I groan as loud as I can and smack my head against the wall a couple more times, which is the only release I'll likely be getting anytime soon.

"Hard day?" I hear the voice of an amused sounding woman and open my eyes to see a hot redhead standing between the open door, in a black business skirt suit and heels. She's smirking as she slowly looks me up and down, eyes lingering on my crotch where evidence of my erection is clearly visible.

I hadn't even noticed I'd arrived at the lobby until she spoke. I force as much of a smile as I can while stuffing my hands into the pockets of my jeans and move towards her to get out of the lift even though she's deliberately blocking my way.

"You have no idea," I rumble and watch her eyes spark with intention.

"I can help you with that if you like?" she offers as she steps into the contraption, unbuttoning her jacket. It's a tempting invitation. The woman is wicked hot, and any single guy would be lucky for the chance, but I deflate at just the thought because she's not the one I'm craving. Even if the one I *am* craving is impossible, I still can't do this right now. As pissed as I am at Kara, and even after what I said to her, I'm still hung up on her.

I sigh as I step up and gently move Red to the side with a hand to her waist.

"You're a godsend just for the offer, but I can't." I step around her then turn to watch her press a button for her floor before she turns to face me with an impenitent smile.

"That's too bad." She waves as the doors shut between us so I wink before turning and heading out, my mind stuck on the problem at hand. *I'm so fucked.*

After the finality of my little speech, I don't know where to go from here. I can't continue hounding her. That will make me look weak and pathetic, which I've done enough when it comes to Kara.

Maybe I need to cut all contact for a while and see what happens? They say, "Distance makes the heart grow fonder." It's worth a try. I can control the urge to contact her and be remote if we happen to be in the same room together. Be the arsehole she's pegged me as. Treat them mean, keep them keen, right? I feel myself smirking as I climb into my Jeep, just having a plan to focus on makes me feel better.

~*~*~*~

THROUGH SHEER DETERMINATION and strong will, I last ten long days into my plan before Kara turns up. I can't be any prouder of myself for sticking to it.

I'm sitting behind the counter at Ink Fix with Kit, listening to her worries about Declan when Kara dramatically storms through the door. She deftly avoids my gaze, acting like I'm not even here as her eyes flit around the room before landing on Kit.

I take advantage of the moment to admire Kara and find myself grinning in appreciation. She reminds me of a badarse Viking chick with her blonde hair artfully braided and messy, grey cotton dress with a leather belt around her waist, with matching brown sandals and a pissed off expression to top it all off.

She's probably the closest I'll ever get to my very own *Lagertha*.

"Where's that chicken-shit boss of yours?" Kara demands as she approaches the counter. Kit gives her a small, tired smile.

"With a customer. So if you're here to serve up an arse whopping, you'll have to wait."

Kara's frown deepens as she folds her arms over her chest. I take the moment while the two of them aren't taking any notice of me to admire the way it makes her tits more prominent in the thin fabric of her dress. If she leans forward just a little more, I'm positive those puppies will spill out.

"I warned him if he hurt Aela, I would make him hurt. She's been a robot for over a week now, and I'm worried and mad, so I'm going to take it out on him and kick his stupid butt."

"Sounds like you." I snicker, and both women turn to look at me. I hadn't meant to say that out loud, but I'm not going to take it back now. Kara has transferred her glaring eyes to me, so I shrug defiantly and throw in a careless grin for good measure, daring her to bite.

"Dec's been the same from the sounds of it. We were just debating what to do," Kit explains as she leans back with a sigh.

"*You* were debating, Miss Meddler. I say our boy's a grown man, who makes his own decisions, and should be allowed to deal with the consequences on his own, so long as he knows we're here if needed," I point out. Kit half-heartedly backhands my arm with an impatient look as though I'm being an idiot, but I'm not.

The three of us are distracted when Dec's voice resonates from down the hall, just before he appears with his cougar client I'd had the *pleasure* of meeting earlier—if you call being fondled by a woman drowning in perfume that makes your eyes water a pleasure.

There's a silent anticipation-filled moment as we politely wait for the woman to pay and leave. Dec emits a tired sigh, shoulders dropping as soon as the door shuts while he messes with a bunch of waivers, clearly waiting for Kara to say her piece while he avoids looking at her. I watch as she scrutinises my best friend, unable to stop my mind picturing her with a sword or axe, ready for a fight, my dick liking the image as much as I do. *I need help*.

"You look like shit," Kara finally announces, and Dec gives a huff of a laugh.

"Thanks for the ego boost. Anything I can do for you?" His eyes are dim and tired when he looks up to finally face her, and I wince.

I haven't had any actual face to face time with Declan for days. He's secluded himself in his workroom and kept his head down or averted as much as possible. His skin is pale, eyes sunken and bruised, and it looks like he's lost a noticeable amount of weight, which is alarming given the short amount of time he's had to fall apart.

So maybe Kit was right, and we need to intervene. And Kara starts said intervention. "Well, I was going to kick your arse, but it looks like someone beat me to it. So just tell me... Do you seriously think dumping Aela and freezing her out, is going to stop the bikers aiming for the target you apparently made her? Because it sounds like useless, wishful thinking to me."

I watch Dec's eyes go cold, his hands clenching into fists at his sides as his whole body seems to tense.

"I'm doing all the damage control that I can. I've been out to the bars where they hang out, made sure I've been seen with other women, and trying to act like I'm happily single—when just the thought makes me sick. What more do you want from me?" Dec's voice is rough and breaks a couple times in his explanation.

"How about a resolution where you aren't *both* walking around like half a person?" Dec steps back like her words hit him with a physical blow. I watch him struggling to swallow as he turns away and without another word, walks off down the hall where a door is slammed shut.

"Wow. Well done, Kara. You really know how to cut a guy down with words. I hope you feel better now." My voice comes out cold, as I recall being on the receiving end of Kara's barbed tongue. I don't like her kicking my brother when he's already down.

Kara flinches, and I feel a little vindicated as Kit looks between us hesitantly and then goes after Dec.

I give in to the urge that's running through every muscle in my body. I've been fighting it, but I can't any longer. I take several steps until I'm as close to Kara as I can get with the counter between us.

"I'm not talking to you," Kara haughtily announces, so I shrug before leaning over, bracing my forearms on the countertop.

"You rarely have something nice to say to me anyway, so I don't really mind. There are better things I'd like you to do with that mouth," I murmur, eyes locked onto her lips, which she licks before stepping back.

"See, you're such a pig. Yet you get mad when I won't have sex with you. You're just like all the others." Kara folds her arms across her chest and rubs her arms as though she's cold. I'm about to argue when she adds, "And you were wrong last time. I'm not giving them power over my future. I'm protecting myself from other arseholes like them. Like you."

"I'm not going to claim to be a saint, Kara, but I am nothing like that prick who took your virginity and you know it. You just won't admit it because you're scared. You're scared of a repeat, so you use it as an excuse to keep your distance and never let anyone see the real you. I get it, sunshine. It's a scary thing to be vulnerable to someone. But you can't run from it and live your life in fear."

Says the kettle to the pot.

Yeah, I'm a total hypocrite, but the difference is I *know* what I'm avoiding, whereas Kara is so deep in denial. I don't think she knows which way is up.

I watch her eyes well with tears as I ache with the need to take her in my arms and apologise, but I hold myself back as she huffs a laugh.

"You're just pissed I'm not one of those stupid girls who throw themselves at your feet and jump at the chance to get in your bed," Kara accuses.

I laugh as I stand back, bracing my hands on the counter before launching my body over it. I take hold of her elbows, making sure she has no chance of ignoring me, and I lean in close to her face and whisper, "Wrong again. You're the only *stupid girl* who has been in my bed since I was seventeen. Yes, I've

167

fucked more than my fair share of women—get over it. I never lied or cheated to get them there, and they knew it was just a one-time thing. *That's* the difference between me and the douchebags of your past, and so help me, God, when you finally come around, I'm going to need more than just one time with you. That's if you haven't put me in the psych ward by then… hell, maybe even then, though it could be difficult in a straightjacket." I realise I'm rambling and sharing more than I need to, so I force myself to stop by leaning in and pressing my lips to hers, fully expecting a fight and bracing for a slap to the face.

What I don't expect is for her to not only accept but return my kiss. Her hands take hold of my elbows in return as she softens against me. I'm tempted to take advantage of the moment and press on, but I pull back, pressing quick pecks to her lips twice more before I take a breath and then wait for her reaction. Kara's eyes slowly open and she looks into mine, so I get a front seat to her panic and confusion. Then she breaks my hold of her, stepping away.

"I—uh… I have to go."

I give a small understanding smile because I know she's struggling with herself, and I've pushed enough. Kara moves to turn away but spins quickly, pressing her lips to my left cheek and then runs for the door, which makes me chuckle as it shuts behind her.

I may not have stuck to the 'treat her mean' plan, but I think we may have finally made some real progress.

THAT NIGHT, I'M working ladies' night and am bouncing on the balls of my feet with energy well after closing time without any help from energy drinks like usual.

I'm whistling the tune of the last song I heard as I exit

through the back door, still buttoning up my shirt. The sun is just starting to lighten the sky as I step out of the alley onto the strip, which is pretty dead with only a couple stragglers police are trying to wake up that are slumped on benches. I check my phone on my way to the garage next door and grin even bigger when I find a text from Kara time stamped six hours ago.

"You have got to stop kissing me like that."

I chuckle and text back, knowing she puts her phone on silent when she's asleep, so I won't wake her.

"You love my kisses ;-)"

I'm about to put my phone away when a shadow crosses my path. I look up to see a tall, lanky guy deliberately stop in my way as though he's looking for a fight. I frown and size him up before raising a questioning brow because he is clearly outweighed if he's looking for a brawl. Judging by his preppy grey dress pants and matching sweater, he isn't the type to go out looking for a challenge even with the cold, calculating look in his eyes.

"Can I help you?" I ask as I slide my phone into my pocket to free my hands in case the dude is packing crazy.

"Yeah, you can stay away from my girl, you piece of shit," he spits out, and I sigh. If I had a dollar for every arsehole that tried to give me crap after a ladies' night gig... I'd have almost enough for a KFC family feed. This shit is old, especially when I don't do more than smile, accept their innocent groping, and playfully touch arses while posing for a pic to give them a cheap thrill.

"Calm down, mate. I was just doing my job, so whoever your girl was in there, I can assure you I'm not interested."

"Don't bullshit me and act dumb. She hasn't acted how she's supposed to for months, and I've seen you two. She's different with you, and I don't like it. You have to leave her alone," he insists, sounding desperate.

I've had enough. I shake my head before stepping around him to continue towards the parking garage. "I'm sorry you're having problems, man, but they have nothing to do with me," I call over my shoulder and notice the security guard step out from his both as the jealous boyfriend starts yelling behind me.

"You are my problem, and if you don't leave her alone, I'll be your problem!"

I turn around but continue walking backwards as I face him to make a suggestion. "Go home, sleep it off and maybe do something nice for your girlfriend in the morning and see where that goes."

I turn back just steps away from running into the burly—yet close to retirement age—guard who is grinning fondly at me.

"You been up to no good again, Alex?"

I hold my hands up innocently and match his grin before we both turn to watch the jealous boyfriend kick a defenceless rubbish bin that's bolted to the ground, causing him to hurt his foot. He hobbles away, muttering to himself.

"Didn't do a damn thing this time, Ron," I swear, and he thumps me on the back with a chuckle like he doesn't believe me.

"You're a scamp, boy. I keep warnin' you it's going to get you in trouble one day. I should know. I used to be the same until I married my Marge a lifetime ago."

I wink playfully and pat his arm as a car comes up to interrupt us, and Ron has to get back to work, slowly going back to his post.

"As long as you're not calling me a tramp," I call out, and he laughs, looking over his shoulder as I follow a few paces behind him.

"Ah… but we both know you are one. I've seen most of the girls you leave with, remember?"

We share a grin, and I wish him a good night before heading

170

for my car.

Just as I get comfortable in bed, my phone alerts me to a text, so I collect it from my bedside table and grin when I see it's from Kara,

"It's a real problem of mine."

I place my phone back down, smiling at her reply, which is an echo of our moment at her apartment—before she backpedalled.

FOUR DAYS GO by quickly without seeing Kara because she's super busy, her only free time, of course, being while I'm at work. But we carry on a disjointed conversation through texts, and I talk her into making plans for tonight since it's my night off. We're only meeting up for a late coffee and a bite to eat on her break between work and a study group, but I'll take what I can get.

I wake up at noon and kill as much time as I can cleaning my place and distractedly playing *Call of Duty*. I become restless and itchy from being inactive, so I decide to leave early and drop by Ink Fix first since we're only going to the café just outside her apartment building.

When I enter the shop, Kit is slowly spinning herself in her swivel seat behind the counter with a big, pleased smile, which only manages to get wider when her eyes land on me. She stops her spinning.

"What's going on, Kitty?" I ask curiously, and she doesn't even bat an eye at the nickname.

"Operation: De-hobo Declan was a success. I got him to shower, go out in public to eat and talk, and right now, he's upstairs restoring that pigsty of an apartment. It's a great day."

I raise my eyebrows at her in shock before grinning. "You

sure he's not up there in the foetal position having a pity party for one? You know he's a stubborn arse."

"He's not. I can hear the washing machine and him thumping around up there. He's keeping busy like a good boy," Kit insists, so I hold up a hand for a congratulatory high-five, which she happily leans over to smack with a long-armed swing.

"Then aren't you the conquering queen of funk. Well done." I move to head down the hall to go see this for myself, but Kit jumps in my way before I can even get to the opening.

"Nu-uh, you're not going up there and ruining this. Sit your butt in this seat, and you can drive me crazy until he comes down when he's finished." She drags me over to the spare stool behind the counter, so I obligingly sit.

"Yes, ma'am," I mock and receive a warning glare.

"You're going to make me regret saying that. I know it," Kit complains before turning to answer the phone as it rings. I contemplate slipping off down the hall, but Kit is some sort of mind reader and turns to shoot me a daring glare. So I stay where I am, picking up her piercing photo album for something to do which, has the perk of having boobs and other bits in it. Skunk comes out just as Kit gets off the phone, and we start talking about grabbing some dinner. Then Kara's ringtone starts blaring from my pocket. There's still an hour until we're set to meet up, so I'm instantly suspicious.

"Sunshine, it's not even eight yet, so you can't be calling to say I'm late, and if this is 'cos you're bailing, I'm going to be mighty disappointed."

I pause expectantly for her reply but am shocked when I hear a broken sob before she stutters out my name.

"Whoa, Kara? What's wrong?" I strain to hear anything I can over the line as though it will help tell me what's happening. All I can hear is my voice echoing over her car stereo.

"Aela's been attacked again. Her boss called to tell me they were taking her to the hospital by ambulance but had to leave it in a voicemail. My phone was on silent in my bag at work, and I missed it. I'm trying to get there, but I'm stuck in traffic. I'm freaking out. I feel like I can't breathe," Kara's hysterics break off into desperate gasps. *Jesus.*

"Calm down. Take slow, deep breaths for me, sweetheart." I coach her in controlled breathing as I curl over to rub my head with my left hand, my elbow propped up on my knee. Belatedly noting the pet name slip up, but I think she's too freaked out to pull me up on it.

"That's it. Now, did Mal say anything else about her condition?" I lean back and look up to see Kit and Skunk listening in with concerned, questioning looks. I hold up a hand to hold them off for a moment.

"He said she's banged up really bad, but she'll live and not to be worried, but I *am* worried, Alex. What if there's internal bleeding or a head injury or… God. She can't die on me." Kara starts crying again, and I feel so useless. I want to assure her Aela won't die, but I've learnt from experience that's not something you can promise.

"How far away are you?" I ask instead. I stand and make sure my keys are still in my pocket.

"About ten minutes away any other day, but it's bumper to bumper here on the highway, and I've barely moved in the last five minutes." Kara sniffles then curses the car in front of her, which makes me smile despite the situation.

"We'll meet you there. Just try not to get worked up and distracted while you're driving—we don't need you in an emergency bed too." I am pleading over her continuing sniffles.

"Okay. Thanks, Alex," she says in a small voice, and I assure her it's nothing before ending the call.

Kit is instantly demanding answers.

"We need to go get Dec. Aela's in the hospital. She's been

attacked."

There's a stunned moment before Kit takes off running down the hall to the stairs, calling out for Declan.

I hear her telling Dec what's going on before I can catch up to her, and my stomach tightens when I see Dec on his knees on the floor with a totally destroyed look on his face. I push the sight from my mind and hope I never see it again.

"No, man. Don't go there. She's alive, just badly beat up. Jesus, Kit. You can't just burst out with half the story," I yell at her as I move to help my best friend up off the floor. I lead the way down to my car while I explain what I know even though he doesn't give so much as a sign that he's listening. He just stares ahead of us.

I head solo towards the emergency entrance, after Dec dramatically threw himself from my moving car before I could even get into the parking lot and I had to stop to let Kit go after him.

I notice Kara on my way and call out to get her attention. She immediately starts jogging for me, barrelling into my chest. I enfold her in my arms and grip her tight for a moment before pulling back to look at her.

Kara's face is flushed red from crying, her ponytail a mess, most of her hair fallen out of it and around her face. The streetlight glints off the fresh tears welling in her eyes. She probably wouldn't believe it right now, but she has never looked more beautiful to me than in this moment—so human.

"Come on. Let's go find out how your girl's doing."

I lead Kara inside by an arm wrapped around her shoulders. I spare a worried glance at Dec and Kit who are in a fevered, whispered conversation just inside the doors. Kit gestures she's got him, so I stick with Kara as she walks to the counter—not like I have a choice with the grip she's got on me. She asks after Aela, saying she's her sister when the lady doubtfully asks if we're relatives.

"She's just been taken for x-rays. I can allow her boyfriend to come get you when she's back if you like?" Kara's eyes go wide at the word *boyfriend,* but she nods anyway.

"I'm afraid only you will be allowed though. As I said to the other gentleman, only family are allowed admittance at this point for that patient."

Kara thanks the lady and then we step away, walking to where Dec has been forced into the back row of chairs.

"I'm guessing that's Malcolm's way of staying with her," Kara mumbles as she takes the seat next to Dec, who looks so forlorn as Kit nudges him in the ribs.

"See, I told you," she mutters at Kara's words. He gives a barely there nod before resuming his very important wall staring.

I take the seat beside Kara, stretching my legs out in front of me in an impossible attempt to get comfortable in the hard plastic chair. Kara leans into my side, so I bury my nose in her hair to escape the cloying antiseptic hospital smell that dredges up memories and feelings from the dark recesses of my mind of all the time I spent in the hospital with Grace.

We sit silently for a while, clearly all lost in our own thoughts, until Kara shivers against me. I notice goose bumps spreading up her arms.

"You cold?" My voice comes out scratchy as though it's been hours instead of minutes since I've used it, so I clear my throat as she nods against my chest.

"I can go find us some coffee, and we'll have our date here," I offer, and Kara tilts her head up to look at me incredulously.

"You want to have a date in the emergency waiting room while I'm worried about my beat up best friend?"

I smother the urge to flinch because put that way, it does sound tactless, and I hadn't meant it literally, but then again… if it distracts us both from our troubles, why not?

"Sure. I've been on dates in weirder places."

I look around the room as though I'm imagining all the romantic possibilities before meeting her gaze. "Do you have something better to do while sitting here for who knows how long?"

Kara raises a challenging brow, and I know I've hooked her with my statement.

"Where were these weirder places?"

I grin, taking it as her concession, and get to my feet before replying.

"Oh, you know, the usual... a couple graveyards at night, a closed church and a chemo ward." I notice my slip up as soon as the words are out and peek at Dec, but he's so deep in his own thoughts, he doesn't even twitch my way. "I'll be right back. You won't even have time to miss me, but it's okay if you do." I wink and receive a timid grin before I spin on my heel and get going.

I silently curse myself for bringing up those dates because my mind seems to have taken it as approval to replay some of those memories. Grace dragging me along on spooky, midnight cemetery tours and a couple of times I surprised her with an impromptu picnic to cheer her up during her chemo sessions that were always rough on her. My hands clench, and I bite the inside of my mouth to ground myself as I blindly seek out the cafeteria or a vending machine. If it weren't for Kara and Aela being here, I'd just walk out. I *really* hate hospitals.

The cafeteria shut hours ago, so I hit the vending machines, loading up on coffees and all the snacks I can safely carry.

Kara's eyes light up with mirth when she notices my return and gets up to help me with my loot. I give the others their coffee before gallantly presenting Kara hers. She rolls her eyes with amusement while lowering back into her seat. She laughs, though, when I continue to empty the stash of chocolate bars in my pockets onto her lap.

"Did you clean out their entire stock or what?" she muses. I shrug as I snag a bag of skittles while reclaiming my seat.

"I don't know which your favourite is. Figured it was best to have a few options."

The way she's looking at me sweetens, like her guard has melted a little, before she shakes it off and murmurs a quiet, "Thank you." Then tentatively sips her coffee.

"You noticed how I have my coffee?" Kara exclaims after her first taste, eyes wide with shock and disbelief, which makes me chuckle as I lean back in my seat.

"I notice everything about you, sunshine. Corny statement but true."

Her eyes do that melty thing again, and then she leans in to press her lips sweetly to mine in appreciation.

We settle in and make small talk as we munch away—I take note that she favours the white chocolate—before a big, tatted dude dressed in all black and rocking a wicked Mohawk, steps out of the secured door but keeps it propped open with a foot as he nods our way in recognition.

It's Mal, the guy we've been waiting for. Kara moves the junk food from her lap to race over to him, and after some murmuring, nodding, and a sympathetic pat on her arm from him, she returns to us as he disappears back through the door. I eye her questioningly as she wraps her arms around herself before meeting my gaze. I feel Dec sit straighter in his seat.

"They're taking Aela into surgery to set her broken arm then she's being admitted. Malcolm says we can move up to the orthopaedics waiting room and he'll meet us there." Kara worries her bottom lip with her teeth, her stormy grey eyes filled with concern and clearly imagining the worst.

I nod then drag myself up out of my seat as she collects her bag. Which we throw all our snacks inside of. I turn to see the others are out of their seat also, waiting for Kara to lead the way.

I take her back under my arm and squeeze her against my side, letting her know I'm here for her as we head for the elevators.

Malcolm is waiting with an amused smirk at managing to beat us to the ward on the sixth floor after we had made a few too many wrong turns. The five of us settle on the deceptively comfortable looking couches which are only marginally better than the chairs downstairs. Malcolm shares what he knows about what happened and Aela's current condition at Declan's desperate demand.

My hands and teeth clench in fury as Malcolm recounts how he came upon the scene. I wince throughout his story, and when he gets to the list of Aela's injuries, all the junk I've eaten threatens to come back up. I have to fight off the burn of tears behind my eyes, blinking quickly before they can appear.

Two breaks in her left arm, a dislocated shoulder, fractured ribs, internal bleeding and bruising as well as minor bumps, bruises and scrapes.

Fucking hell.

Kara starts crying beside me again, so I wrap her in my arms and kiss her hair as I glance at Dec, who is paler than I've ever seen him, slouched back in his seat in defeat with a desolated look that frightens me.

It's as if this is the last straw. The world has thrown so much shit at him that he's battled through with a vengeance, but this, this has him giving up the fight, waving the white flag, and I don't know what to do.

"Oh, God. I have to call her parents." Kara sniffles then retrieves her phone and steps away to the other side of the room. I watch her as she tries to pull herself together enough to make the call.

It may be inappropriate, but I can't seem to take my eyes off her as I get swept up in how beautiful she looks even in sadness.

There's something really, *really* wrong with me.

178

Not even half an hour later, Kara springs from her seat beside me and rushes towards a couple who have barely rounded the corner to where we are sitting solemnly silent. They're a striking older couple, who I'd guess to be in their fifties. The woman is beautiful in a refined way, even though her face is etched in worry and fear as she hastily talks with Kara while the husband places a calming hand on the woman's shoulder.

"I can't do this. I shouldn't be here. I don't deserve to be… it's all my fault. I've got to go," Dec blurts and then bolts up out of his seat and rushes past Aela's family. I can't even think of a word of protest over a shocked stutter. I move to go after him, but Kit places a hand against my arm, halting me.

"I'll go. You stay for Kara. You're more help here than I am. Call me if there's any news?"

I look from her to the corner Dec disappeared behind, then to Kara, who happens to look over her shoulder at me as though she's checking on a lifeline. I can't leave her, so I reluctantly nod and settle back down. Kit presses a quick kiss to my cheek then rushes after our friend, leaving me feeling torn in half.

Kara introduces me to Aela's parents, Evelyn and Jack, when they join us in the waiting game. After some small talk, we descend back into an expectant silence, which is only disrupted when Kit returns, sighing disgruntledly as she resumes her seat. I give her a questioning look but she just shakes her head.

Kara leans against me again. She keeps rubbing her arm and regularly shivering. She shakes her head when I ask if she's cold until I can't take it anymore and tell her I'll be right back.

I head to the nurse's desk just as a couple of them walk away from it, leaving a young blonde in a student uniform to man the desk alone. She looks up as I approach and smiles flirtatiously while propping herself up on an elbow with interest.

"Can I help you?" The tone of her voice suggests just what she'd like to "help" with so I give my best charming smile and lean over the top of the desk toward her.

"I couldn't trouble you for a spare blanket, could I?"

She attempts to tuck some of her short fringe behind her ear, but the strands just fall back into place. She shoots a hesitant glance to where the two nurses had just left before turning back to me.

"Sure. I'll go get one for you." She hurries away, returning a moment later on my side of the desk with a white bundle tucked under her arm, which she presents with another flirtatious smile. "Anything else I can do to warm you up?"

I take the blanket gratefully but shake my head,

"This is all I need. Thank you so much." The girl's shoulders slump as though she's let down. I decide to leave before it gets any more awkward just as one of the older nurses who'd left at my approach, rounds the corner. She frowns as she sees us on the other side of the desk.

"Tell me, Carla, how are you able to take calls if you're running around fetching things for visitors and not at all in reach of the phone?"

Carla's eyes widen, and she stammers until the crabby old lady cuts her off. "You're not, that's how. I don't hand out duties for them to be disregarded for a pretty face. Please come see me in the office when Tara gets back to handle the phone since you're so incapable of doing it yourself." She sneers, levels me with a stern look, and then disappears back the way she came.

"I'm so sorry," Carla and I both whisper simultaneously when we turn to each other and then she nervously laughs as I smile.

"It's fine. I can handle the old dragon. I should get back to my side of the desk, though." Carla winces and hurries around the alcove as the phone starts ringing.

"Causing trouble with weak-willed women wherever you go, huh, Alex?" Kara murmurs sounding amused as I take my seat beside her again. I twist towards her to throw the blanket over her with a flourish before I give her a smirk and a wink as she resumes snuggling into my side.

"My evil superpower," I joke, which gets an eye roll in reply as I wrap my arm around her and settle back. I try not to pay attention to Aela's mother, Evelyn, giving us an amused smirk as she watches us.

MY ARSE IS numb. I have pins and needles in my legs and have no idea how long it's been when a bed is wheeled around the corner.

Aela's parents shoot up off the lounge as though it's on fire before I realise it's Aela in that bed. I gently shake Kara, who is asleep on my shoulder.

The poor woman is exhausted, and I have to say her name twice before she rouses. Kara blinks sleepily at me in confusion a couple times before she jumps straight up in awareness and looks around.

"Aela's been brought up to a room," I inform her. She breathes a sigh of relief before getting up to follow Malcolm to where the others are gathered at the door a couple of rooms down, listening to a guy in blue scrubs that's standing in the doorway.

"Can we sit with her?" Evelyn asks as we join them. The guy, who I'm guessing is a doctor, takes in our group before replying.

"Of course, but only two at a time for now. We don't want to crowd the room. Her internal bleeding will need to be checked again later to make sure it stops on its own. Just be aware, Aela's still under the anaesthetic so it will still be a while before it wears off and she's fully conscious."

We nod our acceptance as Evelyn and Jack thank him then go into the room first when he steps aside. The rest of us head back to the couches while I text an update to Declan.

The mood is a lot lighter now that we've all seen Aela. Kara pulls out the remainder of the sweets in her bag and finds a forgotten deck of cards in there, so we settle in and get a poker game going—using the chocolate bars as currency.

A half hour later, Aela's parents come out to tell us they're going home to get what sleep they can since it may be hours before Aela wakes. They ask that they are called if anything changes and then order us to get some sleep before making their exit.

We decide the two ladies can go in for the next bedside vigil, and it's only when I'm sitting there alone with Malcolm that I wonder why he's even still hanging around just to check on his employee.

I become suspicious of his motives.

"It's awful nice of you as a boss, sticking around even though we know she's going to be okay now," I remark, hoping it will lead to a confession. I shuffle Kara's cards and slide my gaze over to him.

"Aela's a sweet girl, and I promised I wouldn't leave her so I'm not going to if I can help it—until she tells me she doesn't need me."

I squint at him distrustfully,

"Aela doesn't need you, dude. What can you do for her that the staff here, her family or Kara can't?" I demand then snort mockingly.

Malcolm shrugs. "She begged me not to leave her, so I can keep my word and make sure she's okay," he states with a finality in his tone, so I let it go—for now. Because he's a big guy, and I don't want to get into a scuffle with him right here and thrown out.

After forty minutes, I decide to pop my head into the room because I've reached the threshold of my ability to remain idle. Technically, that won't be against the doctor's wishes.

"How we doing in here, ladies?" I ask, surveying the white room before my eyes land on the tiny form on the bed. She is hooked up to cables and intravenous drips, her arm plastered and propped up on a brace and more bandages than skin showing on her head. The sight hits me like a physical blow to the gut, and I press on the ache as I move my eyes to Kara, who is gently brushing back her best friend's hair as she meets my gaze.

"She's been stirring a little. Mumbled Malcolm's name not long ago," Kara informs me as Kit places the medical chart back in the holder at the end of the bed.

"Excuse me, I've been lenient, but visiting hours are long over, and you're disturbing the other patients. Only immediate family can stay now."

Dragon Lady is back and seems to have it out for me as I look over my shoulder to see her glaring at me impatiently.

"How do you know I'm not a brother?" I challenge, so she holds out a hand.

"Show identification to prove it or get out. The lot of you." She looks into the room meaningfully, and the girls squeeze by me a moment later while silently urging me to let it go with insistent looks.

"I'm sorry. Thank you for letting us stay passed visiting hours. But please, let her boyfriend stay? Aela's already been asking for him, and I think she'll need the comfort after all she's been through." Kit tries to be diplomatic as Malcolm wanders over.

I see a hint of compassion bloom in the grumpy woman's eyes as she faces Kit and after a moment, grudgingly nods her acquiescence.

"Fine. But any disruption and you're out." She glares at Mal

183

before turning on her heel and walking away.

"Bitch. I'll go back to the waiting area. She can't banish me from the hospital. Just text me when Aela wakes up, Mal," Kara insists, but I put my arm around her shoulder.

"Instead of causing trouble, why don't you come back to my place with me? Get some shut eye, and we'll come back first thing in the morning?" I lead us down the corridor until she stops suddenly to look at me with a weary sigh.

"If you think I'm going to put out after all this, you're out of your mind."

I ignore Kit's snort and muttered insult about me being mindless and focus on Kara as I turn her body towards me with a smirk.

"Funny that your dirty mind can go there at a time like this, but sadly, no. I'm talking literally *just* sleeping next to each other. I only want to comfort and take care of you if you let me, sunshine." I lean in and finish gently murmuring the last of it a hair's breadth away from touching skin, ending with a quick kiss to the tip of her nose, which she wrinkles adorably before melting into me.

"I'm too tired to argue, so you win. Take me home, Alex," Kara concedes. I can't get us out of there fast enough, only barely stopping to drop Kit off and see her safely inside her place.

"Make yourself at home. If you need a shower or anything before bed, you're welcome to it." I wave Kara inside as I open the front door for her. She emits a tired, needy sound in the back of her throat.

"A hot shower sounds like heaven. And toothpaste. And something clean to wear if I'm not pushing my luck. I don't have anything with me again." Kara wrinkles her nose in distaste as she looks down at her loose cotton shirt, so I push her towards the bathroom with a small smile.

"How about, you go for a shower, throw me out your clothes, and I'll wash them for you to wear in the morning. I'll get you something of mine to sleep in." Kara makes that noise again before leaning over to kiss my cheek.

"You're my hero," she murmurs and then walks into the main bathroom as I chuckle. I like sleepy Kara.

If only she was always so easy to please.

I grab an old shirt and a pair of boxers and wait against the wall opposite the bathroom door until it cracks open. Kara pokes her head out, keeping the rest of herself hidden behind the door.

"You remember I've seen it all before, right?" I smirk as I step forward to offer her the clothes. She frowns at me, thrusting an arm out to take them.

"Doesn't mean you automatically get to see the goods again," she counters as a ball of denim and cotton is thrown at my face and she shuts the door firmly between us. I laugh again and head for the laundry to put it in my washer-dryer combo. I'm too tired and eager for bed to wait for a shower, so I brush my teeth in the my master bathroom, then change into a pair of boxers because I'm sure Kara would kick up a fuss if she finds me naked.

I'm tucked in and waiting, the only illumination from my bedside lamp, as Kara enters my bedroom looking deliciously soft and warm in my clothes, with her hair messily piled up on top of her head and flushed cheeks from the hot shower.

I fold back the covers on her side of the bed invitingly. She lifts her legs until she's on her knees on the end of the mattress and crawls up until she can slip those temptingly bare legs of hers under the covers. She pulls them up and snuggles into my side. It makes me smile like a champ because I didn't even have to goad her into it.

I stretch my free arm out to flick off the lamp and emit a content sigh into the darkness as I wrap my arms around Kara. I settle in, surrounded by her warmth and fruity coconut scent. It calms something deep within me that's always coiled tight to the point I hadn't noticed it until now that it's calm.

If I had more brain power, I would mull this over, but I'm so exhausted and relaxed, I barely get out a murmured, "Goodnight," before I clock out.

IT FEELS LIKE it's only minutes later when I'm woken by my neighbours adopted crow, cawing from its favourite perch on the outside of my windowsill. I groan and mutter a hateful curse at the stupid demon-bird and bury my face deeper into the warm, delicious smelling silk before I realise, not only is the *silk* hair—but just whose hair it is—and what else is pressed up against me. I've rolled to my side during my sleep and have an epic spooning going on with Kara's soft, warm body pressed against the front of mine, from our entangled feet all the way to my nose squished to her scalp.

My nuzzling and complaining, along with the incessant cawing, rouses Kara, and she starts to wriggle in my arms, her sweet arse grinding into my lap—which my morning wood greatly appreciates and shows it by hardening even more. It feels like fucking heaven.

I moan in delight and am greedy for more of it, so I press my hand that's found its way into the waistband of her boxers against her smooth, warm pelvis, which feels just as spectacular.

"Alex?" Kara murmurs sleepily, checking if I'm awake. I lift up to slide my mouth into the dip of her neck where I press little kisses that make her squirm and gasp before I murmur back.

"Good morning, sunshine."

I forgot to close the blinds last night, so I struggle to open my eyes to the harsh light flooding my room so I can take in the sight of Kara in all her sleep-mussed glory as she twists to lie on her back. Her rumpled bed-hair, flushed cheeks, heavy-lidded gaze, and her perfect little pout of protest for being woken up is a sight to behold.

I'm smiling as I reach out to move some of her tangled hair off her face, and she curls into me with a purr like a kitten seeking warmth. I take her hand that snakes out to wrap around my waist, pulling it up to press a kiss to the back of it and notice how pliable she is. I could so easily take advantage and bend her to my will in the state she's in right now. But I said I wouldn't even try, so I fight the urge of my body and focus on just enjoying this moment.

"Visiting hours will start soon. You want breakfast before we head to the hospital?" My hand finds its way under her shirt and glides over her stomach. It takes a moment for my words to sink in, but when they do, her body stiffens as her eyes open wide when reality hits.

"Shit, Aela." She covers her eyes with the palms of her hands in disbelief that she momentarily forgot the drama. I prop myself up on my elbow and reluctantly remove my hand from under her shirt to pull her hands away and drop a kiss to her cheek.

"She's fine. Might even be awake having some terrible hospital food as we speak. So… food?" She nods through a yawn that I can't help ruining by quickly sneaking in a finger to prod her tongue. I snap my hand back when Kara tries to bite it off, and then I get up out of bed with a spring in my step.

"We've got eggs, cereal, or toast?" I call out as I check the contents of my fridge, hearing Kara's bare feet padding down the tiled hallway.

"Jam and toast are fine if you have it. And coffee… extra strong and lots of it."

I chuckle and move to the toaster as she rounds the corner,

and I pause to flick her a grin.

"I knew that. I've already got the water boiling." I point at the red light on the kettle. She leans over as she passes to kiss my cheek.

"You're my hero," she says as she reaches in the cupboard for two mugs.

We proceed to work around each other to get breakfast made. I retrieve the butter and jam as Kara weaves around me for the milk. I get a knife as she fishes for a spoon. I'm amused how we work so easily together. It's as if we've had years of experience making breakfast together and are perfectly cohesive. I think Kara notices it also if the little smirk she shoots me as she makes my coffee by memory is anything to go by.

I turn on the morning news show as we settle in to eat on the couch, eating in companionable silence until I finish and take my dishes to put in the dishwasher.

"I'm going to grab a quick shower. Be ready to go in twenty?" I see Kara nod with a mouthful.

I hear the exhaust fan going in the main bathroom when I exit my room, so I head for the open door as I finish roughly towel drying my hair. My hands pause in the action when I find Kara with her back to me, watching in the mirror as she puts her hair up. She's back in her dark blue jeans and singlet but has thrown my shirt back on over the top, bunching it in the back with an elastic band so it fits tighter.

"Nearly ready?" I ask as I drop the towel on the laundry basket before stepping up behind her.

"Just need to brush my teeth," she replies while finishing her ponytail.

"Oh, good. I didn't want to say something, but you really do… sheesh," I joke, waving my hand in the air as though there's a bad smell. Kara glares at me in the mirror.

"You're a dick," she complains while trying to throw me off

when I wrap my arms around her waist. I rest my chin on her shoulder, but I stay put.

"You like my dick," I correct, enjoying stirring her up.

"No. That's why I haven't had sex with you. I didn't want to say anything but…"

"Shut up. You love my dick. She *loves* my dick," I look away from her reflected eyes to assure my own reflection, which makes her laugh as she shoves my arms away from her to get closer to the sink.

"Nice shirt, by the way," I comment, and she pauses with the toothbrush in her hand that used to be an unopened spare in the cupboard.

"Hope you don't mind, but I didn't want to go in the same clothes, and I think it'll give Aela a good laugh if it's needed." She points to the print on the front, and I couldn't agree more. The shirt is one of my favourites which proudly states *Love all Pussy* with pictures of different cats underneath. It's epic and even better when it's on Kara.

"I'll go warm the car up then. Unless you want me to do as the shirt says…"

Kara points toward the door resolutely so I heave a huge dramatic sigh as I exit, to make her laugh again.

WE GET TO the hospital an hour later because I decided to stop in at Declan's and try to talk him into coming with us, but he was adamant he shouldn't be there despite the fact it was clearly eating at him because he looked like shit.

I felt bad for the guy and somehow wound up agreeing to be his errand boy, making a pit stop down the road to buy some flowers for Aela from him. Though he said to say they were from me, which I didn't really agree with.

When we get to the ward, Aela's parents are at the front desk talking to a nurse with a clipboard, and Kara rushes over to find out what's going on.

I don't want to know what they're saying just yet. I need to see for myself if Aela is okay first because I'm feeling shaken. I've had this feeling of icy dread on my shoulders from the moment we walked through the front doors.

There were a couple of kids that were clearly cancer patients, who had come down to raid the confection stand in the cafeteria. Memories rushed back to doing the same thing with Grace. They had the same look of excitement and happiness over something so small. The look on Grace's face had been the same as the girls when the teenage boy led her by the hand to the elevator we had to share. It got too much, and I came close to vomiting when all the excitement took its toll on the girl on the way up in the small compartment. I had to help the kid hold her up when she almost fainted—until the doors opened up to two sets of very worried-looking parents who immediately swooped in to take them back.

I can't shake the memories and the hollow feeling in my stomach, so I focus on Aela—on sneaking passed Dragon Lady, who is *still* here.

I enter her room and breathe in relief when I see her in the bed and awake, although I seem to have interrupted a private moment with her boss, who is kissing her forehead tenderly.

I clear my throat as I walk more into the room, placing the flowers beside Aela on the bed. I give a blatantly fake apology for interrupting, staring down the guy trying to intimidate him. I lean down to press my lips to Aela's forehead also, intending to wipe out his previous kiss.

My intimidation works on the big guy because he can't get out of the room fast enough as I take his seat.

My left foot will not stop bouncing in agitation as I try to focus on our conversation and on making Aela feel better, instead of the totally irrational feeling I have that Death is hovering over my shoulder.

I make the wrong decision, though, when I come clean and tell her the flowers are from Declan, who isn't here.

Her eyes start welling with tears, and she looks seconds from breaking down as she politely gives me my marching orders. So I kiss her cheek in apology and give her the privacy she desires even though I feel horrible for leaving her like that.

Evelyn is approaching as I step from the room, and I hesitate, blocking her way as I have to make a split-second decision on whether I distract her and hold her off from going in there or let her go comfort her daughter. I don't know the woman enough to know what kind of mother she is, but I consider how she hasn't once looked down her nose at me and my appearance as most wealthy parents would. She's been nothing but nice. Even now, as she smiles warmly at me with a questioning look as I continue to block her way.

I hope I'm not making another mistake as I step aside.

"Ah, Evelyn, aren't you a sight for sore eyes?" I force myself to give a charming smile and wink as I gallantly gesture for her to pass me with a wave of my arm. "I hope the sight of you works on Aela as it has me."

Evelyn shakes her glossy blonde hair with an amused smirk as she taps my shoulder with her purse in admonishment.

"A smooth tongue like that will get you into trouble one day," she warns. I grin playfully.

"I hope so." I waggle my brows, and she laughs as she disappears into the room.

"Hey, you. Where did you wander off to?" Kara asks curiously as I take a seat on the lounge opposite her in the waiting area. I want nothing more than to sit with her and wrap myself up in her, but my head is a mess, and my skin feels like its crawling. I just need a minute to regain control.

"I slipped in to see Aela. What did they have to say about her condition?"

"They didn't know she had woken up yet until Malcolm came out and told us, so they'll be going in to check on her any second now. They did say her internal bleeding has stopped, which is great news. They're still keeping visitors down to two at a time in there to keep her from being too overwhelmed until the doctor can see her, and then they'll go from there."

I nod absently as I stare absently at the floral display on the corner table.

"How is she?" Kara asks quietly as though afraid to ask.

I turn my eyes on her and shrug my shoulders.

"How you would expect her to be? Exhausted, upset and in pain," I answer bluntly. Kara closes her eyes in sympathy for her best friend.

We sit in silence for a while until Aela's father, Jack, exits the room, phone to his ear with a stern expression. He barks a few orders then ends his call, stopping beside Kara to pat her back affectionately.

"Sorry we left you waiting so long, sweetheart. Aela was a bit upset, and Evie made me stay outside until she could calm her down. I've got to get to work, so go ahead, and take my spot. Call me if you girls need anything, okay?"

Kara nods as she stands to kiss his cheek and say goodbye. I realise I'm about to be sitting here on my own and know I definitely won't be able to deal with that. My lungs are already constricting, so I wait until they're done and Kara's gathering her bag to stand up, gaining her attention.

"I'm going to get going too. Are you all right to get home?"

Kara nods, her brow creased with concern.

"I used my uni parking across the road last night, so I'm good. Are you okay?" I nod as I lean over to kiss her cheek.

"Just got some stuff to do. I'll speak to you later," I murmur, then rush for the elevator without looking back.

I inhale deep breaths of fresh air as soon as I reach the freedom of outside, which helps. But my hands are shaking when I get to my car. It takes me a few tries to get the key in the ignition. I sit there with the Jeep idling as I contemplate where to go. I need a distraction, something to help get my head back on straight. I need the ocean. I check that I have my board then get on the road, praying that I'll find a little peace.

Chapter 12

KARA

IT'S BEEN FOUR miserable days without a word from Alex after that awkward goodbye at the hospital.

I have to admit I find myself missing the jerk—his teasing smirk, dirty wit and tempting… *everything*.

I still can't figure out what happened that morning, no matter how much time I spend thinking about it—which is a *lot* despite everything else that should be getting all of my attention. Such as my best friend, who is holed up in her room depressed, my studying and upcoming exams, and not to mention my apparent stalker who has not let up with the *charming* texts and notes.

I'm not going to be the first to reach out to Alex, though. I refuse to be that girl. I hate myself enough for the weak moment I had when I worried if Alex's problem was me.

"Earth to Kara?" Kris whisper-yells, tearing me from my musings. I pull away from his mouth at my ear, glaring at him as he smirks from his seat beside me before he gives a slow shake of his head.

"Just call or text him already and put us all out of our misery," Kris demands then flicks the tip of my nose with his pen.

"Who?"

Yeah, I try to play dumb but receive a condescending look

for my effort.

"You know exactly who. Mister Caramel-delight-I-want-to-lick-him-up-Alex. You know… the guy who was totally sweet and melted your icy heart when you were in distress but now seems to have gone off the grid," he murmurs, pausing to jot something down in his notebook, actually managing to pay attention to the lecture we're in. My book isn't even open in front of me. "You want to do something to cheer Aela up and get her out of the house, and he works at a club, right?"

I clarify with a derisive snort. "Usually a strip club."

"So, use it as an excuse to contact him since you're too damn stubborn. Ask if he can hook you up with free entry or something for her?"

I raise my brows at him sceptically. "You really think going to see hot women take their clothes off as they shake their arse is going to make her feel better?" I ask doubtfully. He pauses his writing to throw me a shrug and a jutted lip of distaste,

"Not my cup of tea, but I'm sure you can make it work for her with enough alcohol."

I purse my lips in thought as I tap my pen on the desk until Kris reaches out to stop it.

"Stop and pay attention to Mister Top Deck."

I shake my head and try not to laugh as I shoot a quick glance at our burly lecturer, who looks like he could bench press a car, but has skipped too many leg days.

"Okay, I give. What is with you branding guys as chocolate these last few days?" I give in and ask because he's been doing it a lot.

"I can't help it. I took a random 'What chocolate are you?' quiz that popped up on Facebook. It was stupid but amusing."

"What did you get?" I ask with an expectant smirk after a beat of silence.

He wrinkles his nose. "Fruit and nut," Kris complains, and I snort.

"Sounds about right." I laugh quietly as he flips me off and then studiously ignores me, leaving me to contemplate his suggestion.

Half an hour later, I've bitten my thumbnail down to the skin. I stare at a draft text to Alex, my thumb hovering over the send button. With uncertainty, I re-read it for maybe the tenth time until Kris fakes a cough and deliberately bumps me. I watch in horror as the text moves into a speech bubble that I read over as though the letters aren't burned into my retinas by now.

"Hey, Alex. Where and when is the next ladies' night? I need to get Aela out of her room and reintroduce her to fun on our lowly student budget. How are you, btw?"

I hate it. But there's nothing I can do about it now. I shoot a sideways glare at Kris who smiles unrepentantly.

I slowly lower my phone to the table as if I don't even care, not at all anticipating the moment the screen lights up with a reply. I'm about to say something to wipe the smug smile off Kris's face when I see the light I'm waiting for and immediately scoop my phone back up, which has him chuckling. I ignore him as I read.

"Morning, beautiful sunshine. I'm good. How are you both? Tonight at Ruby's—chicks get free drinks. I'll leave your names at the door for free entry if you think you're up for it?"

I feel myself smiling and get a warm, giddy feeling like I've been reduced to a teen girl talking to her crush.

Slightly pathetic. But I ignore it to text him back.

"I'm so up for it. Will we be seeing you there? I've kinda missed your face. Though, that could be the delusion from sleep deprivation talking."

I smirk picturing the way his eyes will darken determinedly at the perceived challenge I know he will read in my text—the very look on his face that never fails to excite me.

I get so lost in the mental image that I startle when my phone vibrates in my hand.

"I hope you're up for other things because my face has missed your sweet pussy too, no kinda about it. Be prepared for more sleep deprivation if I get my way."

Holy hotness. I feel flushed and tingly just reading his words. I know my cheeks are flaming as I reply that I'll see him later. I put my phone in my bag before he has me begging like a cat in heat in the middle of my freaking lecture. I reach back to move my hair off my neck in an attempt to cool down as I peek at Kris when I see his torso moving in a silent laugh, finding he's watching me with amusement.

"He can get you hot under the collar with just a text, and you haven't bagged him yet? Damn, girl. You're wasteful." I shrug shamelessly with a grin before turning to pretend that I'm paying attention to the class because I'm not sure that I can speak right now.

There is one thing I am sure of though. I'm done running from Alex. It's time I face him and this thing burning between us head on.

Poor guy's not going to know what hit him.

I SEND OUT word of the ladies' night to those I know Aela would be happy to see and manage to wrangle her into grudgingly complying with my idea. I feel a little bad for bossing her around when she's still injured—especially now it's more for my gain than hers—but I remind myself that it's necessary.

No good, self-respecting best friend could allow her to continue wallowing in self-pity, secluded in her room, and stinking up the place with a lack of personal hygiene and shower snubbing.

I dress to kill in my favourite pair of skin-tight grey jeans that make my arse look curvier with some clever stitching, a loose, shimmery black top that is almost see through in the right light and my 'killer confidence' heels that got their name because I never fail to feel badarse in the chrome heeled stilettos. Even if the only thing they actually *kill* are the soles of my feet, leaving me unable to put any weight on them the next day.

I make a beeline for the bar as soon as we're in the door. Not even bothering to take in our surroundings.

It looks unmanned, but when I lean over the bar-top, I'm greeted by the very welcoming view of Alex's arse on show in a pair of form-fitting, black dress pants. I want to stretch out and bite into it, but if I tried, I'd only end up falling flat on my face. So I refrain and yell out to get his attention.

"What does a girl have to do to get an orgasm and screaming sex with a bartender around here?"

I'm rewarded with that mischievous grin of his that I've grown fond of when he looks back to meet my gaze. He absently shuts the glass door of the fridge he was refilling and rises to lean over towards me.

"You can get both at once from me anytime, babe. All you gotta do is ask," Alex replies in his deep, sensual tone before his eyes dip to appreciate my cleavage on display from my current position. I snicker in an attempt to downplay the effect he's having on me.

Alex winks, letting me know that he sees right through it but turns to select several bottles from the mirrored shelves behind him to mix our cocktails.

I become entranced by the mouth-watering muscles of his arms flexing as he works with a showy flair and skill. I'm sure this would be impressive if I could actually watch the shakers he expertly throws, but I'm much more impressed with his gun show at the moment. Something I will never be caught dead admitting to aloud.

My eyes move to his lips at the sound of his voice as he spills out his effortless charm, but the words wash over me as I get caught up in the warm feeling the timbre of his voice elicits in my body, and words spill from my mouth without a filter.

"You know, something about being behind this bar makes you seem totally fuckable."

My brain takes a split second to play catch up, and then I decide to grin proudly and own it—because it could've been worse. At least I didn't outright tell him to take me now or anything *really* stupid.

Alex quirks a brow and his eyes light with interest as he invites me into the back room teasingly.

I pretend to think about it as he pours our drinks before I reply.

"Nope. You may have better luck after I've had a few of these, though." I wink as I hold up the glass he places before me. We share a laugh before his jade eyes capture me with a heated gleam, full of sensual promise, which has me sinking my teeth into the straw in my glass, wishing it was his bottom lip. I meet his gaze head on, hoping he can read what I'm trying to convey without words just as easily.

"Play your cards right, buddy, and this mouse will finally let you catch her tonight." Or should I be the cat in this game since I'm the one with the pussy? Though he was the one chasing... Maybe we should change the name of the game to Cat and Dog...

Oh, God. I hope whatever he's picking up from me is a whole lot sexier and certain than this line of thought. I throw in another wink for good measure.

Aela shifts her stance beside me, propping her arm cast on the bar and I realise she's looking rather awkward. I feel bad. I momentarily forgot my best friend was even there. Alex is focused on wiping down the bar with a pleased smirk.

"What was with the drink order?" Aela asks curiously while her eyes shoot back and forth between Alex and me as though she's really questioning what's going on between us. Understandable, since I've been very loud and open with my dislike of the guy.

I explain the new rule for ladies' night drinks now having to be dirty cocktails courtesy of Alex, which makes him bow cockily and comment on "changing our life in a profound way." I have a retort on the tip of my tongue, but a couple wave for service further down the bar so I reluctantly let it go so he can do his job. Aela and I wander off towards the main stage where Alex has reserved us a little corner alcove.

We find Kit, Charli, and Jen have beat us to it, and the girls are more than a couple drinks ahead if their enthusiastic greetings are anything to go by, but I love it and soak up the tight hugs and squeals.

I shuffle in line between the twins to sit on the bench seat against the wall which is a very comfy, supple red leather that I can't help running my hand over before remembering where I am and instantly snap my hand back to my lap. Guys are gross in general. Who knows what unsanitary things have gone down in a dark corner of a strip club. I wipe my hand down my denim clad thigh—because that will *totally* save me from herpes—before clutching my glass in both hands and trying to remind myself everything happens in the back rooms, not out in the open, so I'm possibly overreacting and *should* be fine.

I try to pay attention as Charli talks about her amazing trip around the world, but I keep catching glimpses of Alex behind her as he works. It's all I can do to remain in my seat and not go over there. I notice Kit finishing the last of her beer before placing it on the fancy coffee table. I take that as my chance, throwing back my own drink. Before I can take the last mouthful, a pretty redhead in a barely there Red Riding Hood outfit approaches our section and leans over the table, asking if she can get us another round.

Kit points out her bottle since she can't yell over the music. I hold up my glass grudgingly as Red leans more my way to hear my order. I smile as I wriggle forward.

"Can you tell Alex, Kara wants something hard from him?" I offer her a ten dollar note, but she pushes it back to me.

"Your drinks are free with this." She taps the wristband I was given at front reception, but I hold my hand out further as I lean back in to speak.

"It's for your trouble."

She smiles in appreciation as though it's more than just a tenner, and it disappears somewhere in her little costume as she steps back and descends down a couple of stairs to the main floor.

I'm almost giddy as I await his response and wish I could see his face when she relays my request.

I try to distract myself, attempting to join in the twin's discussion that's going on around me, but I've missed a subject change. It takes me a moment to pick up they're talking about Jen's exams now.

Before I know it, Red's little cape catches my attention as she approaches the stairs, expertly balancing a drink tray above the crowd on one hand. She places Kit's beer down on the table then hands me my glass with a slice of lime on the rim—with an amused smile as she leans over to speak.

"He says, he sends a Cock Tease for the cock tease, and he will give you his 'something hard' later if you really want it." Red shakes her head with a laugh as she pulls away, and I give her a smile of gratitude before sipping the drink.

I nearly choke on the unexpected strength of tequila that takes my breath away and burns its way down, before the sweet aftertaste of apple and lime invades my senses.

ASH HOSKING

The DJ takes over the sound system, and the dancers are paraded out on stage as though it's a catwalk and introduced by their stage names before their sets are started. The five of us settle in to watch the show because the noise makes any unnecessary talking nearly impossible.

A handful of dancers later, and I'm bored of the show. There's only so much hip shaking, twerking and self-caressing I can watch before I want to poke my eyes out.

I make sure Aela's okay then excuse myself to go to the bathroom. I spy Alex in the corner of the bar, serving a small group of waitresses who are huddled up in front of him, giggling and hanging off his every word. He is effortlessly charming them while he pours drinks. I have the urge to go and break it up, but I ignore the unwarranted pang of jealousy and continue on my way to the toilets—but not before catching Alex's eyes finding me. I shoot him a quick smirk as I hurry by.

I come to a standstill for a moment when I step through the door, taking in the sight before me. Even the bathroom is extravagantly decorated in this place. The walls are red, matching the round velvet seat in the centre of the black tiled room. The fixtures have been made to look like antiques, the mirrors in a fancy gold framework with excellent lighting. But the best thing of all that I really appreciate—there's no waiting line like in a nightclub. In fact, I'm the only woman in here.

I relieve my bladder in peace then take advantage of the perfect lighting to check my makeup is still smudge free as I wash my hands and then leave the little sanctuary.

I'm distracted by the beautiful historical painting across the small hallway of naked women in a tangled embrace when I catch movement in my peripheral vision. I'm suddenly pinned against the wall behind me, and a mouth covers mine, swallowing my cry of alarm. It only takes a second to diffuse my panic, though, when I recognise the scent of Alex's cologne just

202

as my eyes adjust, and I can make out his face in the dim lighting.

His hands are grasping at my waist as his tongue invades my mouth, and my hands wind up tangled in his soft hair, messing it more than it already is.

Alex pulls me by my waist into him so that my back is arched, our groins meeting and grinding as he dominates my mouth with his wicked tongue and sinful lips. One of his hands finds its way under my shirt, his cool fingertips trailing up the warm skin of my spine. I break the kiss when I draw back with a gasp in a knee-jerk reaction that has me hitting my head against the wall with a thud that reverberates through my skull.

"Your fingers are freezing," I complain in a whimper as his mouth has moved down my cheek to nuzzle into my neck, sending delicious tingles through my whole body. I even feel it in my toes as I curl them and gasp as I grip hard onto his shoulders for fear of my legs going out from beneath me.

Alex withdraws his hand from beneath my shirt, squeezing my denim-clad arse, instead.

"Sorry. I just finished stocking the fridges," he murmurs apologetically while continuing his ministrations on my neck, chuckling when I emit a rather loud moan worthy of a porn star.

"Please tell me you're not planning to get me hard then leave me hanging again tonight?" he pleads with his mouth against my ear that makes me shiver and cling tighter to the thin cotton shirt on his shoulders before I realise he asked a question and is waiting for an answer.

I blink my eyes a few times until my vision isn't blurred and I can see his face as he eyes me with a pleading look. I can't help but smirk.

"You know that doesn't really make sense. He can't really be hanging when he's hard." I palm Alex's crotch and squeeze the hardness I find there playfully, making his eyes close as he utters a curse and moves a hand to cover mine and hold it against his erection.

"God. I've missed that smart mouth of yours." Alex dips in to cover my lips with his, biting my bottom lip when he pulls back. "Seriously, though—no jokes. Please, just tell me what you want," He's begging, and I feel bad for the times I've let things get carried away with us only to retreat.

"I want this," I squeeze him in my hand again. "I want you, and I'm done trying to act like I don't. It's driving me crazy."

He barks out a laugh and shakes his head at the end of my statement. "Driving *you* crazy? Fuck. Sunshine, you have no idea." Alex curses again and looks around us as though he'd forgotten our surroundings. "I only have fifteen minutes left of my break, and I'm not taking you for a quickie in the goddamn toilets. I'm going to need more than this." He looks around thoughtfully again, and I bite my lip to stop myself from laughing because it's kind of adorable, the thought he's putting into this.

"What time do you get off?" I ask. His eyes shoot back to mine as he smirks mischievously.

"After I get you off at least half a dozen times."

I punch his arm ineffectively and roll my eyes, "Ha-ha. Your shift?" I demand and push him back with my hands on his firm chest when he leans in to nip at my lips.

"I'll be done at one if not sooner," he replies, his eyes locked on my lips forlornly. I can't help my smile before we're interrupted by a couple of gigglers walking around us for the bathroom, eyeing Alex with interest as they pass.

"I have to agree. Less than fifteen minutes isn't enough for all I want to do with you. We'll talk once your shift ends." I lean in to press a last quick kiss to his wet lips, but before I can pull away, he traps me in his arms and lengthens the kiss into a hot, tongue-tying, panty-melting make-out that goes on until the interrupting bitches return from the bathroom, giggling when they get an eyeful.

Alex slowly weans himself off me, gentling the kiss to a series of small pecks and then sighs as he steps back and frees me.

"This is going to be damn painful to work with," he mutters under his breath, wincing as he tries to adjust his pants—but that proud and eager monster of his refuses to be tucked away from sight. I have to bite off a laugh in sympathy.

"Aww… poor baby. I'll kiss your boo-boos all better later," I promise with a wink as I turn and walk away. I hear Alex groan behind me, moments before he catches up and tugs my hair playfully.

"You want another drink, sunshine?" he asks just as we re-enter the noise of the main floor.

I nod, leaning in to yell out, "Just water. You were too heavy handed with the tequila in that last drink for this designated driver."

Alex holds up a thumb as he slips back behind the bar. I watch greedily as he fetches a bottle and cracking it open before handing it over to me. The bar is swamped with people trying to get a drink and only two women manning it, so I let him go with a finger wave from my free hand.

I return to my friends and the show that has stepped up leaps and bound while I've been gone—if the dancer hanging upside down, three metres up the pole is anything to go by. The girls are totally engrossed as I slip back into my seat just in time to catch the last dramatic move where she plummets down the pole, stopping just in time to land on her feet softly, bows, and then struts her stuff backstage to a round of applause.

I look over to check in with Aela and am shocked to see Declan standing behind her on the other side of the railing, looking at the back of her head as though he's just found heaven.

Shit. I don't know what to do or what he's doing here, what he's intending to do, or especially, how Aela's going to take it.

My hesitation takes away any chance of interception on my behalf because Declan leans as close to Aela as he can get. Then I watch his lips move as he says something I have no chance of hearing over the music.

Aela's spine stiffens as her eyes go wide.

She tries in vain to act as though he's not there, before snapping around with a glare and yelling at him, which again is drowned out by the music. Aela springs from her seat and rushes from our area as quickly as she can. I stand and yell for her to wait, but she ignores me on her mission to get away.

I move to go after her, but Dec holds up a hand to stop me with a pleading look. After a moment's hesitation, I nod but send him a warning glare, promising a world of hurt if he messes with her, which is received with a solemn nod before he rushes after our girl who is headed for the bar.

I really hope they work things out, because I think he really genuinely loves her, and I want to see my best friend happy with someone who cherishes her.

Unfortunately, Declan is a typical guy and manages to mess up worse. An altercation catches my eye not even fifteen minutes later, just as the bouncers get involved in breaking it up. I notice Dec is one of the idiots being held back by one of the doormen. Aela joins us shortly after with a fresh drink. She looks seconds away from breaking out in tears, but resolutely forces a smile and strikes up a conversation with Jen.

Kit ducks out to smack her boss and best friend in the back of the head before giving him a lecture and then lets him slink off to the other side of the isle, making himself comfortable on a huge white couch where he proceeds to stare after Aela like a lost puppy. It makes me feel a little bad for him, but I'm not about to intervene just yet.

The drinks keep flowing and gradually take effect on the

girls. We end up relocating to a black leather booth down the back near the bathrooms, across from a dark alcove where a fake pole is set up, clearly for amateurs who are inspired by a few too many drinks and watching the show.

Aela laughs when Charli wraps herself around it with an excited squeal and demands her photo to be taken, so I encourage it.

The next thing I know, it's escalated into a challenge for the four of us who aren't handicapped, as Aela watches from the leather booth, nursing her cast as though the arm is giving her some pain. The plastic pole isn't the best material to be trying to swing on. It grips any skin it comes into contact with, which is horribly hilarious when Charli emits a horrible squeak after trying to wrap her legs around it and then hunches over, her hands pressed between her legs on the abused skin. It makes me thankful for my jeans as I manage to pull off the spin she had been attempting.

It's a real workout even though we're only fooling around. I have to give props to the women who do this for a living because it doesn't take long for my arms to shake with exhaustion and for me to be huffing for breath.

I leave it to the others when I catch Alex leaning over the bar, looking my way with clear amusement. I spare a glance at Aela who is giggling at Kit, who is cursing while trying to lift herself up the pole, so I slip away to join him.

"I hope you ladies aren't planning on quitting your day jobs," he jokes as I approach and reach out to smack his arm.

"Shut up. You can't even see us. I have mad skills," I insist haughtily, which he chuckles at before pointing over to where Aela is sitting.

"I've got a perfect view in the reflection."

There's a mirror I hadn't noticed before on the wall above Aela. Sure enough, when he tugs me just a few centimetres over to the right, I get an eyeful of Jen trying to stretch her leg up the pole as she laughs, which makes me laugh also with a conceding shrug.

My laugh dies as I look down to Aela and see how drained she's looking as she fiddles with her necklace.

"Looks like it's time to get Aela home," I state and see Alex follow my line of sight and nod in my peripheral vision.

"You still want to meet up when you finish?" I ask, turning back to him. He meets my gaze with a nod.

"Your place or mine?" Alex throws out. I cringe as I peek back at Aela.

"Yours. I already feel bad for dragging her out. I don't want to keep her up all night too."

He raises a brow when I face him again, his mouth hinting at a smirk.

"*All* night? That's a high expectation there. Good thing I'm up for it."

I grin then smack the bar top with finality as I step back. "We'll see, won't we? Text me when you're done."

Alex starts to nod but pauses.

"Oh. Hold up, take this."

He dives a hand into the left pocket of his trousers, retrieving his keys that he flips through before detaching a blue one and offers it to me.

"My spare front door key, in case you beat me there. I don't want you waiting outside alone."

I smile at his sweet concern for my safety, however misguided it may be since he lives in the 'burbs and a good one at that. Instead of picking on him for it, I go with what I find much more humorous.

"You keep your spare key on the ring with its twin? How is that going to help if you lose your keys?"

Alex grins sheepishly while stepping backwards.

"Actually, that's the key I usually leave in my letterbox. I keep forgetting to put it back. If I need it, Dec has a full set of spares, so it's fine. I've gotta get back to it, but I'll see you soon." He flashes me a wave and turns to deal with a guy who stumbles up to the bar who has clearly had enough to drink.

I turn towards my group, finding them all sitting with Aela looking beat from their failed attempts on the pole, making it easy to call it a night.

Aela heads straight to bed as soon as we get home, so I settle into the lounge solo and try to watch some TV. I can't focus on anything long enough to follow the plotline, same with anything I try to read. I'm unable to relax enough to be comfortable, my stomach feeling unsettled, which only worsens when I realise I'm freaking *nervous* because of a *guy*.

I don't do this. I know better than to get emotionally involved. But my hands are sweaty. I feel as though I'm sitting in a sauna with very little air. My heart is thudding harder than normal, and that feeling in my stomach is seriously in danger of making me vomit.

This is a mistake. My walls are crumbling. I'm falling apart, and we haven't even slept together yet, which is when women are *expected* to get all emotionally attached.

I should just bail out, save myself the trouble.

But when I pull up our text conversation on my phone and type out an excuse, I can't bring myself to hit send.

Against my better judgement, I still want him and the way he makes me feel, more than I want to preserve my sanity, and really, Alex hasn't hidden his 'hit it and quit it' reputation.

I'm going in with eyes wide open and no expectations for more, so how much damage could one night with him possibly do?

Just as I cancel the text, a bubble pops up from Alex as though he read my mind.

"Leaving now. Race you there? First one through the door gets their pick for the first position and location. ;)"

I'm biting my bottom lip, trying to contain my grin as I quickly reply that I'll beat him there. I pocket my phone and rush to gather my keys and shoes before quietly slipping out the front door.

It's time to stop over thinking it.

This is a one-night stand, an itch being scratched, and a good time, nothing more.

I repeat this mantra in my head several times as I restlessly wait for the elevator to stop at the garage then rush to my car. I drive as fast as I can without going over the speed limit enough to warrant a ticket, even though it's unnecessary because the roads that I take to Alex's house are practically deserted of any other cars, so I easily get there first.

I let myself in with the key Alex gave me, flip the light switch that illuminates most of the house all the way to his bedroom door, and then pause as soon as the front door is shut behind me.

Now that I've beaten him here, I don't know what to do with myself. I'm sure he intended for me to make myself at home when he gave me the key, but I don't know how comfortable I want to get. Should I strip off my clothes and wait in his bed? I wrinkle my nose at the thought because it's too cliché for my liking. Kick back on the couch with some telly? Not very sexy.

I shake my head with a laugh at myself then make my way into the kitchen to raid his alcohol cupboard, settling on pouring us a drink for now because I could use something to kill these indecisive nerves. I'm sure he would like one when he gets home to unwind after work.

I snatch his bottle of *Devil's Cut,* collect two tumblers from the other cupboard, then pour myself a quick shot before retrieving a handful of ice from the freezer—which is bare except for the full ice box and a frozen pizza—I pour the bourbon over the ice until the glasses are just over half full, then put the bottle back. I take a small sip from my glass as I lean back against the kitchen bench and look around thoughtfully.

I hear a car pull up in the driveway just as I decide to head for the lounge with our glasses. I get an attack of butterflies in my stomach that make their way up my throat before I can reign it in. I can feel my cheeks flush in embarrassment as though someone caught my reaction, and then I roll my eyes at my own body's stupidity before I clear my throat, take another sip of my drink and decide to meet him at the door.

The front door opens sooner than I expect, as though Alex ran from the car, which makes me smile at his eagerness as I round the divider.

"Honey, I'm home," Alex calls out jokingly while bent over to remove his boots just inside the front door. He gives a cheeky grin my way when he sees me.

I raise a brow as I approach with his drink extended and smile as I decide to play along instead of giving him crap for the shitty endearment.

"How was your day, dear?" I ask with an overly sweet tone while he takes his drink from me. I press myself into his side when he straightens and wraps his free hand around my waist.

"Mm… I could get used to being greeted like this when I get home. Only, you need to be naked," he murmurs with a wink, squeezing me to him before taking a sip of his drink.

"Too bad. You'll have to find someone willing to be your little housewife because that was as far as I'm going with that role play. I can, however, work on being naked," I tease as I play with the first button of his shirt.

Alex finishes off the liquid in his glass in a rush and lowers it to the small hall table beside him before wrapping his other arm around me so that we're now chest to chest. His eyes are shadowed from the above light and are drowning in passion as he stares deeply into my eyes.

"Let me help you with that then," he murmurs, taking my drink from my hand that's pressed between us to set beside his glass. In a sudden movement, I'm lifted off my feet and pressed against the wall behind me, as one of his arms moves to prop me up under my arse, the other hand grabbing a handful of boob while his mouth descends on mine, forcing all thought from my brain.

Alex's lips are cold and taste like bourbon, but when my tongue slides between them, I taste a hint of mint in the warmth of his mouth. The mixture is delicious and ignites a dark, craving need from deep inside of me, causing me to practically maul him.

My legs wrapped around his waist, my hands around the back of his head and threaded through his hair as I fight to get as much of him as I can, as though I can soothe the need inside of me if I just squeeze tightly enough around him.

I moan in complaint when he pulls away an inch, but then comply when I realise it's only to get my shirt out of the way. He pulls it up over my head, tossing it over his shoulder and instantly resumes the frantic kissing, but I need more. I need his skin pressed against mine.

I struggle to find the line of buttons on his shirt, emitting a frustrated growl in the back of my throat when I'm unable to get the first one undone, which makes Alex pause with a grin against my lips.

"Just tear them off. I need the shirt out of the way a hell of a lot more than I ever need to wear it again," he orders, his voice gravelly.

I grin at his urging because it's one of those clichés that I've always wanted to try. I bite my lip as I clench the fabric tightly in my hands, giving it my best sharp pull in delight, but I'm disappointed when only one button goes flying. Alex chuckles at my dismay then presses me firmer against the wall so both of his hands can be free while he assists with the removal of his shirt.

I watch with hungry eyes as his large, talented hands take hold of the gaping parts of his shirt, and with two swift tugs, buttons go flying in all directions. The sides of the shirt part like the Red Sea for Moses. The deliciously bare expanse of his chest and abs are revealed as he struggles to free his arms from the fabric. He lets it drop to the floor behind him to be forgotten as his hands return to glide around my waist—one journeying up my spine to the middle of my back, hauling me off the wall and against his chest as the other drops lower to slide under the waistband of my jeans, managing to find bare arse while our mouths return to each other eagerly.

I curl my back and adjust my legs so I can reach the fly of his pants and get it open but cling tighter to Alex when he stumbles while trying to help me get the pants down his legs.

I squeal indignantly when he winds up tripping on them. The breath is forced from me when I am slammed none too gently into the opposite wall. My exhalation is swallowed by his mouth when it covers mine as his tongue continues its skilful invasion of my mouth, the metal barbell clicking on my teeth harshly, but I can't seem to care about the small pang of pain.

Alex's left hand comes up to apologetically rub my head where it hit the wall, but it's totally forgiven as I struggle with the fly of my own jeans.

Alex joins the fight in this, and we wind up distractedly stumbling into the side table and falling in a heap to the floor where giggling ensues. I take the opportunity to lean back and rid myself of the skin-tight denim that just won't let go, barely even noticing the chill of the cold tiles against my back.

I push myself up into a sitting position by my hands propped behind me once I'm free of my jeans and underwear, raising a questioning brow at Alex because he seems to have produced a strip of condoms from thin air.

"I brought them in from my car. I don't keep any in the house because I've never needed them here."

There's a part of me that goes girly and wants to feel special at his words, but I shove her into a tiny, airless box and push myself up to scramble over until I'm straddling his thighs and then nip at his lush bottom lip.

"Well, aren't you a good little boy scout prepared for anything?" Alex leans back to shoot me a disbelieving look before gesturing towards his crotch.

"What exactly do you find *little* about that?"

I follow his lowered gaze to the very proud and ready erection straining between us, which he expertly applies a condom to, and I bite back a grin.

"This is not the time to be sitting around stroking your ego. Are we doing this or not because—"

Alex cuts off my words by curling his delicious abs so he can seal my mouth with his once again. His hands grip my thighs that he is now nestled between, exactly where I need him to be.

"Hold on, sunshine," Alex orders against my lips then hauls us both up into a standing position as easily as if he were lifting a small child with him and not a fully grown woman.

I gasp in delight when I come to rest against the tip of his cock, and he grins as he stumbles until I'm partially sat on the small side table. I'm so beyond ready for him to take me, but Alex still pauses a moment to rub his tip up and down in the wetness waiting for him before he slowly enters me with ease. *Finally.*

We're both gasping as he takes several shallow thrusts until he's buried to the hilt where he pauses, letting me bask in the feeling of fullness while he utters a curse.

His eyes are squeezed shut as he leans in to kiss me tenderly through his panting and continued curses and nonsensical muttering.

I love the feeling of being so exquisitely full, but I really need him to move. I squeeze my inner muscles around him in encouragement and watch as he bites his bottom lip, looking like he's in pain.

"Jesus-fucking-Christ. Don't do that again just yet, or it's going to be game over before you get your money's worth. Fucking hell, you're tight, woman." Alex growls as his eyes open to glare at me accusingly.

I ignore it as I bark out a laugh before nudging his butt cheek with my left heel.

"Then *move*, dammit," I say with a growl, which has him releasing that dimpled grin of his that I finally get to lick.

"You're so bossy," he mockingly complains. I yell out his name in frustration, which turns into a cry of relief when he draws out to slam back in with the perfect amount of force. I pat his shoulder approvingly while he repeats the movement, adding a little grind of his pelvis against mine that steals my breath.

Alex sets a mind-blowing rhythm that has my eyes rolling back in bliss while he takes over my body like a puppet master. Moving and tilting me to heighten the pleasure, it's all I can do to hold on tight and enjoy the ride.

I hear glass breaking at some point but am too far gone to care, especially when he slips a hand between us to circle his index finger around my clit while his mouth moves to nip and kiss my neck. He hits the tender spot just below my ear, and I'm done for. I'm now the one reduced to senseless muttering while the world explodes behind my eyelids as every nerve in my body sings, every muscle locks and trembles, and my orgasm squeezes around him, forcing Alex into his own shuddering climax with a final curse. His body goes slack, pressing into me more until I'm firmly backed against the wall as he buries his face into my neck. We stop moving to bask in the afterglow with trembling limbs and heavy breathing.

"Wow. That was not what I had planned for our first round at all, but for fuck's sake, I can't make myself feel bad about it." Alex pants in amusement after a long content moment and I giggle quietly while nuzzling his collarbone.

Alex pulls us away from the wall, his right hand lifting to run through my hair tenderly as he moves a foot back a small step and then stiffens at a crunching sound that makes him look down. He chuckles in surprise as he looks around the floor. I follow his look curiously and take in the destruction. There's shattered glass scattered over the tiles and small puddles of water from the ice that was in our glasses that somehow fell from the table while we were distracted. Oops.

I move to carefully lower my feet to the ground, but instead of releasing my legs, Alex tightens his grip, hoisting me up higher, so I'm clear of the table. He then gingerly makes his way to the kitchen where he places me on the bench.

"You stay here so I can clean up before you cut these sexy little feet of yours," Alex orders, stepping back from between my legs. His fingers trail down to trace over the tops of said feet, which kick in reflex because they're ticklish. He grins while I glower, and then aim to kick him, but he dodges with a chuckle as he turns away. He leans down to retrieve a brush and pan from under the sink. I'm sure he's deliberately mooning me because he throws in a teasing wiggle of his hips.

I'm not about to complain, though, because I enjoy the view. In fact, I'm still watching it as he exits the kitchen with a scoffing noise at my ogling. The guy has a spectacular butt. He should win medals for that taut and toned masterpiece.

"You hungry or anything?" Alex asks when he returns, resuming his spot between my legs. I smirk as I grab his arms to pull him closer, locking my legs behind him at the ankles.

"I am, but not for food. You know, I didn't get to choose our first round, which was my reward for winning," I point out then lick at his lips playfully, which makes him chuckle. He leans in to kiss a trail from my cheek, down my neck while his hands squeeze my hips.

"I don't recall you complaining," he murmurs distractedly then nips my collarbone just hard enough to make me jump, sending a jolt of pleasure to my core.

"Oh, I wasn't. Just pointing out it's my turn," I reply breathlessly, catching his grin as he straightens to face me. "Okay. Where and how do you want me?" Alex asks with amusement. I clear my face of emotion to show I mean business as I reply.

"Your bed. On your back," I demand. He doesn't hesitate to carry me to his room, though he does swat my arse challengingly.

I'll show him who's boss.

Chapter 13

ALEX

KARA IS AN insatiable sex fiend and has drugged me. I'm sure of it. There's no other explanation for how I was able to get hard after coming the fourth time of the night and stamina to continue well after sunrise.

She's trying to kill me.

I can see the headline on the news now:

Man dies of heart attack after woman spikes his drink to get herself a never waning wang.

At least, I can't think of a more epic way to go. Except maybe, *Hero dies from smoke inhalation after saving lingerie models and children from a building fire.*

Hey, it doesn't have to make sense—just needs to be epic. I imagine it would earn me a lot of expressions of gratitude from the models before my untimely demise and a medal of bravery on my casket for that shit.

I'm having these rambling thoughts as I try to calm my breathing while lying limp on my back with Kara snuggled into my side. My eyes are shut in the hope that if I don't draw her attention, she won't want another round, because as fun as that all was, I hurt. Hurt in places I didn't know *could* hurt, and I'm so exhausted. If she so much as hints at wanting another round, I will curl up in the foetal position and cry like a baby.

Okay, maybe not physically, but mentally, I will.

I sigh in relief when I feel Kara's breathing and heartbeat slow against me. I risk a cautious lift of my head to peek at her sleeping face that rests on my chest, slowly moving my free arm to prop it under my head so I can watch her. I hesitate when she moves to snuggle into me more, lifting her leg to cover mine and emits a content little sigh as she settles.

Damn.

The woman really doesn't play fair—she's even beautiful when she's sleeping, even as she starts to lightly snore. Just *once* I'd like to find an unattractive look for her.

I gently move my arm that's underneath her until I place my hand in the dip of her waist then relax, letting my eyes close as I relish the feel of her soft warmth at my side and give in to the exhaustion wracking my body, drifting off into an easy, well-deserved sleep.

It feels like only minutes later when I'm torn from sleep by a loud and insistent alarm that I don't recognise coming from somewhere down the hallway.

"What the hell is that?" I rumble as I sit up with a jolt, the fog of sleep still clouding my mind causing me to startle when there's unexpected movement beside me.

"Sorry. That's the alarm on my phone." Kara's voice is huskier than normal as she murmurs, throwing herself out of bed to rush naked from my room while my brain reboots, and I recall everything we did… *Barely three hours ago.*

I curse under my breath when I check the time on my phone to find it's only nine-thirty and fall back against my pillow with a groan as the shrieking sound blessedly stops and all is peaceful again.

I expect Kara to return, but when she doesn't after a few minutes of rustling around out there, I drag myself out of bed and pull on a pair of sweatpants on my way to see what's keeping her.

"What are you doing?" I ask with a disgruntled frown, crossing my arms over my chest when the chill in the air hits me as I watch Kara hop around to pull up her jeans.

"It's called getting dressed. I know you don't understand the concept since you're almost always shirtless, but normal people tend to make sure they are suitably covered up before stepping out in public," she remarks as her jeans slide over her hips.

"But—"

"I'm sorry to rush out on you, but I have an early class. I've got to get going."

I'm at a loss for words. My gaze forlornly searches out my favourite parts of her body that are now all covered—from those sweet rosy nipples to that ticklish spot behind her knees.

I didn't get to say good morning to them, and now she's robbed me of a goodbye? *So selfish.*

Kara's smirking knowingly when I finally look back to her face, which only makes my frown deeper as my arms drop to my sides.

"Thanks for last night. It was fun." She moves in to swiftly kiss me on the cheek. "I'll speak to you later," Kara promises softly in my ear before stepping back to retreat.

I grab hold of her arm, tugging her, so she stumbles off balance and careens into my chest. I stop the complaint about to escape from her lips with my mouth and tongue, kissing her fervently, sensually, lingering while I keep a hold of her so she can't get away until I feel her sink into me with submission.

With a smug smile, I move my hands to cup her cheeks as I taper off the kiss with gentle, sweet little tastes of her lips and then lean back to take in her face.

I have to avert my eyes from her lusciously kiss-bruised lips that are all too tempting, so I focus on her eyes as they flutter open, though I could easily get lost in those stormy grey eyes too.

"Last night was more than *fun*. I wanted the taste of your sweetness on my tongue before I had my morning coffee and made you breakfast, but now you're ruining those plans by leaving. You owe me next time," I grumble, watching as her eyes widen for a split second before she smirks.

"Who said anything about there being a next time?"

I scoff at her cute attempt at denial.

"We both know there will be a next time, so don't try to kid yourself. I've barely begun with you, sunshine," I vow. I guess she sees a glimpse of my intentions in my steady gaze because her eyes pool with lust before she shakes her head to clear it.

"I… but I thought... I've got to go."

Kara pulls away, and I let her, knowing she's not only worried about being late, but she also wasn't expecting me to want more than the one night, and it's thrown her for a loop. I know how she feels because a small part of me is freaking out about getting too close. It's easy to ignore, though, when I want Kara a whole lot more than I want to push her away, so I'm rolling with it for now and trying not to put too much into this.

"We'll speak later. Have a good day. I hope thinking about me doesn't distract you too much from learning, but if it does, don't feel bad. I'm okay with it." I wink as she laughs and then turns away towards the door with a shake of her head.

"That ego of yours. I don't know how your neck is able to hold it up. It's insanely huge," Kara calls over her shoulder while stepping out the door.

I grin before I yell back, "You know my ego doesn't rest in the head you're talking about, and you *know* just how big my other head is." I hear her laugh out loud as she steps out of view.

My apartment feels noticeably colder in Kara's absence. It's more than just being alone here. It's as though she's a vital part to making me feel at home, which is insane but true. I felt the difference of her presence when I came home to find her here last night. I liked it then. Now? Not so much.

It makes me edgy, so I rush to brush my teeth and gather my keys and phone, leaving the oppressive feeling behind and head for the beach.

I LET KARA get away with avoiding me for five days until I decide to intervene when hit with a spark of brilliance. She's been legitimately busy with studying and exams, which have taken over everything, including most of her usual work hours so she can focus. I know because we've been texting back and forth.

So my spark of brilliance—an Exam Survival kit delivery. The corner store just a few streets from my apartment thankfully has everything I need so I can avoid the shopping centre. I get a bright pink metal bucket that's slightly smaller than a washing basket and load it with energy drinks, chewing gum, vitamins, and fruit. Electrolyte drinks, pens, eye drops, her favourite white chocolate, cookies, skittles, and a selection of other sweets and coffee pods that I'm sure are the same box I recall seeing on her kitchen bench. I throw in a cute little bear that's holding a yellow fabric flower that catches my eye as I wait in the checkout line and hope I've covered everything.

I spy a printout on the wall behind the cashier that looks like an attempt at a motivational poster and talk the guy into adding it to my pile for ten bucks which he does with a shrug.

It features a little sand-eating kid that went viral a while ago which always makes me laugh, so I tape it to the front of the bucket with the tape the cashier generously offers.

Once I'm back in my car with the tub in the passenger seat beside me, I text Kara to make sure she's home. I'm sure she will be, though, since last time we texted she said her exam ended at four, and she'd be going straight home to study for the next day.

I feel more than slightly stalker-ish for knowing this, but I ignore it as I text her.

"Hey, sunshine. How's the studying? If you need me to drop by and relieve you of some stress, just say the word."

Kara replies almost immediately, which makes me grin as I start up my car. "That's like asking someone how their Japanese water torture session is going. It's damn painful! But no, I don't need your special brand of stress relief. I don't need to be distracted."

I know that's a not so subtle hint to leave her alone, but I ignore that too as I head for her apartment.

She'll be happy when she sees me.

There's a business woman out front of Kara's building on her smoke break that I charm into buzzing Kara's apartment for me, after many assurances that I'm not about to murder anyone. The woman goes along with a smile after taking a peek at the bucket, informing Kara that there's a delivery for her when she answers the intercom sounding tired and moody.

I thank the woman distractedly and hear her calling me a sweetheart as I race through to the elevator.

Kara's surprised and confused face, when she opens her front door, is priceless. She looks around me as though expecting someone else before turning back to me with raised brows as she understands what I did.

"If you're my delivery, I'm returning you to sender," she remarks dryly before looking to the tub in my hands.

"Ouch. Careful or I'll start to think I'm not wanted."

Kara gives me a bland look, trying to make out that I'm not at all wanted, but I know better.

"Okay, calm down. I just came to deliver this. You can take it and go right back to studying," I assure her, extending the tub for her to take.

"What is all this?" Kara asks, peering into the bucket

curiously.

"An exam survival kit. I think I got everything you might need to get through it, but if there's anything you need while I'm here, I can run down to the shop." I cringe at the thought of having to go to the shopping centre after all, but I'd do it, sucker that I am.

"That's really sweet. But I'm still not sleeping with you right now. I *really* don't have time," Kara insists, but accepts the bucket, making me smile.

"I don't want to sleep. It's not my bedtime yet," I joke, which Kara misinterprets. I guess I should have seen that coming.

"I'm not having *sex* with you," Kara reaffirms needlessly, so I shake my head, holding my hands out in supplication.

"I didn't mean it like that. Honestly. I know how stressed this week is making you and just wanted to do something to help, to show my support. I wasn't looking to get laid. I *may* be using it as an excuse to see your face because I kind of miss it, and if I'm being perfectly honest, I might have been hoping it would result in a 'thank you' kiss, but I know you're busy so I'm not going to push my luck trying for one. I hope all that comes in handy and don't stress too much—you've got this. I know it." I point to the poster on the bucket, which draws Kara's attention to the picture of the kid and she sputters a laugh, sounding emotionally choked up.

Poor girl must be really exhausted if she's tearing up at just a cute picture of a kid eating sand.

Guess my timing was on point. I nod at her in finality then step back with the intention of leaving so she can get back to studying.

"Wait. Let me put this down," Kara orders, disappearing behind the door as she opens it wider, so I move closer to stand in the doorway. I watch as Kara places the bucket on the couch before returning to me with shiny eyes and free arms that wrap around me instantly. I return the unexpected hug, marvelling at the reaction it causes. Having Kara in my arms, her hands pressing against the back of my shirt soothes something deep inside I hadn't noticed was so wound up. It's becoming an odd regular occurrence.

"No one has ever done something like this for me before," she mumbles into my shoulder before pulling back to give me a watery smile. My hand comes up to quickly wipe away a tear that escapes. Her words stroke my deeply ingrained, primal male ego. I like being the only guy to take care of her.

"It's really sweet of you. I think a kiss is the least I can do," Kara murmurs, her eyes already locked on my lips as she licks her own.

I don't give her a second to change her mind. I swoop in and take her mouth eagerly, my arms tightening around her as our tongues intertwine.

I feel her delicate hands pressing insistently against my back in an attempt to get us closer even though it's impossible, her gorgeous tits already squished up as much as they can be against my chest.

I understand her need because I feel it too.

I need more. Need to be closer. Need to consume her.

I tease her tongue with mine while moving my right hand into her hair, cradling her head gently, her silky soft hair sliding through my fingers. I get a whiff of the tropical scent I'm guessing comes from her shampoo that has become my new favourite scent.

Kara whimpers into my mouth before extracting herself from the kiss. I open my eyes to find her looking at me contemplatively, her eyes overcome with sexual need.

"You know what… I can spare twenty minutes." She extracts her hands from under my shirt that had found their way there while I was distracted by her hair and the kiss. Kara takes my hand from her waist to drag me inside, rushing for her room so fast I'm barely able to kick the front door closed behind us while chuckling at her eagerness. I'm grateful, though, because I'm so damn hard, I'm walking funny.

"Is Aela going to be pissed if we get too loud in here?" I ask cautiously as Kara slams her bedroom door then pushes me impatiently backwards to her bed.

"She's with her study group, won't be home for at least an hour," Kara replies, pulling her clothes off—so quickly, you'd think they were on fire. She shoves against my chest with the intention of getting me on my back on her bed, but I smirk as I capture her hands.

I've let her call the shots way too much. It's time I took back some control in this… whatever is going on between us.

"I let you have your fun last time. It's my turn now, and I won't take any arguing over it, so don't try to object if you want to come," I inform Kara assertively, carefully considering her reaction to my tone.

Kara's eyes go around with shock. Her jaw drops, and there's a moment of uncertainty before her eyes dilate with lust. Her mouth closes, and she stands straighter at attention.

I fight off a smirk so I don't lose her.

Just as I thought, Kara needs this just as much as I do, if not more. To be clear, I'm not a Dom. But I enjoy taking control in the bedroom. There's nothing more satisfying than having a woman hand herself over to you completely, pushing her to her limits and rendering her a very sated, happily exhausted, goddess.

Kara obsessively controls everything in her life to a point where she does it naturally without a second thought. Which isn't necessarily a bad thing—who doesn't love a woman in charge? But she's made herself responsible for her own orgasms to the point where her partner is basically just a dildo in human form. I'm sure other guys she's been with were satisfied with that, but I just can't let her do that with me. I crave to show Kara everything she's been missing if she'll just trust me enough to let go. I've pushed her boundaries with oral sex, and now it's time to take it further.

She's naked now, standing before me expectantly. I let her see the appreciation in my eyes as I regard every inch of her raw beauty, before meeting her gaze.

"Climb up onto the bed on your knees and hold onto the headboard with both hands." I spy the goose bumps trailing up her thighs and arms as she complies. "Shuffle down the bed more so you have to stretch your arms out to keep hold, sunshine," I clarify when she misunderstands and is about to settle her stomach against the metal headboard. "That's it. Now stick your arse out for me," I add when she obeys. I could almost weep at how perfect she is while Kara throws in a teasing wiggle of her hips.

I remove my shirt as I approach her side then gently trail my fingertips down her spine. Kara trembles under my touch then has to readjust her grip on the headboard when her hand slips.

"Beautiful. Don't let go," I murmur in her ear then toe off my shoes, before sidling up behind her on the bed.

I can see she's wet and ready, but I tease her for just a moment, trailing my hands down from her lower spine to the bend in her knees and back several times before she murmurs my name like a plea. I press my mouth to her folds and suck gently, just enough to elicit a gasp.

I apparently only have twenty minutes, after all, so I need to use my time wisely. I tease her with my tongue, entering her a few times, and then flick her clit until she tries to push back against me for more. I grin as I give a swift slap to the curve of her arse while leaning back to retrieve a condom from my wallet and get my jeans out of the way.

"Stop trying to be in charge, woman. Accept what I give

you," I command before tearing open the foil packet.

"Hurry up, and I won't have to—Oh, God. *Yes*. Thank you," Kara changes tune quickly when I bury myself to the hilt inside her in one thrust, her heat eagerly welcoming me.

"That's enough lip out of you, or I'll put that mouth to better use and leave you hanging." I stretch over her back to nip her ear warningly. "Now. Don't forget to hold on, sunshine," I remind her with a slight squeeze of her forearms, trailing my hands to her shoulders as I draw back to begin a slow, sensual rhythm with my hips.

I make sure Kara feels every inch of me while I caress every part of her that I can reach, listening to her gasps of pleasure until I know she needs more and pick up the pace and strength of my thrusts.

Every muscle in my body strains as my pelvis hits her arse with an almost punishing force. I reach my left hand out to wrap in her hair, tugging her head back just enough to draw her attention to it as I slide my other hand around her hip, finding her clit with my fingers while being assaulted with the feel of her inner muscles fluttering around me with the impending climax.

I circle my fingers on her clit as I put everything I have left into my repetitive thrusts. She goes over with a scream of ecstasy, milking me so tightly that I'm forced to follow right after her whether I wanted to or not with a final handful of hard thrusts.

My vision goes white, and the energy practically drains from my body, leaving me leaning over Kara's still panting, twitching, and trembling body.

She's managed to keep a hold of the bedhead but is struggling to keep up under my weight. I reach up to gently pry her hands from their death-grip on the metal, holding her torso to mine with the other hand, and lead her body to follow mine. We fall on our side with me spooning her after quickly removing the condom and disposing of it in the small bin handily between her desk and bed.

My face is buried in Kara's hair, surrounding me in its tropical scent. I'm happily content to never move again when I hear Kara's stomach rumble so loud I'm surprised it doesn't echo in the room.

There's a silent pause before we both break out in laughter, and I pat her flat stomach affectionately.

"Think you can spare more time to let me feed you?" I ask as I nuzzle into Kara's neck, which makes her twitch and squeal before pushing me away so she can turn in my arms to face me.

"I don't really have a choice. After what you just did to me, I need fuel to re-energise if I'm going to stay awake even another minute."

I arch a brow as I look down on her, watching as she yawns. "Are you complaining?"

Kara shakes her head while patting my chest reassuringly. "Not at all. You very thoroughly rocked my world within your time constraints. I'm just saying, the least you could do is feed me after robbing me of the last of my energy that I needed to focus on studying my notes tonight." She grins wickedly, which makes me match it as I slide my hand over her hip to squeeze the globe of her arse because I just can't help it.

"Say that first bit again, and I will get you whatever you want," I prod, and Kara gives me a deceptively innocent look.

"Not at all?" She repeats questioningly, trying to fight off a smile as I shake my head then dip to nip at the tip of her nose in admonishment.

"The part after that. Say it again. Loudly." Then I lean back to watch her expectantly.

Kara clears her throat, as she wriggles a little—purposely brushing my semi-hard dick that twitches at her attention—before levelling me with a seriously straight-faced expression.

"Alexei Manzoni, you very thoroughly rocked my world. Now feed me before I starve to death, and you're jailed for my murder," Kara exclaims dramatically, making me chuckle before I slap her adorably cheeky arse, then slide off the bed.

This woman, I swear.

"We can't have that. Get dressed, and we'll get something downstairs," I reply while stepping into my jeans and watch as she pouts while dragging a blanket up from the bottom of the bed to curl into.

"Getting out of bed wasn't part of the deal for me, especially having to get made up to be seen in public. I couldn't even make my legs work yet if I tried."

I lean over and swipe the blanket from her grip, then swat her arse again, much harder this time. She yelps, jumping up off the bed and out of my reach with a scowl.

"Your legs seem to be fine. I'll give you ten minutes to get dressed then I'm taking you out—ready or not."

I'm in no rush at all but know the time limit will stop her moping. It's likely to provoke her, and I love driving Kara mad. Plus, I like seeing her without makeup. Her face is softer and younger looking without the war paint she hides behind so I'm angling to keep her out of it.

"*Ten* minutes? I need at least double that," Kara scoffs with a hand on her hip, still gloriously naked and not even slightly self-conscious.

"Nine minutes fifty seconds and counting. Maybe start with clothes. I know how picky you are about being properly covered up in public. Though I won't object if you're going to let me dine with the girls tonight. I'd like to get to know them better." My eyes drop to her deliciously, perky breasts as I make my suggestion. Kara stutters in disbelief but doesn't make a move, so I look meaningfully at the clock on her bedside table before meeting her gaze again, rubbing my hands together in anticipation with a grin.

Kara searches my eyes, still unconvinced I'm serious. I raise my brow until she practically growls, throwing her hands up in defeat then rushes around the room throwing clothes on as she goes.

I lean back against the nearest wall, watching with amusement as Kara slams her bathroom door between us.

I give Kara exactly ten minutes before walking through the door of her bathroom to find her hastily fluffing her hair.

I grin when the only sign of make-up on her is the shine of her lips.

"Ready or not," I call out. Kara levels me with a glare through the mirror before turning to face me.

"Let's go eat, jerkface."

Kara storms out passed me, and I chuckle. She's just so damn adorable when she's pissed.

The little crease between her brows and the pout of her lips just makes me want to kiss her, but I refrain from doing it right now and take hold of her hand instead, gripping a little tighter when she tries to pull away.

Kara leads the way to a little Indian curry place across the way without even asking for my opinion, which I don't mind in the least because I can eat almost anything. Except for sushi. I can't do sushi. Seaweed belongs in the sea and is gross enough when it wraps around your ankles. I don't need it wrapped around my food in itty bitty portions and don't get me started on the raw fish 'delicacies.'

As soon as we step through the door, we're greeted with a mouth-watering aroma of spices, and I'm hit with a riot of colours from the bright orange walls, yellow chairs tucked under the white tables, and a rainbow collection of decorative flowers that are everywhere in the small restaurant. The curries are in a collection of bain-maries at the counter, encased in glass, and I watch Kara charm the over-enthusiastic server as he dishes our food, giving her extra poppadums for free.

Kara takes her plate and bottle of water with a smile then walks over to a table, leaving me to pay the guy who struggles to take his eyes off her—until I move to block his line of sight.

We have a silent conversation where he smiles unabashedly, stating, "Hey, she's hot and was sweet so you can't blame a guy for looking."

I hand him the cash with a small tip as I smirk and reply, "She's with me, so don't get any ideas."

He nods in compliance before I turn away to join Kara at the table.

She's already tucking into her food with gusto, which I'm happy to see. I love a chick with a healthy appetite, none of that salad picking bullshit. Kara slows down and paces herself about a quarter into her plate then looks up at me apologetically, but her eyes are drawn to something behind me. They go a little wide as she loses whatever she was about to say.

I curiously turn to look behind me, finding a lanky guy in an ill-fitting suit, waiting at the counter but nothing that can be a cause for her alarm. The guy must feel our eyes on him because he turns, and I watch his forehead crinkle in surprise when he finds us both watching him.

"Uhh… hello, Kara. Nice to see you again." He greets her as he steps towards our table uncertain and awkwardly. Something about him seems familiar, but I can't figure it out. I'm more interested in Kara's reaction anyway, turning back to watch her fidget in her seat. She looks slightly embarrassed before reigning in her reaction and giving him a friendly smile, which looks genuine but I can tell it's forced.

"Hey, Ian, it's good to see you too. How have you been?" Kara doesn't make a move to get out of her seat to hug him or give any kind of affectionate greeting like I'm used to seeing when it comes to her friends. It makes me more curious as I watch him crouch down beside her.

"Good. You would know that if you had called like I believed you would, but I can see how you were distracted. I've got to say, I'm surprised. I didn't think you were this kind of woman."

Kara's spine straightens at the implied insult in Ian's words, even though he's tried to ease the sting with a jovial tone and soft smile while his eyes flick to me, making me look at him harder.

"What kind of woman would that be exactly?" I ask with a deceptive calm I don't feel, which makes Ian turn to me again, though he doesn't look happy with my interjecting.

"The type to choose a pretty face over substance. I thought Kara was smarter than that." He pats her arm condescendingly as he rises back to stand over our table with a smirk and interrupts Kara as she's about to speak. "It's a good thing I didn't waste my time on you after all. If you'll excuse me, I have a much smarter woman waiting for me. But hey, call if you ever come to your senses, Kara. I *might* be willing to try again with you."

Ian smiles at the two of us and then walks out of the place like he's better than it and everyone inside.

Bewildered, I turn back to Kara, and she cringes, looking down at her plate as she absently runs her fork through the food.

"Sorry. Ian is the last guy I was with months ago. I ran out on our third date because I couldn't stand the snotty attitude he was giving our waitress. I guess he's bitter about it," Kara explains, leaving me with more questions.

"You dated that guy? Wait. If you ran out on the date, why was he expecting you to call?"

Kara shrugs indignantly while shovelling food into her mouth and makes me wait for her to finish several mouthfuls before answering.

"I thought he was decent until then. And yeah, I didn't want to get into it with him. I just wanted to get away. So I made out I had gastro and may have agreed to call when I felt better as I took off." Kara doesn't look proud of what she did as she stabs her fork into her food. I can't pick if it's because of the guy or for ditching him that way.

"You fought me for ages saying I wasn't your type while the dude you *did* date looks like a poor accountant. So *that's* your type? Nerdy, badly dressed, pale-from-no-sunlight, unwarrantedly egotistical arsehole?" I lean over my plate towards her with a smirk as I continue, "Because I've gotta tell you, that disappoints me, but if it's what you want, I'm sure I could find some similar suits at a second-hand store."

Kara glares at me, not sharing in my amusement at all. "Ian's a dentistry student actually, and I have no idea why I'm trying to defend him. I was wrong. He's a dick. And so are you. Enough judging my past. I want to hear about yours." Kara takes a moment to squint thoughtfully at me as she eats, so I lean back in my seat with my hands held out, gesturing for her to lay it on me.

It isn't long before she grins with a little glint in her eyes. "All right. Since you know more than anyone else who wasn't there for my disaster, I want to know who got your V-card." Kara leans in eagerly for my story with her chin propped up on her hand.

My amusement dies at her unexpected question, and I drop my fork to my plate, looking away from her as though breaking eye contact will save me from this question.

It doesn't work, of course. Kara only becomes more intrigued, leaning far out to her right until she's in my line of sight again.

"Come on. It can't be that bad. It was your first time. I promise not to judge too harshly if you were premature or too young... or scandalous." Kara winks, and I cringe.

My first time wasn't embarrassing even though I was a

fumbling idiot. That's not why I'm hesitating. It was a near perfect moment with Grace that's now a haunting memory I try to avoid, but Kara's dredged it up and not going to let this go, so I might as well share it.

"Can you even remember her name?" Kara asks uncertainly, getting the wrong idea of my silence, so I force words out through lungs that feel airless.

"I remember everything about Grace, even when I wish I couldn't. Believe it or not, my first time was very cliché. A hotel room after our senior formal, with my girlfriend who I thought was the love of my life. I was terrified. Afraid of hurting her and fumbled like an idiot. It wasn't pretty, but it was beautiful, and I wish I could cherish the memory." I look down to my hands on the table as I destroy an innocent napkin in agitation and can feel them getting sweaty as memories tumble through my mind from that night like an over-stuffed box has burst open and released them.

I can practically smell the scent of the rose from Grace's corsage and taste the strawberry flavoured lip balm she used to always wear despite my complaints that it left a bad taste in my mouth. I can feel the silk of her dress slipping through my fingers. But it's the memory of her unwavering deep blue gaze, laying bare all her emotions while refusing to leave mine, during it that is the most painful and has me struggling to remain in the present. I try to keep the memories from sucking me down into the dark void I almost always feel like I'm circling—like water to a drain.

Kara stretches out to place her hands over mine. The warmth seeps into my hands gaining my attention, anchoring me as I look up to find her watching with a tender, supportive gaze.

"I feel like I shouldn't ask, but I'm a curious bitch, so I'm going to, anyway. You can tell me to go to hell if you want, but what happened between you two?"

235

I almost manage a small smile at her bluntness as I turn my hands in her grip so I can hold her back, giving a thankful squeeze, though she seems to be unaware of what she just did for me.

"Grace lost her fight against leukaemia two days later." My words are barely audible, but I get them out. Kara hears because I watch her pull back in shock before her eyes soften in sympathy.

"You ready to get out of here?" I ask, hating that it comes out sounding choked. Kara hasn't completely finished her meal, but I need out of this shop. The aromas in the air that used to be welcoming are now cloying, and I'm desperate for fresh air.

Kara nods in approval, and I move as fast as I can to get us out of there after Kara slips her hand in mine.

"Wait... wasn't Grace the name of Dec's twin who died? Is this the same girl?" Kara asks quietly as I lead the way back to her building. I nod as I pull her to lean against a flower bed in the centre of the plaza.

"It is, though he doesn't know about it. We thought it was best to keep our relationship a secret. I'm pretty sure the only other person who knew was my mum. Hey, another thing you and I have in common."

The moment my words register to Kara, all colour and emotion drain from her face. I watch in confusion until I realise what she must be thinking a moment too late.

She pulls away from me resolutely with a hard, hateful look in her eyes.

"And I bet that was all your idea so your *best friend* wouldn't beat the snot out of you while you chased other girls behind her back. You guys are all the same and disgust me. My God. And to think I was feeling sorry for you a second ago. I've had enough. Stay away from me, Alex." Her voice is quiet but unyielding as she speaks then turns towards her apartment.

"Kara, you're drawing comparisons that aren't there. You

236

don't know the first fucking thing about it. Would you stop for just a second and let me explain?" My voice rises somewhat desperately as I practically beg, rushing to catch up and reach for her arm to stop her retreat, but she pulls away.

"Bullshit. I've heard enough, and if you try to touch me again, I will kick you in the balls so hard that they'll lodge in your throat. Leave me alone." Kara sneers then picks up her pace, bolting through the glass security door to her building as it's shutting behind a couple who had just entered.

She doesn't look back as it closes between us. I helplessly reach the door just as she steps into the elevator. I bang my head against the glass in defeat, exhaling a breath of frustration. That infuriating woman. I'm getting really sick and tired of her running from me.

A feminine throat is impatiently cleared behind me, so I pull back to get out of the way, mumbling an apology as I retreat for my car.

I pull my phone from my pocket before climbing into my seat and contemplate trying to call Kara or send her a text, but I know she doesn't care to hear my side of things.

She's found her newest reason to avoid me and has literally run with it, so there's no point. I'll give her a day or so to calm down before I try again.

I throw my phone onto the passenger seat then head home to get ready for my ladies' night shift. For the first time ever, I'm not even slightly looking forward to a night of being fondled, admired, and coveted by a room of women.

Chapter 14

KARA

TO SAY I'M glad to finally be saying goodbye to Social Sciences after my final exam is an understatement. I've never understood the subjects necessity and it's headache-inducing on the best of days, but today my head is pounding as I leave the building.

Though, to be fair, it was already pounding before I arrived on campus thanks to sleep deprivation caused by a certain arsehole who my mind was stuck on, refusing to focus on anything more important. Like memorising as much of the subject matter that I could cram into my exhausted brain so I wouldn't have to re-take it for a *third* round. No, my mind was an endless loop of the many sides of Alex I've come to know and now loathe.

I can't believe I was starting to *like* that jerk.

After all his trash talking about Nate, he just casually throws out that, oh, he did the same thing to his best friend's sister. Who does that? Idiot guys, that's who, and I'm so done with the lot of them.

I'm a bitch most days, but today there's practically a dark storm cloud over my head, warning everyone to stay out of my way. Or maybe that's just my expression and vibe I'm throwing out. I watch in dark glee as people side-step out of my way as I head for my car. One idiot tries to smile flirtatiously my way as I pass but quickly drops it, looking away when I level him with a venomous glare.

These morons need someone to stand up and hand them their arses, and I'm nominating myself for the job.

I spot Aela leaving the coffee house in a rush, hands wrapped around a mug as though it's her only lifeline, and I feel my frown deepen.

She looks worse than she did in the hospital, which I didn't think could be possible. Her hair is a mess as though she woke up late and barely had time to pull it up into an elastic at the top of her head. Her clothes are rumpled and ill-fitting, her skin paler than usual, and the bags beneath her eyes look like she has two black eyes. They're so dark they stand out even with the distance between us.

I'm holding Declan responsible for this, and I plan to do something about it. I did threaten to make his life a living hell if he hurt her and haven't done anything yet, so it's well overdue.

I drive to Ink Fix with a determination that's most likely illogical and misplaced, but someone is going to catch the brunt of my wrath, and I'm projecting it all onto this problem.

I storm into the shop, the welcoming bell over the door announcing my arrival at odds with my mood. The front room is oddly unmanned, but Kit pops her head out from the door at the end of the hallway, her smile turning to a look of concern when she reads my expression before raising a knowing brow.

"Which idiot are you looking for? I have an abundance to choose from today."

"Your boss if he's available," I reply, and Kit nods her head before slapping her hand against Declan's shut door.

"Hobo, looks like there's an arse-whooping here with your name on it," she yells through the gap then comes my way, grinning with anticipation as I hear a door open.

"What are you hollering about?"

I hear Dec's deep rumbling complaint before he steps out into sight, his eyes going wide when he sees me.

"Kara. Hey, what's going on—is everything okay?" he asks, looking worried as he rushes down the hallway, only hesitating from touching me when he notices my glare.

"What the hell do you think you're playing at? I warned you not to hurt my girl. I let it slide when you stupidly broke up with her, because you looked like you were punishing yourself more than I ever could, but you don't visit her in hospital and then decide to ruin the night out I organise to cheer her up because she had been moping and secluded in her room thanks to you. I won't let you play with her feelings, Declan. You either want her, or you don't. Enough back and forth bullshit!" I punctuate each word of the end of my rant with a thump of the side of my fist to his ridiculously hard muscled chest until he stops me by wrapping his hand around my wrist.

"I'm not trying to hurt Aela. I'm trying to get her back. I handled shit badly, I *know*. But I want to make it right," Declan promises. His eyes locked on mine are filled with sincerity, and it deflates a *little* of my determination to dish out some whoop-arse.

"Then hurry the hell up and fix things, because Aela can't take much more. She's going to make herself sick," I demand obstinately. Dec finally nods, looking to my hand he's still holding.

"I'm working on it, but she's just as stubborn as I hear you are. Now, can I let go of your hand or will you keep beating on me with your fist of fury?"

I'm quickly mollified and let my hand relax from its tight clench before Dec releases my wrist, but both my hands clench instantly when I hear a familiar, irritating voice.

"Kara is much more than stubborn, dude. You have no idea how easy you have it with Aela," Alex interrupts, joining us from the hallway with a happy, unconcerned smile as I glare at him.

"I'm not stubborn. I just won't put up with your bullshit," I counter snidely, stepping away when Alex sidles up beside me.

"If you'd just stop mouthing off and hear me out, you would realise it wasn't like you think," he urges quietly, but I shake my head adamantly before walking away to lean on the counter Declan is now behind rifling through the shelves in search of something.

"So, what's your plan? How are you going to get Aela back?" I attempt to continue my earlier conversation with Dec, who abandons his search when Kit silently hands him a piece of paper before he even shared what he was looking for.

"She's ignoring my texts and calls so far, so I don't know how I'm going to talk to her, but I'm taking care of our biggest problem. I'm looking into selling the parlour and opening a gallery, so there will be no more danger. Well, except for financial ruin, but who needs money to survive, right?" Dec smiles self-deprecatingly as Kit slaps his arm, and I blink in surprise.

"It's going to be awesome. I've already heard back from tonnes of artists interested in showcasing some pieces. Plus, Evie has all her silver-spoon connections looking for pretty things to blow money on. We can't fail," Kit enthuses, but Dec just shrugs while scrubbing his hands down his face, looking like he's in over his head.

"Why do chicks do that?" Alex interrupts again, so the three of us turn to him questioningly. "Why do they get mad and decide to punish us by barring all contact when we all know they actually want to hear from us, and if we could just speak for a minute, we could clear everything up and both be happy instead of downright fucking miserable?" Alex complains, his eyes locked on mine, leaving no doubt it's directed at me, and I scoff.

"In your case, you would have to actually call first in order for the woman to choose to ignore you."

He raises a mocking brow, his lips tugging up at one corner in a hint of that annoyingly knowing smirk of his.

"So if I called, would you answer?" I shrug nonchalantly,

"Not likely, no," I reply obstinately. I don't know why, but he laughs.

"It's simple, dude. Women are stubborn and irrational," Declan throws out, inciting Kit's indignation. She slaps the back of his head so hard even I flinch at the sound of it. Kit gives him a tongue lashing that is hilarious, and I want to pay attention, but I'm distracted by Alex using their moment of distraction to move beside me, leaning in until his mouth is at my ear.

"The only reason we didn't tell Dec about our relationship is we weren't sure how he would react. Then Grace's health deteriorated, and she didn't want to come between us at a time when she said we would need each other the most. You have no idea how much it ate at me. It still doesn't sit right, but there's no point dredging it all up now."

My resolve struggles against the pain in Alex's voice. I have to steel my spine when the others turn towards us, Dec's gaze jumping between us curiously.

"Is there something going on here I don't know about?" he asks, leaning down, so his elbows prop him up on the counter where he patiently waits with an expectant look.

"Uh... *no*?" *Lame, Kara.*

Dec's brow rises at how unsure my reply sounds, but then my phone alerts me to a text, and I use it as an excuse to avoid his gaze.

Aela.

"Exams have been slain! Headed for celebratory drinks at the tavern if you're interested. X"

I reply with a thumbs-up emoticon while trying to ignore Alex's breathing down my neck that's giving me goose bumps.

"Here's your opportunity to talk to Aela again, bro." Alex points over my shoulder where he's clearly read my text. "She's having drinks at the tavern for the end of exams, and you know she'll be surrounded by like-minded douchebags. Better go stake your claim."

I send Alex a glare over my shoulder before turning back to Dec to attempt to talk him out of it. Aela needs at least one drama-free outing to let her hair down.

"I think it's in your best interest if you let Aela have the night with her friends to relax and de-stress. I'll help you get a hold of her another time," I suggest, but my words fall on deaf ears because Alex has triggered Dec's inner caveman. He's pulled back to stand straight, his hands clenched at his sides, as he stares sightlessly through me. I can see the muscle in his jaw tick.

"Kit, reschedule my last appointment. Let's go," he demands, collecting his phone and keys from behind the counter. I look to Kit imploringly, but she shakes her head with a huge sigh as she picks up the phone.

"Do you mind if I ride with you? It'll take too long to get my car out of the shed," Dec asks once he's at my side, so I concede with a shrug, not like I can stop him from going, so what does it matter how he gets there?

He leads the way out to my car as I rifle through my bag for my keys but come to a halt when I hear Alex calling shotgun.

"You're not coming too." I frown at the guy who is waiting at my passenger door.

"You bet your arse I am, sunshine."

I'm about to argue, but Declan interjects impatiently. "Can you two please stop your damn bickering until we get there?"

I snap my jaw shut indignantly, silently glaring at Alex's amused smile as I unlock the car then walk around to drop into my seat.

"Shit, dude, can you move your seat forward? I feel like a pretzel back here," Declan complains as I start the engine.

I look back to see him struggling to get comfortable with his knees up almost in his face because he has more leg than the available leg space, which makes me laugh.

"Hey, you're the one who wanted to ride in the Rio. Not my fault you're related to the daddy long legs." Alex stretches his own limbs out teasingly in his own space with a happy sigh, only to be forced to put his hands out to stop from slamming face first into the dash when Dec pulls the lever that adjusts the seat position.

"Fuck. Watch it, arsehole."

They start bickering over the seat, and I groan exasperatedly before slapping Alex's arm.

"Cut it out, or this car goes nowhere, children." They immediately stop, settling back into their seats as I bite off a smile then pull out of the parking lot.

I'd like to say the drive was a fun one, but that would be a lie. Dec was agitated, his knee bouncing annoyingly in my peripheral vision until I snapped at him to stop it, then had to glare in the rear-view mirror when his hand started tapping rhythmically on the back of Alex's seat. All the while, Alex sang horribly off key to the radio, getting louder the more we protested.

Dec disappears into the crowd the second we enter the bar. I struggle on tiptoes to find Aela or any familiar face, but the place is packed.

"Come on, sunshine. I'll buy us drinks, and we can finish our conversation as best we can with all the noise." Alex places his hand on my lower back to guide me through the crowd as though I need his damn help to find the lit-up bar. I could object and make a scene, but the warmth radiating from his palm seeping into my skin is pleasant, so I let it slide with just a stern warning glance. He looks back with faux innocence, which *almost* makes me smile.

"So, you're still mad at me?" Alex inquires, making himself comfortable against the bar with his first beer in hand. The way he's leaning makes his shirt ride up, revealing a small slice of skin above his belted jeans, which just so happens to be the tempting dip in his left hip.

I struggle to tear my eyes from it so I can meet his gaze, he's amused as he watches me struggle to maintain eye contact.

"Yes, I'm still mad," I confirm resolutely, though I'm struggling to find the reason I'm supposedly angry.

Maybe because he's too damn good-looking for his own good or for my sanity? Not really his fault though, is it?

That's something I have to blame on his parents and God.

"You want to fuck it out? I hear angry sex is phenomenal," Alex suggests before closing the space between us, placing his free hand on my hip.

I'm caught in the heat of his gaze, the sensuality in his tone, and his touch. I want to push him away and break the spell, but I feel like a fly caught in a spider's web, entranced as the spider closes in to devour me.

"Sunshine?" Alex murmurs when I fail to respond, his face dipping closer to mine—so close, I almost go cross-eyed as my gaze lowers to his lips when he runs his tongue along the bottom one temptingly. I was wrong. This guy is definitely the Devil's masterpiece—the embodiment of sin.

"Uh… *Here*?" I stammer uncertainly then look to consider our surroundings—the available positions and the people who would get an eyeful—before I feel Alex laughing against me, the sound breaks me out of my daze as I turn back to him with a raised brow, hoping he doesn't notice the flush I feel heating my cheeks.

"Not what I meant, but if exhibitionism makes you happy,

I'm willing to put on a show. The cops might get called though, so we'd have to make it quick."

I slap at his chest, feeling embarrassed as Alex's hands come up to hold my face so I can't look away.

"What do I have to do for you to trust that I'm not as much of an arsehole as you think? And that I like you a lot, and I'm not out to hurt you?"

The sincerity in his gaze and words has my heart thumping hard and fast. My throat feels like its closing, as though I'm going into anaphylactic shock.

Maybe I'm allergic to the male sincerity act.

I shrug my shoulders.

"Don't take it personally. I don't trust any guy easily." *Or at all,* I amend silently.

I don't like Alex's sudden serious side. It's disconcerting. So I force myself to give a teasing smile as I change the subject. "Now, how about that public quickie? I hope you weren't just teasing because I'm totally game."

Alex's brow quirks at my obvious avoidance, and I wait a heavily silent moment before he smiles and, for whatever reason, decides to let it slide without comment.

"I don't know about public, but there's a storage room with our name on it if you really need it right now?"

I down the rest of my drink at his words then set the empty glass on the bar before facing him daringly.

"I *really* do," I affirm. Alex tries to read if I'm serious before placing his half empty beer on the bar to take my hand in his then force our way through the crowd to the hallway.

"CAN YOU SEE Aela anywhere?" I ask anxiously as I exit the ladies' room to find Alex leaning against the doorjamb that leads back to the main part of the tavern.

Our quickie in the supply room was exactly that—quick. Hard, hot-as-hell, and exactly what I needed, but I feel guilty for getting swept up in Alex and not even thinking about my best friend who I'm supposed to be here for.

"No. But I see a solo, sorry-looking Declan, sitting at the bar." Alex turns his head back, gaze softening when it lands on me, and I have to fight the urge to jump him. He hasn't even tried to tidy up. His hair is still messed from my hands being tangled in it. There's a mark on his neck from when I got caught up in the moment and bit him, which has a smear of my lipstick.

I reach to wipe it off, but Alex captures my hand and presses a kiss to the back of it sweetly, the feel of his soft lips against my skin distracting me. I'm severely tempted to drag him back to the storeroom until a bunch of chattering women jostle me on their way to the bathroom, and my concern for Aela returns.

"I'll call her and see where she is."

I pull my phone from the pocket of my denim shorts and call as I search the crowd for her, but it rings out before going to message bank. I hang up and head for Declan because I'm positive he has something to do with her disappearance.

"Want to tell me why I get the feeling I have a bitch slapping to serve with your name on it?" I ask as I lean back on the bar beside Declan so I can face him.

"I told your best friend I love her for the first time and scared her off," he answers dully, his eyes glued to the glass in his hand, before taking a large gulp of his drink.

I watch his Adam's apple bob with wide eyes while slipping my itchy, slap-happy hand into my pocket to save for later.

"Wow, you used the L word. You don't mess around huh? Just go right for the big guns. I can't believe she didn't instantly fall for it, Casanova."

"Your sarcasm isn't helpful," Dec mutters, eyes flicking to

mine with annoyance to see my unapologetic shrug.

"Wasn't trying to be helpful, lover boy. You're supposed to save that shit for a more romantic—less desperate moment." He rolls his eyes at my mocking then returns to his drink.

"Well. Since you run off my girl, who was our reason for coming here, are you ready to be dropped back home, or are you going to stay and drink your stupidity away? Because I'm heading out to check on Aela to make sure she hasn't barricaded herself up in her room."

Alex slaps Dec's back who winces and puts his glass on the bar top. "Come on, man. Let's jet," Alex encourages. The sap nods silently, sliding from his stool. Alex cuts a path through the crowd for us with Dec lagging behind.

"Thanks for the ride, Kara. Sorry I caused more strife, but I do want to fix things." Dec leans forward from the backseat to apologise as we pull up out front of his shop where I keep the car idling as I wait for the guys to get out.

"It's fine, Declan. But you have to start being smarter and less impulsive when it comes to Aela. She's hurting, and going all caveman on her isn't going to get you anywhere." He nods without comment while opening his door, placing a foot in the gutter.

"See you guys later," Dec murmurs and then gets out, shutting his door as I call out goodbye before his words register—and I turn to look at Alex who is still buckled into the passenger seat.

"Where do you think I'm taking you?" I ask sarcastically, and he just grins with a wave of his hand to gesture to the road ahead of us.

"I'm coming to your place."

I scoff at his statement, shaking my head and am about to object, but he continues, "You can shake that pretty head of yours all you want, but we have things to talk about, and I want to make sure Aela's okay too. We don't even have to have sex if you don't want. Though I'd like it noted that I'm up for it."

I shake my head again but ease into traffic without argument as I head for home. I don't really believe his concern for Aela, though, and I make sure he knows I'm on to him.

"I'm not buying your concern for my best friend," I point out, flicking my eyes his way to see him shrug.

"I know you're worried and won't rest until you know she's okay, and I have an important proposition to discuss with you, so it will just have to be at your place instead of mine. And I do care for Aela. She's a sweetheart and a good friend."

I raise my brow and shoot him a disbelieving look.

"You know you don't need to proposition me. We've already had sex multiple times," I point out, and he chuckles as I turn into my driveway.

"And if it suits you, I'd like to make it a more permanent thing," Alex suggests casually, as though it's not a big deal. I press so hard on the brake that we lurch forward in our seats.

"You mean like a *relationship*?" My voice has a very high pitched, unattractive screech that makes Alex wince before he gives me a thoughtful nod.

"If that's what you want to call it, sure. But can we talk about this once we're out of the car where you can't kill us?"

I continue to stare at him incredulously until there's an impatient horn blasting behind us. I robotically drive into my parking space. Alex can't be serious. He's the ultimate man-whore. I know—I've heard many stories. Why would he suddenly want to give that up?

I'm thoughtfully silent on the trip to my apartment until I dump my stuff on the couch beside the door and can barely look at Alex as I turn to face him.

"I'm going to check on Aela," I mumble then hurry to put

some distance between me and the absurd man who has lost his damn mind.

I knock quietly because I don't want to wake Aela if she's asleep, and then focus on hearing a reply.

"Is she even here?" Alex whispers over my shoulder, and I jump because I didn't even realise he'd followed.

"Oh, my God. Give a girl a heart attack why don't you. Make some damn noise when you're following someone," I scold, smacking his arm then shush him with my finger to my lips even though I was way noisier in my surprise than he was. "I don't want to wake her if she's sleeping."

I try to noiselessly open the door, cringing when it squeaks as I peer into the dark room. I can just make out the outline of Aela curled up in the bed, swallowed by shadows since the only light is filtering in from outside.

"Aela, are you awake?" I whisper and wait expectantly. She doesn't move or make a noise after a long moment, so I step back and shut the door, feeling like the worst best friend in the history of best friends.

"She'll be okay. You worry too much," Alex murmurs, picking up on my train of thoughts as he wraps an arm around my shoulders to lead me toward my room. I let him automatically as my mind runs a million miles per second, worrying about Aela and the coming conversation about what Alex wants from me. Not to mention the fact that he wants something other than sex in the first place.

My nerves become too much to contain when Alex shuts my bedroom door, trapping me inside with him. I turn to face him, hands out to stop his approach as he walks towards me in the middle of the space before my bed.

My nervousness explodes from me in a torrent of word vomit before I even figure out what I want to say.

"Okay, before you start with your *proposition*, you should

know, I don't do the typical relationship thing. I can't do the messy feelings bullshit, never have, and probably never will. But I can do friends with benefits, and I think—if you're interested—we could do that. I mean… the sex is great. It'll be nice to not have to teach a guy what I like for a while. I'm too busy to go through that at the moment just to get sex that isn't as great as it's been with you. So, yeah…" My words trail off and dry up as Alex starts laughing. He steps up to take me in his arms, pressing a kiss to my lips as his body shakes with laughter.

"Fuck, you're adorable when you get nervous. I *almost* like it more than you're confident, sexy-as-hell ballbuster side."

I wrinkle my brow at him and open my mouth to complain, but he places a finger over my lips and continues. "I'm not ready for a 'typical relationship' as you called it, either. But I'd like more of what we've got going between us, so I can agree to your terms so long as you agree to two of mine." Alex grins wickedly as his hand that's at my mouth moves to the back of my neck.

"What are your terms?" My question comes out breathy because the pads of his fingers start massaging the tired muscles at the nape of my neck, which is heaven and blissfully distracting.

"Well, for starters, I'd like for us to be exclusive. I already have limited time with you as it is, I don't want to be vying for it against some other douchebag that you know in the end won't satisfy you like I can anyhow. And you need to get back into that General's costume sometime. I'm still plagued by fantasies of you in that thing, and I'm pretty sure you owe me play time with that whip."

I laugh, my body melting against his as Alex pulls me in.

"I can do that. Are you sure you can give up your 'freebies' with the dancers you work with, though?" I ask against his shoulder while Alex makes a trail of kisses down the side of my neck. I enjoy the slight grazing against the tender skin from his

251

stubble, which I usually hate.

"Definitely. Won't be a problem at all," Alex insists without hesitation while lowering the straps of my top from my shoulders.

"Okay. Should we get all this in writing? Seal the agreement with a handshake, a kiss, or something?" I joke, mainly to distract myself as he nudges his face into the left cup of my bra, extracting as much of my breast as he can, which he nips, kisses and licks. Heat builds in my core, the greedy muscles there clenching with need.

"Sure. I'll seal it with a kiss," Alex murmurs sinfully.

Then I'm suddenly lifted from my feet. I squeal as I'm placed on my back on my bed, Alex between my legs, where he works to remove my shorts and underwear. Then his mouth is on me, licking, nipping and sucking at my clit while I grip my pillows tightly, whimpering in a mixture of pleasure and need.

He picks up on how needy I am and enters me teasingly with his thumb, thrusting it inside me with a steady pace as his tongue laps at my clit. It all feels phenomenal, but it's driving me crazy. I *need* more.

"Alex… not enough." I pant desperately and look down as he pulls back with a devilish grin that is gleaming wet. The sight of it breaks the last of my control. I lean up, reaching out for his arms to drag him down over me, simultaneously wrapping my legs around his waist and lift my pelvis in search of his erection, only to let out a frustrated growl because it's still trapped behind his jeans.

Alex chuckles with amusement but smartly slides a hand between us to remove the offending denim.

As soon as I feel flesh, I tilt my pelvis and sigh in relief when I'm finally stretched and filled.

Oh yes, this will be the best decision I've ever made.

Alex emits a throaty rumble of pleasure once he's fully

seated inside me but doesn't waste a second, getting a perfect rhythm going with shallow thrusts of his pelvis into mine.

"Oh, God, yes. I love your cock." I tighten my legs around him in an attempt to get impossibly closer.

"Alex." He pants his own name emphatically between thrusts which give me pause.

"What?" I question, hoping he's not into himself so much now that he's calling out his own name during sex because, if so, I'm reneging on our deal.

"It's Alex's huge dick in you, and me who you should be praising. Sure, the Big Guy created it, so he should get some credit, but the move of my hips is all me, baby, so enough calling his name and scream mine, instead," Alex insists with extra force in his next thrust, which has me throwing my head back with a gasp that chokes off my laugh at his cocky statement.

It isn't long after when he gets what he wants. A tidal wave of orgasm crashes over me, and I call his name out so loud, it leaves an itchy ache in my throat when we're both finished.

When the blissful haze fades, I find myself curled up against Alex as he lazily strokes his hand up and down the curve of my thigh. The warm, tender moment feels even more intimate than what we just did. This is exactly what I have to put a stop to because it's in the content, post-orgasmic haze where misplaced feelings sneak in and take hold.

"What are you doing?" I ask, my voice huskier than normal. My tone comes out languidly curious instead of the admonishment aimed for.

"Taking advantage of you being blissed out so I can get my snuggle on during our intermission," Alex murmurs into the top of my head, wrapping his arm around my back to keep me still when I try to pull away.

"We can't snuggle. That's for couples, and we're like, frenemies with benefits. We need rules for this thing. That's too affectionate and a big no-no." I stress my point but can't bring myself to stop caressing his hand.

"Does this no affection thing mean no kissing either? Because if so, I'll have a problem with that and break this stupid rule of yours. A lot."

At the mention of kissing, my gaze locks onto his lips, and I can't imagine depriving myself of their perfection. Just the thought of it makes me mourn their loss when they're right in front of me.

"Not in public. Speaking of public... I can't believe I'm going to say it, but we should keep this between the two of us. Aela will eventually give in to Declan, and I don't want her getting any ideas of double dates or anything."

Alex raises a sceptical brow.

"You really think you can hide this from your roommate?"

I nod resolutely though the disapproval is clear all over his face.

"I'll make it work. This is only sex between us—however phenomenal it may be—the moment lines get blurred, it ends." My breath hitches at the thought, but I ignore it as Alex searches my gaze for a long, heavy moment before he shakes his head with a resigned sigh.

"Whatever you say, sunshine," Alex concedes then hauls his body over mine, so he's covering me with a playful smirk.

"Enough talk now. I'm ready for more of this *phenomenal* sex you speak of." He dips his head to nuzzle my neck, making me laugh and squirm as he attacks my ticklish spot.

I can do this. I hope.

I WAKE UP to the blindingly bright sun shining in my eyes and the sound of Alex's laughter reverberating through the walls of my room and groan as I try to block it all out with a pillow over my head that carries the infuriating jerk's scent.

He stayed the night. He didn't even last a day with the boundaries I set before breaking one. I huff in frustration though he isn't the only one to blame. To be fair, he *had* been dressed and about to walk out the front door before I jumped him, and what I had meant to be a goodbye kiss, turned into round three of the night over the back of the couch before he carried me back to bed to continue.

I hear Aela's muffled voice as she snaps at him, and I give up on sleeping because God knows what he's telling her.

He's already broken a rule once.

I snatch up my black silk slip draped over my chair in the corner, slip it on with some underwear, and then storm straight towards the coffee machine for my desperately needed cup before I can deal with the sneaky charmer.

"You two are loud arseholes," I complain as I pass the two sitting in the lounge room and catch Alex's amused grin before I round the kitchen counter and am out of sight.

"Funny, that's what I thought about you two all night."

Aela says this at the same time Alex says, "No, but I'd like to get up in yours."

The sound of a slap follows as I snort with contempt at his comment while feeling guilty about waking Aela up when we were supposed to be keeping things on the down-low.

"What are you even doing here? I thought your motto was *have fun with the clit then time to split,*" I ask Alex scornfully, forcing my point across that I'm not happy about any of this.

"You wore me out, sunshine. I couldn't leave if I wanted to," Alex justifies, his voice sounding a little too controlled, and I get my second serving of guilt for the morning before I can even get my coffee.

Oh, it's going to be a great day.

I'm trying to think of what to say in front of Aela when she enters the kitchen to rinse her cup and place it in the dishwasher.

"I'm going for a shower," she states in a rush, then hurries off to her room, doing her best to not be here, just as my coffee finishes brewing.

I take my mug in both hands and blow on it lightly as I cautiously head out to join Alex on the couch.

"What the hell do you think you're doing? What happened to our agreement of keeping this to ourselves?" I whisper-yell so hard my throat hurts while trying to ignore how delicious he looks all sleep rumpled and warm looking.

Alex's eyes are glued to my chest, so I look down and quickly fold my arms over it when I find a little more skin on display from my slip than I had expected due to the position I'm sitting in. Doesn't help that my nipples are high-beaming through the silk either.

"Aela was already up when I woke up. What did you want me to do? Remove the flyscreen on the tiny window in your bathroom and scale the building in my underwear? I'm sorry I'm not Spiderman," Alex argues. I grudgingly accept that he has a point, but that doesn't mean I'm not still annoyed at the situation.

"Look, you can tell Aela it was a one off thing if you want. I didn't say anything that would contradict that," he suggests. I nod dully, hating the idea of lying to Aela. It's harder than just not telling her.

"So long as you emphasise on how awesome and multiple the *off* you received was. I have a rep to uphold after all," Alex adds, nudging my arm. I laugh quietly as I turn to see his smug grin.

"Sorry, I don't want to lie to her more than I already have to," I tease and then work hard to keep a straight face when his brow rises in challenge.

He leans towards me, his arm moving to rest behind me on

the back of the couch.

"Excuse me, but my count was sitting at six orgasms when you passed out. Do I need to give you another to remind you?" His hand moves to slip between my thighs, slowly venturing underneath my slip until I trap it tight between my thighs to still it.

"Nope. I remember."

For goodness sake, I'm already panting at the memories as the well-used muscles of his target clench greedily with a twinge of pain. I'm literally saved by the bell when a harsh buzz from the intercom distracts us, and I practically fly from my seat to get it as Alex rests back into the couch.

"Hello?" I pant out curiously as I try to tear my eyes from how tempting Alex looks in his relaxed pose.

"Good morning. I have a delivery from Miss Daisy's for Aela Montgomery?" A bubbly female voice greets me so I buzz her in, intrigued by what it could be as I cast a questioning glance Alex's way to find him grinning knowingly.

"That's a flower shop around the corner from Declan." We're both grinning like fools at each other as we wait to see what he's done when there's a knock at the door. We both scramble to answer it, me getting there first, of course, since it's only a couple steps away, and I wasn't hindered by the lounge.

"Ooh, pretty," I exclaim, taking a rainbow of roses from the cute blonde woman. I sign for them before reading the note attached and send a mental high-five Declan's way for being so swoon-worthy. Alex tries to peek at the card, but I pull the bouquet away from him in protest.

"That's personal. Not for your eyes." I hold it out of his reach as I walk the flowers to the kitchen and retrieve the vase that's gathering dust on the bench.

"But you just read it. Come on, I bet it's sappy as hell and he deserves to be mocked well for it. It's my job to do the mocking, let me see."

Alex makes grabby hands for the vase after I fill it with water and place the flowers inside. I place it in a spot against the wall then push him away while I turn to face him.

"No. I had to read it because I signed for the delivery and had to BFF-approve it. Leave it alone. They're adorable."

I pull Alex away from the kitchen, though he doesn't take his eyes away from the bouquet until I press my chest up against his.

"I'm not leaving here until I read that note unless you give me a worthy distraction," Alex insists as his hands slide over my hips, resting at the top of my arse.

I give him a thoughtful look as I think of what I have to offer out of the bedroom because we're not going there again while Aela's here. I could just send him on his way, but now that I'm properly awake and marginally less grumpy, I find myself enjoying his company.

"What about Zombies and a bacon sandwich? I have the latest episode of *The Walking Dead* to watch and bacon in the fridge," I explain, and he doesn't even take a second before nodding his acceptance.

"Sounds good. But you may have to pin me down if you don't want me wandering over to peek at the card."

"I'll sit on you all right," I threaten disgruntledly, shoving him to sit on the couch where he grins as he slides back to get comfy.

"Why do you make that sound like a threat? You know I loved when you sat on me last night. Both my face and my dick were very appreciative."

I scoff at his crassness, rolling my eyes and fighting to contain a smile as I return to the kitchen at his knowing chuckle. Damn the incorrigible man and his dirty, magical mouth I can't get enough of.

~*~*~*~

I SHOVE THE last piece of my sandwich in my mouth. So engrossed in the drama on screen as I lean forward to place my plate on the coffee table, I jump and almost choke on my mouthful when Alex's hand snakes around my waist to pull me against his side. I mumble a complaint.

"Hush. I'm not breaking your rules because this isn't snuggling. You're my body shield against the zombies. I'm totally scared right now," Alex murmurs, sounding sultry and not scared in the least. His hand trails up and down my arm as I swallow my mouthful. There hasn't even been a zombie on screen yet, so I know he's lying.

"You're full of shit," I point out and feel his mouth move against my hair.

"If you don't want me peeking at Declan's sappy love note, then you will let me hold you and enjoy it, sunshine."

Alex squeezes his arm around me, and it takes a split second before I give in and relax against him

It's for our friends, not my own enjoyment, I tell myself as I wriggle to get a comfier position then refocus on the television, my subconscious whispering that I'm a liar while Alex starts playing with my hair.

I become so relaxed that I'm close to falling back to sleep when Aela ventures out of her room. I know I should move before she gets any ideas, but I'm much too comfy to give a damn. I inform Aela of her delivery then watch the big, goofy smile that occurs as she reads the note. I send Dec a telepathic pat on the back.

I continue watching as she fiddles on her phone because it's been so long since I've seen her smiling like this. An old love song starts playing from her phone, which is quickly cut off as she laughs out loud. I swear I almost tear up at the pure sound of happiness which has also been missing these past few weeks. I'm sure that too, has something to do with Declan, and I could kiss the guy for it.

"Haven't heard that sweet sound in a while," Alex murmurs in my ear, echoing my thoughts. I don't hesitate or think twice about turning to kiss his cheek, so caught up in the happy, relieved moment.

He's staring at my lips with a look of shock when I pull away, which of course is when doubt hits me. I could mentally kick myself for breaking my own freaking rules like that, even if it had been an innocent act.

I bite my bottom lip regretfully as Alex's eyes slowly lift to meet mine. His hand comes up, thumb running over my lip to release it from between my teeth.

"You can kiss me whenever you want without feeling guilty, sunshine. I'm not the one making up rules against it." He says it affectionately, and I pull back in a rush, needing to regain my senses and put some distance between us.

"I think—"

"It's such a gorgeous day. You guys want to come down to the spit for some fresh air and sun?" Aela asks in between bites of the toast she's holding in her casted hand as she steps out of the kitchen, unaware I was about to suggest Alex should leave.

He eagerly accepts her offer before I can even utter a noise.

"You mean I get to have you two beauties in bikinis all to myself? I'd be certifiable to refuse."

Aela shoots him a gracious smile before heading back to her room. I turn to glare at the sneak, certain he knew I'd been about to send him packing.

"What?" he asks with all the innocence he can muster, but he can't hide the smug smirk on his lips.

"You're really pushing my boundaries," I warn, though we

both know he is well aware of what he's doing.

Alex sits up a little straighter and levels me with a serious expression. "We were flirty and friend-like before we added sex to the mix. I think our friends would be more suspicious if we stopped it all together in front of them than if we continue. I agreed to go to the beach because it looked like it would make Aela happy, and we both know that sweet woman could do with a dose of happiness and laughter. Luckily, I have a knack for making her laugh when she doesn't even want to smile, and I damn well intend to use it." His little heartfelt speech and care for Aela makes my guard soften a little toward him. There's no way I can argue, so I give in with a small nod and pat his arm that's stretched across the back of the lounge behind me as I get to my feet.

"Guess I better go get into a bikini then."

I start for my room, jumping when Alex grabs at my arse with a little squeeze.

"Make it the tiniest one you have, and I'll reward you later," he requests huskily. I roll my eyes, though I have the perfect red string bikini in mind for the cause.

And despite my reservations, I have a great day at the beach.

Chapter 15

ALEX

THE TWO WEEKS following my not so accidental sleepover are an amazing, crazy whirlwind. I continue to go along with Kara's wishes, and we have covert hook-ups in between helping Declan get his gallery ready for its grand opening tonight and Operation: Keep-Aela-Happy-and-Distracted, as well as our own daily stuff.

It's been fun. Kara is so easy to be with, giving me many fond memories in such a short amount of time and I swear the sex just gets better, which I didn't think was possible—but she always finds new ways to blow my mind. She's also started up a theme for our hook-ups in the last week since she granted my request and wore her Russian General getup. Now she's all about the roleplay and dons a new sexy costume each time.

I don't need all the acting and sexy costumes to get excited for her. But I'm not about to complain. The confidence emanating from her as she portrays her characters is hot as hell.

The gallery opening is in full swing and judging by the people packed into the place, I think it's safe to say it's a huge success. Declan has closed Aela and him off in his office for the modicum of privacy it provides with the clear glass windows giving us an unobscured view of their every move.

Not that I'm watching as much as the others are. I've been

having difficulty keeping my eyes off Kara. She looks incredible. Her dress is a creamy, pale shade of pink that almost matches her skin tone and hugs her body perfectly to her hips where it flows out to her knees, swishing around her legs as she moves. It's unexpectedly sweet and girly for the little spitfire. Combined with a pair of cream and gold heels, her shoulder length hair casually down and curly and that beautiful smile that lights up her eyes with the happy flush in her cheeks, she's absolutely stunning. I can't believe I'm the lucky bastard that gets to call her mine.

Well, not *really*... but I'm the closest to it. Not that I have any intention or inclination of claiming any woman as mine again. I'm just confusing myself now.

I rub my hand hard over my forehead to relieve the tension brewing there from my thoughts, which gets Kara's attention and she gives me a concerned frown.

"You okay?" I nod and wave it off, fighting the urge to pull her close and kiss her in gratitude for her care, but luckily, I'm distracted when my eyes find our best friends getting a little too hot and heavy considering their mothers are watching.

I laugh along with the others who notice then start clapping loudly, which gets Declan's attention as he detaches his mouth from Aela's to look up with an unapologetic grin. The light is back in his eyes when they meet mine, which is a relief. I give them a thumbs-up and whistle loudly as Kit, Kara, and the mother's cheer and holler, making the happy couple laugh while Aela gives an awkward little wave.

We back off when they break apart, and my eyes find their way back to the only object of fascination for me in this place. I'm thrown to find Kara frowning down at her phone before shutting it off and burying it in her purse. There are shadows clouding her grey eyes when they lift and meet my gaze. It's now my turn to be concerned. I step forward, crowding her into the corner away from the crowd.

"What's wrong?" I ask as I search her eyes, hoping for a way I can bring back the carefree happiness of only minutes ago.

Kara forces a smile and straightens her spine, but those shadows in her eyes don't disappear as she replies, "Nothing." Her voice wobbles on the single word, belying the happiness she tried to force in her tone.

"And pigs fly. What was on your phone, sunshine?" I push, not liking the idea of her keeping whatever upset her from me.

"It was just someone with a wrong number. I'm fine, promise. But I appreciate your concern." She reaches a hand up to pat my cheek in a move I'm sure is meant to be affectionate. However, it feels condescending as she forces her way around me to go hug Aela with a flurry of happy squeals, laughter and jumping around.

Fine. I can let it slide for now, but I don't believe her, so we'll be talking about it later—maybe after I loosen her tongue with a few orgasms.

A couple of beers and as many hours later, a majority of the art in the place sports proud little gold "sold" stickers beside them. I don't think anything could wipe the exuberant smile from Dec's face as he keeps Aela at his side, constantly touching and fussing over her.

His pussy-whipped actions are begging to be teased, but I'll let their reunion night slide since I'm happy for them.

Kara is currently across the room from me, talking to a pair of preppy looking douches as she gently sways to the music from the overhead speakers. I would intervene to steal her away if it weren't so amusing to watch the guy in the floral shirt slowly losing patience trying to charm the oblivious and more than tipsy woman who keeps gesturing to the art around them distractedly. Poor sucker.

I decide to take pity and cut him loose after his third failed attempt at casually throwing his arm around Kara.

I drain the rest of my beer and salute Dec and Aela when I catch their attention as they're busy schmoozing a rich looking old couple who are showing interest in one of Dec's weirder looking metal sculptures. The blissed-out couple give me a wave before being drawn back to the old geezer, so I take the opportunity to slip out of their sight and walk up behind Kara.

"I have something much more impressive I'd like to show you if you'll come with me?" I murmur in her ear and snake an arm around her waist.

Kara melts into me until her back is pressed into my chest then giggles, tilting her head to look at me.

"I always come with you." The vixen purrs, grinding her sexy arse into my groin, which has my hand reflexively clutching her stomach.

Christ. She had more to drink than I realised.

"Let's go, sunshine. Say goodbye to your friends." I waggle my fingers teasingly at the douche who looks very unhappy with this turn of events.

"Bye!" Kara waves at the guys who are instantly dismissed as she turns to eagerly take my hand, regardless of who may be watching in her rush for the door.

"You in a hurry, sunshine?" I chuckle as she drags me to my car, which she stops in front of, and turns to shove her hands in the pockets of my pants, searching for my keys. She pauses, momentarily distracted, when she rubs against something else that's eager.

"I needed you hours ago," Kara insists, tugging her hand with my keys in it from my pocket. I take them from her and unlock the car myself as I tug her towards the passenger side.

"Well, why didn't you say something?" I ask, opening the door then scoop her up to place her in the seat.

"I'll drive fast," I promise, taking Kara's hand in mine to

stop her efforts when she starts trying to undo the fly on my pants just as I'm starting the ignition.

"Are you sure you can wait that long?" Kara sighs while taking over my hand on hers, guiding it to place between her legs then thrusts her pelvis against it, so I feel the soaked status of her lace underwear.

I bite back a groan as my fingers push into her like heat-seeking missiles with a mind of their own. I could easily take her right here, right now and not give a damn who sees in this well-lit and busy parking lot, but I know Kara wouldn't be so eager if she were sober—especially when people we know could come out to find us at any minute.

It takes every ounce of self-control I have to extract my hand from heaven and use it to grip the steering wheel so hard it creaks under the pressure. Putting the car into gear is my only reply to the little tease since I can't speak through my clenched jaw.

I have to fight to keep focused on driving, but it's made easier a handful of minutes later when I hear a small snort and turn to find Kara fast asleep, her head against the passenger door, quietly snoring. It's impossibly cute. I chuckle under my breath while wiping a hand over my mouth, turning back to watch the road.

Kara's still out like a light when I pull into my driveway. Barely stirring when I open her door, she practically falls into my arms. It's awkward to get her out, the seatbelt caught between us making it difficult with her dead weight.

"Lex?" Kara mumbles into my neck as I hoist her in my arms for a better hold, shutting the door with my back. I grin as I head for the front door.

"I've got you, sunshine," I assure, and she snuggles more into me contently. It takes great skill to get inside without dropping Kara or smacking her head on anything. I exhale with great relief when I place her on my bed, safe and sound.

I remove her heels and throw the blanket over her before heading for the bathroom. I strip off my Italian leather boots, button-up shirt and slacks on my way to give my teeth a quick brush.

I slip in beside Kara who reacts like a magnet, rolling over to snuggle into my side. Her hand trails down my stomach towards my dick that twitches, anticipating her attention, but I stop her hand again with mine, holding it against my sternum and take a deep breath.

"Sexy time?" Kara murmurs questioningly into my shoulder, making me grin in the dark as I lift my head to place a kiss to hers.

"Not tonight, sweetheart," I whisper, more than content with the opportunity to just hold her as I fall asleep since she so seldom allows it. There's peace in this quiet moment. Our almost in-sync breathing and heartbeats the only sound filling the space around us, which I've become almost addicted to.

I *love* the sex, the heated arguments, and teasing the woman who has the knack to drive me crazy like no one else, but it's the moments like this that I look forward to the most. It's dangerously toeing a line I don't want to cross. But I refuse to think about it and force the consequences from my mind as I pull her warm body against me tighter and relax into the bed with a deep exhale.

AFTER WAKING UP to Kara's mouth around my morning wood, and a spectacular round of morning sex, Kara takes me up on my offer to make breakfast as she showers.

Stupid idea on my behalf. It's difficult to focus on the bacon frying before me when my mind is conjuring up images of her naked and soapy in my shower.

267

I'm distracted from my thoughts when my phone on the counter alerts me to a text. I lean over and click on the icon as I peer at the screen and instantly wish I hadn't when I read the words and realise its Kara's phone, not mine.

"You looked like a cheap whore in that dress with nothing underneath. And needing that lowlife to carry you from the car? Classy, bitch. Can't wait to see what you wear today. Pick something red for me."

What. The. Fuck?

I check the top of the screen for the sender, but it's just a bunch of numbers. I flick the screen with my thumb, and it scrolls up to reveal a whole lot more vitriol that makes the blood in my veins boil as my shock turns to rage.

Who the hell thinks they can say this shit to Kara—or any woman for that matter?

I clench the phone tightly in my grip and find myself storming into the bathroom before I realise I'd decided to act.

Kara is just opening the glass door and stepping from the shower in a cloud of steam. A black towel is wrapped around her and tucked under her arms, hair slicked back and shiny, skin flushed from the heat and still coated in droplets of water.

She looks fucking edible, but it barely registers through my haze of anger and need for retribution.

"Who the fuck is this?" I seethe, my anger harsh and uncontrollable, as I hold the phone up between us.

Kara shoots me a questioning glance before focusing on the screen and visibly baulks before raising her brows at me. "You snooped through my phone?" Kara deflects my question, but I refuse to be deterred from the real issue here.

"I want a name, Kara." My voice comes out low and threatening, but it's not directed at her, even if she is trying to avoid giving me what I need right now before I lose my shit.

"I don't know who it is, Alex. Do you see a name on there?"

Kara snaps back edgily, snatching her phone from my hand. "It's not even a phone number. I've tried calling it, and it just makes a sound like it's a fax or internet line. All I can do is text back, and that would only encourage them." She sounds defeated, and I hate that even more.

"Have you tried to take it to the police or anyone?"

Kara laughs harshly like I've just suggested she try shitting rainbows or something.

"Yeah, I'm sure they'd make my bullying texts their top priority and not give me shit for wasting their time. I don't know why I haven't thought of it myself," she mocks, pushing by to walk into the bedroom where she roughly yanks her towel free to dry off then pulls her dress from the night before back on over her head in quick, impatient movements.

"This arsehole is not just bullying you, Kara. He's fucking stalking you. The police would have to be concerned and so should you!" I shout in frustration, feeling like she isn't taking this threat seriously at all.

"Stop yelling at me!" Kara yells back, before continuing more calmly, "This has nothing to do with you anyway. You had no right going through my phone, no matter what's on there."

I get in her way when she goes to storm out of the room, wrapping my hands around her arms to keep her still when she tries to dodge me.

"I didn't mean to snoop, but now that I've seen that shit, you can bet your sweet arse I'm going to do anything I can to stop it," I swear, but she stubbornly shakes her head.

"I don't need you to do anything for me, Alex. You're not my boyfriend, so stop acting like a possessive jerk. It's my problem, and I'll deal with it how I see fit—as I have been for month's now—without your input."

Jesus Christ, this woman is infuriating.

"Sorry, sweetheart. But your way of dealing with it sucks, so

I'm stepping in whether you like it or not." I regret how condescending that sounds as soon as it's said, but she drives me crazy, and I'm not about to take it back. I meant every word even if it came out wrong. I'm not even shocked when I receive a stinging slap to the side of my face before Kara pushes by me and rushes for the front door, barely stopping to collect her shoes and purse.

"Fuck you, Alex," she yells before slamming the screen door out of her way, so it makes a loud clanging noise against the brick side of the house as she makes her exit. *Shit.*

I rush to grab my keys from the kitchen bench to go after her and take her home if that's what she wants when the smoke in the room catches my attention. I curse again at the forgotten breakfast I left cooking, which is now beyond charred black as I turn it off, removing the pan from the heat.

There's no sight of Kara by the time I get outside. I get into my car and head the way I would drive to her place, but after several turns, it's clear she didn't head this way. I try calling her phone as I change direction, but the line is busy, and after a couple turns, I still don't see her anywhere.

I start to worry—she does have a fucking stalker, after all—but I try to be calm as I drive down the last option she could have gone, and what I figured was the least likely since it's the opposite direction of her home.

I breathe a sigh of relief when I spy her approaching the little corner café on the other side of a busy crossroad. I speed up through the amber traffic light through the intersection then slow down, so I come to a crawl beside an oblivious Kara who is on the phone.

"Kara, get in. I'll take you home," I yell across the passenger seat, and she turns to glare at me while finishing her call.

"Fuck you. I have a ride coming." She flips me the bird and flounces into the café without a backwards glance.

I hesitate. Tempted to get out and make a scene in order to get her in the car, but she's spitting mad.

There are no parking spots free, so now I know she's safe, I decide to leave her to it and give us some time to cool off instead of arguing more.

I pull a U-turn and head back to my place, but I'm not about to let the problem of her stalker slide.

Once I'm in my driveway, I call Kane. Kane works security at Ruby's and is an ex-cop who lost his badge for beating up a domestic violence offender whose wife was admitted to the hospital, barely clinging to life. He still has connections and works part-time as a private investigator. He's the only person I know who can and will help me. I keep the call short because the guy isn't one to like needless chat, especially from me.

I give him Kara's number and tell him I need any information he can find on the non-phone number with all the messages to her, telling him why, so he has some incentive because the guy takes threats against women by arseholes really personally.

Kane insists that I'll hear from him as soon as possible with everything he can find before ending the call. I sit there in the resounding silence, my head back against the headrest, and pinch the bridge of my nose. *This is all just fucked up.*

I don't know how long I sit before finally heading back inside, but my legs and back are stiff, so I'd say it's a while. The place is too quiet for my liking, so I blast some angry, fast paced music to drown it out before I start cleaning up the mess from the disaster of breakfast, winding up on a cleaning spree through the whole apartment without really paying attention. My body is on auto-pilot as my mind is consumed with Kara.

By the time the place is spotless, I'm no closer to clearing my head. There are too many emotions. I'm feeling too much when I promised myself I'd never feel like this again because it would kill me in the end. Kara slipped through my defences without my realising and stole a part of me that I can't afford to give, and I don't know how to take it back.

Dread sits heavy in the pit of my stomach. I can't ignore or shake it, no matter what I do. I get desperate and decide to go for a run because I know that's what Dec and Aela do when their heads are too busy.

I push myself until my lungs feel like they're on fire, and I'm drowning in sweat, but the dread doesn't lessen. I breathlessly curse everything under the sun as I make my way back home at a snail's pace, hunched over like the weight of the world is on my shoulders.

It's dark when I get out of the shower and notice my phone is lit up. I go over to check it and at first, feel a pang of disappointment when I see it wasn't Kara trying to call. It was Kane, so I instantly swipe to call back, hoping he has something.

"Bout time, pretty boy. I thought this was important to you?" His gruff voice rasps over the phone. I ignore his bitching because it wasn't even a minute before I returned his call.

"What have you got?" I ask eagerly and hear him chuckle throatily after what sounds like a draw of a cigarette.

"I have a name. A copy of a driver's license, credit card details, place of work, a rap sheet, and an address," Kane replies smugly, and it's a good thing we're not having this conversation in person because I could kiss the guy right now. and he would beat my arse if I did. I know, because I've kissed his beautiful, bald head in a drunken stupor before and swear I almost needed a kidney transplant after he introduced his giant fist to it.

"That's more than I could wish for. Seriously, I feel like *Aladdin,* and you're my mountain-sized genie, only not blue. I love your big bald head, man. I owe you huge."

"Yeah, well, my head just isn't that into you, so cut that shit out before I introduce it to your nose next time and ruin your pretty face. I'm sending you an email, excluding the rap sheet so no one can get in trouble if it's somehow found in your possession by the good boys and girls in blue. You tell your girl to carefully watch her back, though. This guy has a history of sexual assault and stalking charges. A list so long, I seriously doubt he could ever be reformed of such fucked up ways by anything other than a bullet to the head or a lengthy lifetime behind bars."

I feel a chill roll down my spine at the picture he's painting and hear my phone creak in protest when my grip on it tightens.

"Thanks for the heads up. I'm going to see her now and make sure she takes this more seriously." I prop the phone in the crook of my neck as I start pulling out clothes.

"Good. And listen, if you need help with this cockroach, let me know. I volunteer to drop him a visit, free of charge," Kane offers, and I nod though he can't see it.

"I'll keep that in mind. Thanks, man."

I end the call, tossing the phone on my bed so I can get dressed then collect it and my keys on the way out the door. I try to call Kara on my way to the car, hoping she's had enough time to calm down and will actually answer, breathing a small sigh of relief when she does, voice small and hesitant.

"We need to talk. Are you home?" I ask soberly, unable to force any pleasantries with the current situation. There's a moment's pause before she replies.

"Uh… yeah. We do, and I am." She sounds uncertain and shaky, probably thinking I'm coming over to yell at her some more.

I try to project calm vibes when I reply, "Great. On my way."

"Great," Kara bites out then ends the call.

I frown with confusion at her tone before shaking it off and focus on driving. That woman's moods give me whiplash.

273

Chapter 16

KARA

"HE'S COMING OVER. Says *we need to talk*," I inform Kris, as I drop my phone on the coffee table before sitting back into the couch. I lean my head against his shoulder and snag a piece of popcorn from the bowl he has in his lap.

"Ouch. The words of doom and you're not even in an *actual* relationship. Can't be good. You want me to go?" Kris asks while pushing me from his shoulder so he can wrap that arm around me, attempting to be comforting while he shoves a handful of popcorn into his mouth.

"No. Stay, and we can continue this pity party once I tell him our deal is off." I try to say it casually then toss a couple more kernels into my mouth but feel Kris become still around me.

"You want to beat him to the punch? What if that's not what he's coming to do?" he asks cautiously. I shrug as though it's no big deal, but inside, I feel like all my vital organs are being squeezed in a vice.

These last few weeks with Alex have been amazing.

But I had myself fooled thinking I could keep it just sexual with him. He's sweet, thoughtful, fun, and protective—everything I had been dreaming of before Nate fucked me over. I didn't realise just how much my feelings for him had grown, though, until I heard those four little words of dread over the

275

phone and my stomach twisted.

I ran from him earlier when he found out about the stalker—not because of the yelling, but because I had liked the way he had been so worked up and concerned for me.

I liked it too much. To the point where I was about to roll over and let him deal with the problem however he saw fit. I can't do that. I'd be relying on him, and that's against my rules. I have to sort out my own problems. The minute you rely on a guy is the minute you hand them the power to crush you. Best to put a stop to it now and go back to normal than to let things get any more out of control.

I can do this. I *have* to.

Kris allows me to sit introspectively silent as I mentally prepare myself until he makes me jump when he slaps my hand from my mouth. I've been biting my thumbnail down to the skin without even realising and it's starting to bleed.

"Stop that. You want something to bite? Here, stuff your face." Kris shoves the popcorn bowl at me with disgust which makes me laugh a little.

"You're enabling my emotional eating?" I tease because he's usually the one taking my comfort food away and trying to make me actively deal with my problems.

"It's a less disgusting habit than tearing your nails apart with your teeth, and you could do with some fattening up, not that it will happen. We both know you can eat what you like and never gain a thing like your insides are coated in Teflon. I hate you for that."

I chuckle, but any amusement quickly dies when the intercom rings.

"I think that's for you, sweet stuff." Kris prods when I hesitate too long, nudging me when I still fail to make my legs move. I stumble up to answer when the intercom rings again.

"Alex?" my voice sounds pathetic to my own ears, so I clear

my throat as his gravelly voice confirms it.

I press the button to let him in then wring my fingers as I pace before the door until I catch myself.

Reign it in, idiot.

I take a deep, fortifying breath and force my hands to my sides, my spine to straighten, and my feet to still.

Every muscle in my body obeys but for my heart—which is thumping so hard it's thrashing against its cage in a bid to break free.

There's a knock at the door before I can fully calm down, and I ignore the shake of my hand as I reach for the handle. I have to lean against the door while holding it open because the moment my eyes land on Alex, my legs begin to shake, and I'm not sure they'll hold me up. The sight of Alex before me makes my breath hitch. He always looks great, but it's like I forget just how much until that moment every time.

His head is hanging lower than normal on his shoulders with an apprehensive look on his face, hair wet and pushed back as though he's just come from the shower, flexed arms on display in a loose white singlet. His hands are shoved deep into the front pockets of his dark-washed jeans.

"Hey," Alex murmurs when my silent appraisal stretches on too long into awkward territory.

I can't talk through the lump forming in my throat as I meet his gaze, so I tilt my head, gesturing for him to come inside. The scent of his shower gel teases me as he passes, and I know I'm going to be hunting down a bottle of the smoky sandalwood scented goodness once he's gone.

For now, I settle with breathing it in deep as I follow him.

Kris catches my not-so-discreet sniffing of the guy like a hound when he shakes Alex's hand over the back of the couch—looking at me as though he's ashamed to know me at that moment—before focusing on Alex.

"Hey, man, good to see you again," Kris exclaims, setting the popcorn to the side to get up as Alex returns the greeting. He looks around hesitantly, clearly not expecting an audience for the dumping he was planning.

"Excuse me. I need to go release a radioactive-looking waterfall since energy drinks are the only thing Kara had in the fridge." Kris scrunches his face in clear disgust then turns towards the hallway.

"TMI, Kris. No one needs to know *any* of that," I call out with amusement, knowing he's using it as an excuse to give us a semblance of privacy for the coming conversation. I know without a doubt, he'll be listening with his ear pressed to the door.

"Sharing is caring, sweets," Kris calls out in reply with a dismissive wave of his hand before slipping out of sight.

There's an awkward pause before Alex and I turn to face each other, simultaneously starting to speak then both stopping to listen. I laugh awkwardly, gesturing for him to talk first as he smiles sheepishly.

"I'm sorry for yelling at you today. I was pissed off and worried, but that's no excuse to take it out on you."

I shrug off his apology because it's not like it had hurt my feelings. My problem was that I had liked it.

"No, don't just shrug it off. This was my problem in the first place. You don't take your own safety serious enough. The only things you're cautious about are feelings and your heart—you guard that like a fucking Pitbull. It's stupid and dangerous, and this guy stalking you is—" I cut him off mid-rant because I can see where this is going, and I've had enough.

Gone is the sentimental idiot Kara. It's time to get this over with.

"It is none of your damn business. We're done. I'm calling an end to our agreement!" I yell over his words.

Alex is momentarily thrown, stunned into silence.

"You— You're not serious," he stutters in disbelief, his eyes searching mine for a sign that I'm lying, but I've shut off my emotions and stare back with a grim resolution.

"I am. I told you—the minute this was no longer fun or got messy, it was over. Well, guess what? This isn't fun." I gesture between us with a wave of a hand, hoping he doesn't notice it's trembling.

"You're running because I actually give a shit about you enough to want to help when some douchebag is threatening you?" Alex's glare is challenging, daring me to admit he's right.

I shake my head. "Not at all. I'm alleviating you of the misconception that you have the right to tell me what to do in my life, simply because you're the only guy getting to fuck me. You don't have a say. You don't have a fucking *thing*, except my request that you leave right now, lose my number, and never come back." I have to breathe deeply to catch my breath at the end of my outburst and cautiously back away from Alex because he looks livid. I worry that I may have pushed him too far. I'm not scared he'd ever physically hurt me. I just don't want to be at ground zero when he explodes.

"You're so fucked up and delusional."

He looks at me with pity, which is bullshit, and I'm about to reprimand him for it when he shakes his head, looking resigned.

"You know what? I've had enough shit from you. You want me gone?" Alex sneers as he steps back with his hands in the air. "Fine. I'm out of here. Go find someone else to ride shotgun on your drive into crazy town."

He turns his back and storms out, slamming the front door behind him loud enough to make me jump. I make my way around the couch, feeling numb and empty as I collapse back into the cushions.

Huh. That was easier than I thought it would be.

I hear the sounds of the toilet flushing before Kris joins me, tucking me back under his arm that's thrown around my shoulders as he presses a kiss to my hair.

"That was ugly. You sure this is what you want?" Kris murmurs and I choke out a laugh.

"It's done. Not like I can take all that back, even if I wanted to, and I seriously doubt he'd just accept it."

His hand comes up to wipe at my cheek, and I realise my eyes have sprung a leak.

Stupid eye ducts have to get with the damn program—*we don't care*.

I shrug it off, trying to act nonchalant as I wipe my other cheek.

"It was time to cut him loose anyway," I state glumly, and he sighs, tightening his arm around me.

"What a sad, self-destructive pair we are," Kris murmurs self-deprecatingly, referring to the main reason he stuck around after coming to pick me up—to escape the aftermath of his freak out from Corey suggesting they move in together.

"Yeah. Welcome to Commitment-Phobes-R-Us," I quip, then feel his chest move and a hit of hot air against the side of my face when he huffs out a laugh.

"How about I go grab us some munchies then we can hole up in your room with the Xbox. I'll let you kick my arse in whatever game you want?" Kris suggests after a long moment. The idea of pounding out my frustrations on a control to beat up virtual people sounds much better than just sitting here wallowing, so I nod eagerly as I sit up in order for him to move.

"Sure. But we both know there's no *letting* me win. I own you, every time," I state cockily. Kris laughs as he gets to his feet. I don't know why. He knows it's true.

The guy hits like a little girl in Mortal Kombat, and I clean the floor with him every round. I make a mental vow to not tease

Kris so much this time, bless him. Video games just aren't his forte, but I really appreciate him enduring it amiably just to cheer me up.

MISERY LOVES COMPANY. And sweets. Lots and lots of sweets. In the last week, I've really put Kris' theory that I can eat whatever I want to the test, as my sullen mood inevitably spread to anyone unfortunate enough to have to deal with me.

I'm well aware and don't like it, but I can't control it. My contagious mood was so bad today that Josh finally had enough and sent me home early. *Josh*, who is generally nine times out of ten too difficult to work with for most people due to his attitude, sent *me* home for being too negative. It spoke volumes of how miserable I am to be around when even *he* couldn't handle it.

I unlock the door to our apartment with a sigh of relief, looking forward to a hot bath and then curling up in bed with zombies on the telly and some Chinese takeout.

I dump my gear on the couch then look up and roll my eyes when I find the loved up couple getting hot and heavy, entwined on the lounge. Don't get me wrong, I love seeing the two of them back together, but I don't need to see *so* much of them.

"You guys suck. It's enough I have to hear you two, I don't need to *see* you in action," I complain as I walk behind the lounge with a hand blocking them from view on my way to the kitchen.

They break away from each other with a laugh before Aela calls out, "Sorry. I wasn't expecting you to be home so early." Her voice is thick with amusement.

"Well, hang a sock over the doorknob or something next time to warn me, yeah?" I start to retrieve what I need for a jug of frozen daiquiri since I'm in the mood for something teeth-achingly sweet and strong.

"Everything okay?" Aela asks after coming to join me in the kitchen and watching for a moment as I shut the cupboards and fridge a little harder than necessary.

"Just having one of those days. How was both of yours?" I deflect her question with barely a glance as Dec joins us, standing behind Aela with his hands resting on her hips and chin on her shoulder.

"Frustrating. We had an experiment in lab that was set to fail because we had the wrong equipment, and instead of getting the right ones out of storage because our teacher is a lazy cow, she claimed it was a test to see how we wrote out our detailed findings for failures. Total waste of resources." Aela's disgruntled annoyance is clear in her voice, and I have to hide a smile, focusing on what I'm pouring into the blender. I love my little nerd.

"My day wins in suck factor. I had to do a foot tattoo for a chick with a low pain threshold, who wouldn't keep still," Dec announces, shuddering as he moves to lean against the bench when I turn to shoot him a doubtful look because it doesn't sound so bad.

"What?" he asks indignantly, taking in mine and Aela's expressions as she smirks, amused.

"Do you know how gross feet are? I had to spend two hours holding it down, right in front of my face." Dec's face is scrunched up in distaste, which makes me laugh and something inside me lightens as the two of them playfully bicker over whose day was worse while I turn on the blender to drown them out.

"Want some?" I offer with the jug held out once it's mixed, and Aela waves it away as Dec scrunches his nose again.

"Men don't touch that girly crap," he says as he moves to the fridge to retrieve a beer.

"They don't get squeamish over feet either," Aela adds teasingly. Dec turns to give her an indignant look as he twists the cap off his bottle.

"You dissing my manliness?" Dec asks incredulously then quickly steps up to sweep Aela off her feet, hauling her over his shoulder one-armed as she squeals.

"I'll teach you, trouble." He shoots me a quick wink before carrying her off towards her room. I shake my head in amusement as I take the jug with me for my bath, making sure to grab my headphones on my way so I can drown out any noise they may make.

When I re-emerge an hour later in anticipation of a takeaway order, the lovebirds are back, snuggled up on the lounge and freshly showered. I don't mean to, but as I'm getting myself a bottle of water, I overhear Declan talking about another inspection he has with a real estate agent tomorrow for an apartment. I roll my eyes as I walk out to join them. The guy has been struggling to fit inspections into his busy schedule between two jobs and so far, hasn't liked what he's seen. I don't know why he bothers. He's here every night that Aela isn't at his place. He may as well stay.

"Why don't you just move in here?" I butt in. They both turn to look at me with alarm, as though they've never thought about the inevitable. I shrug because I don't see it as a big deal, at least not for me.

"You practically live here anyway. You stay at least five nights of the week. Stupid to blow all that money on another apartment."

The buzz of the intercom interrupts, and I happily bounce over to let my food into the building, my stomach growling at the thought. I pat it as I turn back to see the lovebirds having I silent conversation as they peer at each other, their expressions making words unnecessary. Dec's is questioning and more than a little hopeful, as Aela thinks it over before smiling brilliantly and sliding up more against his chest with shy excitement.

"You really wanna be my roomie? You don't think it's too soon?" she asks uncertainly.

Dec smiles down at her as he smooths her hair back from her face, his hand stopping to cup her cheek.

"Nothing's too soon if it's right. Plus, you're a better roommate than Tom. You don't fart half as bad as him, and you're less demanding," Dec jokes and Aela smacks him on the chest. They laugh then begin a celebratory kiss as a knock sounds at the door. I eagerly answer before the knocking even finishes. I could kiss the stuttering delivery guy in appreciation for saving me from the moment and bringing me my food if I didn't think it would freak him out.

"Speaking of that handsome little gentleman of yours, bring Tom over tomorrow. I could do with some snuggles," I speak affectionately of Dec's kitty as I turn from the shut door and see they've stopped with the kissing. I was never much of a cat lover until that big furball won me over with his charm the night I met him. I forgot all about my aversion to fur that gets everywhere. He's so soft, affectionate, and adorable.

Dec grins at me with a little shake of his head.

"Tommy strikes again," he murmurs to Aela who giggles against him. I don't bother asking what that's about because I have my precious food to take to my room and devour that I'm clutching like *Sméagol's, Precious.* Seriously, I would imitate the creepy little voice and stroke the containers if I didn't know the other two would look at me like I need a time out in a padded cell.

"Well. Welcome to the apartment, roomie. If you need help moving, let me know. I can lift light stuff like it's no body's business. Now, if you'll excuse me, I have a bed date with some zombies and this deliciousness." I shoot them a peace sign as I hurry by, which makes them laugh, but I don't care. I'm feeling better than I have in days. Well, until I'm in my room and see my phone lit up with a message from my hater and not the one person I'm secretly pining to hear from. I don't even read it. I just slide my thumb across the screen to delete it, then go back to ignoring my phone, climbing into bed to focus on my food and television.

"WHAT THE HELL was I thinking volunteering for this?" I mutter under my breath, dumping another box in the corner of Aela's room.

Well, I guess I should call it Dec and Aela's, since he's moving in today.

It took Declan a week after my suggestion to organise his stuff and free up the weekend to shift it all. I don't mind the physical labour, especially when they've designated only the light stuff for Aela and me to carry. No, my problem is who else offered to help.

I should've known Alex would be involved. But no, I stupidly didn't even think of the possibility until I came down to the basement this morning to start and came face to face with him. Well, face to side, because the guy refuses to look my way.

It hurts. But then, just seeing him hurts, and I have no choice but to suck it up, to act as though it doesn't affect me. Easier said than done, though. I can't keep my eyes from finding their way over to him, watching as he works. It doesn't help that when they came back with the second load, he had shed his shirt, so now I get a clear view of all that beautiful bare skin and muscle-flexing on display.

It's so unfair.

He looks so damn perfect while I'm rocking yoga pants, a

loose sweater, and a messy bun with no make-up and feel pathetic every time I find myself watching him.

Actually, it's probably a good thing he doesn't see the mess I am.

"Just quit if it's *so* hard for you, princess. Don't go working up a sweat. Heaven forbid you should do something for someone other than yourself," Alex gripes behind me. I jump, not realising I wasn't alone when I'd muttered my complaint.

"Excuse me?"

Alex turns at my sharp question, levelling me with a glare that would make a weaker person step back, but I put my hands on my hips and remain still in defiance.

"You're not deaf, and I'm not taking it back." Alex shrugs then swings around to leave the room.

Oh, hell no.

I go after him and pull back on his shoulder.

"I'm not some selfish *princess*. I wasn't complaining about carrying this stuff. It's easy, and I'm happy to help Declan. Otherwise I wouldn't have offered." I defend myself against his assumption, and he cocks a brow in impatient disbelief.

"Then what's your fucking problem?"

I stutter in panic because I'm not about to tell him what he does to me.

"I— it's none of your business. I wasn't even talking to you," I retort then make my escape.

Chapter 17

ALEX

IT'S BEEN TWO long arse weeks without her, yet Kara is still under my goddamn skin. I knew I'd have to put up with her when I agreed to help Dec out today, but the moment she showed up in the basement—before my eyes even found her—I felt her presence, and my whole body tensed in awareness.

I'm still mad at her and the whole situation between us. I can't find it in me to pretend to be polite or even acknowledge her, so I don't. Dec notices and gives me questioning glances, but I play dumb and act like I don't catch his meaning.

But I can't keep my eyes off Kara for long. Especially her perky arse in those stretchy pants as she climbs the couple steps to the lift. I'm careful to keep my looks her way on the down low, only side glances and long takes when her back is turned, but it's enough to notice how unusually tired she looks. Beyond the comfy clothes that look like cosy pyjamas, her makeup free face and messy hair. It's her whole demeanour. She's quieter, paler, and the skin around her eyes is puffy and dark. It's concerning, and I worry about the cause of it, which just makes me even more annoyed because she made it clear she doesn't want me to care.

I finish helping Declan place his drawing desk beside Aela's, which is piled high with books with complicated titles, then wander back through the apartment to find Kara babying Tom, who is purring up a storm, his arse planted on the kitchen bench as she feeds him treats. The way she's petting and talking to him affectionately makes me irrationally jealous of the damn animal, and I find myself reacting before I can stop it.

"That bastard is fat enough without you plying him with treats," I mutter as I approach. Kara straightens to glare at me while covering the little beast's ears as though he can understand.

"He's not fat, just really furry. Don't pick on the innocent kitty just because you're a bad-mood-bear." She defends the damn thing. I shake my head at her ridiculousness. The cat weighs a tonne and is the size of a small toddler. He's definitely overweight.

"What is your damn problem? You've been bitchy all morning. Are you on your period?" Kara goads.

I emit a low, derisive rumble in the back of my throat then move around the bench to stand beside her as she turns to face me defensively.

"That's rich coming from *you*," I growl out as I back her up against the countertop, placing my hands on either side of her, so she's trapped.

"Your stupid, stubborn arse is my problem," I continue as I lean in, breathing the words beside her ear, feeling a sense of gratification when her body trembles against mine.

"You call me the nicest things. Really, what girl could resist that?" she mocks, and I pull back to find her eyes, smirking when her gaze locks onto my lips as she licks her own.

"You can't resist though, can you?" I murmur as the air between us electrifies, and everything around us fades away. It's just the two of us and our little bubble of undeniable attraction. I lean in until our noses are millimetres apart then continue to taunt her. "Even now, you're thinking about kissing me. Remembering the feel of my lips on yours and every other delectable inch of your body they've been. Admit it, and I'll give you another taste," I whisper, my gaze steady and focused on hers, almost cross-eyed as her eyes flit between mine with a mix of emotions.

She wants it. Badly. I can see the yearning in her gaze, but it's almost drowned out by fear.

Before I can push her that little inch into giving in, her hands are pushing against my chest, forcing me back several steps until her arms are fully extended.

"Never going to happen. Let it go, Alex," she bites out, her eyes clearing of all emotion before she turns away and walks around the kitchen bench heading for the front door.

"Easier said than done," I mutter bitterly under my breath.

I lean back to rest my head on the cupboards behind me, banging it against them for good measure, wishing it would scramble the thoughts in my head, though the hits are barely hard enough to feel as I release a sigh of frustration.

"What's going on between you two?" Dec questions suspiciously. I startle at his voice breaking the silence. I didn't even notice he was still in the apartment.

I drop my head and see him standing on the other side of the bench, arms crossed over his chest, an expectant look on his face.

"What do you mean? You know we've had this bickering thing going on since the day we met." I automatically play it down, but his look tells me he isn't buying it. Dec knows me too well and continues to wait me out, his all-seeing, soul-stripping eyes staring me down.

He knows I hate that.

He also knows it's damn effective.

The FBI could use those creepy peepers of his for interrogations and have the toughest of criminals crack with just a stare down.

Dec clears his throat, letting me know he's still waiting in case I had somehow forgotten when I'm looking right at him.

"I don't know what to tell you, man," I begin truthfully, throwing my hands out to my sides in supplication,

"We hooked up a few times. It was hot but nothing serious." I give as much of the truth as I'm willing to share, hating how it comes out sounding so trivial because, if I'm honest with myself, the time with Kara meant more than just sex to me. *She* means a hell of a lot more, even though it pisses me off, and I try to live in self-denial.

"That doesn't explain the animosity between you two," Dec prods, and I can't meet his gaze any longer.

I look away—everywhere but back at him as I shrug nonchalantly.

"I'm trying to prove to her that she called an end to it prematurely, but Kara's being stubborn," I complain and look to Dec grudgingly when he starts to chuckle in amusement. *Arsehole.*

"You want more with her. This is too perfect after all the crap you gave me about Aela."

He laughs more when I frown in denial at his words but can't manage to get out a word of protest, settling with a rumble of denial from my throat.

"Dude, your silence speaks volumes. You hooked up with her *a few times*, yet this is the first I've heard of it. Usually, I can't get you to shut up about details of your sex life. The last time this happened was with Grace, which was a good thing because I would have had to beat you up for bragging about that shit."

Jaw, meet floor.

I'm pretty sure everything in my body shuts down in shock, including the blood in my veins and all vital organs as his words sink in. Not the bold claim about Kara—that's momentarily forgotten.

Dec knows about Grace. And he's acting all cool about it.

There's no fist flying for my face or condemnation and betrayal in his eyes, only amusement. I feel light headed, black spots blurring my vision as I stumble sideways a little before my lungs remember how to inflate and I take a long breath.

"You? How?" Obviously, my brain still needs time to reboot because I can't produce words.

"You two weren't as covert as you thought you were back then, and you still can't lie for shit. I knew something was up and then Grace confessed in the journal she left for me."

I knew about the journal. Grace had written a veritable 'goodbye' book for every person she loved during her alone time in the hospital. I have my own tucked away in the closet of my room at my parent's house that I've barely read. I didn't know what she had written to her brother, though. A little warning would have been nice.

"All this time. You never said anything."

Look at that, almost a full sentence. *Go, brain*.

Dec shoves his hands into the pockets of his jeans then shrugs his shoulders.

"I didn't know how to. Figured if you ever wanted to talk about it, you would." He looks contrite now as I let out a tired, self-deprecating laugh.

"You don't know how many times I fought with the need to tell you over the years. Keeping that secret ate me up." I move around to his side of the counter to drop my arse into a stool. Declan takes the one beside me shortly after.

"Alex, you can always talk to me—anytime about anything. You're my brother. Sure, I was mad when I found out. But it wasn't because of your relationship. It was because you guys couldn't trust me to support it, and I felt like I let you both down because you should have known without a doubt that I was there no matter what for you two. Don't think I didn't notice the way you looked at each other or the way you were there for her when she got sick. You bent over backwards to make her smile every day, and I can never thank you enough for that."

I look over through blurry eyes to notice his have welled up also. I have to swallow hard around the lump in my throat. I don't know what to say.

"I loved Grace. A piece of my heart went with her when she died that I didn't think would ever grow back," I admit, my voice gruff with emotion. Dec gives me a sympathetic grin.

"Believe me, I know that feeling." His eyes have a tiny light of hope when he continues, "But then you let Kara in, and that love turned into *loved* and the pain got easier to bear," Dec states knowingly, and I growl before I can control myself.

"Kara's not replacing Grace. No one can. Ever. I'll never forget her."

Dec holds his hands up in surrender, brows raised as he tries to calm me down. "Hey, I never said that."

I inhale deep and slow to calm down, feeling like I'm in emotional overload.

"I'll always love your sister, but you are partially right. I wouldn't say my feelings for Kara are *more* than Grace or replacing her, but it's like the remaining part of my heart has a different feel to it. With Grace, it was tender and sweet, easy and natural. With Kara, it's intense and maddening. Like being caught up in a cyclone. Honestly, it scares the shit out of me," I admit, focusing on my hands as I press them to the granite counter before me.

"Grace wanted you to move on and be happy, and I reckon she'd love Kara. They're a lot alike really—blondie doesn't take your shit just like Grace never did."

I grimace as Dec chuckles and slaps me on the back.

"She has the same stubborn streak too," I add as he slides from his stool and rounds the bench into the kitchen.

"I don't know about you, but after all that sharing, I need a beer. You want?" he asks as he bends behind the fridge door.

"You have something stronger to grow back some of our chest hair first?" I ask hopefully. He chuckles as he steps back with two *Coronas* dangling from one hand then reaches into the cupboard above, extracting a bottle of *Fireball*, waggling his brows when he turns back to face me with it held up.

"Bring it," I encourage. Dec places the bottles on the bench before collecting two shot glasses.

"To the women we love, who drive us crazy and make life worth living." He holds out his full shot glass for a toast, and I roll my eyes as I tap it with my own.

"Enough of the feels. Let's drink already," I mutter then down the shot, revelling in the sharp burn as it warms my chest before I wash it down with the beer.

We sit there in a peaceful moment, and I realise how lighter I feel after our chat, but the peace is broken as Aela enters the apartment, emitting a disgruntled noise of protest.

"Oh, hell no. You two are not relaxing while we girls do all the work moving your stuff in," she exclaims while dumping the box she awkwardly carried with her cast in the way, propping her good hand on her hip and glaring at us in a way I'm sure is meant to be intimidating, but she's so small it just looks like an adorable tantrum that has me struggling to contain a grin.

"Sorry, sweets. We had some important stuff to hash out that couldn't wait." My apology distracts Aela as Dec puts away the *Fireball* and she steps closer, holding her cast to her chest as she eyes us warily.

"What's so important? Is everything okay?"

I shoot her a smile to ease her concern as I slide from my stool, tucking her under my arm so I can steer her towards the door, waving my hanging hand in her face dismissively.

"Super-secret-manly stuff. Everything's fine though," I insist. She rolls her eyes, stepping out from under my arm so she can turn to shoot me a glare, which is cute as hell. I sip my beer to prove how intimidating she isn't as I continue to pass her.

"Right. Get your arses moving downstairs, bludgers." Aela swats at my arse cheekily then squeals when Dec throws her over his shoulder, ignoring her protests as he palms her butt cheek through her jeans in retaliation.

"Declan Lewis, what the hell do you think you're doing?" Aela gripes after we step into the elevator. I jab the button for the basement parking with a chuckle.

"I'm getting *my* arse downstairs just like you said." Dec affectionately pats the cheek he hasn't let go of as he makes his claim. Aela emits a frustrated groan before pummelling his lower back with a tiny fist. He ignores it as the elevator starts to descend until she slumps against him in defeat.

"*Please,* put me down?" Aela asks quietly. Dec finally relents, bending until she's on her feet, then wraps her in his arms as he straightens and covers her face in little kisses. *Geez.*

I can't get out fast enough when the doors start to open.

Forty minutes later the moving in is complete, and I can escape the sickeningly sweet, loved-up couple if I want to. But I notice how relieved Kara is at the prospect of me leaving and decide to torture myself more by sticking around. I share a knowing grin with Declan when I announce my plan then watch Kara's shoulders slump as he hands me another beer, slapping me on the back as he goes after Aela who is already in their bedroom trying to organise his stuff.

Kara slips into the kitchen, so I follow, claiming a stool to watch as she makes herself some coffee.

"What are you doing for the rest of the day?" I ask as she works determinedly to ignore my presence, which I don't like one bit. I want her damn attention.

"Taking this into my room to watch a movie," she mutters grudgingly when I wait her out to the point she can't stand *not* answering.

"Porn? It's the only type of movie worth watching. Satisfaction is guaranteed, and there's always a climactic finale," I tease, trying to goad her into looking at me and grin victoriously when she does, even if it is through a death stare.

"You're a pig," Kara exclaims over the noise of the machine kicking in.

"That wasn't a no," I point out, and she growls in frustration, turning her back on me to watch her cup filling. "It's even better to watch with someone else. Want me to join you?" I add, unable to help myself.

Kara doesn't look the least bit amused when she turns, cup in hand and sends a lethal glare my way.

"No. Feel free to go home, though. The door is there, in case you forgot." She points sarcastically to the front door then makes her way around me.

"You know what you need?" I throw out, hoping to stop her from walking away from me. I'm not ready to let her leave yet. Kara only slows her steps towards her room, not even bothering to look my way.

"An oral attitude adjustment. Luckily for you, I'm an expert cunnilinguist." I can't help the smirk when she slowly turns to face me. I catch the spark of desire in her eyes. She bites her bottom lip before shaking her head as though trying to rid it of images or memories of me going down on her that my words induced.

"You just can't stop, can you?" Kara states with resignation. I find myself moving to stand before her, almost toe to toe.

"Nope. I'm not willing to give up on you just yet. Despite what I said when you tried to end things, I'm going to keep pushing until I wear you down again. And I will, we both know you can't resist my charm," I vow quietly, fighting the urge to take her in my arms when her body sways a little towards me, proving my point as her eyes widen with alarm.

"Why?" she asks incredulously, eyes darting between mine. I can't fight the need to touch her any longer. I reach out to slip my hand around the nape of her neck and draw her to me, tempted to reply with a joke about why she can't resist me, but I know she needs an honest and serious answer right now.

"I miss us. And as much as you try to push me away because of your hangups—I think you need someone to fight for you, even if they are only fighting *you* to be with you. I want to be the guy to do it. I want to be with you, and not in that friends-with-benefits thing you tried to enforce, but a very real, very *public* and in-all-their-faces-till-they-want-to-puke *relationship*." I pause to let my words sink in as I wrap my other arm around her back, pressing her against me where she can no doubt feel how hard my heart is beating, because saying these words aloud is fucking terrifying, but I want Kara to know I'm right there with her.

I make sure I have her trapped in my arms in an unbreakable hold before I continue.

"Because as much as you drive me crazy, I've fallen more than a little in love with you. And I know that's going to freak your freak and ignite your instinct to run big time. But I want you to take a breath, accept my words, and make peace with them before I let you go do your thing. I'm not going to smother you into submission because I know that won't work. You take as long as you need to wrap your head around it, but I'll be here every day, fighting the fight to gain your trust until you're ready to take that leap of faith with me."

I watch the emotions wash over Kara's face after my vow and swear I could watch the show all day. Her mind is so busy searching my words and expression for any sign to doubt me, she hasn't even thought about keeping up her barriers.

I don't know how long we stand there before Kara finally

blinks her watery eyes and seems to stop her search. Her gaze settles on me steadily as she takes a slow breath then releases it.

"I— I don't know what to say," Kara admits in the smallest voice I've ever heard from her, before looking down to our feet. I release her hair so I can use that hand to tilt back her chin until I can see her eyes again.

"You don't have to say a thing, sunshine. Just accept my words and get used to the idea that I'm going to be around so much you'll get sick of me." I grin, trying to lighten the mood and receive a poor imitation of her typical bitchy smirk, the sight of it making me want to kiss her.

"Who says I'm not already sick of you?"

My resolve to not spook her more breaks. I swoop in to kiss her quickly. My intention of only getting the barest taste dies instantly just like every other time between us, evolving into more as tongues, teeth, and hands get in on the action. I kiss her with fierce determination and feel the hope in her growing as the timid actions of her tongue and hands turn bolder.

Suddenly, she's trying to climb my body, wrapping her legs around my hips, and if I had a free hand, I would so fist pump the air with this small victory.

The sound of footsteps down the hallway slowly breaks into my consciousness, interrupting the moment as Kara tears her face away from mine and drops her legs, kicking them in silent urging to be put down. It goes against every fibre of my being that just wants to hold on tighter, but I lower Kara to her feet and back up just as Aela appears, grinning and totally oblivious since she's focused on the blob of fur in her arms, scratching Tom's chin.

Kara looks desperate to bolt, so I go easy on her even though I really want to continue that kiss.

"I'm gonna bounce now that the slave labour is over. Ladies, stay beautiful."

Aela snorts and looks down at her clothes, thinking I'm

297

poking fun at her messy hair and glasses paired with tiny denim shorts that are mostly covered by the navy shirt she's swimming in, which I'm sure is Declan's. She's always beautiful though, no matter what she wears, but I'm not going to point it out and embarrass her. I kiss her cheek with a one-armed hug then do the same with Kara and have to force myself to let her go and make my exit.

I DON'T SEE much progress with Kara in the following seven days. Every time I drop by, she's her usually moody self and makes her escape within ten minutes. I'm not deterred though and have high hopes for today.

The lovebirds are having a Sunday afternoon barbecue in the entertainment area beside the rooftop pool, so there's no way Kara can ditch me. There's a spring in my step as I head to my Jeep, despite only getting three hours of sleep after getting home from work this morning.

I load the cases of popular girly drinks and beer in the back that I got discounted from work—best perk of being close to the boss—as well as a bottle of Jack and make sure they're secure before driving by the gallery to collect Kit.

She's just closing up when I get there, looking like she already had a big night, donning her bug-eyed shades and wrapped in a cardigan even though it's no less than twenty-three celsius out, with a barely-there breeze.

"You all right, Kitty?" I ask as I approach and take the cooler bag she's struggling to hold while pulling the door shut.

"Fine. This feels like the longest day ever though," she complains as we walk, and I take a peek inside the cooler. I grin when I find a glass dish of her speciality berry trifle inside and get a better hold of the bag so I can sneak a hand inside, under the lid to snag a chocolate drizzled strawberry half from the top that is coated on the bottom with whipped cream. Kit catches me as I'm putting it in my mouth and smacks my arm in outrage.

"Oi, keep your dirty fingers out of my dessert until we get to the party at least."

I grin shamelessly and reach out to wipe my "dirty" fingers on her face, but she ducks away with a squeal as I bite into the strawberry in my mouth. The strong taste of gin assaults my taste buds, but I was prepared for it. Kit's famous for drowning her trifle in more alcohol than custard or any other ingredient.

"Hey. My clean, angelic fingers want nothing to do with your dirty dessert. Geez, incest much?" I scrunch my nose up at her as I reach back into the bag, but she grabs hold of it, taking it from me. Probably for the best. I still have to drive, and those strawberries are potent.

Kit texts Declan when we pull up so he can help with hauling the alcohol in, and I'm surprised when he arrives not even a minute later, looking agitated and uneasy.

He fusses with rolling up the long sleeves of his white button up, which is dressier than I would expect from him for a pool party, even the tan cargo shorts, which are suspiciously wrinkle-free, and I notice his lip ring's missing.

"What's up, bro?" I ask as I unzip the canvas to the back of the Jeep, watching Dec run his hands through his hair. It's his nervous tick that gains Kit's attention too. She slides her sunnies to the top of her head while watching with concern.

"I just needed to get out of the apartment for a breather. All the parents are up there, and Aela's dad's scrutiny is getting to me. I knew how protective he was of her and thought I was prepared, but geez. Those intense eyes follow me everywhere, and I keep saying the wrong thing and second guessing every move I make, so I look like I have spasms. Aela tried to hug me in front of him just now, and I panicked. I dodged it to give her a fucking high five. She's going to hate me if I fuck this up," Declan rambles, sounding like he's on the verge of a panic attack.

I feel bad for the guy, but damn if I don't have to fight off a laugh. I look imploringly to Kit who is unsuccessfully biting off her own grin, and Dec catches it as his eyes flit between us.

"If you two fucking laugh right now, I will drown you in the damn pool!" He growls, and I have to disguise the laughter that bubbles up as a cough that has me doubled over while Kit thankfully steps up to grab his arm and attention.

"Declan Lewis. You've started a brawl in a bikie compound without a second thought, but meeting your girl's dad has you in a panic attack?" she asks incredulously. I look up in time to see her trying to shake him out of it, though she's too little to get much movement from his body before adding, "You have to man up."

Dec frowns down at her, but already looks calmer before he comments, "The pep in your talk is severely lacking."

Kit shrugs as she steps back.

"I'm the arse kicker to get you motivated. If you want the cheerleader, turn to today's optimist." Kit points her thumb my way before they both look to me.

Well, shit. I shrug also and hold my hands out to my sides as I lean against the rear bumper.

"I'm fresh out of pompoms. But seriously, dude, you don't need it. Aela loves you already. Hell, you're shacked up together, and his wife is your business partner. I doubt there's anything dear old dad could do or say to change anything now. I get that you want his approval but fuck him. Take a breath, check your balls, ignore his staring, and show the guy that Aela's *your* world now, and you're not going anywhere."

Both of them stand there stock-still and silent, staring at me after I finish. It drags on long enough to weird me out, so I shrug and throw out, "In other words, go… Dec," I cheer and throw out some fist pumps then break out into a revised version of that eighties song, 'Hey Mickey'—name changed to Declan though, throwing in some kicks and clapping, before they're both laughing, begging me to stop.

I get some catcalls and applause from a group of teens walking by and take a bow before Dec slaps me on the back and brings me in to man-hug it out.

"You good, brother?" I ask as we break away, and he nods, smile back in place.

"Let's get the goods up there and crack one open. You're right, fuck him—just not literally." He winks then we laugh as Kit shakes her head at us and mutters something about us being weird.

Dec leads us to the rooftop where people have started to congregate, and I spot Nicola, Aela's parents, and an unfamiliar couple also their age admiring the view of the Broadwater from a corner of the terrace.

My eyes immediately search for Kara but fail to find her as I follow Dec to where he wants the drinks beside the barbecue.

Aela happily jumps up to say hello, engulfing me in a hug that feels larger than her. I sweep her off her feet, squeezing her tight enough in return to make her giggle as Dec removes his fancy shirt, making himself comfortable. I spy a new addition to the ink covering his chest that sparks my need to tease him but first thing's first.

"Where's your other roommate?" I ask Aela when I release her, and she points inside while stepping back.

"Kara's organising salad stuff back in the apartment," Aela replies, so I nod as Declan snakes a bare arm around her waist, pulling her back into him and kissing the side of her neck, which makes her eyes cloud with lust before she turns to face him. I grin at his claiming of her as I snag a beer.

"I might see if she needs help," I announce, though the lovebirds are too wrapped up in each other to care, despite having caught the attention of Aela's dad while the others in the parental group are distracted by Kit. I move to walk away, but Jack starts heading over, so I pause and settle back against the bench to watch expectantly.

The old man walks between us and clears his throat loudly while he takes a beer. The sound bursts the lovebird's bubble, Aela's back stiffening, and Dec's hands tightening protectively on her waist before they pull apart.

Aela turns to face her dad who looks blasé as can be while opening his beer bottle before looking over at them.

"If you're done mauling my daughter, it would be nice to get the grill started. Some of us were made to skip lunch for this thing and starving."

I have to fight off a grin, but Aela giggles as Dec flashes a grin of his own. "I've barely started, sir. But it's no problem, I can multitask."

Aela laughs at Dec's reply while reaching up on her toes to wrap her arms around his shoulders.

"Sorry, Dad. I'll bring out some snacks."

She smacks a kiss on Dec's cheek then leaves with her father grumbling behind her.

I look back to Dec and am reminded of his new ink then grin.

"So… *trouble,* huh?" I pointedly look to the script over the top of his ribcage before adding, "You don't waste any time, bro. It makes me scared to blink 'cos I might miss you slipping a rock on the girl's finger before she knows what hit her," I tease and expect him to baulk at the idea, but he shrugs with a grin, running his right thumb over the ink in question.

"I'm working on it. Don't say anything though," he says casually like he were commenting on the weather or something and didn't just drop a bomb. I blink speechlessly for several seconds as I watch him stand there, awaiting my reaction with pride and self-assurance in his eyes. I've never seen him so sure of something ever.

My best friend, who only months ago was adverse to opening up to caring for someone else he could potentially lose, is grabbing life by the horns with no reservations.

It makes me proud, and a spark of hope ignites inside me before I let out a celebratory shout and rush him.

I lift Dec up by his legs over my shoulder like how we celebrated a win back in our footy days, bouncing him around. I shout out a few curse words that get some displeased looks from the real adults as Dec laughs, then I run us into the pool with the biggest splash possible.

I kick off the bottom of the pool and resurface in time to see Declan come up spluttering and choking through water and laughter, his eyes landing on me lit with amusement.

"Dick. She still has to say yes when I ask her." He wipes his face of water, smile dimming slightly as he looks towards Aela's parents while we tread water.

"I want to talk to her dad first too. I know I'm not likely to get his permission, but I think the guy deserves a heads up at least."

I splash him to regain his attention and throw my hands in the air. "Fuck him, remember? And Aela will say yes, you two are practically hitched already. You should maybe go feed him, though. Your barbecue skills might butter him up," I suggest then we climb out of the pool to find Aela offering towels with a look of affectionate amusement as she struggles to be stern.

"We have guests to feed, guys. No time for a water fight."

Dec leans down to kiss her as he accepts a towel with a murmured, "Yes, ma'am."

I wrap my towel around me and shoot her a wink as Dec

heads for the grill. "I'll dry off and then go check on Kara's salad then."

Aela shakes her head but doesn't comment.

I let myself into the apartment with a grin, anticipating time alone with my girl, but draw back when I hear her agitated tone coming from the kitchen accompanied by a low, unknown male's voice. It's unexpected and alarming enough to stop me in my tracks as they continue.

"You have to grow up and let it go eventually, Kara. It was a mistake. I was young and stupid and you—"

"I was just a gullible fool who loved you and didn't know better. You might have been young, but you were old enough to know what you were doing. I can't and won't forgive you for using me, so save your breath."

Ah, right.

Understanding sinks in with their words, and I walk until I get a view of them in the kitchen. The douchebag has Kara backed up in the corner where she was clearly cutting up vegetables. He's lucky she's not using the knife in her hands on him.

I take a moment to apprise the uptight, preppy looking bastard who clearly didn't get the memo it's a pool party because he's dressed in a grey button-down, tucked into black slacks, his dark hair glued back with product.

We're about the same size, but he doesn't look like he uses it for any physical activity—not that I can really tell through his fancy clothes. I round the kitchen counter without getting his attention, but Kara notices, and I catch the relief in her gaze, which says a lot considering her looks my way have been guarded of late.

I fake a relaxed lean against the bench opposite them, snagging a piece of chorizo from the cheese platter beside me.

"Nate, I presume?" I drawl, popping the morsel of meat into

my mouth, watching expectantly as his back stiffens warily then he turns my way.

"And who the hell are you?" he bites out haughtily, eyes scanning my appearance then sneering at my black *Avenged Sevenfold* singlet that shows all the ink of my arms, paired with my graffiti styled board shorts and flip-flops. I allow him time to judge me as I casually eat a piece of cheese before replying with a level gaze, so he knows I mean my words.

"I'm the guy that knows what you did to her, you piece of shit. You don't get to talk to Kara like that. In fact, I don't want you even looking at her anymore."

Nate bristles, puffing his chest like he's trying to be intimidating as he scoffs.

"You don't know anything. If you did, you would know this hero act is unnecessary. Kara gives it up all too easily."

I don't see red. I see black. I see the venom of his words and the shame in Kara's eyes behind him as the need for retribution bubbles up inside me deep and thick like tar. The next thing I know, my fists swing out. My hand sinks into his stomach just before the other connects with his jaw. He doubles over, dropping to the floor on his side and curls up in the foetal position around the pain as he tries to catch the breath I forced from him.

Kara has her hands over her mouth in shock and tears in her wide eyes, so I step over the weak arsehole to take her in my arms as she trembles.

Shit.

I hope I haven't just irrevocably fucked things up for us. However justified it felt—I know their families are close.

Chapter 18

KARA

I'M EXHAUSTED AND more than a little shocked.

It's the only excuse I have for breaking down in Alex's arms after watching him drop Nate with two swift, precise and unexpected, but well-deserved punches.

Nate's words were cutting like he'd intended, no doubt in retaliation for the disdain in Alex's words, but I'm used to him being an arsehole—and was almost expecting it.

What I wasn't expecting, though, was Alex's reaction. There was pain in his eyes when they came to me before his look turned dark and punishing just before he struck out.

I've never had anyone, but Aela ever stand up for me. I didn't know what to do with that and the myriad of feelings it invoked, but the moment Alex wrapped me in his arms and held me tight against him, I was cocooned in the strongest sense of protection and safety I've ever felt, and I finally broke.

For weeks now, I've felt itchy in my own skin, like it no longer fit. Felt like the ground beneath me was seconds from crumbling and everything around me was topsy-turvy. But now, with just a simple hug, suddenly everything is settling and calm like I'm right where I'm supposed to be. And that is terrifying because Alex *shouldn't* feel so right.

"I'm sorry if I scared you, but he deserved it," Alex murmurs into the side of my head, his voice tinged with concern. I shake my head against his chest, rubbing my nose against his sternum and feel how soaked his shirt is. I lean back, swiping at the tears under my eyes with a cringe of embarrassment.

"I'm not crying because you punched Nate. I wish I could have done it myself with the same result. It's been a long time coming."

I tilt to look over Alex's shoulder then go to move around him to face the idiot still on the floor. Alex's grip tightens before he complies and releases me. I step around to crouch before the jerk, so I have his attention before I speak.

"We may have to be in the same place a lot for the foreseeable future because I'm still not going to tell our families and make shit awkward for them, but I won't be bullied into playing nice with you, Nate. I'll even stop being bitchy towards you because I admit it was my childish way of getting even. I thought I loved you. I gave myself to you, and you used me then discarded me. I don't want anything more to do with you. So from now on, feel free to act as though I don't exist, because I'll be doing the same with you."

Movement to my left catches my attention as I rise back up on my feet, and I find Aela looking at me with sad, knowing eyes. Panic hits me in the stomach, rendering me still and silent as a statue as I wait for her reaction with dread.

Aela rounds the counter, eyes welling up before they find her brother still on the floor, though he's at least moved to a seated position against the cabinets.

"It was *you*? God. I'm so stupid—of course, it was you. Everything makes sense now. How could you do that to Kara?" she accuses as she stares down at him, kicking his foot in frustration when he doesn't even acknowledge her. "*How*, Nate?" Aela demands louder, and Alex moves to hold her back when she looks ready to dive on her brother, but she breaks out of his hold to turn my way, flinging her little body at me.

I flinch, expecting her to wail on me, but she wraps herself around me and whispers, "I'm so sorry, Kara."

Say what?

"You're the only innocent person in this room. What the hell do you have to be sorry for?" I exclaim as I hug her back and feel Alex move beside us.

"Excuse me, how am I gui—" Alex starts to protest my words until Nate gets our attention, slowly climbing to his feet while holding his jaw which looks like it hurts if the redness peeking out around his hand is anything to go by.

"Oh, right. Never mind," Alex smiles sheepishly for interrupting. His smile is turning smug while watching Nate tenderly prod the already noticeable swelling on the left side of his face.

"If I'm innocent, I won't be for long. Can you two give us a moment? I'd like to speak to my idiot brother." Aela deviates from her steely glare to said brother to shoot me a look of concern.

"We'll talk later though, yeah?" She squeezes my arm while releasing me, and I nod my acceptance before stepping back, dragging Alex from the pose he's settled into against the bench because he looks like he's not inclined to leave at all.

It isn't until we're enclosed in the lift that I worry about what I look like after my little breakdown and turn to check my reflection in the mirror with dread, imagining the mess of my makeup dripping down my face and the look on my mother's face when she sees it.

Thankfully, it's not too bad thanks to the genius who invented waterproof mascara—just a little blotchy.

"Stop it. You look beautiful. Just breathe," Alex insists, taking my hands in his to stop my repetitive rubbing under my eyes and fussing.

I notice the angry red swelling of his left knuckles before doubtfully meeting his gaze in the reflection that's right behind mine. Alex frowns before using his grip on my wrists to spin me to face him, pushing me, so I'm pressed back against the mirror. He holds my hands on either side of my head as his chest leans against mine.

"We need to work on your trust issues. When I say you're beautiful, you best believe it because I damn well fucking mean it." He growls before his lips take mine demandingly in a possessive, all-consuming kiss that forces everything else from my mind until my only thoughts are of him and the way he makes my body ignite.

The dinging sound of the elevator announcing our arrival and the doors slowly opening invade the moment, and Alex releases me, pulling away as my eyes languidly open to find his pleased grin.

"You tell me to breathe just to take it from me?" I question breathlessly. He shrugs, stepping backwards out of the lift.

"Tell me you didn't enjoy it?" Alex challenges, knowing full well that I can't honestly say that. I'm not about to encourage his ego, though, so I match his grin with a shrug of my own.

"Eh, I've had better."

His eyes glower, but his knowing smirk doesn't waver as he leans in, reaching out to snag my hand, tugging me out hard enough to make me stumble into him, his arms instantly wrapping around me.

"I'll show you better," Alex murmurs, but I hold him back with a hand at his chest, because we're out in the open now where eyes are curiously watching—including my mother, who I spot over his shoulder.

"Thanks, but no thanks." I use my hand holding him back to pat his chest then slip by him, but Alex still has hold of my right hand and refuses to let me go.

I turn back to find his face devoid of all amusement. He looks pissed off, and if I'm not mistaken, more than a little hurt.

"I'm still only good enough to fool around with so long as no one else knows?"

I open my mouth to speak before I can find the words I want to say, so I pause, and Alex takes that as an admission, releasing my wrist with a tired sigh as his eyes drop to the ground. I struggle with myself as I watch him process whatever is in his head before he gives it a little shake, runs a hand through his hair and then walks away without another word to join Declan at the barbecue.

Hell, if that doesn't make me feel like crap.

I've been so worried about getting hurt that I didn't even stop to think I might be hurting *him*.

Honestly, I never thought I *could* hurt Alex. I know he's made some determined and almost sweet speeches lately, but I thought it was more because I had ended things and bruised his ego, so he wanted another chance to end it on his terms.

Since when do guys catch feelings and want more than just sex when it's offered with no strings attached?

I consider everything he's ever said and done as I watch him talking animatedly with Skunk while Buzz, Declan, and the small group of other guys listen on with amusement.

Can I trust him? I'm still unsure.

But that's due to my own reservations and nothing he's done to deserve my mistrust.

Do I *want* to? I think… maybe I'd like to.

First, though, I need to apologise.

I'm not one for public displays of emotion unless I'm handing someone their arse, and I can't make myself swallow my pride and start now, so I opt for a gesture that I hope he'll understand. Which is doubtful given how thick his skull is, but it's as far as I'm willing to go in front of an audience. I approach the barbecue area behind the group and tear off a piece of cloth from the roll of wipes and use it to grab a handful of ice from the cooler turning it into a makeshift icepack with the hair tie around my wrist.

I step up to Alex, tapping him on the shoulder. He turns around reluctantly, obviously knowing it's me. His eyes are guarded when they meet mine. I hold out the ice pack in offering as I reach out to take his injured hand that's clasped around his beer bottle and then balance it over his knuckles as I take his free hand and place it over the cold pack to keep it in place. I look up apologetically into his beautiful jade eyes and hold them for a moment before I offer a little smile and then release him and walk away, rushing back inside to get the salads I was working on before all the drama.

My quick escape is delayed by the elevator's slow rise, though, and by the time it arrives, I'm no longer alone.

I step inside and press the button for our floor before turning to face Declan, who joins me in the suddenly smaller contraption, his eyes watching me with concern as I lean against the wall opposite him.

"You all right, sweetheart?" he asks quietly, so I nod, not feeling the need to fight the pet name because he's the only guy I know that makes it feel familiar and genuine when he uses endearments.

"Shouldn't you be manning the grill so we can get the food out before the guests turn into a starving mob out for our blood?" I suggest dramatically, intending to make him laugh, but Dec waves it away.

"Buzz has it covered for a moment. I just can't be too long, or the meat will be more beer than barbecued."

I scrunch my nose at the thought as we arrive on our floor.

I figured Declan had come down because he needed something for the barbecue, but when we step inside to find Aela and Nate coming from the hallway, I watch curiously as Declan heads their way, looking imposing and seeming to be using his body as a shield… for *me,* though I step to the side so I can see what's going on.

Dec barely glances Aela's way before focusing his intimidating gaze on her brother.

"Nathaniel. I know the two of you are practically family or whatever and I know I'm an outsider who doesn't know the dynamics of how you all operate, *and* I don't even know exactly what happened. But I *do* know that you don't come into Kara's home and disrespect her. Not while I'm around. I don't care who you are. If you can't show the women under this roof the respect they deserve, then you can get the fuck out."

Wow. I'm touched that Declan would take up for me too, but should have known he would. The guy has a knack for taking on a protective role for all the females around him. The guys are locked into the stare-down-of-all-stare-downs as I look to Aela with wide eyes, but she just gives me a small, proud smile.

Yeah, her boyfriend is a keeper. I kinda want to hug him for it.

Eventually, Nate steps down from the challenge, looking off to the side before grudgingly meeting my gaze with a clenched jaw. He stares at me for a long moment before huffing out a breath which seems to take his anger along with it as his expression turns regretful and his stance slumps slightly.

"He's right. I'm sorry for what I said. It was uncalled for. We both need to move on, so I'll do as you suggested and leave you alone from now on," he vows before turning to look at Aela and Declan. "If you all don't mind, I'd like to stick around for a bit longer?"

They both look to me for approval, so I shrug.

"Fine. Just don't be a dick to anyone," I concede and bite off the urge to add how doubtful I am of that happening because he's a naturally born arsehole. He has the audacity to smirk at me sheepishly, though.

"I'll do my best but can't promise anything. I've been told I'm a douche of epic proportions, after all."

My glare of warning-and-promise-of-painful-things follows him as he slips by me and exits the apartment.

"Well, I better get back to the grill." Declan lays a loud kiss to Aela's cheek then makes his way out also, but I stop him with a hand at his elbow as he passes, leaning up to kiss his cheek lightly.

"Thank you. I really don't need anyone fighting my battles for me, but I appreciate it anyway."

He nods, flashing his dimple-making smile that I'm sure he's reaped loads of trouble with in the past.

"It's no problem, sweetheart. I know you can handle your own shit, but sometimes it's nice to know you have people in your corner, and I'll have you know, I have a gift for setting arseholes straight." He winks and pats me on the shoulder before walking out.

Aela links her arm with mine as I watch her guy go with gratitude, leaning her head against my shoulder as I turn back toward her and she tugs me toward the kitchen.

"Come on. Let's get this damn food up there before they come searching for it."

So I extract myself from her to load my arms with as much as I can carry.

THE PARTY GOES off without a hitch after all the drama, and I'm kept so busy trying to be the perfect host, I don't really get to talk to Alex again before he has to leave for work. It was disappointing, but I squashed the emotion down as best I could with a smile and a hefty drop of Jack.

Two days later, and I haven't stopped thinking about Alex once, and am just as conflicted about what I want with him as ever. Even now my leg is jittering as I pass my phone around in my hands, fighting the urge to contact him, sightlessly staring at the boring beige wall across from me. Aela shifts uncomfortably in the creaky plastic chair to the right of mine, drawing my attention as she sighs impatiently, struggling to prop her cast up on the armrest between us.

We're at her appointment with the specialist to hopefully break her free of the cast, and as the minutes pass, her agitation rises. It's highly amusing.

"You've had that thing on for months, a few extra minutes can't be so bad," I comment and Aela shoots me a disgruntled look.

"The stupid thing's itching more than ever right now. Like it knows it's time of torturing me is coming to an end, so it's going all out. I swear I will start biting it off if they don't hurry up and call me back there."

I look down to said offending plaster and can't help a small reminiscent smile when my eyes land on the chicken scratch writing I can only make out because I know it's there which claims: "Master Alex's harem member #69" with a bold cross through it that was hastily added after Dec threatened to unman Alex. It was later turned into a skull and crossbones, which didn't quite cover the writing completely.

I recall memories of the night Aela passed out on the lounge from her painkillers, and Alex suggested we should decorate her cast because it was too pink and boring.

Good thing Declan was there to cover up the worst of our art—if you call crass caricatures, childish flower doodles, and varying statements of our awesomeness, art—with a beautiful, almost life-like, floral design. It was a great night. I have no idea how we didn't wake Aela between my laughing and the guys bickering. Those pills must have been super strong. I'm kind of sorry to see the cast go.

"Once I'm free, I can have it framed and give it to you if you want?" Aela prods, clearly catching my mood. I shake my head with a snort as her name is finally called and she bounces up out of her seat.

I stay behind as I continue reliving that night of Alex joking he should take up tattooing as he proudly appreciated his crudely drawn gangster rabbit caricature with a cigar hanging from its mouth. I also remember how sweet he was later on when we were curled up in my bed, laughing as we exchanged childhood memories long after Dec had carried Aela to bed.

There was nothing sexual that night, just sweet kisses and caresses. I miss the connection we had. I felt like I could tell him anything and never be judged. The loss of it sits like something sour in the pit of my stomach.

Before I can stop myself, I type out a text then hit send, hoping this isn't a huge mistake I'm going to regret.

"I miss us too. I miss you. I'm sorry."

Okay, that's enough confessions for now.

I shove my phone in my bag and zip it up to keep me from adding more, tucking my hands between my knees.

"Kara, everything okay?" I cringe at the familiarly soft voice and shut my eyes, wishing the owner would disappear if I squeeze my eyelids together hard enough. *Thinking of mistakes…*

I open my eyes and slowly take in the person hovering over me. The horrible boat shoes with no socks, too much exposed ankle under the ill-fitting faded jeans, the white polo tucked in. His sharp angled face that could get him modelling gigs galore if he knew how to use it and an attitude to back it up, with his blue-eyed, blond-haired, boy-next-door look. Instead, he's a radiographer, and unfortunately, as meek as a mouse and doesn't know how to carry himself or care for his looks. I dated Jameson for three months before I couldn't take any more of being the one in charge of *every* aspect and decision in our relationship and cut him loose. It was like kicking a puppy but had to be done.

I try to force a friendly smile, which I'm sure is anything but.

"Hey… Jameson," I drag on my greeting with a weird little wave and then mentally shake myself to recover my composure. He looks me over, clearly looking for a reason for my being here as he awaits my answer.

"I'm fine. Just waiting for Aela to have a cast removed," I uselessly gesture down the hall feeling awkward as hell, but I can't summon the urge to be a bitch to him. The guy is just too nice, so awkward is all I have.

"I hope she's okay. I'm just going on my break. Do you want to join me for a quick coffee across the road? It would be nice to catch up with you."

Hell. Of course, he works here. I stare back apprehensively as Jameson eagerly fidgets waiting for my reply, way too eager for just catching up.

I can see he's trying to contain it, but he just reminds me of a puppy wanting to play. The last thing I want to do is give him false hope by accepting the offer. Damn it. Sometimes, it's easier to just always be the bitch.

"Uh… that would be nice. But I can't. I have to get Aela home as soon as she's done and get to work. Sorry."

I cringe as his face falls, but immediately, perks up.

"Some other time then. You still have my number?"

Sure I do. In my blocked list. Thankfully, I'm saved by Aela's appearance down the hall as she practically skips our way with a huge smile while rubbing her left wrist.

"I'm free, finally free!" she exclaims loudly, not even caring where we are, which makes me laugh as she bounds into me and starts jumping around.

"I'm driving home. God, I missed driving. *Jameson*, how are you?" Aela reigns in her excitement when she notices our company.

Jameson nods politely with a smile her way.

"Very well, thank you. Congratulations on the cast removal."

Aela grins exuberantly as she thanks him then turns to me, "Are we going for coffee now?"

Dammit. Aela turns back towards Jameson and looks about to invite him along, so I jump in to cut her off immediately.

"I have to get work," I blurt, and Aela closes her mouth to frown at me, no doubt confused because we had planned to grab coffee afterwards.

"Oh, okay. Well, nice seeing you again, Jameson." Aela gives him a friendly half-hug, and I settle on smiling with another wave from my very safe and impersonal distance.

"Bye, Jameson." I grab hold of Aela's arm and drag her away as he seems speechless, taking advantage of his silence to make an exit before he can stop us.

"I liked Jameson. He was nice," Aela comments thoughtfully, rhythmically tapping her fingers on the steering wheel before her to the beat of the catchy pop song on the radio while we sit at the set of traffic lights directly in front of the doctor's office.

"He *is* nice, like a damn boy scout without the fun rope-tying skills," I admit, and she shakes her head as the green light illuminates.

"I don't even want to know what you mean by that," Aela remarks wryly, so I grin her way.

"I'll leave it to your imagination," I tease, and she laughs, focusing on the road ahead.

"Are we really not going for coffee now?" She deftly changes the subject, and I snort derisively.

"Like hell we aren't. I have time and need my caffeine fix if I'm going to get through the mind-numbing drive to work."

Aela nods at my insistence as I feel my phone vibrate in my bag against my foot. I try not act as eager as I feel as I retrieve it and see Alex's reply.

My stomach flutters with butterflies and my chest expands with anticipation as I open it and read.

"Have dinner with me?"

Damn. I'm disappointed because I have to tell him I'll be working late. After I respond, I wait with my phone in hand but don't receive anything more before we pull up to the little café Aela chooses.

I shove my phone dejectedly into my bag and try not to be annoyed. The guy could just be busy.

Hours later, though, and still nothing. I've tried to not let it get to me, even locked my phone in the drawer of my desk at work after a couple hours of surreptitiously checking it—turned up to the maximum volume of course so I can hear if he *does* reply. I need to be able to focus and get my work done. Otherwise, I'll never get out of here, and I plan on dropping by his place with dessert since I know it's his night off. I already picked up some chocolate eclairs from the bakery across the road and hid them in the back of the fridge in the little kitchenette.

Good thing I thought ahead, because it's nine-thirty by the time I finally start on my last package of edits. Everyone else is gone, Josh being the last to ditch me over half an hour ago, who turned the overhead lights off as he went, urging me to follow his order to call it a night.

Every workstation in the place is swallowed by darkness apart from mine since I switched my little desk lamp on because I was too busy and lazy to walk across the warehouse floor. This works better for me anyway. Now I have fewer visual distractions and am able to listen to my music without the headphones that give me a headache after too long.

I already have a tension headache, though, and my eyes are straining to focus on the computer screen in front of me, feeling dry and gritty, and they keep blurring, so I take a moment to close them and rub my eyelids to get some relief. I look around the pitch black room, the only illumination outside of my space being the green exit sign above the emergency stairwell at the very back since the blinds have been pulled over the windows. I can't see the front reception from my spot, only a faint glow of outside lighting at the entrance.

It should probably be creepy, but I've never been afraid of the dark. Quite the opposite, actually. I embrace it and the solitude it provides.

I leave my desk to stretch my back and legs, snagging a small juice bottle from the kitchenette while I'm up and then wander back. I hear a click that sounds like the closing latch of a door, and I halt mid-step. I look around, straining my ears in search of anything else, but nothing seems to be amiss. All I can hear is the low music from my computer and the hum of the fridge after a long pause, so I brush it off and slide back into my chair. I take a long drink of juice. I catch the movement of a large shadow cutting across the dim light at the main entrance and frown as I finally hear footfalls over the wooden floorboards. My body goes on high alert at the obvious and unexpected presence.

"Hello?" I call out questioningly and politely when really, I want to demand they tell me who the hell they are with a few choice swear words thrown in for good measure.

I'm starting to get a little weirded out. The hairs at the nape of my neck are tingly with apprehension. I don't like it one bit. The darkness surrounding me that only a moment ago felt peaceful and calming, has now turned against me and feels heavy with the promise of danger.

I have to fight the increasingly strong urge to hide under my table as I try to talk sense to myself. For all I know, my mind is playing tricks on me, and it's just the cleaner, even though I know they're not due tonight and never work this late—or a colleague coming back because they forgot something. I can just picture the mocking that would entail if Josh came in to find me huddled under my desk.

The footsteps suddenly halt, but I still can't see anyone, and they haven't replied, so I start to think it's someone deliberately messing with me. The list of possible suspects is a short one, and the longer I think on it, the more I decide I know who it would be and feel my lips stretching into a grin.

Alex.

I can just picture him deciding to take my unavailability as a challenge and opportunity to surprise me, which is why I didn't hear back from him. The guy doesn't take *no* for an answer.

"Alex, if that's you, stop messing around and get your butt in here. If you brought dinner, I have two choices for dessert." I call out leadingly, leaving no doubt to what one of those options will be, picturing the way we could make use of my desk.

The footsteps come again, louder and faster this time, and I'm grinning as the shadow of a male form appears at the entrance before the lights are turned on, the sudden brightness momentarily blinding me, and I have to blink against the harshness of it before I get a clear view of the person standing before me.

Alarm travels down my spine as my eyes widen and my grin falls away when I find the last person I could've imagined, and the dark, predatory look in his eyes that I've never seen before.

"No, not the man-whore scum. Sorry to disappoint. I know how attached you've become to him. Which I don't understand. He's the complete opposite of the men I've seen you date since I've known you," he states. The tone of his voice is off, airy like he's out of his mind on something as he ambles his way towards me.

"Jameson. What are you doing here?" I ask cautiously, not really knowing what to say in return, but he doesn't reply to me anyway, just continues rambling.

"Why him? I put in months of work, figuring out your type and perfecting my fit into that profile before we even had a proper conversation. And you didn't appreciate any of it. I did everything you asked, followed every rule you set. I gave you everything, and then you just cut me off when you decided you'd had enough. Like I was nothing."

Jameson pulls a plastic sandwich bag from his back pocket, tossing it onto my desk where it lands with a heavy *thunk* before me.

It's filled with photos. Of me. And Alex. The one on top is a shot of us in a compromised position in his bed, taken from his bedroom window.

The invasion of privacy, of such an intimate moment, makes my stomach churn and my eyes well. My skin crawls. I feel invaded and defiled. I look away before I throw up, and I wind up finding Jameson's hate-filled gaze.

Blinking away the blurriness of tears threatening to spill, I swallow harshly as I straighten my back and level him with a glare of my own. I don't know where he's going with this, but I'm going to put a stop to it.

"You're so happy to be the stripper's slut, though, aren't you? Despite all my warnings," he continues snidely, and I shoot up out of my chair to face him evenly.

It was *Jameson* tormenting me this whole time. I'm done with being talked down to and judged by this psycho, and I'm not listening to him trash talk about Alex.

"That's enough. I don't know what you're expecting to accomplish from all this, but I'm not listening to any of it. What I do with my life is none of your business. Stop following me and get a life of your own, preferably in a padded cell with a comfy white jacket. Get the fuck out of here now, you creep, before I call the police."

I move to retrieve my phone from the drawer only to remember I locked it when the drawer doesn't budge as I tug on the handle. I mentally curse myself, rifling through the mess on my desk in search of the key, but immediately freeze at a clicking sound that turns the blood in my veins to ice and every one of my muscles to stone.

My brain scrambles to make sense of what is happening because this can't be real.

"I thought that might get your attention." Jameson sounds pleased as he steps into my line of sight, arm stretched out between us, so the gun in his hands is mere centimetres from the tip of my nose.

It's so close that I go cross-eyed looking at the ominous metal reflecting the low light of my lamp.

"You're no longer the one in charge. I'll make you a deal, though. I'll go easy on you if you get on your knees for me like you did the stripper. I really liked the look of you that way." He motions to the floor with the gun, rounding my desk, so there's no longer anything between us. Jameson's expression turns smug as he reaches out with his now free hand to swipe his thumb across my cheek, ignoring when I flinch away from him as he puts it to his mouth and tastes it, looking very proud of himself.

"Not so emotionless and detached now, are you?" he remarks, and that's when I realise not only am I trembling, but tears have started to freefall from my eyes. I've completely lost control of myself.

"Please, don't do this? Put the gun away, and we can talk, I won't call the police," I plead, but he shakes his head with an amused chuckle, the glint in his eyes filled with dark, violent promises.

I have no idea who this monster is in front of me. He's definitely not the Jameson I thought I knew.

"Take off that pretty little top and skirt," he commands, following when I try to step back from him.

After a moment of me trembling in disbelief, he presses the barrel of the gun into my forehead menacingly.

"Get it off and get on your knees!" He is seething mad with impatience, spittle hitting me in the face.

I ignore it and force my numb muscles to move, pulling my tank top up over my head, and thankfully, forcing some space between my head and a bullet as I do. My fingers fumble to grasp the waist of my skirt, and I whimper when he makes a disgruntled noise, but I manage to hook my thumbs in the elastic, forcing the fabric down to my knees where it drops to the floor without resistance.

I slowly straighten and face him, my stomach churning at the ravenous look in his eyes as he leers at me covered in only small scraps of orange lace.

Jameson's gaze flicks up to mine, his brows rising impatiently.

"I won't ask again, Kara," he urges me with a wave of the gun again, and I feel like I'm dying inside.

I can't do this.

I won't survive this intact even if he doesn't put a bullet in me. I don't see any way out, though, short of divine intervention. I'm praying for a miracle as I slowly get to my knees on the rough carpet that garners my intent stare.

Jameson taps the side of my skull none too gently with the barrel of the gun, forcing me to look up at him.

"Beautiful. Remove your bra, and then undo my belt."

I have to fight the urge to throw up on him or punch him in the balls as a surge of anger fills me. How dare he think he has the right to do this to me—make me a victim when I worked so hard to be the one in charge of everything in my life, all because I bruised his ego?

That damn gun. I need to get it out of his control.

My mind races, coming up with plans and discarding them for being too risky as I comply, releasing the front clasp on my bra then slowly pulling the straps down from my shoulders. My chest, unfortunately, thrusts forward as I reach my arms behind me during the removal, and I damn near vomit on Jameson's shiny leather shoes when he reaches down to palm and squeezes my right breast.

My breathing is harsh in my ears as I fight the encroaching panic, gritting my teeth against the growing, frantic urge to lash out in a bid to escape.

But then I notice something. Jameson is so caught up in fondling my boob that his gun hand has dropped to his side, forgotten.

I form a plan. It's risky, and I may have to go along with his orders more than I'd like, but it's better than flat out giving in. I reach out with both hands to slowly slide his belt free, unbuckling it before peeking to see him watching intently.

My heart is beating erratically, and the adrenaline pumping through my body feels like a livewire under my skin. Jameson nods his head towards his obvious arousal behind his pants.

"Release me," he urges, his voice thick with lust. I have to flex my hands because all the emotions flooding me make them shake. I release the button and zipper teasingly slow and feel a small victory because Jameson seems so enraptured that he's content to let me take my time, no longer pushy and impatient. But then, he's so close to getting what he wants that, of course, he's savouring it.

I swallow back the bile that rises up my throat when I have to reach a hand into his open pants and retrieve his hard on. *God, please don't let me die like this.*

324

Jameson's free hand fists in the back of my hair, pulling my face towards his groin, and I really, *really* have to fight not to be sick because this is it. Do or die. Or do *and* die, but I can't think that. I place my hands on the front of his thighs like I need it to balance, feeling his body stiffen with anticipation as I take a calming breath, but come up short when I hear the most unexpected, welcome yet panic-inducing sound ever.

"Sunshine, you can stop right there. Please take the gun you were going for, though—he won't stop you."

Talk about divine intervention.

Alex growls at Jameson to move his fingers as far from the trigger as possible if he doesn't want a broken neck. I can't take the handgun fast enough.

I scramble backwards until I've jammed my chair into the wall, and it stops me from going any further, then look up to see Alex behind Jameson, his arm wrapped around the psycho's throat in a chokehold, his face a mask of lethal fury.

Chapter 19

ALEX

AND TO THINK I'd been having such a good day until I came upon this sight.

I woke up after a long, shitty night at work to Kara's text of timid surrender and practically sprung out of bed to start planning how to show her she made the right choice and that she had nothing to fear because I only want her, with no ulterior motives.

She said she would be at work until late, so I decided to surprise her by dropping in with dinner.

I called Aela to ask what Kara's favourite meal was and she sounded shocked, rattling off a bunch of answers.

"Chicken, spicy stuff, and pasta." All of which is not a favourite dish. I pointed out her failure as a best friend disgruntledly, making her laugh as I hung up. So after wracking my brain and googling randomly, I decided on trying to make lasagne. One call to my mum while at the store to find out which packet pasta would be best to use—because, as always, there were too many choices—I had a rather disgruntled 'helper' in my kitchen, by which I mean my mother compulsively trying to take over.

She was so excited about what I was doing and insisted on showing me how to make the pasta from scratch with *her* recipe. It was a good thing I had the day to perfect it.

While the dish baked, I got grilled by my mother, who decided to stick around for a glass of wine, barraging me with questions about Kara and demanding to meet her immediately. Thankfully, once it was safely out of the oven and her glass had long gone dry, I managed to get her out the door after having to promise and swear that I would introduce her and Kara real soon, knowing full well that she'd be dropping by unannounced in the very near future.

Time flew by, and it was already dark out by the time I had everything ready to go. I had a salad and garlic bread (bought frozen much to my mother's dismay) for sides, the rest of the wine, even though either of us are big wine drinkers. I figured whisky might be too much, as well as dessert since she was supposed to be working. I didn't want to take up too much time. I just wanted to feed her and show that she was cared for.

I also brought along a white bouquet of roses, and finally, the stack of information I had printed off about her stalker because it's beyond time to share it. The more time went by with her determined to live in ignorance, the more dangerous I felt the situation becoming.

The parking is down the side of the building and empty, but for Kara's Rio, so I took the spot beside it.

As I lugged my haul back up the slope to the footpath, I made a mental note to make sure she didn't walk down there by herself at night because it's barely lit by the streetlights. They don't even reach her car in the middle of the lot, and the back is completely blacked out—prime stalker estate. My woman has to be more careful.

There's a fancy BMW parked on the street right in front of the doors to the building, and I snort because there's a clear 'tow away zone' sign right before it. *Ignorant*.

It's practically screaming to be towed.

I'm about to turn my back on it when something niggles the

back of my mind, forcing me to check it out again.

That's when I recognised the numberplate. That seemingly inconsequential sequence of letters and numbers filled me with dread like I've never felt before. I almost dropped everything I was carrying. It's burned into my brain from my memorising it in hopes of being able to spot it, but I never imagined it would be like this.

But here I am.

I want to run in there and make sure Kara's okay, but I don't know what's going on inside and worry I might make things worse, so I call Kane.

I don't even know what I say in my panic, but once I stop talking, he tells me he's on his way and will bring in his buddies from the force.

He also says to wait for them but fuck that.

I'm not about to sit here and twiddle my thumbs as God knows what is going on inside. I have to get to Kara. Now.

I put everything down beside the entrance out of the way, then open the door just enough to see through, moving slower than everything inside me is screaming to do.

I can't see anyone in the reception room or hear anything, so I pull the door wider and slip through, making sure it shuts soundlessly before I release it and then move across the room, listening for any noise when I hear a voice.

"Undo my belt." I make out the end of what the guy is saying and have to fight for control to not blindly rush in.

I hear a low, pleased growl and find myself peeking around the corner into the lit up room before I even think of moving and what I see has my veins igniting with rage.

The guy I'm certain is Jameson in the file from Kane has his back to me, standing behind a desk to the side of the room.

I can't really see Kara, just the top of her head as she's on her knees in front of him behind the desk. But I can clearly see the Glock in his hand that's being used to threaten her into submission, although at the moment, he is so distracted with what she's doing that it's being held limply by his side.

"Release me," he croaks out.

I can't ignore where this is going. I still can't see if Kara is hurt or in any other danger apart from the gun, but I'm about to find out.

I'd rather take a bullet than stand by and let him violate her, but I'm going to do my best to get us both out of this alive.

I move low and quietly into the room, my heart thudding so loud in my chest it's like the stupid organ is trying to give me away as I try to ignore it's thrumming in my ears.

I'm careful to stay out of his possible peripheral vision as I move swiftly, even though the guy's entire focus is on Kara at his feet. I doubt anything could distract him, but I'm still careful.

I see Kara's hands slide around the sides of his thighs, slowly gliding up towards his hips. I watch the hand nearing the gun and recognise her plan, which makes my already erratic heart speed up with fear because it's a huge risk. Not that I can judge, I guess.

But I have to stop her before he catches on.

I rush the last few feet and sling my arm tightly around his throat so fast that I have him firmly in a chokehold before he realises what's happening.

"Sunshine, you can stop right there. Please take the gun you were going for, though. He won't stop you."

I can't see Kara over his shoulder when I speak but hear her exhale of relief as I squeeze my arm tighter around his oesophagus to discourage any sudden moves while turning my face towards his ear.

"You'll get those slimy fingers of yours as far from the trigger as you can if you want your neck to remain intact. Be a good boy now, and I'll release you once Kara's safe." I hold my breath as I hear Kara scrambling around and then could almost weep when I can finally wholly see her when she scrambles backwards.

Covered by only her underwear and shaking like she's about to vibrate her way out of her skin, but physically unharmed. It's the most beautiful sight I've ever seen.

Kara struggles back into her clothes on the floor as I drag Jameson back a few steps until he can no longer see Kara, turning us around, so I'm standing between them for good measure.

"I did what you wanted so you can get your filthy hands off me now." Jameson has the hide to sneer, which just blows my mind. The audacity of this guy.

I tighten my hold until he's choking and struggling before I relax again.

"I've seen your rap sheet. You stalk, take dirty photos of women without their knowledge, sexually assault, harass, and bully. You hold Kara at gunpoint to get yourself off, yet *I'm* the filthy one?"

I ask incredulously then push him away from me, so he stumbles into the neighbouring desk, falling into the chair that I lean over, trapping him there.

"You're not even a man. You're a rabid, diseased animal that needs to be put down," I practically growl, the need for revenge singing in my veins, begging to make him hurt.

"She deserved it. She treated me like I—"

I don't even let him finish his bullshit. My arm swings back and my fist slams into his face so hard I feel things crunch and pop on both sides of the connection. It feels so good, strokes my need for violence so sweetly that I want to keep going, but I have something more important I need to do.

"Sunshine, how you are doing over there?" I look back to where Kara is huddled under her desk, looking up at me with eyes that are too wide and shimmering.

I need to hold her, feel her in my arms so I know she's safe. Then I can hopefully breathe properly again. I look back to Jameson, who is hunched over and howling about his face, which I ignore, shoving him back against the seat, so he's pinned and then twist back, holding my hand out to Kara imploringly.

"Come here, sweetheart, please?" I plead softly then wait as Kara just stares back warily before finally scrambling out to fling herself into my side, burying her face in my chest as she breaks down into body-shaking sobs.

I pull her in as tight as possible, pressing my face into her hair, and take my first deep breath in far too long as my heartbeat finally starts to recede to a more normal rate.

This feeling of completeness with her in my arms is overwhelming and worth everything. I want to keep her there forever, and for once, the thought doesn't send me into a downward spiral of panic that has me running.

Nervous maybe, but I need this feeling—I need *her*, enough to deal with my insecurities of the inevitable yet unknown future, and I'm not going to let anything take Kara without a fight. Death itself should be wary of taking this one from me.

I keep an eye on Jameson as I attempt to soothe Kara, murmuring repeated assurances of safety while holding her tight, because it feels as though she'd shatter without my support.

Before I know it, all three of us jump in surprise as the room is suddenly swarmed by a team of at least ten law enforcement officers pouring in from the front and back of the place.

I drag Kara several steps away from Jameson as he is forced to the floor and is searched and cuffed by three officers who easily manhandle him, ignoring his protests and the blood still freefalling from his misshapen nose.

There's a flurry of activity around us, a barrage of voices and orders being made, camera flashes and a lot of noise when someone comes across the gun.

It's overwhelming watching investigators paw over the place for evidence while Jameson's escorted out.

"Miss, can you please come with me so we can have you looked at by the medics and get your statement?" a male officer asks gently beside us, gesturing with a hand for Kara to walk away with him, but she whimpers, grasping the sides of my shirt and holding tightly, fearful of being separated.

"He didn't—I don't… Jameson didn't touch me. Not like *that*. Can't we just stay here?" Kara stutters and the poor guy looks out of his depth. A small, older looking female officer joins us, patting him on the shoulder.

"Why don't we trade off? You get Mr Manzoni's statement while Kara and I take a seat just over here to get hers." The female officer points to the desk before Kara's and turns to address Kara with a warm smile.

"You look like you're dealing with a fair amount of shock there, sweetheart. Let us get you off your feet and make you a little more comfortable."

Kara looks between the officer and the desk she indicated warily, before turning her panicked gaze to me, eyes glittering and welled with tears.

"You're going to stay right here?" she asks uncertainly with a small, shaky voice that has my throat clogging up, making me even more unwilling to let her go.

I nod and smooth back some of her hair that's fallen into her face as I promise, "I'm not going anywhere without you."

Kara's eye flit between mine, her hands flexing their grip on my sides before she whispers, "I need you."

Three little words that absolutely slay me coming from the fiercely independent woman in my arms because I know how much it costs her to say them.

I smile affectionately as I cup her cheeks in both hands.

"I need you more, sunshine."

I press my lips to her forehead when I see the doubt in her eyes because now isn't the time to get into it—with an audience and all.

"Are you all right to walk or do you want help to the chair? Because I'm more than happy to carry you anyway you want, bridal, fireman, superman… turtle style, you name it," I say, trying to lighten the mood with a lame attempt at being comical, but I'm actually concerned Kara won't be able to hold herself up with how badly she's shaking from shock. I smile when she gives me a dubious look with a slight grin, extracting herself from my arms and takes a step back.

"I'm not going to ask what turtle style is because I'm sure you're making it up, but either way, it's unnecessary. I can walk the five steps on my own two feet," Kara assures, voice laced with humour as she leans over to kiss my cheek. "Thank you," she whispers, then follows the policewoman's gesture to walk ahead of her, looking much steadier.

Kane shows up, muttering about traffic as I finish giving the officer my statement. I included the information I had dug up on Jameson and the reason why I got it, informing him I have the folder here. When we're done, he leaves, returning minutes later with all my stuff from outside but the folder, which he'll be keeping. I don't mind so long as Jameson gets put away.

It takes Kara a while longer to finish with hers, and it has me worrying about what I've missed that she has so much to share. I do my best to hide my concern while Kara keeps checking I'm still in place, though I haven't moved. Watching her talk comforts me a little, and I notice she's stopped shaking now with a blanket draped over her and a mug of hot chocolate cupped in her hands that someone made her. I'll feel a whole lot better when she's done, and I can have her back in my arms.

It feels like everything drags on at a snail's pace, but

eventually, we're free to go. Kane does me a solid, letting me know he's organised to have Kara's car dropped off at my place. I can't thank the guy enough for all his help, though he dismisses it and tries to claim he didn't do enough. The fact I get to walk out of here with my girl under my arm is all thanks to him as far as I'm concerned. It was his information that led to me recognising the car in the first place.

"What's all that?" Kara asks curiously from the passenger seat of my Jeep as I'm returning the food carriers to the backseat. I snag the roses and step over to open the door I'd just helped Kara in and offer them to her.

"Oh, you know, just my magic kit to make you fall in love with me." I mean every word but make it sound like a joke to keep things light. I'm rewarded with a pleased smile and the blush rising in her cheeks as she takes the roses before smelling them.

"These are beautiful," she murmurs, glistening eyes meeting mine, and I don't hesitate to correct her.

"*You're* beautiful."

I lean in to steal a kiss because I can't help myself, but I need to get her home, so I keep it quick.

"Let's get home so I can make you love me."

I shut her door and jog around to climb in my side to find Kara watching me pensively. I wait for her to say something, but not at all expecting what comes from her mouth.

"Whatever it is isn't necessary. I already love you. Have for a while now."

Kara gives me a small smile as though she just one-upped me, but I can see the uncertainty grow in her eyes the longer I watch her in shell-shocked silence before reaching over to take her face in my hands.

She looks nervous as I reign in how I feel to look at her sincerely, so she has no reason to doubt me when I reply.

334

"You've been *it* for me for months now. I don't understand how you haven't noticed already. I love you like I've never loved anyone before. It's terrifying, exhilarating, and sometimes debilitating, but in a good way. You made me feel again when I didn't think I could. You drive me crazy, and we fight like cat and dog, but I wouldn't have it any other way, and I'm done letting you run from me. So if you chicken out and try to run again from this, you better know that I'm going to give chase. You're not getting any more space from me. I'm going to be on you like a fat kid on the last piece of cake at the party."

Kara scrunches her nose at my bad analogy before giving me the biggest, most brilliant smile I've ever seen. She then starts simultaneously laughing and crying.

Well, shit.

I don't know what to do with myself and am about to panic when she grabs my face and kisses me forcefully before leaning back to look at me.

"Okay then," Kara whispers with a grin, leaning back in her seat as though all is well in the world. I sit there dumbstruck, feeling like that was rather anticlimactic before she turns to look at me questioningly.

"I hope that kit of yours contains food because I'm kind of hungry now."

Right. Time to get us home.

I start the engine and get us on our way, hearing a giggle come from Kara that's like a sweet sledgehammer to my chest.

"You have some clothes in your car or want to stop at your place first? Because I plan to keep you for a while." Kara shakes her head, reaching over to run her fingers through the back of my hair.

"Just get us home. I want to get into your bed and have you feed me as soon as possible." She grins then tries to smother a yawn as I notice the toll tonight has taken on the both of us and,

335

of course, I agree with her idea, though I have a feeling she's going to regret not having any clean clothes tomorrow.

This night didn't go at all like I'd planned, but I can't complain about the outcome.

We're both alive. And together.

That's all I need really.

Chapter 20

KARA

I WAKE UP feeling surrounded by warmth and security. I languidly open my eyes to find myself wrapped in Alex. We're facing each other in the middle of his bed, my head tucked under his chin, so I'm breathing into his neck, his right arm tucked under my pillow while the other is draped over my hip. My hands are both curled up against his bare chest and our legs entwined so that even our toes are touching.

I tilt my head back so I can see his handsome face softened with sleep and have to fight the temptation to run my fingers over it because I don't want to wake him just yet.

I need to wrap my head around everything that happened last night.

I found out who my stalker and messenger-of-hate was.

Jameson held me at gunpoint for a blowjob and god knows what else he had planned.

Alex dropped by with a beautiful surprise, risked his life to disarm Jameson, punched him in the face and then we were surrounded by police.

I stole evidence from the scene and now have Jameson's photo collection in my bag.

I swallowed my fear and told the second guy ever in my life, who I'm not related to, I love them.

After what felt like forever, Alex told me he loved me too in his special kind of way.

I fought my feelings for the man before me from practically the moment my eyes landed on him—because I was afraid.

I wanted him and thought I could work around it, but the more I knew about him, the more I fell and the scarier it became. So I did everything I could to push Alex away. I thought loving him would only result in him leaving when he knew, so I was forcing him to leave before it came to that.

Only he kept coming back. More determined each time and fighting against myself and him was tiring.

I want to love and be loved.

I took the risk and leapt when I voiced my confession, and thankfully, he was there to catch me as I fell.

Love is terrifying. The scariest and easiest thing we put ourselves through.

"Stop thinking so hard while staring at me. It's too early to worry you're having second thoughts about us," Alex mumbles against his pillow, his voice rough with sleep.

His eyes slowly open, beautiful jade gaze meeting mine before his hand comes up to tap my forehead.

"Turn this off and let me enjoy morning snuggles a little longer," Alex grumbles adorably, closing his eyes as I grin and finally, let myself stroke the side of his face, making him purr in appreciation, which ignites a tingling between my thighs.

"I wasn't having second thoughts, just thinking," I promise and one of his eyes barely open, searching my face for affirmation before he snuggles in impossibly more.

"Good. Because we're a done deal," Alex asserts. I'd chuckle if he wasn't restricting my air intake.

"We are?" I ask sarcastically, and he nods, pressing his face into my neck, nose skimming my skin with the movement, making my breath catch.

"You admitted you love me so, yeah, you're stuck with me now."

I sigh dramatically as though I'm put out by that, and Alex pokes me in the ribs, making me giggle.

"There could be worse things to be stuck with I guess," I comment just to tease him. Alex levels me with a mock glare before commenting,

"Yeah. It's a good thing I'm not your type. Your exes I've met so far have all been giant, gaping arseholes."

The reminder of Jameson makes my smile and amusement dim, which Alex notices because his face softens.

"How are you doing with all the crazy that went down?" he asks quietly, his teasing tone replaced with concern as his fingers run through my hair, brushing it back from my face.

It makes a warm, pleasant feeling spread in my chest.

I'm still not used to having him genuinely care about me.

"I'm dealing with it," I answer shakily. He squeezes me in his arms comfortingly.

"If you want to talk about it, I'm here," Alex offers, so I give him a small smile of gratitude but don't want to talk about what happened. I need to process it myself when I'm ready, which is not now. Right now, it's all I can do to keep the images and feelings at bay.

My stomach growls embarrassingly loud, serving to break the heavy moment as we both break into laughter, and Alex leans back to pat it affectionately.

"Time to tame that beast. Any requests?" Alex smacks a kiss on the top of my head then rolls out of bed. He pulls on a pair of grey boxer briefs then looks at me expectantly.

"Mm… something sweet?" I suggest, and he grins.

"I'll see what I can do."

Alex winks and is out the door.

I take a moment to indulge in a whole body stretch before

getting up to follow, stealing his shirt from the end of the bed to wear since my clothes are where I left them on the bathroom floor, and I have no desire to put them back on. Ever.

"How does chocolate fudge sauce, sprinkles, and cornflakes sound?" Alex asks as I round the corner into the kitchen. I scrunch my nose, glad I decided to follow before he tried to serve up that concoction.

"Horrible. That's the best you can come up with?" I shove Alex aside so I can search the pantry, but he pulls me back with his hands at my waist. I'm suddenly turned, lifted off my feet, and placed to sit on the bench with Alex forcing his way between my legs.

"How about I have the first two and you for my breakfast?" Alex suggests with a throaty growl, nuzzling into my neck as his hands find their way under the hem of my shirt.

Well, his shirt.

I'm about to order him to feed me first when the front door suddenly opens, and a barrage of footsteps and voices intrude on our moment.

I turn that way in shock as Declan and Aela, accompanied by an older lady, step into view, and all come to a standstill at the sight of us.

"Uh… can we help you guys?" Alex is first to break the silence, and they break into chaos.

The woman, who now I've had a proper look at her, I recognise the resemblance and take a guess that she's Alex's mother, jumps with a happy shriek, hands clasped to her chest as she hurries over while the other two simultaneously start yelling.

"I knew it! You owe me, Aela." Dec looks smug, fist pumping the air like he just won the lottery as his girlfriend rushes me.

"*Can you help us*? You could try answering your damn phone, bitch. I've been so fucking worried. I had to use the Find

My Phone app!" Aela yells in outrage. I know it's bad because she hardly ever swears.

It's all just noise after that as everyone talks over each other, until Alex produces an ear-piercing whistle.

"One at a time," he orders and is then jostled aside so Aela can fling her arms around me. I have to quickly grab the hem of my shirt to keep from flashing everyone.

"Why didn't you call me? It was on the news. They interviewed Josh and a cop and filmed Jameson being led into the station in cuffs. Are you okay?"

Wait, what?

My stomach twists with dawning horror as her words sink in, and I look over Aela's head to see the guys talking quietly together against the opposite bench while Alex's maybe-mother thoughtfully stares at me, which is even more unnerving.

I need clothes. Especially underwear.

"I need to change. Follow me to the room, and we'll talk," I suggest to Aela before sliding off the bench in front of her, and then we slip out of the room.

"I don't suppose you have any clothing I could borrow in that bag?" I ask hopelessly once we're in Alex's bedroom with the door shut behind us.

"I have a cardigan," Aela offers helpfully, and I curse.

"This is just perfect. Of course, I would be the idiot with no clothes to wear when meeting my boyfriend's mother. She must be so super impressed right now. Probably thinks I'm one of the strippers he works with."

Aela's mouth and eyes are wide open when I stop to look at her while gnawing on my left thumbnail.

"Did you just call Alex your boyfriend?" Aela asks in disbelief, and my impending freak out makes me snarky. I give her a sarcastic look as I rush into the bathroom to inspect the condition of my clothes in there.

"No. I'm talking about another guy whose mother just happens to be here and resemble Alex. Keep up, Aela," I retort, and she huffs.

"I'm trying, but I have more questions than I do answers. You're going to have to catch me up."

I exhale slowly as I throw my wrinkled and wet shirt and underwear back to the floor but keep my skirt and bra with me as I move on to hunt through Alex's closet, snagging a grey button up. I get dressed as I give Aela the short summary.

"Jameson's been stalking me. He came in, ordering me around at gunpoint. Alex showed up to surprise me with dinner and intercepted. The police came, I told Alex I love him, and he returned the sentiment. We came here, ate dinner in bed, talked a little, and then went to sleep."

I tuck the shirt into my skirt and roll up the sleeves before a mirror check and instantly undo the work because the shirt is too big and looks ridiculous. I switch it out with one of Alex's singlets, which is still loose but looks much better.

I quickly brush my teeth and hair, noticing Aela hasn't made a sound the whole time, so I look out to find her sitting on the end of the bed, watching me with watery eyes, her bottom lip wobbling.

"Hey, I'm okay."

I stop my fussing to go over and wrap my arms around her. Aela returns the hug fiercely tight with a small sniffle.

"I'm signing us up for self-defence classes. This shit has got to stop happening," she states resolutely, needlessly reminding me of her own attack not that long ago, which I've nowhere near forgotten. It's still hard for me to think of her walking around campus or anywhere alone.

I give her a squeeze as I move to sit beside her with a sound of agreement when there's a knock at the bedroom door.

"Yeah?" I call out nervously as the door opens, and Alex's

head pops through, regarding us sitting on his bed.

"You know, I had a dream like this once. Only there was less clothing, and I was in the middle," he enlightens us as he steps inside, and I snort derisively as Aela and I separate. "Everything all right in here?" Alex asks cautiously as he steps closer. Aela nods as she stands, and I assure him it is while he puts on a pair of shorts then pulls me into him, pressing a kiss to my head as Aela watches with a small, indulgent smile.

"Mum's making us all pancakes and is eager to fuss over you after hearing what went down last night, if you're done hiding out in here," Alex informs me, so I pull away to look at him beseechingly.

"She's staying a while? Alex, I can't meet your mother like this," I wave my hand wildly at myself, but he doesn't seem to see the problem. He just smiles, gesturing for us to walk out of the room, which Aela complies with.

"You look beautiful," Alex states, leading me to the door, so I snort again as I push against his hand at my back.

"I don't even have underwear on," I mutter, and he chuckles, palming my arse and squeezing.

"I told you you'd want clothes. But I like this. In fact, new rule—this is now an underwear-free establishment as far as you're concerned."

I glare at his smirking face as he pushes me down the hall.

When we get to the kitchen, Alex wraps his arm around me to stop me from bailing, clearing his throat to get his mother's attention from the frying pan she's ladling batter onto.

"Mum, I'd like you to properly meet my girlfriend, Kara. Sunshine, this is my mum, Josephine." Alex sounds way too prideful considering the circumstances.

His smile is so brilliant it stuns me stupid, and I have trouble looking away until Josephine steps up, brushing some of her dark, unruly hair away from her face. She immediately enfolds me in a tight embrace. Even her hug reminds me of her son.

"Call me Josie. I'm so happy to meet you," she says in a sweet, gentle voice that feels like a hug in itself, before stepping back to meet my gaze with the same eyes as her son, only lightly wrinkled in the corners.

"It's nice to meet you, Josie," I return. She smiles then releases me to shoo us out of the room.

"You two go sit and relax. I have pancakes to make."

We do as we're told and join the others at the small dining table where Dec is hogging into a container of biscuits like they're going to disappear if he doesn't get to them fast enough.

"Declan Lewis, you share my biscotti, or you'll never get another one," Josie calls out with her back turned to us. He pauses mid-bite as Alex rushes over to snatch the container away that is less than half full, glowering at his best friend.

"You greedy arsehole. There are hardly any left. They weren't even for you."

Alex goes to snatch the one in Dec's hand, so he quickly shoves it in his overstuffed mouth.

"They're so good. I missed them," Dec complains through his mouthful and then tries snagging another, but Alex slaps his hand away, offering the container to Aela and me, Alex's glare not leaving Declan. He hesitantly takes a seat but keeps the biscuits out of Dec's reach, refusing to give in to his pleading and bribery for the little bites of heaven.

Josie is an absolute delight, and I get a kick out of watching her lovingly tease both of the guys, but eventually, she has to leave for a charity meeting, doling out kisses and hugs to all on her way out. Aela and Declan leave shortly after so he can drop Aela off at work, and I talk Alex into going to my place so I can at least get some clean clothes.

I check my phone on the drive and am taken aback by the number of texts and missed calls I have from overnight.

I listen to the ten voicemails that were left, deleting Aela's since I've spoken to her, and listen to a couple from Josh. He sounds concerned as he tells me to have the next two days off. *So nice of him when I'm already rostered off the next three*, but he does say to call if I need more time or just to talk, which is actually sweet of him.

There's also one from Detective Miller asking for me to call her back because she has an update for me, so I hit the button to return her call, and she answers on the third ring.

"Hello, Kara. Thanks for calling back, how are you?" genuine concern clear in her voice. I'm hit with nervous butterflies in my stomach.

"I'm fine. What's going on?" I feel rude for not asking how she is in return, but I'm worried she has bad news, and I just want to get it over with before the nerves tightening my stomach bring my breakfast back up.

"I've just left Mr Whitby's arraignment hearing and thought you would like to know that thanks to the extensive evidence we collected, the clear escalation of Whitby's behaviour combined with his history, the judge deemed him a danger to the community, refusing his bail and set his hearing for two months from today. You will be notified if they require you to testify, but I spoke to the prosecutor, and he's certain your statement, and all the evidence along with the fact Whitby pleaded no contest, should be more than sufficient."

I'm momentarily stunned silent as I absorb her words and then I'm overwhelmed.

I want to jump and shout, cry and laugh, curl up in a ball and weep. What I actually do is shake uncontrollably and close my eyes in relief as a sob slips passed the lump in my throat. I cover my mouth with a shaky hand.

"Thank you," I manage to force out after a long silent moment over the line.

I can hear the smile in the detective's voice when she replies. "It's my pleasure, sweetheart. I'm going to enjoy finally going to sleep in the next few hours, knowing there's one less monster on the streets. Take care of yourself. Keep my number and use it if you ever need it."

I mumble I will and thank her again before the call ends.

I open my eyes to find Alex pulled over to the side of the road during my meltdown and is watching me warily.

I give him a watery smile then launch myself at him, wrapping my arms around his back and bury my face in his chest as Alex holds me, being the sturdy rock I need to pull myself back together and calm the barrage of emotions.

"Talk to me, sunshine," Alex murmurs gruffly, running his hand through the back of my hair soothingly once I've quieted down. I pull away from his chest, wiping the wet spot on his shirt from my tears.

"I'm sorry. It's just such a relief, no more creepy gifts and belittling texts to deal with, or looking over my shoulder wondering who the hell it is."

Alex shakes his head with sympathetic eyes.

"You don't ever need to apologise for how you feel, Kara. I just wanted you to let me in. You can snot cry all over me if you need to."

A shock of laughter bursts out of me, making Alex smile then consider me for a long moment before pulling back onto the road.

Alex stretches out across my bed, making himself at home as I grab an overnight bag to pack because he's adamant he is keeping me at his place—preferably restricted to the bed—until I have to go back to work.

I place my laptop on the bed beside my bag because I need to take it with me in case I manage to get some time to get any work done before classes resume next week. I retrieve my laptop bag and some clothes from the wardrobe and return to find Alex with my laptop on his stomach as he opens it.

"Your laptop is password protected? What do you have on here to hide?" I'm not hiding anything, of course. I just have my personal and school stuff to protect in case the laptop is misplaced or stolen, but I tell him what I'm sure he wants to hear.

"Porn. Lots of porn."

Alex takes the bait. He gets excited, rubbing his hands together as he looks my way.

"I'm going to need the password to check this out if I'm going to be sure you're a viable partner for the rest of my life."

I give him an incredulous look then go back to filling my bag but can feel his patient stare drilling holes through me. I'm flushed when I give in not even a minute later.

"Cannon EOS," I admit and he raises a brow at me questioningly, so I shrug. "It's part of the name of my favourite camera. I'm not going to forget that," I explain, and then head back to the wardrobe as he keys in the password.

"I was only kidding about the porn, by the way. You won't find any." At least, I don't think he will.

"That's blasphemous," I hear Alex grumble, making me laugh and stick my head back through the door.

"Well, then, while I'm at it, do you want to have some fun with a naughty nun later?" I grin impishly when he drags his eyes away from the screen to look my way.

He gives me a considering look before shaking his head, his eyes going soft and serious.

"The roleplaying is fun. But I'd rather have just Kara, the woman I love. No bells and whistles or distractions."

Seriously, he's going to have to scrape me up off the floor. I'm overwhelmed by the emotions this guy evokes. I like seeing myself through his eyes. It's intoxicating. I'm not inadequate.

I'm not my past or my insecurities, and I'm not letting my fear hold us back. I see a sparkly, bright future of hope and possibility for us, and I'm going to put in the hard work to get it.

My eyes mist up as I exit the wardrobe, dragging my bag off the bed to the floor as I make my way around to Alex's side. I take my laptop, placing it safely on the bedside table then climb up to saddle his lap, dropping my forehead to rest against his as we lock gazes. Close enough that he turns into a cyclops in my vision.

"You have me," I whisper, running my hands through his hair, then lean in to kiss him with all the feelings bubbling up inside me.

Alex gentles my impassioned kiss into a sweet, slow seduction as his hands glide up and down my sides.

His ministrations make my head spin, and before I know it, I'm losing the ability to hold myself up, pressing into Alex more until he rolls us over and braces himself above me as I sink into the bed with ease.

He pauses to search my face as though trying to burn the image into his retinas while his hands keep busy, the left running through my hair as he braces himself on that elbow while the other hand roams my body. He moves slowly, appearing to not suffer the same urgency I feel while his kisses and soft caresses have me craving more.

I impatiently tug his shirt, needing help to get it over his head, but thankfully, he complies, and I throw it across the room with glee. The barbell through his nipple catches my attention and I lean up to take it into my mouth. Alex groans as I get to work on the fly of his jeans, but then his hand comes down to cover mine, halting my effort.

I look up to meet his gaze impatiently and watch him fight off a smirk.

"Slow down, sunshine. I want to take my time getting

reacquainted and shower you with all my love and affection. You've been deprived of it for too long and deserve it."

I pull his head down for a kiss because his words and intent gaze have my throat clogging up again, and I refuse to be *that* chick, who cries during sex, especially when we haven't even got to it yet.

"Lose the pants, and I'll let you go as slow as you like," I counter against his lips, and he chuckles, shaking his head before leaning back on his shins.

"You always have to get your way," he remarks dryly, so I mimic his raised brow.

"Are you complaining because I want to get you naked and get my hands all over you?" I mock. Alex groans derisively, guiding my hands still caught in his grip above my head, pushing them into the bed.

"You're going to get me too worked up and distract me from my plan," he complains petulantly. I laugh until he grinds his groin against mine. My breath catches when I feel how worked up he already is.

"Maybe that's what I want," I gasp out, enjoying the pressure when he presses against the pulse point that is begging for him most. I don't even realise my eyes shut in bliss at the contact until he pulls back, and I open them to plead for more. Alex chuckles but shakes his head adamantly.

"We're doing this my way, sunshine. You can have it your way later—relationships are all about the compromise."

He grins wickedly then proceeds to make sweet, slow torturous love to me like I've never imagined him capable of doing, and when he finally lets me climax, I swear my heart explodes right along with the rest of my body.

I knew Alex would be trouble for me the moment I laid eyes on him. But I didn't know he would also be the best thing that could ever happen to me. He taught me there's strength in letting love make you weak, and there's nothing wrong with that.

It's essential to living—because a life without love isn't really living at all. And I plan to love this man with everything that I am, for as long as I can.

Acknowledgments

FIRST, I'D LIKE to thank every single person who read and enjoyed Draw Me In. Your kind words and enthusiasm, plus your anticipation for this book, continues to blow my mind. It means the world to me, and I hope Alex and Kara's story is everything you were looking forward to in book two.

Michael, for all that you are and all that you do, I love you most and always.

Thank you to Chritty. The Louise to my Tina, who puts up with my three a.m. plotting texts, can't get enough sneak peeks, loved my characters before I could even get them written down, and cracks the proverbial whip when I procrastinate too much. Love you, brosis.

To Kahlia, Kate, and Kayleigh, thank you for your encouragement and opinions when decisions started to make my head spin. You ladies are goddesses!

A HUGE thank you to Rogena of RMJ Manuscript Service, editor extraordinaire with the patience of a saint. She has the ability to produce diamonds out of coal! You're a superstar! I can't thank you enough for all your work. Anyone looking for help with a manuscript—I can't recommend Rogena enough!

To Natalie and her ladies at B&B Promotions, THANK YOU! For all your help, hard work, support and super organisation. Sending you all the love!

Thank you to Tracey from Soxational Cover Art for the beautiful cover!

To Tash from Outlined with Love Designs, one of the sweetest and crazily talented ladies I've ever known. I'm going to find you and squish the stuffing out of you at FYM in September! Thank you for your beautiful work!

A special shout out to my GReeps! I love and miss you ladies!

Big thanks to all the wonderful bloggers who participated in the release blitz for Draw Me In, for everything you did from sharing teasers to the wonderful reviewers! Books and Boys book blog, Perfectly Perez, The Power of three readers, AC Squared, 2 girls who love books, Through the eyes of a book goddess, Abigail Davies, All the feels, Harlie's books, Maddy's reading, The Reading spot, Maari loves her Indies, The Phantom paragrapher, G&T's Indie café, Bit'n book promoters, Schmexy girl, Blog on the run, Book Addicts reviews, Wicked babes, Nerdy, dirty & flirty, Jambookblog, Next Book review, Naughty smut readers, SpunkyNsassy, Sassy southern, IrishdaisylovesRomance, Warrior Woman Winmill, La Jersey Chika Reads Indie Books, The Romance Rebels, Books and War paint, Paranormal Romance Trance, Men behaving badly, Rad Review Repeat, Lucky 13 Book reviews and news, Virginia Lee, New England Naughty and Nice, Secrets in books, Karen Fernandez, Best Book Boyfriends, Stacie's love of books, The book fairy reviews, JoandIsalovebooks, Gypsy treasures and fairytale dreams.
I can't thank you all enough!

And many, many thanks to YOU for choosing this book and taking the time to read it. I hope Alex and Kara didn't disappoint! Whether you loved or hated their story, I would appreciate your feedback. Leave a review on the site you purchased it from and/or contact me. I'd love to hear from you!

Also by Ash Hosking

Draw Me In
Drive Me Crazy
Drive Me Wild

About the Author

ASH HOSKING is an admitted daydreamer and hopeless romantic with a dirty mind from the Gold Coast, Australia.

She lives with her husband and adorable furbaby, Prim, who loves to snuggle on Ash's lap to keep her from getting anything done.

When not at her day job in catering, she can usually be found either working on her next book or reading, including on her lunch breaks.

She enjoys warm days at the beach, is addicted to Zarraffa's mocha fusions and can never say no to a Tim Tam.

Contact or follow Ash at:
Facebook: Ash Hosking,
facebook.com/ashhoskingbooks

Instagram: ash.hosking

Email: ash.hosking@gmail.com